S0-AWJ-458

BEFORE THE PERSONAL COMPUTER, before the microchip and even before the fragrant expanses of prune orchards, there was the Santa Clara Valley. After the Americans took control from Mexico, an event nearly coinciding with the Gold Rush, immigrants began to arrive in droves, quickly turning the humble pueblos into a multicultural society by necessity. In *We May Choose*, the hardy descendents of four diverse families find their way to San Jose from far-flung points on the globe, where they mingle with established Californios struggling to preserve their lands and lifestyle. Over the next five decades their linked life stories are, by turns, refreshing and heartbreaking, violent and life-affirming, productive and painful. Collectively, the old families and the new lay the foundation for astounding growth in the century to follow.

We May Choose

Choose

A Novel of California's
Santa Clara Valley

Don A. Dugdale

Aventine Press

Cover & Graphics: Judy Anderson
Cover Photo: Don Dugdale
Editor: Steve Hoar

Copyright © 2013 by Don A. Dugdale

Without limiting the rights under copyright reserved above,
no part of this publication may be reproduced, stored in or
introduced into a retrieval system, or transmitted, in any form or
by any means (electronic, mechanical, photocopying, recording,
or otherwise), without the prior written permission of both the
copyright owner and the publisher of this book.

Published by Aventine Press
55 East Emerson St.
Chula Vista CA 91911
www.aventinepress.com

ISBN: 978-1-59330-816-2

Library of Congress Control Number: 2013905151
Library of Congress Cataloging-in-Publication Data
We May Choose/ Don A. Dugdale

Printed in the United States of America
ALL RIGHTS RESERVED

The Families

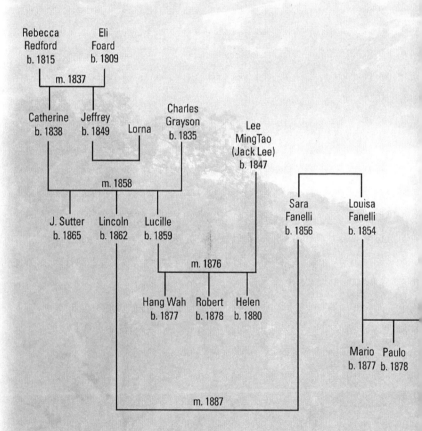

Rebecca Redford b. 1815 — Eli Foard b. 1809
m. 1837

Catherine b. 1838 — Jeffrey b. 1849 — Lorna — Charles Grayson b. 1835 — Lee MingTao (Jack Lee) b. 1847

m. 1858

J. Sutter b. 1865 — Lincoln b. 1862 — Lucille b. 1859

Sara Fanelli b. 1856 — Louisa Fanelli b. 1854

m. 1876

Hang Wah b. 1877 — Robert b. 1878 — Helen b. 1880

Mario b. 1877 — Paulo b. 1878

m. 1887

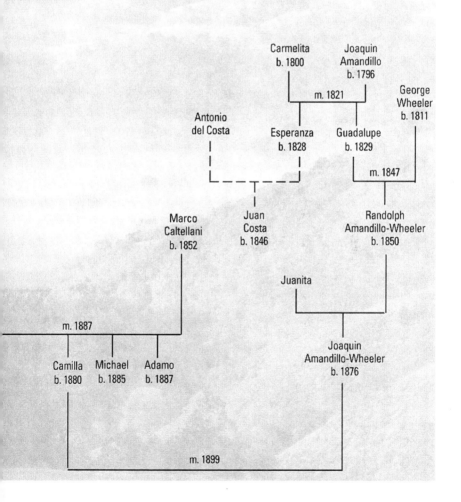

"Don't you see? . . . The American Standard translation *orders* men to triumph over sin, and you call sin ignorance. The King James translation makes a promise in 'Thou shalt,' meaning that men will surely triumph over sin. But the Hebrew word, the word *timshel*—'Thou mayest'—that gives a choice. It might be the most important word in the world. That says the way is open."

— *John Steinbeck's character Lee, in* East of Eden

So when at times the mob is swayed
To carry praise or blame too far,
We may choose something like a star
To stay our minds on and be staid.

— *Robert Frost, from "Choose Something Like a Star"*

Prologue

Mission Santa Clara, California
July 1799

PADRE MAGIN DE CATALA lifted his head from the hollow of his adobe pillow. He blinked in the morning light just now penetrating the narrow window in the two-foot-thick mud-brick wall of his quarters at the mission. It was time to get started, for today would be an important day for the Lord's work.

The hard pillow was Catala's gesture toward asceticism. But it had evolved into more than his personal cross, more than just a daily reminder of the suffering of Christ. It had become his signature, part of his identity. *Everyone* knew that Father Catala slept on a stone pillow. He held his head a bit higher, carried a touch more authority because of it. In his heart of hearts, he knew he was nurturing this pride, but chose not to look too hard at that. Besides, it would feel odd now to lay his head on anything soft.

As he did every morning, the padre knelt on the cold tile beside his narrow bed, facing the wooden crucifix on the wall, and began his hour of prayer. He prayed for the Holy Father in Rome. He prayed for his family members in Spain. He prayed for the other padres in the missions of California. He prayed for his neophytes, the local Ohlone

Indians who had converted to Christianity and were attached to the mission under his care. And today, as he had for the past four months, he prayed for the safety and success of his special work crew, the planters of trees.

One day this past January, as he had often done in his five years in Santa Clara, Father Catala had risen from his hard pillow with a vision. In his vision that morning, he had gazed from the Mission down the long irrigation canals, the twin *zanjas* that brought water from the Guadalupe River to his crops, the canals he had ordered built as one of his first projects here. But instead of seeing things as they were – a mostly open expanse, muddy with winter rains and dotted with an occasional oak and a few head of stray cattle – he saw in his mind a broad avenue between the two canals, shaded on both sides by rows of majestic trees. And between those trees, striding purposefully up the avenue, he saw the villagers of the nearby pueblo of San Jose, on their way to Sunday mass at the mission.

Surely, he thought, this was something that was meant to be. Red and black willow saplings could be obtained from the banks of the Guadalupe and from around a few local ponds. In a few years, these trees would begin to mature, and then the pueblo's populace would see what he had done and would be grateful to have such a beautiful tree-shaded path for a Sunday morning walk – so grateful that they would mend their errant ways and come up this three-mile avenue to the house of the Lord.

He would call it The Alameda, which in Spanish meant, in this sense, "shady walk" or "public walk." In a way, it would be Father Catala's peace offering to the community. Out of zeal for the true path and in their concern for the settlers' spiritual health, he and the other padres had often condemned the pueblo residents' backsliding ways – their bullfights, their bear fights, their places of debauchery and poor repute. These people were a bad influence on his neophytes, Catala thought. But the wayward had not always appreciated the high motives of the clerics, and the swampy path between the pueblo and the mission had not helped attendance at mass, despite his church being the only one in the area. During rainy winters, a dry trek of three miles could easily turn into a sloppy, circuitous six. This new road would help unite the mission and the pueblo, Catala was sure, and might even help settle the boundary disputes that had cropped up.

So Father Catala had put his people to work. The man directly in charge was Padre Jose Viader, Catala's assistant. But the one who really made things work was a wise Native American named Chief Ynigo. According to legend, Ynigo was born in 1760, headed a small tribe that made its home in a place called Posolmi a few miles to the northwest on the shore of the great bay, and had the blood of kings in his veins. Ynigo had attached himself to the Spanish padres soon after Father Thomas de la Pena planted the cross in front of the first Mission Santa Clara, the seventh in the mission chain, in 1777, and then had stayed. In time, he would become a legend among the Mission Indians and would live to age 104. But in this year he was just another servant of the Lord and of Father Catala.

Father Catala knew that he depended on the loyalty of Father Viader and Chief Ynigo for the completion of this great work. But for the future – and Catala always looked to the future – he had his eye on Ynigo's 14-year-old assistant, an overgrown Indian named Marcelo. Marcelo's size – he had already grown to nearly six feet and dwarfed the typical Ohlone native – gave him a natural position of authority and potential for leadership. Marcelo could carry twice the load of the average neophyte. And Catala noticed that even now, when Marcelo spoke, the two hundred neophytes listened. If the willows of The Alameda were to survive and grow, Catala knew he would need someone such as Marcelo to take on the responsibility.

So Father Catala had groomed Marcelo. He had shown Marcelo special attention, had personally tutored him in language, history and theology. Most important, he had shared with Marcelo his vision for the mission as a spiritual and educational center, with The Alameda its natural gateway. By now he knew that Marcelo had taken these things to heart and would carry the vision forward.

Under Ynigo's foremanship and with Marcelo's zeal, the neophytes pulled the willow saplings from the ground and hauled them on their backs to the planting site along the avenue. For four months they planted, cut irrigation ditches from the *zanjas*, and nursed the 3,000 saplings through their first few weeks. As they went, they built up the road, filling in the swampy areas and creating a level walking surface. It was the first inter-urban road in California to be built so purposefully. Father Catala could see that soon it would carry the two-wheeled *carretas* pulled by oxen, wagons, perhaps buggies and coaches. Still beyond his vision were the horse-drawn trolleys, electric streetcars, and finally motor traffic that would come that way. But for today, his road was for walkers.

After his prayers, Father Catala rose slowly, for even now, at thirty-eight, he was bothered by chronic rheumatism. He washed, dressed and went to the mission to celebrate his daily mass – he never ate before noon. After mass, he collected a jug of water and walked out toward his Alameda. In the distance, he could hear, faintly, the strains of a song from his native Catalonia being played on a guitar. It was a perfect day – one of a string of quiet, perfect days typical for July in this valley of Mediterranean climate. The forested mountains to the west and south still harbored a wisp of mist that was evaporating quickly. To the east, the mostly grass-covered Diablo range had taken on its tawny summer tone, a vivid contrast with the cloudless blue of the sky. Father Catala gazed, taking it all in, breathed deeply and went out to meet his planters and builders, to see the last of his trees be placed into the ground and to take a long walk down his new road. Praise the Lord. It was a day to rejoice and be glad.

PART ONE
WINDS OF CHANGE

Chapter 1

Monterey, California
March 1846

BEFORE HE SPOKE IT out loud, the question had been gnawing at Antonio del Costa for weeks, keeping him awake at night, distracting him at work:

"What's to become of us?"

Across from Costa in his little room sat Esperanza Amandillo, daughter of one of the wealthiest men in Monterey, Don Joaquin Cervantes Amandillo. Even as Costa questioned his future with Esperanza, his eye focused on her collarbone, dark hair covering part of it, the cleavage of her breasts, her magnificent skin.

Esperanza sighed, grimaced and tried to change the subject.

"Don't spoil the day, Antonio. We have an hour left. Let's not waste it."

It was early afternoon. This was Esperanza's fifth, maybe sixth visit to the room of Lieutenant Costa, an officer of the Mexican Army assigned to the Presidio of Monterey and a customs official. Her parents believed she was with her friend, Clarita, a few blocks away. Only Esperanza, Clarita and Costa knew the truth.

Not far from Costa's room, near the Custom House, her father was working in his import-export office. On the

Amandillo ranch, a few miles outside town, her mother, Carmelita, was going over plans for the evening meal with her kitchen help.

The lieutenant pressed his concerns with his lover. "We have no future," he said, fingering his wine glass and frowning into it. "If we had a future, I would be calling on you at home like a proper suitor. If we keep on like this, we'll be caught, and then it will all be over."

"We're not going to be caught," she assured him. "I've told you, I have a plan. I just need time to work on my father. At the right time, I'll get you invited to the ranch. You'll have a chance to get to know my parents. Everything will be fine." She reached for his hand, but he drew it back and clasped both hands behind his head, staring now at dark rafters of the ceiling. The light from the small window emphasized his scruffy beard.

"Your father doesn't like me – I can tell – and you know it too, or else I'd have been invited out by now. I keep trying to send business his way, but he pays no attention. And after – you know, after the trouble – he'd never trust me. I know men like that. He'll never have me in his house."

She dismissed his qualms: "You're worrying too much."

He parried: "You're not worried enough."

"I can handle my father," she insisted. "He's not going to stand in our way. What you did is done all the time."

"But don't you see," Costa protested, "that's not important to your father. He's an upright man from the old school. He'd never even associate with me as a *compadre*, much less as a potential son-in-law."

"Antonio, the ranch is going to be mine someday. I have no brothers. And when I'm of age, I can marry whomever I want. I always get what I want. My parents are not going to turn away if I approach them the right way."

Costa was not persuaded. "Your father wants a businessman running the ranch," he said. "To him, I'm just a corrupt official with no background. And besides, what about your sister?"

"Guadalupe doesn't care about the ranch," Esperanza declared. "She's a ninny. I'll own it and she'll be happy about it. She'll probably go off with whoever she marries." She took his hands and put her face close to his. "If it'll make you feel better, I'll start working on them right away. I'll bet I can get you invited to the ranch within a week. And while I'm doing that, you can work on him some more. Be friendly. Send him some more business. He'll want to repay you for that."

"I can do that part all right," he agreed. "But he won't change his mind so easily."

"He will. Wait and see."

She put her hand in his dark hair and brushed it out of his face. Then she smiled as he looked into her eyes and she kissed him, a long, seductive kiss. He came around the table and pulled her up to an embrace.

"You're right," he said. "We're wasting time."

Later that same afternoon

"It's a ship, Señor Amandillo, and a big one. I'd say 10 miles out, bearing in, full sail."

Joaquin Amandillo nodded at his harborside assistant, who was poking his head into the inner office of the small whitewashed adobe building, and the man disappeared. Amandillo, immaculately dressed for work, left his desk carrying a telescope and walked quickly past the Custom House to the shoreline. Trade was his business, and in Monterey, the capital of Mexico's province of California, ships were the engine of trade. He scanned the horizon with his scope. There it was just below a layer of fog – a clipper ship, all right, almost certainly carrying goods. Amandillo waited and watched. When a ship came in, there was money to be made.

Aboard the *Golden Eagle*, George C.M. Wheeler piloted his vessel carefully into Monterey Bay. Over the next hour he barked orders for furling one sail after another, and just before 4 p.m. he eased the ship to an anchor point as the crowd at harborside grew. Wheeler and his men hadn't been ashore in weeks, so the little town was a welcome sight. They could see twenty-five or thirty adobe buildings, mostly one story, sloping up gradually from the water's edge. Two little lanes led through the town to some low hills, sparsely covered with pines. The high fog was clearing but a few clouds remained, casting ephemeral shadows on parts of the landscape. Directly in front of Wheeler, a dozen or so people collected at the shore, curious about the arrival of this large vessel, as his men rowed the captain's boat toward the wooden dock.

George Wheeler was the son of a carpenter from the Isle of Wight and a lady of high breeding who visited the island and never left. In his veins flowed the pure Anglo-Saxon blood of his ancestors who predated the Norman invasion. George was born in Dartmouth, Devonshire, where began many a life spent at sea. When George was still a boy, his father died and his mother took him to live in Massachusetts. There, after schooling, he turned to the sea, did well and eventually bought his own ship. But now his mind was moving in a different direction – toward family and a more settled life.

The townspeople knew Wheeler was bringing trade to Monterey, and trade was the lifeblood of this the town. The economic center of West Coast commerce, Monterey fed off shipments such as the one Wheeler carried from the Far East – lacquerware, porcelains, silks, cottons and teas, as well as a selection of fine furniture handmade from exotic woods. After the captain dealt with customs officials, Wheeler and his crew would receive a hearty welcome.

As the captain entered the Custom House, Lieutenant Antonio del Costa reached to shake his hand. "At sea long, captain?" Costa inquired.

"Six weeks, three days," Wheeler said.

"Goods from China?"

"Hong Kong and Singapore, mostly."

"How long do you plan to port in Monterey?"

"Not sure. The crew is sea-weary and I'm due for a respite myself. I'll need to find buyers and then load up again. Maybe a few weeks, maybe longer. You in charge of customs?"

"Captain Hernando Flores is the customs officer. I'm Costa – taking his place while he's gone to Los Angeles for a while. I'll be checking your goods and collecting duties. You'll probably want to rest a bit before you unload."

"We'll keep it onboard until I find a warehouse. You can direct me to the local buyers and storage people, I trust."

"Whenever you're ready, señor. I suspect they'll find you first, though."

"No doubt. My men will need a place to unwind. I can't keep them on board another night – they'd desert. Now would you be good enough to direct me to the offices of the Fortino Trading Co.?"

"Señor Fortino's in the small building directly behind the Custom House. But you might also be interested in talking to Señor Amandillo, whose office is in the same building. He often has goods ready to ship. Right across the plaza is a hotel with a cantina. There's another place just up the street with more lively entertainment." Costa gave Wheeler a wink.

"All right," Wheeler said, staring at Costa straight-faced. "My men will be coming ashore soon – fifty-two of us. I'll drop by tomorrow to see about the duties.

"Tomorrow for certain," Costa said. "You know, we have to keep watch all night on your ship until you bring the goods ashore."

"Of course you do. But there will be no evasive maneuvers by my crew, you can be sure."

"I wouldn't suggest otherwise. But before you go, I'll need you to come inside my office and register your arrival."

Costa led Wheeler to the small room at the end of the first floor. Wheeler, who was six-foot-two, a full seven inches taller than Costa, ducked to avoid the lintel beam over the doorway. Costa pulled the wooden door to as Wheeler eyed him curiously. Costa opened the log book and handed Wheeler a pen.

"You know, captain, my men do a good job inspecting and cataloging goods," Costa said as Wheeler wrote in the log. "But sometimes they overlook things. If you and I made a special arrangement . . . well, I think you know what I'm getting at."

Wheeler had heard this kind of proposal many times. "If you're suggesting that I should pay you to avoid tariffs on part of my cargo, I have no interest in that at all," Wheeler said. "I will not be accused of flouting the law, and you would be well advised to take the same course. Do I make myself clear?"

Costa met Wheeler's steady gaze. "You make yourself clear. No one in my customs office can be bribed, captain. We'll want to make our inventory tomorrow morning. And we will have you bring every last item ashore to the Custom House, I assure you."

"I would expect nothing else, lieutenant."

By this time, Wheeler was weary and impatient. It was getting late, and he knew his crew would be expecting to go ashore. If he didn't release them soon, some of them would be jumping ship anyway, so as he stepped out of the Custom House, he met his first mate's inquiring gaze with a quiet nod. As the mate relayed the signal to the ship, a great cheer could be heard from across the water. Within seconds, boats were in the water, full of thirsty, lusty seamen headed for the dock.

Wheeler heaved a sigh, turned and started down the narrow dirt path that led around the corner of the Custom House, to begin arrangements for the sale of his cargo, for he would need to make his crew's payroll right away. But no sooner had he turned the corner than he was met by Joaquin Amandillo, striding purposefully toward him. Since Amandillo's man had been listening at Wheeler's dockside arrival, the trader already had the basic information he needed.

"Captain Wheeler, I believe," Amandillo said, extending his hand. "I was hoping to find you. I am Joaquin Amandillo. We haven't had the pleasure of meeting but I am *alcalde* here, and I do a lot of exporting. We are happy to have you in port."

"Thank you, sir. It's a pleasure indeed. I was just on my way to see Fortino about ..."

"Yes," Amandillo interrupted. "Of course. Unfortunately, Mr. Fortino has been called away from his office. I was coming over to save you the trip. He has a note posted on his door to the effect that he won't return until late this afternoon. I also thought you and your first mate might be looking for lodging. Our hotels are not first-class, I need to warn you. Would the two of you be kind enough to accept hospitality at my villa tonight?"

"It's a generous offer, but we have only just met. Are you sure ..."

"Any ship's captain doing business in Monterey can vouch for me, señor – you'll be safe at Rancho de los Palos."

"Oh, I wasn't questioning ...." Wheeler and Amandillo looked at each other and then broke into simultaneous laughter. "Of course, Señor Amandillo. We will be happy to accept. I suppose my business with Fortino can wait until morning. And by the way, sir, if I may …" Wheeler lowered his voice as he hesitated and looked Amandillo in the eye. "Lieutenant Costa – I wonder if you could tell me … can he be trusted?"

Amandillo raised his eyebrows. "It's interesting that you ask," he said. "He has been known to make deals under the table. If he has made any illicit offer … "

"No," Wheeler said, "just a feeling I had," Wheeler said. "I thought I'd ask."

"You would be wise to have your crew keep a close eye on your cargo. And make no deals with Costa. Nothing good will come of it."

"Mmm. Thank you. I'm getting a feel for things in Monterey."

"Very good, *señor*. Now, I will have a buggy pick you up at the dock in an hour. My family will be interested to hear about your journeys."

"The pleasure will be mine. In the meantime, I hope you'll excuse me while I make sure my crew isn't making a shambles of your cantina."

"*Hasta luego, señor.*"

Rancho de Los Palos, 6 p.m.

BACK AT HIS HACIENDA, Amandillo toyed with his practice *reata*, twirling it in a tight loop beside the comfortable oak and leather desk chair where he sat. Casually, he tossed the loop toward a four-inch post, placed for that purpose in the far corner of his study. The roping post was made to bend flexibly at the base, so the reata could be pulled off easily. Amandillo was thinking; he did his best thinking when his hands were busy. But at that moment his train of thought was interrupted by voices in the hallway.

"It was supposed to be a yellow dress, mama, yellow. And the sleeves are all wrong. I can't wear it. I hate green."

"But it's a lovely dress, Esperanza. Why don't you at least try it on?"

"No – I can't stand it. It's horrible."

Amandillo grimaced and sighed. When he heard a door slam, he knew his daughter had gone to her room, probably not to emerge until supper. He sighed again, trying to regain his train of thought.

When Amandillo wasn't outside – and he was outside most of the time – he was most at ease here in this little hideaway, reading, doing correspondence, keeping his financial records in order. Outside, he lived large, roamed freely, letting his imagination run loose. In this room he made firm plans, came to practical, well-considered decisions. Today, before he went out to tend to matters with his ranch foreman, he had something to think through.

Here in Monterey, Amandillo was building what he hoped would turn into a family dynasty. Twenty-five years before, in California as a young Mexican military officer, Amandillo happened to befriend the man who was to become governor, Juan Bautista Alvarado. In 1834, Alvarado was handing out huge land grants like party favors. Amandillo ended up with 22,489 acres of good ranch land extending northeast from the Monterey pine forest into rolling, bare hills ideal for grazing cattle. His Rancho de los Palos was known for hundreds of miles around.

Of all the land grantees in Alta California, Amandillo had been the most successful. In only twelve years he had made a fortune, mainly in the cattle business, building his herd and trading with shippers eager to take his hides and tallow to the ports of the world where they were in high demand. His whitewashed ranch house had grown from a bungalow into a sprawling hacienda, its walls of three-foot-thick adobe providing warmth in the winter and a cool respite from summer's warmer days. Often, when the fogs had Monterey in a chill, his family, five miles away, basked in sunshine. On summer nights, guitars, violins and castanets played into early morning as his guests danced the *fandango*, the *jarabe* and the sensual *jota* on his private patio.

Now, at 50, Amandillo could still ride and rope with the younger vaqueros, and he often joined them at branding time. But he saved himself more time for relaxation lately. His children were grown – though they still lived in the villa. Amandillo and his wife, Carmelita, liked to sit on their terrace and play cards while they sipped a cool drink and enjoyed the warm noonday sun. As evening approached they lit fires, even in July and August, to keep warm against the chilly ocean air.

The study door opened and Carmelita Amandillo appeared, worry on her face. "I can't handle our daughter," she said. "She's takes more out of me every day."

"She'll be all right," Amandillo answered. "We've been handling her for years. Esperanza has high spirits."

"You mean I've been handling her for years, and maybe she'll be all right but she'll kill me off. When there's trouble, you just go out and herd your cattle. They don't give you any sass."

"You're upset, I know, but things will calm down. Esperanza still has some growing up to do. And when she's married, her husband can deal with her."

Carmelita shook her head. "I pity the husband. What I'm afraid of is that no one will want her for long. I'm worried. She's unstable and I don't know what to do."

"Like I said, she'll grow up. You'll see." Carmelita just stared at him, slowly shaking her head, then turned and started to close the door behind her, but stopped when she heard her husband's voice again.

"*Mi preciosa.*" He used the term often when trying to console his wife. As she turned back, her face softening, Amandillo motioned for her to sit in the comfortable chair beside his desk. "I have something else to talk about."

"What's that?" she said, putting her hands on the chair but not sitting.

"The northeast parcel, the 7,000 acres. I think I can trade it for the ranch, the one in the Carmel Valley I've been looking at. What do you think?"

She cocked her head for a moment, thinking. "You're after your vineyard, no? You want it and you're going to have it."

"It's not just for me," he said. "We have two daughters. We need to provide for both of them, so we need to leave a dual legacy. The ranch won't hold both of them."

"But why a vineyard? You don't know wine."

"I can find someone who does. Monterey is going to grow, and the people here will need a good supply of wine. Even if it were just for us, it would be a good idea. We can never get enough good wine."

She shook her head slowly, smiling at him in resignation. "Fine, then. Have your vineyard. I'm sure you'll make it a success. You always do." She came around the desk, kissed him on the cheek, then patted him on the shoulder.

"*Gracias, amor,*" he said.

Amandillo was used to these conversations. They had become so frequent lately that he had prepared responses to anything Carmelita might say. Immediately, he went back to tossing his *reata*.

Lately Amandillo had been troubled by some political instability – the Mexican government, he knew, might not be able to hold California for long. Only two months before, an American officer named John C. Fremont had come to town. Fremont was said to have sixty armed men camped at Sutter's Fort, 185 miles to the north, but for some reason

he had come to Monterey alone. He claimed that he was
a scientist, not a soldier, and that he was surveying the
best route from the East Coast to the Pacific. Amandillo,
as *alcalde* in Monterey, had met Fremont and didn't trust
him. He had been relieved to see Fremont leave to rejoin
his troops. He had no feeling of attachment to the Mexican
government and no particular fear of the *Americanos*. But
the last thing Amandillo wanted was a military altercation.
It would be bad for business.

Aside from the politics, only one thing troubled
Amandillo: God had not given him a son. He doted on
his two daughters, who were both of marrying age and
would soon, he assumed, be choosing husbands. But what
sort of men would they choose? What abilities, values,
goals and character traits would they bring to a marriage?
And above all, what sort of loyalty would they have to the
family? With no male heir of his own, how could he be
sure his legacy would be preserved?

Amandillo loved his daughters, but he was sure neither
of them was hard-headed enough to run a working ranch.
Esperanza, the older sister, was materialistic enough, but
her concerns were entirely outside the business realm. She
was a consumer, and she consumed with great dedication.
In fact, Joaquin and Carmelita had spent quite a bit of effort
lately keeping Esperanza's consumption in check. If she
had a new dress, she needed new shoes. If she had a new
outfit, she wanted another. If she were attending a party
this Saturday, she wondered why she was not invited to
a second or third party. Luckily for her figure, she did not
show the effects of overeating, because she ate with a zest
that bordered on gluttony. And when it came to men, she
was equally voracious.

Esperanza's shiny black hair, dark eyes and striking,
blemish-free face had attracted the interest of dozens of
young men, and she had developed the knack of keeping

several interested at a time. But none of them satisfied her for long. She seemed to be always flirting and toying with a good-looking boy. But as soon as one came too close, made some unfortunate gaffe, lowered his guard or glanced in the direction of at some other woman, Esperanza would cut him off. She could be giggling and vivacious one minute and off somewhere pouting the next.

Joaquin was most proud of Esperanza when he saw her on a horse. She was passionate about horses – had been since she was a small girl. And always, whatever the occasion, she rode bareback. She knew the ranch better than most of the vaqueros that worked it – had covered every acre of it on Guapo, her much-admired paint stallion.

Guadalupe, on the other hand, was as even-tempered as Esperanza was volatile. She loved life and welcomed it with open arms. If the sun was shining, she would bathe in it. If it rained, she found something fun to do inside. She socialized easily and never seemed to be without a friend. Her eyes widened with excitement when some new adventure beckoned, and she never, ever seemed to worry. Now that she was grown, she had not drawn the attention that Esperanza had, but she had her own kind of beauty – softer, more understated. Perhaps in reaction to Esperanza's outbursts, Guadalupe never made a fuss. When times were pleasant, the sisters got along well. When Esperanza created a storm, Guadalupe quietly went her own way and found shelter. These were things Amandillo knew.

It was with his daughters in mind that Amandillo contemplated his next big decision – the division of the family land. God willing, he had many years left as a rancher, but he wanted to put his mind at ease now. Rancho de los Palos was not the sort of business that could be successfully split in two. It needed a single strong leader, someone who could command the respect of both the surly ranch hands who did the work and the unscrupulous business people he sometimes had to deal with on the outside. He hated the thought of leaving the ranch to anyone he did not consider his equal in intelligence, fortitude and character – and he was sure neither of his fuzzy-headed daughters could do the work alone. Splitting the ranch between them would be disastrous. He could only hope that one of them would choose an acceptable husband. Then the question would remain: what to leave the other.

Rancho de los Palos was sprawling and diverse. The best land for cattle was the 15,000 or so acres southwest of the Salinas River, which included the villa. The 7,000 acres to the northeast wasn't bad land, but it was divided by sloughs and harder to traverse. Amandillo did not consider it essential to his ranching operations. The potential vineyard in Carmel Valley would be a good trade. Some horse breeders owned it now, but Amandillo was already thinking of a building site for his winery. It was time to act – time to prepare for the future.

WHILE HER FATHER PLANNED, Doña Esperanza Amandillo brooded in her room. Antonio del Costa had been her lover for the better part of three months – an era in Esperanza's experience. One of the things that made Costa interesting was that he was *prohibido*. And things were actually worse than Costa suspected: Don Joaquin had banned him from the hacienda and commanded Esperanza to drop him. Perhaps she might have done so except for her father's ultimatum. Now her lover was forbidden fruit and as such, much more tempting.

When the two first met, Costa had been a visitor in her father's office. Soon they became intimate. The man was everything Esperanza thought she wanted – handsome, well built, confident and suave. But then he had run afoul of his superiors. Caught red-handed taking kickbacks in his role as a customs official, he had been disciplined and demoted. The news spread through the town, and Joaquin Amandillo chalked this man off his list – he was no longer a suitable son-in-law. Now, months later, Costa was back in his old job, inspecting ships and collecting tariffs. Esperanza, not to be so easily turned aside, pursued the relationship. She could not stop seeing him – she was sure now that he was the best-looking, most irresistible man she had ever met, and she was choosy.

At some point, she knew, she would have to change her father's mind. She would somehow have to come up with a way to convince him that Costa was a worthy heir and capable of taking charge of the ranch. She thought as much about the future of the ranch as her father did – not how to make it productive and preserve it but how to make it hers. She wanted it. She wanted it to be hers alone. As the elder child, she was entitled to the ranch, she thought. Her sister might continue to live there, but the ranch would be Esperanza's – she would make sure of that. And Antonio would be hers too. They would command the estate like royalty, the toast of Monterey. It was only a matter of time.

But now Esperanza had a more immediate problem – she had to either keep putting Antonio off or convince her father to give him another chance. Which tactic she chose might prove critical to achieving her goals.

Chapter 2

THE BUGGY CARRYING Captain Wheeler and Lieutenant Meadows from town pulled within sight of Rancho de los Palos. As they crested the hill above the ranch and headed down the narrow lane toward the front door, perhaps a quarter of a mile ahead, Wheeler eyed the low-slung, whitewashed adobe critically. The last rays of sun just caught the top of the Amandillo house and reflected off the windows near the far front corner. A few Coast Live Oaks dotted the dry landscape in front, partially hiding a well-tended orchard to the side of the house. Each of the windows, framed in green, contained several small panes sheltered by a sloped awning covered in clay tile that matched the roof.

Amandillo opened the heavy oak front door and walked out to greet the two seamen before the buggy stopped: "So kind of you to join us, captain." The driver pulled the horses to a stop and Wheeler hopped to the ground immediately to meet the handshake offered by his host.

"I owe you all the thanks, *Señor* Amandillo. May I present my first mate, Joseph Meadows." Meadows and Amandillo shook hands.

As the three men entered the house, Wheeler noticed the change in atmosphere. Outside, it had been warm, bright, dusty. Here it was cool, dark and clean. Oil lamps lit the room, and he detected the pungent aroma of braised meats. The guests were led through a large tile-floored room lined with heavy furniture, then to a central patio shaded by cypress and olive trees, where fireplaces burned at the corners.

"May I offer you some punch, *señores*, perhaps some *aguardiente?*"

"Please, Papa, let me serve the gentlemen."

At the sound of the woman's voice, both Wheeler and Meadows turned to see a girl, perhaps 19 or 20, with jet-black hair, long and playing off her shoulders, which were bare except for the strap of her sleeveless yellow dress hanging over the end of her shoulder. Her lips were partly open, her eyebrows raised. Wheeler could not stop looking at her eyes, which were almost coffee-dark but lightened by just a hint of hazel.

"Well, which will it be?"

"I'll try the punch," Wheeler said, almost as if from a trance.

"Yes, by all means, punch," Meadows said.

"May I present my daughter, Esperanza," Amandillo said. "Esperanza, Captain Wheeler and Lieutenant Meadows have been trading in the Far East."

"It must seem boring here after all your adventures," Esperanza said as she ladled punch at a table a few steps away. As she filled the cups she glanced back at Wheeler. Her lashes were striking even at that distance.

"You can't conceive of boredom until you've been on a long sea voyage, Miss Amandillo. It's been months since my crew has been ashore and I seriously doubt if they're bored just now. Nor am I."

Wheeler caught himself staring at Esperanza, and then tried to look at the others instead. But he couldn't help stealing glances – at the orange flower in her hair, her naked shoulders, the profile of her face.

"Here's my daughter, Guadalupe," Amandillo said, and just in time Wheeler realized he was being spoken to and shifted his eyes. A girl with a sweet, open face, more round than Esperanza's, stood in front of him.

"*Buenos noches, señor,*" she said. Wheeler nodded, smiling. This was also a pretty girl, he thought, in her own innocent way.

"You have a wonderful family," Wheeler said, looking at Amandillo. "You should be proud."

"*Gracias, señor.* And now, let me hear about your adventures on the high seas."

The evening passed, as did several thereafter, with Wheeler, Meadows and the Amandillos sharing adventure tales and speculating over the shaky status of the Mexican government. On the third such evening, after he had been in Monterey a week, Wheeler managed to get a seat at dinner next to Esperanza. The two of them talked the evening away, she apparently intrigued by this adventurer, he mesmerized.

After two weeks, Wheeler found himself almost a fixture in the Amandillo household. He wondered if he was overstaying his welcome, but he could not turn down an invitation when he thought of the delicious meals and Esperanza waiting there in one of her colorful outfits. It also quickly became obvious that Wheeler and Amandillo, even with their cultural differences, spoke a common language, that they were forming a bond.

On sunny mornings, Esperanza and Guadalupe would go riding with Wheeler and Meadows, Esperanza mounted bareback on Guapo while she showed the men her favorite spots on the ranch, all the best views. This lithe, energetic girl was beginning to captivate Wheeler's attention, helped along by the scenic backdrop of the California coast. He began thinking about Esperanza night and day.

One morning Wheeler decided he knew Amandillo well enough to say directly what was on his mind. He approached the rancher in his study. "I see that your daughter, Esperanza, has no suitor at present," he said.

"No," Amandillo said, still busy with his papers.

"I would like your permission to fill that void."

Amandillo smiled and looked up, curious. "I was wondering how long it would take you," he said. "But I need to know some more about you before I can give that permission." He stood up and walked around the desk toward Wheeler. "What kind of husband would you be to her, sailing all over while she languishes at home?"

Wheeler had anticipated the question. "I will be curtailing my activities as a ship's captain," he said. "My last short voyage will be coming up this fall, and then I plan to settle in Monterey and lease my ship to a younger man while I establish myself as an importer/exporter. I have tired of the sea."

"All well and good, but are you financially able ... "

"I have all the capital I need to support a family and do well in business, if that's what you're concerned about."

"And so you will stay in Monterey?"

"I have purchased land in the town, and I'll be building a house there."

Amandillo smiled. "That's good," he said, and then he looked Wheeler straight in the eye. "Now tell me about your past. You must assure me that you have not been married, that you are a man of good character ... "

"I assure you, sir, that I have not been married. As for my character, you can ask my shipmates. Meadows knows me well."

"Thank you – I'll do that. And now there's one more thing. If you're serious about marrying my daughter, you need to understand that we are Catholics, and a Catholic can only be married in the Catholic Church by a priest. We would also expect our grandchildren to be raised in the Catholic Church. Are you a religious man?"

"I was baptized in the Church of England, but that was long ago. In Massachusetts my mother and I were Episcopalians. But personally, I think all of us believe in the same God. If it suits your family, I would be happy to join the community of Christians here in Monterey and become a Catholic."

"Really?" Amandillo said, taken aback. "I didn't expect that, but I don't know why it wouldn't be possible. Why don't you speak to one of the fathers about it at the Church of San Carlos? I like you, George. I would be pleased for you to court my daughter." The two men shook hands.

Just as Wheeler was about to leave, Amandillo put a hand on his arm. "*Señor*, I think it's only fair to tell you – you may not know – well, it's about Lieutenant Costa, the one you met at the Custom House. He and Esperanza were seeing each other. When he was caught taking his under-the-table payments, I told him he should stop seeing Esperanza. She was upset with me, of course, but I banned him from the house and I forbade her to see any more of him. If this concerns you, you should bring it up with my daughter."

"I'm not worried. But thank you for the information." Wheeler was confident enough not to let something like this get in his way. But in the back of his mind, a seed of caution was planted.

Esperanza sat at her dressing table staring blankly at her own face in the mirror. Carefully, she pulled an ivory-inlaid brush through her hair, tilting her head back, her eyes unfocused and half-closed.

The arrival of Captain George Wheeler in her life had opened up new possibilities and created new problems. Wheeler was attractive enough. He was experienced and confident, qualities Esperanza admired. She was intrigued by his stories. And he had two things that Antonio del

Costa did not have – money and her father's respect. It had also become obvious that Wheeler was interested in her. But then, most men were.

At first, Esperanza had played the coquette because that was just what she did with good-looking men. Then she began to see that Wheeler could fulfill her needs in a way that Costa never could. If the captain became her husband, he could follow in her father's footsteps and run the Rancho de los Palos. He had held a position of authority, she reasoned. And he looked as if he could make people listen to him. Those qualities were important because although her father had never broached the subject with his daughters – nor would he – Esperanza knew instinctively that neither she nor Guadalupe would be entrusted with the ranch alone.

It would never even occur to her father that a woman – or worse, two women – could handle the responsibility of a large ranch. But with a man such as Wheeler for a husband, the matter would be all but settled. Esperanza noticed the attention and time her father had given to Wheeler. No other guest had been allowed such an extended stay or had captivated Joaquin Amandillo quite so much as this British seaman. "He likes Papa too," she thought. "They're going to be friends, I know. This could work."

Almost unconsciously, but decidedly, Wheeler replaced Costa in Esperanza's mind as her husband of choice. And yet, she hated that she had to do it. She still loved Costa as much as ever, still wanted him and refused to give him up. When she was with him, he satisfied all her needs. But on another level, she had begun to edge away, to prepare herself for the day she would have to give him this news. It was becoming harder to make excuses for delaying Costa's visit to the ranch, so she had made her visits to town less frequent. Interestingly, as she did this, their trysts had become even more delicious, more spontaneous and fulfilling. But the time was approaching, she knew, when she would have to make the break. And she was also prepared for the probability that Costa would learn it for himself. Already he had asked her about Wheeler's extended stay at the hacienda – what was he up to, what were his plans? There was a hint of jealousy in his voice. When Wheeler's feelings for her became apparent, as Esperanza knew they would, she would have to forestall any rash action by Costa. Just how to do that, she had not thought through.

WHEN GUADALUPE AMANDILLO heard her sister say that George Wheeler was her "new beau," she had a little surge of pleasure. It meant that this interesting man, this gentlemanly sea captain, would remain a regular visitor and might someday be joining her family. That meant many things to Guadalupe, all of them good – well, almost all. It meant another man about the house, a welcome relief from the current female-dominated chatter and hubbub. It meant that the ranch would have an heir apparent, which would alleviate the uncertainty she knew her father felt over that issue. And it could mean that her volatile, self-indulgent sister might finally have someone who could keep her appetites in check – maybe even keep her reasonably happy. It was too much to hope that Esperanza would ever be fully content, but this man was not like the others. He was older than Esperanza's usual boyfriends and a man of the world. And he exuded confidence. A strong man like this could meet the challenge if anyone could.

For weeks now, Guadalupe had noticed the sidelong glances, the flirting, then the whispered conversations, the sly smiles. But she knew Esperanza and distrusted her. She had seen her manipulate people over and over, was sure Esperanza would try to do the same with Wheeler. Her first instinct was to want to protect him, maybe even to warn him somehow without betraying her sister outright. This was a good man, she thought – not someone who deserved a grasping malcontent for a wife. But she didn't want to scare him. Then she began to see that Wheeler was no fool. He was clearly enjoying this flirtation, but had also held something back. This was not one of the overeager, wide-eyed boys who usually fell hard for Esperanza – the ones she could easily keep dangling indefinitely if it suited her purpose. Here, finally, was a man who would not be played. Still, she couldn't help but think that Esperanza would find a way to alienate him. "She doesn't know what she has," Guadalupe thought. "She doesn't have a clue." Guadalupe looked at Wheeler and saw her model man – an Anglo, seagoing version of her father. It wasn't long before the official announcement was made – Captain Wheeler and her sister were engaged.

WHEN DON AMANDILLO first revealed Esperanza's romance with Costa, George Wheeler had not been unduly surprised or concerned. It was to be expected that a girl as beautiful as Esperanza would have had suitors. What was past was past – something that could be brought up and disposed of at an appropriate time. It did not even bother him that Costa was a sleazy sort – girls are often deceived by that kind of man, the charming, handsome smooth talker. With his own influence, he was confident that Esperanza would become a devoted wife and a loving mother to their children. What he did not expect was what happened on a weekday afternoon in mid-May.

Wheeler happened to be strolling in Monterey, down a path he was not used to taking. On his way from the dock to the cantina, he noticed a narrow alley that seemed to lead to a garden of some kind, and then back out to the street where he was headed. Curious, he entered the unfenced garden just in time to see two figures emerge, laughing, from a doorway on the opposite end of the garden. Thinking he might be intruding on some private space, he shrank back behind a tall hedge. But just then he heard the voices distinctly and stopped, frozen. As he peeked around the hedge, his first impression was confirmed – it was Esperanza, and with her was Lieutenant Antonio del Costa. Their body language told him all he needed to know– that he was watching two lovers linger before parting. Their faces held close together, they toyed with each other, both smiling. They kissed playfully, again and again, and then held each other in a long embrace.

When he had seen enough, Wheeler edged away and retreated quietly the way he had come.

His mouth went dry and a knot formed in the pit of his stomach. His breathing became heavier. Not only had he been deceived and betrayed, but it was now evident that Costa and Esperanza had never ended their liaison. She preferred this chiseling low-life to him, had promised to be his wife knowing that, and for what purpose? In his fury, he saw this woman in a new light, garish and unflattering. Suddenly, he didn't think he could stand the sight of her. How could she be this treacherous?

That afternoon he returned to the Amandillo villa to collect his things. Esperanza had not returned, but Wheeler told Carmelita Amandillo what he had seen and made clear that he would not tolerate it. The engagement was off.

"Your daughter has continued her relationship with Antonio Costa," he told her in a confrontation in the front hallway. "I have seen them with my own eyes."

"But are you sure? What ... "

"Nothing could have been more plain, *señora*. If you need any more information, I suggest you ask your daughter!" He continued out the front door, which he left standing open, tossed his bag into his buggy and started to pull away, but was caught short by the shouts of Guadalupe, who had come out of the house at a dash.

"George!" she called, in a shriek that brought Wheeler's hands back on the reins. The horse reared and stomped in a loud complaint. Guadalupe rushed to grab the buggy by its side.

"Don't run off, please," she said, coming to tears. "Whatever's happened, it can be fixed. You can't just leave!"

Wheeler brought his horse under control and stared at her, mystified. "No, you don't know what you're talking about," he said, shaking his head. "What could you possibly ... ?"

"I know something awful has happened. I'm not surprised," she said, shocked at her own sudden frankness. She had overheard the exchange between Wheeler and her mother. "But I don't want you to leave. Promise me."

Wheeler continued to stare, still not comprehending, yet suddenly full of compassion and affection for this girl in obvious distress.

"Don't worry," he said, now calm and reassuring. "We'll see each other again. I just have to be away from here for a while. Don't be upset, but you have to understand that I've had a shock."

Guadalupe took her hands off the buggy and edged back toward the house. "Yes, I can see you have," she said. "I understand. I'll see you again, then, when you're ready."

Still Wheeler stared at her, his face mellowing, his eyes softening. "*Hasta luego*, Guadalupe," he said, and started on his way. She watched until he had ridden out of sight over the nearest hill.

Carmelita Amandillo, who had been witnessing this scene from the doorway, glared at Guadalupe, catching her daughter by the shoulders as she moved slowly to the door, tearful. "What's all this?" the mother asked, her face full of worry and frustration.

"I don't know, Mama. I don't know. Do you?" She put her face in her mother's bosom, sobbing uncontrollably.

Chapter 3

Independence, Missouri
May 1846

NEAR DAYBREAK ON MAY 12, the day George Wheeler
stormed out of the Amandillo villa, the Foard family,
recently of Franklin, Missouri, prepared to leave for
California. In the family's hotel room, Eli Foard couldn't
sleep, so he carefully slid out of bed, trying not to wake his
wife and eight-year-old daughter. He shivered a little and
reached for his overalls. A faint smell of frying bacon tinged
with wood smoke hung lightly in the darkened room, and
muffled voices could be heard from the street, through
the half-open window. Morning light was glowing on the
eastern horizon, but it hadn't yet penetrated the tiny room
where the Foard family was spending what would be their
last night indoors for many months. Somewhere a rooster
crowed.

Eli's wife, Rebecca, was already awake. "Is it time?"
she whispered.

"You're awake," he said.

"For hours. We might as well have slept in the wagon.
What a waste."

"I'd better go look after the supplies. You and Cathy
can stay here while I get things ready."

"We're going with you. I can't wait to get out of here."

"Cathy's still asleep."

"She'll be fine. She won't want to miss the excitement."

Rebecca looked at Catherine, lying asleep with an embroidered coverlet over her in the corner of the room, which was still dark, and hoped they were doing the right thing taking her on such a risky trip. There was so much they couldn't know. She lit a lamp as Eli pulled on his clothes, and she looked out to the east at the light in the sky, toward what would from this day on be their old world. It was time to go.

In less than three hours the Foards would be climbing aboard a canvass-covered hardwood wagon containing all their belongings, to begin a cross-country trek of some two thousand miles and unknown duration. Pulled by four oxen, their wagon would traverse the northern plains of the American West. They would keep as close to water as they could – along the Platte and North Platte rivers, then the Sweetwater River in latter-day Wyoming, skirting south of the Granite Mountains and then crossing the continental divide at South Pass. After a stop at the Fort Bridger trading post, they would follow the Oregon Trail northwest to Fort Hall, the Hudson's Bay Co. post in Oregon Country, in what was to become Idaho. The California-bound wagons would then branch off to the south, following the Humboldt River though 300 more miles of semiarid lands, then across a forty-mile bone-dry desert until they found the Truckee River. They would follow the Truckee up into the imposing Sierra Nevada, crossing the crest of the great mountain range and continuing on to their destination at Sutter's Fort in California's central valley. If their food lasted, their health withstood the journey, and they all survived any Indian attacks, severe weather or equipment delays, they could then begin their new life.

Now, in the semidarkness, Eli, Cathy and Rebecca walked to the edge of town where their wagon and oxen were standing with those of the rest of the party. Eli heaved the oaken yokes onto the oxen, hooked them to the tongue of the wagon and led the animals to the small warehouse where the party's provisions were stored. Already, four or five families were loading up. For supplies, Eli had bought 700 pounds of flour, 180 pounds of lard, 500 pounds of bacon, 200 pounds of dried beans, seventy-five pounds of dried fruit, seventy-five pounds of coffee, twenty-five pounds of salt, twenty pounds of sugar, a little keg of vinegar and a bushel of corn meal. In addition, they were taking a thirty-pound case of hardtack bread, which they hoped they wouldn't need, for emergencies. They had a good horse, a rifle, a shovel, a hunting knife and cooking utensils. A bucket of axle grease – actually a mixture of lard and pine tar – would hang off the rear axle for keeping the wheels lubricated. Otherwise, the family had room for little else in the bed of their four-foot-by-twelve-foot wagon. They each had one change of clothing and some bedding. Rebecca put up a strong case for taking her family dishes, but Eli argued that the extra weight would be an unnecessary burden on the journey, where excess pounds could lead to delays and death. So they left them with her parents in St. Louis. The wagon could carry more than 2,000 pounds, but Eli wanted to keep the load as close to 1,600 pounds as he could, to save wear on the animals and the wagon itself. He had experience with those things. If their supplies ran short, he could hunt for food as long as the weather cooperated. Rebecca knew he'd be good at that.

On this warm morning in early May, the sun rose in a cloudless sky. Eli loaded their goods, adjusting the weight carefully. Cathy and Rebecca watched, chatting with a few of the other families as they prepared to go. By the time Eli had the wagon loaded, the street was noisy with men getting things ready, hitching teams to their wagons. In Independence that day, at least three groups were organizing to leave immediately, for they were all in a critical time window for beginning the trek. Any earlier and winter weather, especially floods, would have been an immediate threat. But if they waited even two more weeks, there might not be time to traverse the Sierra before the snows hit.

"Foard!" bellowed someone to their left, as Eli started to lead the animals off toward the assembly area. It was the self-assured voice of Jack Benedict. Rebecca was on the opposite side of the wagon and couldn't see Benedict, but she saw Eli turn just as the sun came out and caught him in the face. As he tried to shield his eyes, Benedict appeared and put one hand on his shoulder, grabbing his right elbow with the other. "Good that you're ready early," Benedict said, putting his face a little too close to Eli's. "Some o' these other shitheads aren't even up yet. We need to get going. And can you help Gagnon and Price? Gagnon's got family problems or something. Hell of a time."

Just then Benedict glanced at Cathy and Rebecca. "Oh, excuse my language folks, I didn't see you there," he said, smiling and waving as he walked away.

"Uh, yeah, sure," Eli said. Benedict was already moving on before Eli could raise any objections. Benedict's attitude bothered Eli, but Rebecca thought there was something else wrong, too, something she couldn't put her finger on. In any case, it was clear that Benedict was taking charge.

Eli and Rebecca had met Benedict just six days ago, but those six days now seemed like half a lifetime. He was that kind of man. Six feet four and swarthy, he towered over others, a physical presence wherever he went. He was intimidating. But beyond that, the man was more confident than he had a right to be. Whatever the topic, Benedict would dominate the conversation. Whatever the question, he thought he had the answer. Maybe he was right, maybe not. But anyone who wanted to argue was in for a battle because if there was one thing Jack Benedict could not tolerate, it was losing an argument. Fervently, loudly and persistently, he would bluster, build his case and steadily wear down whoever opposed him until the only options were to agree or to wave him off in disgust and walk away. Considering Benedict's size, a fistfight didn't seem the way to go.

Eli should have been captain of the train, Rebecca knew. He was the adventurer, the former trapper, the blacksmith, the horse trainer and trader. He had far more backwoods savvy and knowledge of the West than Benedict did, and she pushed her husband to put himself up for leader. But competent as he was, Eli never tried to impose himself on people. Leading wasn't his cup of tea – too many headaches, he said – and that frustrated her. Eli wouldn't take charge, so it was Benedict, big and brawny, who filled the gap.

Now their fate was in his hands as they made their way from the Midwestern plains to the fertile valleys of California – a migration that they knew was fraught with far more peril than Benedict was prepared for. In theory, Eli was second in command as well as chief scout and pathfinder. But in the inevitable contests of wills, Eli would have to use all his powers of reason and persuasion to keep the party on the right track. It was those confrontations that he dreaded, and Rebecca knew it.

What confidence the group placed in Benedict was based almost totally on his ability to command. He was open, usually positive, and engaging. A thirty-nine-year-old mining superintendent from Indiana, Benedict had come to Independence heading up six parties, fifteen wagons in all – by far the largest single component of their forty-wagon group. In the meeting to select a captain, Eli had summed up his own wilderness background factually, but never contested Benedict's election as leader. Immediately after Benedict took over, he sought Eli's advice and enlisted his support. That, at least, spoke well of his judgment. Despite Benedict's forceful manner and bluntness, Eli thought he seemed reasonable, though prone to stubbornness. Their relationship had been friendly and without conflict. But the trip had not yet begun.

"What's going on with *him*?" came a voice from behind. "Morning, Rebecca, Cathy." It was George Enderle, a young doctor from St. Louis. Dr. Enderle, a beefy thirty-year-old with prematurely gray hair and a twinkle in his eye, had been a neighbor to Rebecca's family before she married Eli. Rebecca had known him most of her life, and she felt hugely relieved that he was in the party, for medical emergencies and general support. Like Eli, Enderle had a quiet confidence about him, and he obviously was an orderly man, which Eli appreciated. The Enderle wagon was outfitted carefully, with precision – no excess baggage but no essential item missing.

"Oh, he's trying to get things organized, I guess," Eli said in answer to Enderle's question. "You know, the burden of leadership. We're only going to get started when the last wagon is ready, so he has a worry about that last wagon."

"Well, maybe I can help out," Enderle said. "When I finish loading I'll go see how the others are doing." He signaled his leave and walked on toward the warehouse to collect his supplies. Eli followed Benedict's order and went to check with Jacob Price and Horace Gagnon. By that time, the sun was up. Rebecca and Cathy sat on a sunny patch of grass near the wagon.

"They seem to have things in hand," Eli said when he returned. "Let's go over to the café and get some breakfast." He had one of the men keep an eye on the wagon and team while they walked over to the Collingwood Cafe.

"Daddy, I'm all packed," Cathy said as they crossed the main street. Their daughter, always eager to please, was as even-tempered as anyone they knew. She adored her father.

"We are ready and we are *hungry*," Rebecca said.

"This will be our last chance to eat in a dining room, and we want to save our supplies," Eli said. They squeezed into the crowded restaurant/tavern after a short wait and ordered breakfast.

"So we are really doing this, are we?" Rebecca said with a smirk, as they waited for their food.

"It seems we are," Eli said. "Are you excited?"

"*I* am!" Cathy said. "I want to see buffalo and bears and Indians and mountains!"

"Well, I don't know about bears, but you'll be seeing a lot of interesting things," Eli replied.

"Daddy will keep the Indians away, honey," Rebecca said. "Won't you." She was eyeing him, and it was a directive, not a question.

"But I don't want to keep them away," Cathy persisted. "I want to talk to an Indian."

"We'll make sure they're friendly first, honey," her father said, grinning. Rebecca scowled.

Eli had put himself in perilous situations many times, but now he had a wife and a child. Now he had to think of how to keep them safe. Eli would do his best, Rebecca knew, but some dangers might be out of his control. Eli had warned her that the journey would hold risks well beyond her imagination. She trusted him, but her trust had limits. If faced with danger, she was prepared to take action.

Chapter 4

REBECCA FOARD MADE no secret of her reservations about going to California. Like her husband, she sought out adventure, so she was intrigued about what they might find in the West. But she doubted Eli's resolve, his ability to stick with a plan until it produced results. His dedication seemed as fleeting as hot breath on a windowpane. One day he would be happily making wagon wheels, the next day off tracking deer. Rebecca had willingly taken on the venture in Franklin, making a home for them, canning berries, growing vegetables. But she was bitter about how quickly the dream there faded for Eli. She didn't want California to be just a repeat of Franklin.

Eli was a mountain man if anyone was. He had spent years in the West before he met Rebecca. He was a fit thirty-eight years old, bright-eyed, and an experienced trapper and backwoodsman. He was just medium height and not impressive physically, but his blacksmithing had made him powerful. His only facial hair was a bushy mustache. Born into a strict Moravian family in Bethlehem, Pennsylvania, he had felt misplaced in the devout religious community. At fourteen, he took one of the family horses, without permission, to go squirrel hunting with friends. After he was punished, instead of reforming, he hardened. At sixteen, he refused to attend church anymore. He had gone west at eighteen, learning and working as he went. After ten years of beaver trapping and trading in Oregon Country, he took his stash and returned east, looking for a wife. He first thought he might find a misfit like himself at home among the Moravians in Bethlehem, where his family still lived; but he made it only as far east as St. Louis. There, in the restaurant of the Planter's House Hotel, Rebecca was having dinner with her parents and noticed him at the next table. He introduced himself, a conversation ensued, and she found herself spellbound by Eli's tales of the far West. He was invited to the Redford house for tea. Three months later, Eli and Rebecca were married.

Eli always said that he found Rebecca, but the truth was that she had a plan to marry Eli from that first day at the hotel. "You don't get in Becky's way when she wants something," her mother would say, recalling the battles the two of them used to have. Until age twelve, she was a tomboy. Snakes, spiders and mice didn't scare her, and she never backed away from a challenge. She became a crack shot with a pistol while still a teenager. Today she was no different, and she hadn't lost her red hair and freckles. Eli seemed to like her spunk – until he had to deal with it himself.

Their married life had not been easy. They decided to settle in the central Missouri town of Franklin, then a frontier settlement, where Eli opened a livery stable and blacksmith shop. Rebecca was determined to be the ideal wife and mother. She loved Eli's playfulness, his bravery, his sense of adventure. But as time went on, she became frustrated with his casual attitude toward life. She wanted him to begin using his talents to create a better life for the family. She didn't mind the rigors of frontier life, but she was disappointed with the meager financial returns from Eli's new business. They needed to do better, Eli knew, but he resented Rebecca's hounding him about it. He resisted, but Rebecca kept pushing.

At first, Eli had been content, busying himself with the details of getting established in a new location. But after the second year he became restless, bored with the day-to-day routine. Business was slow. He began thinking more of his old life in the West, the grandeur of the mountains, the thrill of blazing new trails. The birth of their daughter gave them both a new commitment, but soon Eli's attention seemed to wander again. He began spending days away on hunting trips, leaving an assistant in charge of the stable. The couple argued more frequently. Then there was the incident of August 16, 1845. After that, nothing could be the same for them in Franklin. They tried to put it in the past, but wherever they went, it haunted them. Franklin was a small town and Rebecca became a marked woman.

The following winter, after Catherine barely survived a severe bout of influenza, Rebecca told Eli they were in the wrong place. They had a choice to make. Eli had never seen California, but in his years trapping in Oregon Country he had heard tales of the vast, fertile lands to the south, of enormous vegetables and wheat growing as tall as a man. People seemed to be happier there. He thought this new place offered great opportunities, and that was all the convincing Rebecca needed. They sold their property, acquired a proper wagon, returned to St. Louis for a final visit with the Redfords, and set out for Independence. Joining them in St. Louis, with their own wagon, were George Enderle and his wife Earlene, friends of the Redfords who had, coincidentally, been planning a trip west. The two families bonded immediately. Now they were moving ahead, into the unknown, on the greatest adventure of their lives.

"WITH A MIXTURE OF EXCITEMENT, fear, hope and expectation, we packed up in Independence and began the trek to

California, first moving southwest along the Blue River, then west following Indian Creek," Rebecca wrote in her journal. "The Benedict-Foard party is comprised 136 people and forty wagons. A few families brought two wagons and most have a few stock animals as well. Our wagon has sides two feet high, secured to a sturdy undercarriage. The wheels and axles are of oak. Critical spots are reinforced with iron, but the metal was too heavy to be used extensively."

Eli took precautions that other parties did not – he was smart that way. He carried an extra wheel strapped to the side of the wagon. He would also spend 45 minutes each evening removing the wagon wheels, chaining them together and leaving them to soak in the river, securely staked down. He knew that in the dry western air, the oak wheels could shrink and separate from the four-inch iron tire around their circumference, with disastrous results. Eli preached this soaking practice to every one of the thirty-six parties, but on the first night, he noticed that Jack Benedict and a number of others had not taken his advice. After a week on the trail, only three or four parties were still soaking their wheels. Also, many wagons were overloaded, Eli thought. He had advised against too much weight and had been strict about limiting his family's load to 1,600 pounds. But by the time they assembled, most parties were already committed to the load they had and couldn't be swayed.

"They'll learn later," Eli said to Rebecca privately. He also mentioned this to Benedict, but Benedict brushed him off.

Water, along with food, was always the critical and overriding need on the journey. No more than a day or two could go by without access to a good water supply, so the course of rivers and streams would dictate the route. Without water, the animals would die. That would put everyone's life in danger. But when the wagons had to cross streams and swamps, those with heavy loads would come to grief.

Just before noon on the fourth day on the trail, the train crossed over the "Indian line," which was the Western border of Missouri, into present-day Kansas. Then they were no longer in the United States. As they stopped for a noontime break, Eli noticed, far in the distance, what looked like a dust cloud. "Might be another party," Eli said to Rebecca. An hour later, the dust cloud disappeared. The following morning, they saw it again, only more of it, so they prepared to meet up with what they assumed was another group of wagons, and Eli alerted Benedict. Sure enough, on the seventh day, as they approached the expected crossing of the Kaw River late in the morning, they pulled within sight of a party of fifty or sixty wagons. When the two groups merged at a side creek, Eli mounted his horse and rode ahead to make friendly contact. As he approached, he noticed that one of the wagons, pulled by six oxen, was oversized – wide and tall. Everyone was stopped at the creek by now, and he rode up to this wagon and signaled a greeting.

"Forty-wagon party coming up behind you," Eli said to a bearded, fiftyish man in a black hat, who was leading his ox team to water. The man nodded. The other folks nearby gathered around.

"I'm Eli Foard," he said.

"James Reed. My wife, Margaret, right here. Over there's George Donner and his group. We're from Springfield, Illinois. You going to Oregon or California?"

"California. Our party's just behind you. And you?"

"The same. We're all headed there."

"Planning to reach Sutter's Fort by October 1, then?" Eli inquired. Most people thought that beyond then, snow might make the Sierra Nevada impassable for wagons.

"At least by then," Reed said. "Why don't you and your family join us for a midday meal? We can talk some more."

"That's nice of you," Eli said, nodding. "I'll let the others know."

The wagons of the Benedict-Foard party pulled even, circled and prepared for their break. Rebecca chatted with Margaret Reed as they prepared the food, and Eli spoke quietly with her husband. Rebecca felt the men sizing each other up as they talked. Margaret said they had owned a successful sawmill, store and furniture-making business in Springfield. She and James had three small children and a twelve-year-old stepdaughter by Margaret's previous marriage. His wife's mother, Mrs. Keyes, also traveled with them, but she was bedridden inside the wagon. As Rebecca heard snatches of the men's conversation, she thought James Reed spoke with a slight Irish lilt, or maybe Scottish.

The unusual thing was that big wagon of theirs – about the same length as an ordinary wagon, but fatter and higher. Whereas most people just crawled into their wagons from the front or back, the Reed wagon had special doors with folding steps on both sides for access. Inside were custom-built compartments for storage and even a small wood stove with a chimney jutting high up through the canvas. Margaret said James had built it so her mother could be comfortable. Rebecca was impressed, but Eli thought the added weight was unnecessary.

Margaret and Rebecca joined the two men as they sat on logs, had lunch and told of their lives and plans. Reed's ambition was to someday handle all U.S. relations with Native Americans west of the Rockies. In this he hoped to enlist the help of a politician neighbor of his from Springfield named Abraham Lincoln, with whom he had fought against the Indians in the Black Hawk wars in Illinois. Since California still belonged to Mexico, and she had not heard of any problems between the United States and the California Indians, Rebecca wondered what this job would entail. But Reed seemed to think it would be important.

Then Reed pulled out a book. It was a thin volume titled *The Emigrants' Guide to Oregon and California,* published the year before. Neither Eli nor Rebecca had seen the book, but a shiver went through Rebecca when she saw the name of the author: Lansford Hastings. She looked at Eli. His jaw tightened, then froze.

"This fellow seems to know a lot about California," Reed said. "You might be interested in his suggestion for a more direct route."

Rebecca decided to keep quiet. Eli nodded silently, apparently considering what to say and how to say it. She knew he did not want to reveal everything they knew. He tried to keep a calm demeanor. "I would examine anything Lansford Hastings had to say with great care before acting on it," Eli said, finally, "for I have met the man."

"You have met Hastings? And how was that?" Reed asked, cocking his head.

"He was in central Missouri on a speaking tour, promoting temperance. Friends of ours took us to hear him." Eli paused before going on. "He said he had been in California – he did not mention a book. But I was keen to speak with him, to get his impressions, for this was before we had decided to make this journey. He is an engaging gentleman, that's true. But I would say he cannot be trusted."

"Oh, and why is that, sir?" Reed asked.

"Because I found many factual misstatements in what he told me."

"And you say this not having been to California yourself," Reed said, his piercing eyes fixed intently on Eli.

"I did not question his statements about California, but about Oregon Country, with which I have years of experience. To test his knowledge and reliability, I led our conversation there as if I had no information on the place. He told me a number of things that I knew to be wrong. The man has a way of speaking with authority but on a base of ignorance."

"So you deliberately misled him," Reed said.

"I did, and with a purpose. I learned a good deal in my conversation with Lansford Hastings, but pertaining to the man, not the West. This gentleman is not what he pretends to be."

"I do not take your opinion lightly. But he has published a book, and a highly recommended one it is. We have sent a message ahead to him, and we may be employing his services later on as a guide. I understand he would be available for this service, from the point where our trail splits from the one bound for Oregon."

"Is that right?" Eli said. "Well, I wish you the best. I have only spoken from my firsthand experience."

"And I thank you for that. Now perhaps we should have some food."

Later, as the Foards returned to their group, they looked at each other, silently. There was so much else they might have said to Reed about Lansford Hastings, but couldn't.

"If Reed chooses to ignore my warning, then so be it," Eli said. The tension in his jaw was back.

"So be it," Rebecca said.

Chapter 5

As THE TWO WAGON GROUPS approached the Kaw River crossing later that day, it became apparent that the Foards would have plenty of company on the trail to California. Already grouped at the crossing and camped for the night was a third group of perhaps seventy wagons. When the Benedict-Foard and Donner-Reed parties joined them, nearly 150 wagons stood quietly by the river, a virtual army of migrants waiting to cross the water the next morning.

The river had risen after recent rains, and that made the crossing a long, tedious process. The water was far too high to risk fording, so the wagons had to be ferried on little barges. "A white man named Jones was operating a concession there, employing fifteen to twenty Indians in poling the wagons across, two wagons to a barge without teams," Rebecca wrote. "The wagons had to be unloaded, then moved close to the water, unhitched and lifted onto the barge by several men. After crossing, the wagons were assembled again on the other side. The animals, goods and people were ferried across separately. The fee for the crossing was one dollar per wagon."

Some of the women were encountering their first natives on the trail and were reluctant to approach them. But the Indians looked fairly harmless, Rebecca thought. As far as she could tell, they were only interested in getting their jobs done. The sky clouded heavily by noon, and a thunderstorm struck before one o'clock, making the work all the harder. By the time all the wagons had been taken across and reassembled, most people were muddy and soaked and out of patience.

Rebecca was watching Eli reassemble the wagon when suddenly she had a start – where was Catherine? She was not around the wagon. Suddenly alert, Rebecca looked back toward the river and was seized by fear. Down by the riverbank, her daughter was with one of the Indians – and no one else. Rebecca headed for them at a run and then, as she approached, slowed to a fast walk. The two of them seemed to be talking. The Indian looked up, calmly.

"You mother?" the Indian asked.

Rebecca barely nodded. "It's time to go, Cathy," she said.

"I told him they should build a bridge and charge people to go over it," Catherine said. "He thought it was a good idea."

"Smart girl," the Indian said.

Rebecca managed a tight-lipped smile. "Let's go, honey," she said. Hand in hand, mother and daughter returned to the rest of the group.

It was late afternoon and nearly time to camp again. During that day, the three parties had time to talk about the problems they might find ahead. Sometime that night, Eli heard that the Donner-Reed group had joined with the larger Bryant party. Apparently the Donners and Reeds were looking for the additional protection provided by more wagons. Some Indians might be friendly, but everyone knew that out on the plains, anything could happen.

"Horace is the shy type," Judith Gagnon was saying at the campfire that evening, Rebecca and Earlene Enderle listening. "I wish he would assert himself more. Benedict is the sort of man Horace hates. He doesn't like having to stand up for himself." Judith was sweet-natured, Rebecca thought, but was showing the wear and tear of raising a brood of kids. The Gagnons had five young children. As far as Rebecca could tell, Horace was dedicated to his family. He seemed to be a good provider and devoted to his brood. Yet, since the group left Independence, the Gagnons had constantly found themselves in trouble. The children were young and curious, and Judith had a terrible time keeping them corralled. Horace seemed to be a procrastinator by nature, so the result almost every morning was that the Gagnons were the last ones ready to leave camp. Rebecca could tell Benedict was having his patience tested. On the morning after the Kaw River crossing, he confronted Gagnon as Eli happened by.

"We're losing time because of you," Benedict said. "I am not going to let this train get stalled and delayed because of one family. Either you get ready to move out when everybody else is, or we will have to leave you. I have been as patient as I can, but this has been a consistent pattern with you. If you need help, get it – other people will help you. What is the problem?"

"There's no need for that tone," Gagnon said. "We have a big family. We need a little extra time."

"I am giving everyone enough time to prepare to move in the morning, and nobody is having a problem with it but you," Benedict said. "Tomorrow, when the other wagons are ready, we're moving out. If you are not ready, you will be on your own. Find a way to get it done." Benedict wheeled and stalked away, not waiting for an answer.

Eli tried to smooth things over by giving Horace and Judith a few practical suggestions about their equipment. "He's not being fair, singling us out," Judith told Eli. "This is supposed to be a community, so we should get help if we need it. There's no need to threaten us."

The next morning, Eli made a point to get his own work done early so he could check with the Gagnons. They had no trouble that day, but early the next morning the older Gagnon boys accidentally broke the wagon tongue in a rough-and-tumble game, and it had to be repaired before the oxen could be hitched. Eli informed Benedict, who blew his stack, but Eli persuaded him to allow extra time for the repair.

DAY AFTER WEARY DAY, everyone's main job was to walk. Only the little children and the infirm rode with the supplies in the wagon. The wagon ride was bumpy, and the animals needed to be saved. Most often they covered ten miles a day, sometimes fifteen or more. As the Foards moved on, through hazy sunrises followed by humid mornings leading to oven-baked afternoons, they began to absorb the full extent of the challenge they had taken on – or thought they did. Rebecca now felt completely drained each day by the time they made camp. Then there was more work to do. And yet, they still had half the continent left to traverse. All of them began the trip knowing how many miles they would have to travel. But few expected it would be so hard.

"They should have a railroad train," Catherine said one day. "There should be a railroad all the way to California."

"St. Louis doesn't even have a railroad yet," Eli told her. "It's going to be a long time before there's a railroad clear out here."

The harder it got, the more determined Rebecca became. They had to stick it out, after all, or die, she reasoned. But she still had no inkling of how trying the next three months would become.

They seemed to progress without incident for the next two weeks. Horace Gagnon, with Dr. Enderle and Eli's help, had his family better organized. The children seemed to be more under control. After a few more days, they reached the Platte River, where they turned due west to follow the trail along the south bank of the Platte to the Rocky Mountains.

Then one morning there was an incident. The Gagnons' five-year-old daughter and six-year-old son could not be found. Apparently they had wandered into the brush along the river bank. Five or six families helped look for them, but when it was time to leave, they were still missing. Benedict became impatient. He insisted on moving out and gave the order.

Trying to make peace again, Eli went to Benedict. "We'll stay until the children are found, then we'll catch up," he said. "I'm sure it won't be long."

"Yeah, yeah. Fine. Well, I hope you make it," Benedict replied. He returned to his wagon, and most of the party moved out with him. But the Foards, the Enderles and three other wagons stayed behind with the Gagnons, all of them mad at Benedict. One group was sent upriver, another group downriver, to search the banks for the missing children. Judith was beside herself, distraught over her children and now worried they all would be separated from the main part of the wagon train.

By the time the children were located, the rest of the party had moved out of sight, so the six families were in a hurry to get started. They all felt they needed the security of the larger group, especially if there should be trouble with Indians. Horace was the most flustered and angry. He yelled at the children – unheard of for him – and they shrank back, in tears. Then he turned to his team, giving his lead ox an extra-hard hit to get them moving.

The ox team lurched. But out of Horace's sight, his six-year-old son, Stephen, had started climbing into the wagon. Rebecca saw the lurch of the wagon jolt the boy to the ground, just as the oxen were pulling forward. The timing was just wrong. As Stephen hit the ground, the heavy wagon moved, the front wheel catching Stephen's left arm and crushing it under the load. Stephen screamed and Gagnon immediately brought the team to a halt, but it was too late – the damage was done.

Dr. Enderle heard the commotion and came immediately. He had Stephen, who was in agony, put on a blanket, and examined the injury carefully. He had treated a few sprains, cuts and internal disorders on the trip, but this was the first bad injury. After a minute, he turned to the Gagnons, who waited anxiously.

"I'm sorry," he said. "I can save his life, but the arm will have to come off. It will kill him if I don't take it off."

Horace tried to console his wife, who could not speak through her tears. Gagnon nodded to Elderle, who nodded in return. The doctor left to get his medical tools.

Dr. Enderle performed the amputation on Stephen, who had gone into shock. Afterward, he administered a sedative and gave Judith orders to keep her son warm and under constant watch in the wagon. A half-hour later, when the Gagnons had settled down a little, Eli quietly advised everyone that it would be best to get moving. In a subdued mood, they started onward. Eli thought they had lost perhaps two hours.

Although this kind of accident could have occurred at any time, the Foards blamed Benedict for it. His impatience and dictatorial style had cost the boy his arm. Rebecca knew they were right, and also knew the Gagnons must feel the same, although Horace had gone inside himself and had spoken just a few words since the accident. Judith was sobbing, and Rebecca helped her tend to Stephen while Catherine looked after herself.

"There has to be a change before Benedict gets us all into serious trouble," Rebecca told Eli. "You know that, don't you?" she said.

"Benedict's got the welfare of the whole group to think about," Eli said. "He knows we have to keep on schedule if we want to beat the snow in the Sierra."

"I can't believe you can be so callous," she said. "What would a few minutes of waiting have hurt? Can you look me in the eye and say he's a good leader?"

He stared at her for a few seconds and then turned away, grim-faced.

Chapter 6

Night fell, and the delayed six-wagon group had not overtaken the rest of the party, so they were forced to camp by themselves. When Rebecca finished her work, and while Eli was doing a wheel repair, she spread a blanket on the ground so she and Catherine could lie back and look at the stars, which seemed especially brilliant that night. Although she didn't know why, she began to feel calmer. It didn't make sense because they were in real danger, just six families isolated and vulnerable to attack. Maybe it was being separated from the tension and resentment that Benedict seemed to generate just by his presence. Maybe the quiet made her feel more rested.

The moon was nearly full, but all six families agreed that they needed to rest and shouldn't travel by moonlight trying to catch up. So they planned to rise extra early and start at first light, hoping the lead party might wait. And in fact, it did. Benedict's group persuaded him to lay over a few hours to see if the rest would catch up. When the two groups merged, and after everyone had heard the news about Stephen Gagnon, heads were shaking and women were talking among themselves in murmuring huddles. Benedict himself said nothing.

That night Rebecca said to Eli, "You should talk to people, see if they want you to take over as captain. They can't be happy with Benedict after this. You should be in charge. If you don't do this, I'm afraid of what might happen."

"I haven't had anyone ask me," Eli said. "This can't be a mutiny, because that's even worse. We can't have a split in the party, and some still think Benedict is right. They'll side with him."

"Oh, and how do you know?"

"I know – I've heard what people are saying."

"Well, the women are against him, and the women will control what the men do – you'll see. You need to take some action! You can't just stand by and wait for trouble."

"I just don't want to cause worse trouble. You can't push these things. I'll see what the feeling is, but I'm not going to start a civil war here."

"Well somebody needs to push something, and I want you to take charge. You should have, from the beginning. It's your choice. Are you going to be timid all your life?"

Eli grimaced. The word *timid* was the clincher. He went silent. Rebecca later regretted using it, remembering how he had braved the wilderness for 10 years; but what else could she say to get him to act? Eli thought he would just let her stew awhile. They were both exhausted.

Eli never said what his plan was, but over the next few days he quietly, methodically made contact with all the families in the party, subtly getting their take on Benedict's leadership. It was apparent that many of them thought Benedict had been rash, but a number of men, especially those who knew him well, still respected his authority. Eli was careful not to suggest that he thought a change was needed. Eventually he told Rebecca he had decided to let things alone for the present.

By the third week in June, the wagon wheels were becoming a serious problem. Because most in the party were not soaking their wheels at night, the dry air had shrunk them. They now had to face the fact that someday soon, the wooden wheels would start separating from their iron tires and break apart. On June 15 a wheel broke near midday, and the party had to camp while it was repaired. Eli performed a stopgap fix; but because there was no timber, he could not make a fire hot enough to do a proper blacksmith's repair, one that would last. He told Benedict they would have to find timber soon because dozens of wagons were now at risk. Broken wheels would have to be repaired so the wagons could go on, and the work might take days. Only then did Benedict pass the word, and everyone in the party began soaking the wheels in the river each night. Some managed this by tying their wagons securely on the bank and backing them into the river, allowing the wheels to soak to a point above the hub but not wetting the wagon bed. Eli thought it was a lazy and inadequate method.

As wood for fires became scarce, many began using buffalo chips for fuel. These hunks of dried dung burned well and gave the camp a distinctive smell during the evening and morning meals. Some complained, but the smell was nothing compared to the real dangers – Indian attacks, starvation, keeping the animals alive. More and more, the talk centered on those fears. The buffalo and elk meat that the hunters brought back was satisfying most everyone's hunger, and some even said the dung gave it a hickory-like flavor. Rebecca had a different opinion.

One day just before noon someone spotted two Indian braves sitting on their horses far in the distance. Rebecca watched them closely, seeing that they barely moved as the wagons passed. The tension kept everyone on edge. That night Benedict put extra men on the watch, but nothing happened. After another day, the incident was nearly forgotten.

Five days later, a supply of deadwood was found large enough to build a good fire, and Eli spent two days repairing all the wheels that were loose. The other men took a break to do other kinds of repairs. Some of the best riflemen went on a daylong hunt; others in the party stood admiring Eli's skilled workmanship. While they waited, much of their talk centered on how his earlier advice about the wheels had been ignored, leading to the current delay. Rebecca thought she detected Eli's stock rising, and Benedict's falling.

On June 17, they passed the point where the Platte River splits into the South Platte and the North Platte. Two days later, the wagon train had to cross over the South Platte to continue along the North Platte toward Fort Laramie. They found the place where the river was lowest and began to ford the mile-wide stream. Three wagons became mired in quicksand and had to be unloaded and hauled out with extra teams. At times the water came over the wagon beds, but most of them came through without damage to the contents. They all did a bit of drying out that night.

Four days later they caught sight of the striking vertical formations of Courthouse Rock and Chimney Rock. As these imposing landmarks gradually came into view on the horizon, most of the travelers couldn't stop staring; they had never seen such a thing. Several people said they felt they had finally arrived in the West. Four days after that, they pulled into the place officially named Fort John, a fur-trading outpost that most people were now calling Fort Laramie. As they approached the fort, a large group of wagons came into view, clustered near the buildings. To the Foards' surprise, the wagons turned out to be those of the Bryant party – which now apparently was led by a man named Russell. They had arrived just that morning, meaning that the Benedict-Foard group had been only a day or less behind despite its problems. Eli soon found James Reed and George Donner, whose group was still with the Bryants. The three men talked a bit and arranged for the families to share an evening meal while they caught up with trail news.

"My mother-in-law died a few weeks back," Reed told the Foards that night. "I never thought she should make the trip, but she insisted. She and Margaret were close. We buried her before we reached the Platte. Otherwise, we are well."

"I'm sorry," Eli said. "Any word about Hastings?"

"No, but the route by the Salt Lake is looking more necessary for us. We're slower on the trail than we thought, and we will need the extra time we could gain on the shorter route."

Eli let the comment pass.

As they finished their meal a rough-looking stranger approached the group. "Looking for James Reed," he said, and before anyone could respond, the man pointed at Reed. "There you are, Reed. Remember me from the war against the Sauk? James Clyman. Somebody said a Reed from Springfield was here. You've come west."

"Clyman!" Reed said, getting up to shake the man's hand. "What in the world … "

"I'm a fur trader. Been in the mountains for years. We're on our way east from California. You going to Oregon?"

"California for us," Reed said.

The conversation soon turned to the available wagon routes. At the mention of Hastings' southern route via the Salt Lake, Clyman shook his head. "I've come that way on horseback, but it's no good for wagons. There's no road. Take the regular wagon track and never leave it. It's barely possible to get through if you follow it, and maybe impossible if you don't. If you go south, you have the high mountains south of Fort Bridger, then the great desert, and you must find a way through the Ruby Mountains to boot, which also has no wagon road."

"But we can save a lot of distance, according to Hastings – maybe 400 miles," Reed said.

"Maybe, maybe not," Clyman said. "You'll be safer going to the north."

"Have you read Hastings' book?" Reed asked.

"Don't know about any book," Clyman said. "Besides, I can't read."

The talk turned to Indians and then to life in California, and no one brought up the route again. After the others had left, Eli and Clyman spent a while telling fur-trading stories. Rebecca noticed that Reed, Benedict and Donner spent some time talking among themselves. That night, for the first time, Eli revealed his worst fears to Rebecca.

"This Reed is bent on taking a southern route," he said. "I saw him and Donner talking to Benedict. In this book they have that Hastings wrote . . ."

"The Hastings book! I should have known."

"Hastings can't be trusted, as we know," Eli said, "and this Clyman confirmed it, so I hope Benedict isn't tending that way."

"I can't believe it! You'll have to change his mind if he is," Rebecca said. "Are you ready to make a stand?"

"On that point I am," Eli said.

The next morning, Eli learned that Benedict had agreed to join the Russell-Donner group for the trip along the North Platte and then up the Sweetwater River, which would take them nearly over the continental divide, close to the parting-of-the-ways, where a decision would have to be made on the routes. Finding Benedict, Eli raised the issue of Hastings' cutoff.

"It's not decided," Benedict said. "Even Reed and Donner don't know which way they'll go. We'll have to see where we are when the time comes."

"Well, there's no sign of Hastings, and he can't be depended on," Eli said. "I would trust this man Clyman before relying on Hastings." Benedict just nodded.

So on Sunday, June 28, all three groups moved out together, but it soon became apparent that the Donner group was lagging behind. With their heavy wagons, loaded down with household goods and items to sell and trade, they could not keep pace with the others. The Russell party soon separated from the rest, moving out ahead and then out of sight. The Benedict-Foard group could have moved with them, but for some reason Benedict insisted on waiting at each critical juncture – every meal and every stream crossing – until the Donner group had caught up. Rebecca could feel Eli getting impatient. Since this practice ran directly counter to Benedict's earlier haste, Eli finally confronted him.

"It's Indian country here, according to the talk at Fort Laramie," Benedict said. "We're a small group to be caught alone if they should attack."

"I know the tribes here, and I heard the talk too," Eli said. "The Sioux and the Crow are headed for war, but they're likely focused on that, not on wagon trains. I haven't heard of any attacks in this area."

"I still feel safer this way," Benedict said. "Don't want to alarm the women." Eli didn't argue any more. An evening or two later, as if to confirm Benedict's judgment, there was an incident. It had been an especially hot day, the temperature probably over 100. Eli, Benedict and several other men had gone hunting, taking advantage of the light on the long midsummer evening. When they returned with meat, Rebecca made a fire. She carved up some buffalo steaks from a hunk that they had brought in, and she put them on the grill to cook. As she did, the men and several women went to the river to clean and dress the rest of the meat. Catherine and Rebecca found themselves alone in the fading light. A few minutes later, Rebecca heard a noise behind her. Thinking it must be one of the women, she glanced around to find a full-grown Crow brave sitting by the fire, not five feet from her, stark naked.

She jumped and whimpered involuntarily. But shocked as she was, she didn't cry out in fear. Then she felt amazingly calm. Instinctively, she felt that causing an alarm would be the wrong reaction. Her first real thought was for Catherine, so she quickly surveyed the area she could see, finding her daughter absent.

"Cathy," she called in a voice that trembled just slightly, but was otherwise close to normal. She kept her eyes glued on the Indian.

"I'm in here." Catherine's voice came from inside the wagon.

"Honey, I want you to stay there until I tell you to come out, okay," Rebecca said, as firmly and evenly as she could. But Catherine had already crawled out. She saw the naked Indian immediately, and gave a little squeaky gasp as she put her hands to her mouth.

"Just stay where you are, honey," Rebecca said, still in an even voice. "I won't let him hurt you." Catherine froze. A tense few seconds went by in silence.

"Do you need some clothes, Mr. Indian?" Catherine said, as if she were addressing a neighbor.

"Don't talk to him, Cathy," Rebecca said anxiously. "He can't understand you."

The Indian did not move an inch, or utter a word. Rebecca didn't know what was going to happen, but she just thought it was best, above all, not to act afraid, so she didn't call out. She subtly felt her apron pocket to be sure the carving knife was still there – it was. Still grasping her fork, she turned the buffalo steaks on the grill, keeping a steady eye on the naked brave, who was eyeing the grill but still hadn't moved or spoken. Within a minute a steak was ready to take off the fire, so handling the steak with the fork, she placed it on a plate, which was resting on a tree stump. The Indian grabbed the steak immediately and, before her eyes, tore it apart with his teeth and downed it. By the time he finished, she had placed a second cooked steak on the plate. The Indian took that steak and ate it as quickly as he had done the first.

"You sure must be hungry," Catherine said.

Now Rebecca was growing impatient, angry and fearful for her daughter's safety. Catherine was still and watching calmly from her position, leaning her back against the front wagon wheel. Rebecca, with her right hand on the butcher knife concealed in her pocket, placed a third steak on the plate with her left hand, thinking that this Indian must be satisfied by now. But no – he reached for the steak. In a flash, she had the knife out and brought it down hard, point first, on the Indian's wrist, pinning it to the tree stump.

The Indian let out a wild scream as blood spurted on Rebecca. Horrified at what she had done, she pulled the knife out with both hands, and the Indian, wild-eyed, tore off into the semidarkness as fast as he could go. Rebecca staggered backwards and fell on her backside into a patch of dry sagebrush as Catherine looked on, open-mouthed and unable to move. The others soon came running up from the river and from the other wagons.

Rebecca tried to tell exactly what had happened but she did a poor job of explaining herself. When everyone had heard about it, most of them seemed startled and afraid. They didn't seem to care what Rebecca had just been through. They began to speculate on what this injured savage would do, what he would tell his people, what their reaction would be. Even the other women didn't seem to sympathize with Rebecca.

"There'll be an attack for sure," one man said. "They'll chase us down and try to kill us." Others agreed. The brave might bleed to death or live to lead an attack on the whole wagon party. Would they all die? Even Eli didn't have any ready answers. Taking quick action, he and Jacob Price, the best riders, had jumped on their horses and ridden out, trying to locate the Indian, but it was dark, and he was not to be found.

After they had all eaten, there was a meeting, attended by everyone in the two parties. Some were still angry with Rebecca for placing them in danger, wanting to ostracize her, but Rose Enderle, her closest friend, came to her defense.

"No one knows what this Indian's intentions were aside from getting something to eat," she said, "but for all we know Rebecca has saved herself from a worse fate. Would you expect someone to just do nothing with an Indian sitting next to you?"

The argument persuaded just enough of the others so that in the end the Foards were allowed to remain with the group. Most people were on edge for a day or two, but the incident soon faded into the lore of the journey, and no one ever found out what had happened to the unfortunate steak-loving brave. Eli, when he spoke of the incident later, couldn't help smiling at his wife's decisive self-defense. But then, he had seen her in action before.

Late that night, Catherine, Eli and Rebecca sat outside their wagon in the warm, still air, looking at the dying embers of the fire that had cooked the buffalo steaks.

"Why did you stab the Indian, Mommie?" Catherine asked at last.

"I don't know, honey. I did what seemed right, what came to me in the moment. What do you think, Eli? Do you think I did right?"

"There's no right or wrong. You did what you had to do at the time," Eli said. "I don't know if I would have done the same thing, exactly. But you felt like you were in a crisis and you made your choice. You always do."

"But what if more Indians come?" Catherine asked.

Rebecca nodded. "People are against us now – they're blaming me," she said.

"Let them blame," Eli said. "We're going to get through this. And if they think about it, they'll realize that you were just defending yourself and Cathy."

They sat there a long time, thinking. Then Rebecca glanced at Catherine and realized she was asleep. Carefully, they put her to bed and got into their own bedding and talked some more, in whispers. Long after Eli had gone to sleep, Rebecca lay awake, looking at the thousands of stars above them, wondering what lay ahead. Now, for the first time, she almost wished they had not come at all.

Chapter 7

Monterey, California
May-June 1846

As THE WAGONS MOVED west from Missouri on May 13, the day after George Wheeler discovered Esperanza Amandillo and Antonio del Costa together in a Monterey garden, in Washington, D.C., President James Polk signed a declaration of war against Mexico. The war would eventually lead to bloodshed in Texas, some scattered fighting in California, the eventual surrender of those territories to the United States and the expansion of the country into a bi-coastal nation. But no splashy headlines appeared anywhere in the West that day. In fact, news of the war would not reach Monterey until July.

In the meantime, Wheeler's accusation against Esperanza sent the Amandillo household into turmoil. Carmelita confronted Esperanza that evening in the kitchen. Esperanza admitted she had been seeing Costa, then immediately turned on Wheeler. "What – does a ship's captain have nothing better to do than prowl the dark alleys of Monterey, spying?" she asked with a sneer. "Are you telling me he was thinking high-minded thoughts when he found us or did he have something else to do in that part of town? I'm sure he wasn't there by accident."

"You really have no call to make such accusations, Esperanza," her mother said. It's you who should be apologizing to him."

"For what? I'm not the property of that man, and he has no claim on me."

"You know you led him to think you were available, and then you agreed to marry him. You deceived everybody – including us, I could add."

"I see who I want to see."

"You told us you had stopped associating with that man – that criminal. He should be in jail. That's not someone I want my daughter running after. Why did you lie to us?"

"What was I supposed to do? If I'd said I was still seeing him you would have locked me up here – or had him sent away. What would you do if you were in love with someone?" Throwing her hands up, Esperanza stormed out of the kitchen.

"In love?" Carmelita shouted after her. "Daughter, you had better *decide* who you are in love with because until you do you are only going to cause more trouble."

Esperanza's frustration and resentment was compounded when she found out about her sister's newfound attachment to Wheeler. When she heard about the scene at the front driveway, she blew up and marched into Guadalupe's room.

"You shameless little wench," she shouted, throwing two pillows and a candlestick at Guadalupe, forcing her sister to duck. "If you wanted to steal my boyfriend, why didn't you just come out and say so. You've been going behind my back the whole time, haven't you?"

"No – no, it's not like that," Guadalupe said, but Esperanza wasn't listening.

"Have you been sleeping with him?"

"What? What are you thinking? Do you think I planned this, do you think I wanted it? You're the one who spoiled everything, you did it to yourself. How could you be so two-faced – leading him on while all along you were still in love with Antonio?"

"You're so jealous, you reek with jealousy. I can have anyone I want. It's not my fault that you get stuck with all the losers and the ugly men. You couldn't get anyone else so you had to go after mine. Well, fine, you can have him now. Take him if you want a stupid *gringo* that prowls around the streets at night."

"It was daytime."

"Oh, you've got all the dirty little details, don't you? The two of you probably planned this together. Fine – take the pasty-faced gringo. See if you can keep him away from all those whores he must be keeping in every port he's been to. He has high standards, I'm sure." She started to leave.

Steaming but momentarily speechless, Guadalupe shook her head and glared at her sister. "You don't know anything about him," she said at last.

Esperanza turned back and glared. "Oh, really?" she said, her voice now dark and muted. "And how much do you know?" She stared at Guadalupe for another few seconds before walking away.

The turmoil continued in the Amandillo household for two weeks. It was then, on June 15, in Sonoma, 150 miles to the north, that a former schoolteacher from Vermont made a crudely fashioned flag lettered with berry juice and raised it over the little town, declaring himself and his associates a "California Republic." The flag featured a crude grizzly bear that could have been mistaken for a pig at first glance. On the same day, the Amandillo family gathered for a midday meal on their sunny patio. Thomas Larkin, a family friend and a Monterey businessman who was the official U.S. consul to California, happened to be at the ranch to see Joaquin and stayed for lunch.

"I've pushed as hard as I can for a peaceful settlement, but fighting now seems certain," Larkin said as he sat at the table. "The Americans are bound to win in the end. I only hope it's over quickly."

"I can't run a ranch when my men are off shooting at Americans," Joaquin said. "As for me, I can live as well under the U.S. flag as under the Mexican one."

After the meal, when Larkin announced he had pressing business in town and left, Esperanza, Guadalupe and their parents were left at the table.

"Mother, do you think your grandchildren will really be growing up under an American flag?" Esperanza asked nonchalantly. She was looking at Carmelita but snuck glances at her father.

"Those things are for men to decide," Carmelita said. "They don't concern me. I only want us to be safe."

"It's entirely possible," Joaquin said diffidently, his eyes half-closed. "Whatever flag flies here, the world will still need hides and tallow. Besides, we don't have any grandchildren."

"Not yet." Esperanza wore an enigmatic expression, a smile working its way to her lips. Curious eyes turned to Esperanza.

"What are you trying to say?" her mother said, suddenly alert and suspicious.

"That you're going to have one soon, that's all."

All three of them stared at her, stunned. Joaquin's face turned red. "What have you done?" he shot back.

"Are you … are you sure? You're pregnant?" Carmelita blurted, stunned. Esperanza only flashed a broad smile.

"How could you let this happen?" Joaquin fumed.

Carmelita was already out of her seat. She started to huff, pressed her lips together, and then held herself back as she exhaled deeply and then went to one knee beside Esperanza's chair.

"Whose is it?" she asked, tight-lipped and whispering. "Who did this to you?"

"Not *to* me. And who do you think? It's Antonio's. I want it. You wouldn't let him in the house, but that didn't work, did it?" Esperanza had a sardonic smile still playing on her lips.

"You did it to spite me, didn't you," Joaquin snapped. "You did it to spit all your venom on me."

Horrified at the scene, Guadalupe sat frozen in her seat.

"I'd have thought you might be happier to be getting a grandchild," Esperanza said. "Didn't you want more family?"

Joaquin, his face now a deep purple, slammed down his napkin on the table, rattling the dishes with force of his fist, and stalked off to his study. Carmelita heaved a sigh and suddenly softened, putting her arm around Esperanza and squeezing her tenderly. Guadalupe, still unsure how to respond, sat in her place, toying with the frijoles left on her plate. Esperanza stared vacantly at the cumulus clouds now mounting in the sky.

Already incensed by his daughter's deceit, Joaquin now had more reason for worry. In spite of all his careful planning and work, nothing was playing out as he expected. Now that Esperanza had a child on the way and no prospective husband, the chances of finding a good son-in-law to take over the ranch had suddenly sunk to nothing.

He could not fathom what to make of Guadalupe's new attraction to Wheeler. Although he placed all the blame on Esperanza for her breakup with the Englishman, Joaquin was not ready to see him take up with Guadalupe so suddenly, as if jumping from one horse to another in the middle of a ride. The propriety of it did not sit well. But he did not want to cause another family blowup so soon after Esperanza's bombshell. He would not consent for Guadalupe to visit Wheeler – even properly chaperoned, of course – not even after she quietly and patiently explained herself one night in his study.

"Papa, I never meant for this to happen," she said, sitting by his chair on a little stool, looking at him in the eyes. "I didn't even know how I felt. I wouldn't have had it happen at all – I wouldn't do that to my sister. I liked his company, but it was only when – you know, when he found out – when I saw he was going to leave and not come back. Then I realized I couldn't let that happen. I couldn't let him just go. I love him, Papa."

Joaquin looked at his daughter calmly, with concern in his face. "I know how that can happen," he said. "I trust you. But this is not the way things are done. A young woman does not go chasing after a man. He's an honorable man, but he won't be rushing into anything. If he wants to see you, he will call. You're young, and you have time."

Guadalupe felt crushed, but she would not cross her father. "I know, Papa," she said. "Thank you, Papa." But she was hurt. And she was angry at being so unfairly restricted while Esperanza seemed to be suffering no penalty for conceiving a child out of wedlock. That night, alone in her room, she cried for over an hour. Then she took out a pen and paper and started composing a letter.

At his hotel in Monterey, George Wheeler could not sort out his feelings. He felt like a fool for thinking he could tame Esperanza after hearing her father's warning. When he had seen her with Costa, at first it seemed not to be happening. He had wondered whether he was dreaming. When he realized it was real, a huge wave of anger swept over him and kept receding and then returning for days. During one of those waves of anger he had charged into and out of the Amandillo house. Guadalupe's words and desperate plea as he left were too much to think about just then. Even now that he had been able to sort out the situation for a week, he couldn't put his anger aside long enough to think of what to do.

Then he received the letter:

Dear George,
   Please don't think that I am just having a girlish infatuation. I love you. I want to see you again. Please talk to my father – he'll understand.
                                        Love, Guadalupe

Wheeler sighed. Guadalupe was a nice, pretty girl, but he was not in love with her. Nor did he really want her in love with him just now, when such a situation might require more interaction with the Amandillos, just when he wanted them all out of his life. He couldn't picture himself ever comfortably socializing with that family. When word reached him of Esperanza's pregnancy, he realized that even without his discovery, any relationship with her would have been doomed. But as he read Guadalupe's note again, he was touched.

Then, after almost a month had passed, Wheeler had an unexpected visit from Joaquin Amandillo at his hotel.

"My daughter Guadalupe is disconsolate," he said when the two had settled down to glasses of whiskey at the hotel bar. "Can you tell me why this would be?"

"Your daughter is sensitive," Wheeler said. "I could see that from the first time I met her. She's probably feeling sorry for her sister."

"That is not the reason. It appears that she has harbored feelings for you, my friend."

Wheeler's expression did not change. "Well, I can't account for it," he said. "I never made any ..."

"Without intention, perhaps, you made some gesture or perhaps touched her in a friendly way."

"I can't recall. She's a happy, vibrant girl. I enjoyed her company. In a moment of fun I might have ... "

"Girls are quick to pick up signals, whether intended or not. At any rate, I need to get my family back together, to reach some stability. So here is my question, and you need to be very frank in your answer: Do you have, or could you possibly have, any interest in a relationship with either of my daughters? Esperanza, as you know, is with child. If you have any remaining feelings for her, that would preclude your seeing Guadalupe as far as I am concerned."

"I am over Esperanza, you can be sure. She hurt me too badly."

"Just as I thought. So if you have any intentions toward Guadalupe, I need to know now."

Wheeler thought for a long time, taking two or three good sips of whiskey and savoring them on his tongue while he thought. Esperanza had faded now. He could focus on Guadalupe's soft eyes, her young, tender face. He knew that he wanted to comfort her – that was all.

"*Señor*, what you ask is a hard choice to make on the spot. I like Guadalupe very much and I have also enjoyed the hospitality of you and your wife, and your good company. If you think it wouldn't create too much disruption in the household, I would like to return for a visit sometime. Where that would lead, I don't know."

"I hoped you would say so," Joaquin said, smiling. "I have been holding Guadalupe back, much against her wishes, and preventing her from coming into town. Perhaps before you come out to the hacienda, you two should meet here for, say, a chaperoned afternoon walk along the shoreline." And so it was arranged that Wheeler and Guadalupe should meet. That first meeting led to another, and those led to a succession of dinners at the hacienda. Although Esperanza was invited to these dinners, as a member of the household, she did not attend, to Wheeler's relief. She remained in her room, dining alone and refusing even to appear in the drawing room or on the patio when Wheeler was visiting. It was an uncomfortable situation, but Joaquin and Carmelita could not find a better solution than to simply let Esperanza sulk and prepare for the birth of her child.

She didn't sulk for long. Soon she was thinking, and then she was plotting. Now that she was to have a baby, it was even more important for her to have security, to be provided with a safe, respectable home to raise the child in. Since Guadalupe had stolen her captain, it seemed a virtual certainty that if they married, Guadalupe and Wheeler would inherit the ranch as well. Esperanza couldn't envision a future in which she could be happy under the thumb of her former suitor and his new wife. That was an absurd thought. There had to be a way to prevent that from happening. There had to be a way to make sure she got the ranch. She could not do it on her own – she would need Costa's help. The problem just now was that she was not allowed visits to town – her father had restricted her to the hacienda because of her condition and because of her transgressions. She needed to get messages to Costa, and to do that, somehow, she had to get her sister's help. Guadalupe was a trusting sort. Esperanza knew she could use that to her advantage, particularly in her current state. Guadalupe was probably eager to get back in her good graces and smooth things over, Esperanza thought. And she was right.

Her chance came one day when she was taking lunch on the patio. Guadalupe came out to sit with her. The two had barely spoken since the recent upheaval, and Guadalupe, ever the peacemaker, had decided to test the waters.

"It's good to see you getting out of your room," Guadalupe began tepidly.

"My room is my life now," Esperanza snorted. "I can't go anywhere. I can't see anyone. Those four walls are my only friends."

"I know. It must be a terrible time for you right now. I just ..." she sighed and looked away. "I just wanted you to know that I never intended ..."

"Yes, I know, you never intended to steal my boyfriend. Well, you don't have to worry about it. He was never really my boyfriend. He thought he was. I guess he would have married me, but I never wanted him – not really. You know who I love. Antonio was always the one – the only one. And now that I have his child, I can't even see him. I'm in prison here. My baby is going to be born and grow up without knowing his father. That shouldn't happen. No child should be kept from knowing his father."

"You're right – every child should have a father – and a mother."

"Papa hates Antonio. He'll never let him anywhere near here. I can't talk to him – can't even get a message to him. Sometimes I think I'm going to die of loneliness."

"You should at least be able to write him a letter. Don't you have a way to get a letter into town?"

"How am I going to do that? Mama won't take it. She's too worried about crossing Papa. If I trusted one of the servants, they might read the letter or tell on me. The servants all hate me."

The two sat in silence for a minute. Finally, Guadalupe said, "I'll take a letter to Antonio. You can give it to me. I'll make sure he gets it and I'll bring you his letter back if he wants to give me one."

Esperanza looked at her sister and saw that her eyes were shining. She was so eager, like a little puppy, Esperanza thought. "Do you think you could do it without anyone noticing?" she asked. "I don't want any word to get to Papa about this."

"I can do it. No one will know. I'll just slip over to the Custom House when no one is looking. Put the letter in the mailbox. It's simple. Make sure the envelope is sealed with wax. And along with it, I'll give him a note to let him know where I'll be at a certain time, so he can give me a reply. No one will ever know."

"You're good to do this. It means a lot to me."

"It's only right. They can't keep you two apart forever."

And so, unwittingly, Guadalupe chose to become the go-between in a nefarious plot that nearly sabotaged her own marriage. The idea came from Esperanza, the execution from Costa. Esperanza's first letter spelled out the problem:

My Dear Antonio,

We have to discredit the gringo. He's been all over the world, so he must have a past, something or someone that could be exploited, like a former mistress. Or, even better, a family in some foreign port? Someone from his ship must know.

Love, Esperanza

In his return letter, Costa said he had already asked around about this. Wheeler was said to be strictly proper in his dealings with women. But there must be something. Nobody was perfect. Maybe one of the hands could be bought off – paid to say something, to tell a story that might be true, that would sound plausible. They could make it up. Every seaman has something he wouldn't want known. They would decide what Wheeler's secret was and put it in someone else's mouth. It had to be a story bad enough to repulse such an upstanding man as Joaquin Amandillo – something that would show beyond any doubt that Wheeler was unworthy, unsuitable as a son-in-law and prospective heir. Then, when Wheeler was out of the way, Esperanza would have time to work on her father, to placate him, to show that she had changed and make him fall in love with his grandchild. It would also give her time to restore Costa's image, make her parents see that the child needed a father. Someday the ranch would be theirs. It all sounded workable to Costa.

He knew Esperanza was his if he wanted her. Through her he could become a privileged landowner. He wrote out his plan, sealed it in an envelope and waited for her sister, the messenger, to return.

Chapter 8

Monterey, California
July 1846

ON HIS WAY INTO MONTEREY on horseback, Joaquin
Amandillo began to think now that his plan to provide
for his daughters' security while protecting his legacy
was right all along. He liked George Wheeler and wanted
him for a son-in-law. Guadalupe was a better match for
him than Esperanza would have been. If things between
Wheeler and Guadalupe went well, then …. He knew
he shouldn't count on it, but he wanted his daughters to
prosper. The ranch would then be preserved and passed to
his grandchildren through the care of someone he trusted.
It was all fine with him as long as his daughters were
happy, and lately Guadalupe and Esperanza seemed to be
getting along fine. He had even seen them whispering to
each other, sharing girl talk and giggling in a way they
had not done since they were pre-teens. It was a healthy
sign, he thought. They were maturing and learning to
live together as adults. When Esperanza's child was born,
Guadalupe would become a doting aunt, and the child a
good companion for his future cousins. Now it was time
to go ahead with the rest of the plan.

Joaquin was riding into Monterey to see his lawyer,
Eusebio Garcia, as he did every Wednesday. Garcia had

drawn up the papers that would transfer ownership of his 7,000 acres north of the Salinas River to Ricardo Gutierrez, owner of the 5,000-acre tract in the Carmel Valley that Gutierrez was using for breeding. The Carmel Valley land would become Amandillo's property, a place where the climate and soil were perfect for a vineyard and winery. Gutierrez would get the space he needed to expand his breeding operation. Someday the vineyard land would be passed to Esperanza and the ranch to Guadalupe. That was the plan, and Amandillo had also asked Garcia to draw up a new will, putting all those intentions into writing.

As Amandillo was dismounting in the Plaza he happened to see Thomas Larkin. Larkin walked quickly over to see him, clearly excited. "It's happening," Larkin told him, his eyes wide. "President Polk has declared war. The U.S. fleet is on its way to Monterey!"

"What does this mean?" Amandillo said. "Are we going to be occupied? Blockaded? There's no one here to stop them."

"Of course not," Larkin said. "No gunpowder. Few troops. It should all be over quickly. The only change will be the color of the flag and the uniforms on the soldiers."

This conversation was on Amandillo's mind as he went to Garcia's office to do his business. When he had signed the papers and pocketed the deed and the copies of the new will, Amandillo went by the shoreline before having his lunch at the hotel. As he stood looking out to sea, wondering how he would fare with the Americans in charge of Monterey, he became aware of a man standing nearby, a seaman by the look of him – dark clothing, greasy hair, haggard look. At first the man seemed to be just gazing to sea as Amandillo was, but then he began to move closer, slowly put purposefully. Amandillo started to move on, for he wasn't in the mood to converse, but the man signaled a greeting.

"*Señor* Amandillo, is it?" the man inquired.

"Yes, and who are you?"

"Jenkins, sir. Yes, Mr. Jenkins. I was a boatswain's mate on the *Golden Eagle*, the ship of Mr. Wheeler, sir. Hasn't been any crews goin' out lately, sort of a lull, ye might say. Hard on an old sailor's livin', you know?"

"Yes, I suppose it is. Well, I'm sure the ship will be sailing soon." Amandillo turned to leave.

"'Scuse me for buttin' in where I shouldn't, but Mr. Wheeler is said to be a marryin' yer daughter, if I have 'eered correctly."

"Perhaps, yes," Amandillo said, snapping around. "What is that to you, may I ask?" His tone was impatient.

"Oh, 'snone o' my concern, none at all, except that bein', you know, privy to certain information, certain things most don't know about, I could provide ye with facts ye might find interestin'. If ye catch my meanin'."

"I catch no meaning at all. If you have something to say, say it straight out."

"Well, it's a hard thing t' put jes like that, one-two-three. If I was to have a little shot, to wet me whistle . . ."

"You want me to buy you a drink? Is that what this is about? Look, I'm in no mood to socialize. So please excuse me." Amandillo again started to walk away.

"'E's not what ye think," Jenkins said loudly. "'e's got quite a 'istory, that man." Amandillo turned and stared. "A woman 'ere, a woman there. In Singapore he 'as a whole brood, they say. Oh, yeah. Several little ones 'e has there, along with 'is wife – or maybe she isn't. But in Singapore . . ."

"Why would you say something like that to me? What do you hope to gain? Jenkins, was it? Just what are you trying to do?"

"Me, sir? No sir, no. I just 'eered Mr. Wheeler would be a marryin', and I, well, you know, I think the perspective family deserves . . ."

"Look here, this has gone far enough. First of all, I'm not interested in any rumors or gossip about Captain Wheeler. He's a substantial, upstanding man, which it's obvious you are not. So if you were expecting some gratitude on my part, I'm going to disappoint you. And don't approach me or any member of my family again – have I put it clearly enough?"

Amandillo strode off purposefully. But instead of heading for the hotel, as he first intended, he made a beeline for the horse he had left at the stable and left town immediately for the ranch.

For the rest of the afternoon, Amandillo busied himself with some chores he had been putting off. He repaired a hinge on the patio gate. He patched a crumbling piece of adobe in the garden wall. He organized and conditioned his riding tack. But he couldn't get the encounter with Jenkins off his mind. Suppose some of what Jenkins said was true, he thought. Every sailor has had some experiences. What of it? Probably Jenkins was just a disgruntled jack-tar looking to make trouble or bum a few pesos. Just the same, he decided to confront Wheeler, who would be coming for dinner that night.

It was a subdued evening, without much animated talk. Only Guadalupe was her usual bubbly self. As the table was about to be cleared, Amandillo invited Wheeler to join him in his study. The don got right to the point.

"You had a sailor named Jenkins on your last voyage?" he opened.

"Garson Jenkins – yes, an older fellow. Not one I'd want to have again. Usually got his work done but always causing a stir – cheating at cards, fighting, arguments, that sort of thing. Just troublesome. No one trusted him. The boys kept a close watch on their stash when he was around, let me tell you. Bit of a drunkard, too, and I had to confine him when he got out of hand. Why, is Jenkins still around town?"

"He found me today. I was taking a stroll down at the harbor as usual before lunch. I don't think it was a chance meeting. He wanted to talk about you."

"Really?" Wheeler's eyes widened, but only slightly. "Hmm. Nothing good to say, I'd bet."

"Said you had a family in Singapore. What about it?"

Wheeler stared vacantly for a few seconds, gathering his thoughts. Then he inhaled and exhaled deeply. "Yes," he said. "It's something in my past. I should have brought it up before now."

"Should have? Don't you remember I asked if you'd been married?" Amandillo asked, his voice rising. "*Por Dios*, you've got a lot of nerve. After all we've been through with both my daughters, and now this? What were you thinking?" He was shouting now.

"I'm sorry," Wheeler said. "I should have brought it all out in the open, and I intended to. I was waiting for the right time. But I didn't lie – I haven't been married."

"Well, the right time was weeks ago."

"Yes, of course you're right. Here's the real issue. They're my former family – not my family now."

"Oh, I see, you've abandoned them. Well, I'm glad we've cleared that up. That's damned reassuring."

"No – not abandoned. They were taken from me."

"Taken. I can't wait to hear the explanation for that."

Wheeler nodded, letting go another sigh and then fixing his eyes on Amandillo. "It's all documented. I can show you the papers. Or you can ask Meadows – he testified for me, but it didn't help. I loved Suyen. She was a wonderful companion and gave me two beautiful children. And I provided well for her. Her family looked after her during my long absences. That should have been enough, but I wanted more security for her, to keep her protected. So I made a mistake. There was a man there called Charon. He was half French, half Malaysian, and he was a government official. I knew him pretty well, I thought, and I considered him a family friend. But I didn't know he secretly loved Suyen. You see, I asked Charon to look after Suyen the last time I went away from Singapore for several months. I thought with him being in the government, he could help her with any problems that might come up. But while I was gone he … he seduced Suyen, and then he used his position to claim legal guardianship of the children." Wheeler choked a little as a well of feelings came up and suddenly his eyes were moist and red. "He was a lawyer, you see," he said, regaining his composure a bit. "And he, uh, he knew how to use the courts over there. He claimed I had deserted the family, and it looked bad because Suyen and I were never married. I wasn't there to defend myself, so he won. Suyen didn't even know what was going on at first, but by the time she did it was too late. She was told she had to go along with the court decree for the sake of the children. So when I returned it was all decided, and I had no legal recourse."

Amandillo looked at Wheeler and shook his head slowly. "Didn't you want to kill this man, Charon?" he asked.

"Yes I did, and I thought of how I would do it and what the consequences would be. The result would have been disastrous for the family. I might be caught. And then, in all probability, the children would have no father at all. And even if I weren't caught, I didn't want to leave the family with such a legacy – to teach them that murder was the way to solve problems. I did have a fistfight with him. But I stopped before I killed him."

"So you left your family in the hands of this usurper."

"I thought I had no choice. If I had been able to reverse it in an honorable way, I would have done it. The family had to have a protector."

"What about a legal challenge?"

"The courts there are difficult. I contacted a lawyer, but he advised me that I had virtually no chance. I thought it better to leave the family in peace."

The two sat in silence for a few minutes. Finally, Wheeler spoke.

"I'll tell Guadalupe the story, if you'll permit me."

"I think it would be better coming from you – yes."

"If she will still have me, do we still have your blessing?"

"I'm not going to stand in the way."

On July 2, Thomas Larkin watched from shore as Commodore John D. Sloat led his U.S. Pacific Squadron around Point Piños and into Monterey Bay. Sloat, a cautious man, had been at sea when he received word of President Polk's declaration of war, along with instructions to occupy California's Pacific ports but not to disturb the populace. The first thing he wanted to do was salute the presidio, but he could see no Mexican flag.

It was left to Larkin to go on board the flagship *Savannah* to meet Sloat and inform him that the post was so depleted it had neither a flag nor gunpowder to return a salute. Sloat waited in the harbor for five days while the residents of Monterey were left in suspense. Then on July 7, after he had received word that Fremont had taken command of Sonoma, Sloat went ashore. The Mexican captain in charge told him that he had neither the authority to surrender the port nor the forces with which to resist. At 10 o'clock that morning 250 Marines and seamen went ashore, Sloat read a proclamation in Spanish and English, and the American flag was raised over Monterey to a twenty-one-gun salute.

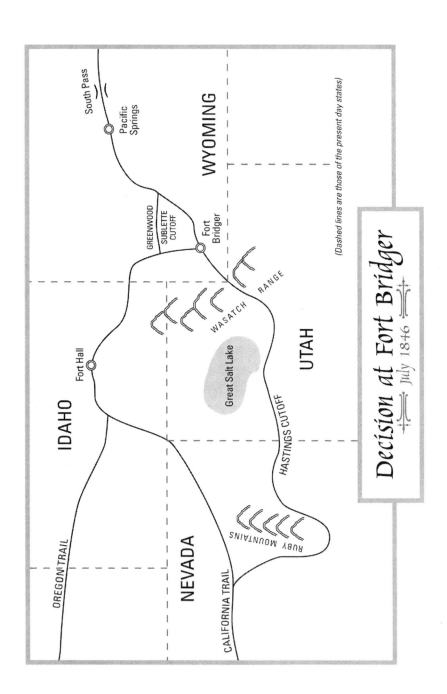

Decision at Fort Bridger — July 1846

(Dashed lines are those of the present day states)

Chapter 9

On the California Trail
July 1846

As THE WAGONS of the Benedict-Foard party moved past Independence Rock on July 11, they knew they were behind schedule. It was said that to be sure of escaping the Sierra Nevada snows, a wagon party should pass this hunk of granite, a third of a mile long, by Independence Day, July 4.

About the same time, the wagon train met a group of frontiersmen on horseback, coming from Fort Bridger on their way to Fort Laramie. One carried an open letter to wagon trains from Lansford Hastings, a copy of which had also been given to the Bryant-Russell party, now apparently a day ahead. James Reed was the first to grab the letter and read it to his party. It explained that Hastings was on his way to Fort Bridger from California via the Salt Lake, and that he would be happy to lead any wagon parties from Fort Bridger through the new cutoff – for a charge of $10 per family group. Eli thought Reed appeared to be pleased by this proposition and that Reed seemed especially reassured that Hastings himself would have had time to survey the mountain passage ahead of them. Eli and others still had serious doubts.

July 18 dawned bright and just a little cooler, but Eli predicted they would all be sweating by mid-morning.

Today the combined wagon party – now numbering some 250 people and ninety wagons, would have to leave the camp on the Sweetwater, seeing that river for the last time. They would gradually gain altitude for eight miles to the broad saddle called South Pass, which bridged the continental divide. From there, all water would flow west to the Pacific. It was a deceptively benign passage, and Eli said that often a group would pass there unaware of its importance. But it was in fact about 7,500 feet above sea level and represented the most significant geographical demarcation between East and West. It was also the only practical pass for wagons coming this way.

"What people even more often don't know is that on this route they'll have to travel the next 30 miles with only one drinkable source of water," Eli told Rebecca as they were getting ready for bed the night before. "That source is the Pacific Spring two miles west of the pass. After that, it'll be another twenty miles to the next good water at the Little Sandy. That means that with our oxen pulling heavy wagons uphill, we *have* to camp at the Pacific Spring because a thirty-mile day under these conditions is out of the question. The animals will dehydrate." Eli knew those things because he had been that way several times.

"Tomorrow will be a decision point," he said. "This party could split apart. And if it's not tomorrow, it'll be before Fort Bridger. I think Benedict wants to join the Donners on the Hastings route."

Rebecca didn't say anything for a few minutes, but then she asked, "What if the rest of the party goes with him? Are we going on by ourselves?"

"They won't. And even if some of them do … well, we'll cross one bridge at a time. You've been wanting me to make a stand."

"I know," she said. "But are you going to strand us out here by ourselves?" Eli didn't answer. She knew he was fuming inside.

The next morning, Eli went to explain the facts about the water to Jack Benedict, but Benedict didn't seem worried. "Donner and Reed are keen to get down to Fort Bridger to meet Hastings," he said. "A day could make a difference. They've been told there's another stream between the spring and the Little Sandy."

"It's an unreliable stream, sometimes dry," Eli told him. "Even if there is water in it, you cannot let your oxen drink from there. They'll get sick."

But Benedict was still unconvinced. "We could go eighteen miles on a downhill course without water, if we needed to," he said.

"It seems as if it's downhill, but that only lessens the effort – it doesn't lessen the need for water," Eli argued. "And it's not entirely downhill, and it's very exposed."

"We'll see," Benedict said.

For three days now, they had all been able to see the snow-capped Wind River Range to the northwest. Now, as they crested South Pass, the peaks formed a backdrop to the line of wagons working their way west. The easterners who were seeing these vistas for the first time shook their heads with amazement at the craggy peaks, so white and lofty while they endured 90-degree heat at their lower elevation. It was a reminder of what could happen in cooler weather if they were delayed into fall, especially in the Sierra Nevada.

They lunched at South Pass, and by early afternoon had come to the Pacific Spring, lush and green amidst the dry landscape they had come to accept as the norm since leaving the Missouri Valley. Now was the point of decision, Rebecca knew. If Benedict chose to move on at this point, to try to reach the next water by nightfall, he would be putting the whole party at risk, so Eli would have to stand in his way – the confrontation he had been dreading, and one that could divide the party and have unknown further consequences. As Benedict approached him after the meal, she saw Eli bracing himself, and she knew he had made his choice. While most of the wagons prepared to leave, Rebecca moved closer to listen, as did Dr. Enderle and a few of the other men.

"Let's get ready to move," Benedict said, his big jaw set, pointing his thumb down the trail and staring Eli in the face, daring him to disagree. "The cattle will get mired in the mud if we let them water here overnight." Eli sneered and spat on the ground.

"It's not worth the risk, Jack," Eli said. These animals can make the eighteen miles to the Little Sandy tomorrow, with time to rest today. They're not going to make it today before nightfall."

"It's only twelve miles, Reed and Donner's people say; and besides, they've heard there's water in the other stream, the Dry Sandy. We're going to make it fine. We want to keep with the other group for safety, so stay with me on this."

"I don't know exactly why you're thinking this way, but there's no way I can do that. I know this country and you don't, and neither do Reed and Donner. You'd do well to listen to me."

"It's decided, Eli. We're going."

"I have to let the rest of the folks know what they're getting into," Eli said, starting to move past the trail captain, who stepped directly in his way and put his palm against Eli's left shoulder.

"You're not going to stir up shit in my party," Benedict said with assurance. Benedict was 6 inches taller than Eli and outweighed him by a good 50 pounds. But Benedict clearly was not expecting a fight, and Eli was ready for one. With electric quickness, all of his frustration with Benedict came to a point. He disabled Benedict with a sharp punch to the solar plexus. In the second it took Benedict to slash a massive forearm in the direction of Eli's neck, Eli ducked and caught Benedict square on the side of his jaw. The big man went down, shaking his head to get his senses back, and then slowly crawled to his knees. Eli kicked him in the stomach, leaving him supine, gasping for breath. Three blows had put him out. Rebecca stood with her mouth open. She had never seen her husband in a fight.

Eli gathered the men of the two parties and told them what he knew about the water sources. "Jack has made a wrong decision," Eli said, breathing hard himself, but his voice confident. "You'll be taking an unnecessary risk to try to reach the next good water source today." The Donner-Reed wagons, standing to one side, clearly were going to try to make it. Benedict, still gasping and angry, recovered enough to try to shout him down.

Leaning on one arm, he said, "Here's a man who thinks he's so fucking smarter than the rest of you, he wants to split us up. If you want to be part of a mutiny, stay with him. I think I've been a good leader so far."

There was a lot of shouting. As the family leaders were about to get together for a vote, George Enderle gave a shrill whistle. He mounted a wagon, and everyone turned as he began to speak. By now, Enderle was one of the most respected members of the group. He had treated members of every family for some malady, injury or ailment and had consistently gone out of his way to be helpful to everyone.

"I've come to know Eli Ford like a brother on this trip," George said. "You know him to be a competent and able tracker, hunter, workman and guide. He's quiet about his accomplishments, but I know something more. He's got the best judgment of anyone I know, and he knows this country. You all remember what happened with the wagon wheels." There was a general nodding of agreement. "If Eli says we should camp, then we should camp. I'm staying."

In the end, Benedict convinced only the six families he had brought from Indiana. The other families with their twenty-five wagons sided with the Foards, announcing they would split and camp at the spring. That night, they chose Eli as their new leader.

The next day, as Eli led his train, now twenty-five wagons strong, down from Pacific Spring, the wisdom of their decision became plain. They passed Dry Sandy Creek, which was standing in stagnant pools, and Eli warned everyone to steer their oxen clear of the water. As the day dragged on, they saw the effect on the other group from the day before – the carcasses of two oxen that had apparently drunk from the Dry Sandy and been poisoned. Before they reached the Little Sandy, four more dead oxen appeared. And, as Eli had predicted, they found the Donner-Reed-Benedict party still encamped at the Little Sandy, exhausted and dispirited from the misspent effort of the previous day. Benedict had lost one ox, the Reed family had lost their best oxen pair from poisoning, and none of them had gained any time, since they had needed a rest day after the ordeal anyway.

To avoid disharmony, Eli camped his entourage a few hundred yards downstream from the others, where he found something he was looking for – a trail junction with the right-hand turn marked with a wooden sign marked "Greenwood." This was the place that was to be known as the parting-of-the-ways – the northern cutoff that would become standard for later wagon groups bound for Oregon or California. But it was new to Eli, having been documented only a year or two before. He had learned of it at Fort Laramie, in talking with fur trappers there. It was said to save two and a half days over the route via Fort Bridger, but Eli was extremely skeptical.

"I haven't traveled the route, but I suspect that after crossing the Big Sandy, there won't be any water for 40 miles," he told Rebecca. He called a meeting to explain the pros and cons of taking this cutoff, and it was unanimously decided to continue on the older trail to Fort Bridger. Eli also sought out James Reed after dinner, to make sure Reed understood the option. Reed was worried about the loss of his oxen, but he still seemed confident about the prospects for meeting Hastings at Fort Bridger, so he had no interest in bypassing Fort Bridger by taking this cutoff.

To Eli's mind, it might have been better to take the Greenwood, since the party would then be committed to the northern route around the Salt Lake, and any potential dissention that might come up regarding the Hastings route at Fort Bridger would be avoided. But in the end he didn't want to risk the water shortage, so they were going to take the safer option. Six days later, at Fort Bridger, Eli would have reason to second-guess himself.

Chapter 10

Fort Bridger, Oregon-California Trail
July 1846

THE SCENE AT FORT BRIDGER on July 27 was frenetic, even chaotic compared with the atmosphere the Foards had been used to for the past few weeks. The place was virtually a one-man operation. Jim Bridger, a frontiersman from way back, had built two primitive log buildings, connected by a pen for horses. Within sight of it stood perhaps 200 wagons – some leaving, some arriving, some staying a few days. Everybody going west – that is, almost everybody there – now had less than half the journey left – perhaps 950 miles from there to the Sacramento Valley. No one, but no one, was crazy enough to think the worst was over. The overall mood was a mixture of hollow-eyed hope and poorly disguised anxiety. Most parties were behind the schedule they had wanted to maintain, and they hoped to find some way of either increasing their travel pace or shortening the route, so as to get through the Sierra before the snows hit. That could occur as early as October, they all knew. The danger had not been spoken aloud by many, but at the current pace, they all would be hard-pressed to make their destination by October 1. For the slower travelers such as the Donner-Reeds, the chances were even slimmer.

From his old trapper friend Elisha Stephens, Eli knew that the Truckee River route over the Sierra was passable. Two years before, Stephens had been the first to lead a wagon party over the route. He had sent word to Eli that he could use this route and had given him hand-sketched maps and descriptions. But the Stephens party had nearly been trapped by snow, and Stephens warned Eli not to push into mid-October.

Many of the new arrivals came hoping to buy animals at Fort Bridger to replace ones they had lost, but there were few to be had, and only people with lots of hard cash could claim them. Everybody wanted the latest updates on optional routes, and some were hoping to find supplies for equipment repairs or replacement. Few would be completely satisfied with what they found. A blacksmith shop could do repairs. Liquor, some food staples, a few weapons and some wagon parts could be bought. Some of the trappers who lived there were willing to trade their furs and hides for necessities, but furs were not in high demand just then. It was a critical juncture, the last chance for supplies before reaching California.

Reed was the first to be disappointed. He learned that Lansford Hastings, instead of waiting for all the wagons that might want to try his new cutoff to the south, had left a day or two before with a 60-wagon party that was anxious to get moving. That group was now working its way over the Wasatch Range with Hastings as guide, the first wagon train to try the route.

But the Donner-Reed party had already voted, back at the Greenwood cutoff. The men and boys over 14 years old had gathered, and decided to try Hastings' route and elected George Donner as their leader. Bridger himself assured the still-undaunted Reed and Donner that Hastings had been over the route on horseback and reported that it was passable for wagons. Reed told the rest that they were sure to come upon Hastings if they set out soon.

For the Foards there was no question of route – Eli would be leading the party northeast on the main trail via Fort Hall. Benedict, who had arrived at Fort Bridger with his six families shortly after them, had conferred with his friend Reed and was lining up his now-small party to join the Donner-Reed group on the Hastings cutoff. But by then Rebecca had talked to George Donner's wife, Tamsen, and knew she was *not* convinced. Even from their short time together on the trail, Rebecca knew Tamsen Donner was an independent and cautious woman. Aware of James Clyman's warning, and hearing of Eli's strong opinion, Tamsen Donner took matters into her own hands. She was not going to directly oppose her husband, but she was determined not to lure others to join what she considered a dangerous venture into the unknown. So she lobbied the women, focusing on the families in Benedict's group.

That evening, there was a gathering outside the log cabins to discuss the Hastings route and to air all opinions. Getting wind of the doings, nearly everyone in the Donner-Reed, Foard and Benedict groups were soon gathered, along with another wagon party that had arrived, all of them concerned with the choice of routes. The men gathered at the front, the women at the back listening, all of them standing. Rebecca stood at the side, with her arm around Cathy. Jim Bridger, as owner of the premises, was allowed to speak first.

Bridger, it turned out, had a lot riding on the success of the Hastings route. Since the opening of the Greenwood cutoff to the north, some wagon trains that might have come by his trading post – and spent money – had been bypassing him. That trend seemed likely to continue unless the Hastings route were found preferable and drew more wagons to come his way. Bridger stood to lose substantial business, maybe his entire investment.

Bridger was known to be a teller of tall tales, most of which were taken as such by his audiences. But in describing the Hastings Cutoff, he told an outright lie.

"You'll find an easy, wide path through the mountains, with lots of grass," Bridger said. Your biggest challenge will be the forty-mile desert going west from the Salt Lake. "You'll need to stock up on water for that, but you'll save days of travel."

Eli looked at Bridger in amazement, shaking his head. He knew that Bridger knew better than this, so he immediately jumped onto the log Bridger had been standing on to speak his piece.

"I know Mr. Bridger very well, but some of you may not, so let me tell you a little about him," Eli said. "Over the years, he has acquired one of the biggest collections of yarns in the West. He takes delight in spinning these tales, and many people have been greatly entertained, no doubt. But let me give you fair warning – he is not to be taken seriously. He may not realize that most of you are unaccustomed to such kidding and are about to make a very important choice with serious consequences. Don't make this mistake."

Bridger had kept his place beside Eli on the log. "Oh, let me assure you that I am serious," he chimed in. "The southern route is a fine one, and one that you would be well advised to take. Mr. Foard has not been west for some years, so he is probably not the best source of information on the latest routes. Even now, Lansford Hastings is escorting wagons to establish this trail, so those wagons that follow should have an even easier time."

"I have received no information that leads me to believe this is a feasible route for wagons," Eli persisted. "And the desert is much more of a problem than is being said.

Some of you will die from dehydration, and your animals certainly will."

At this point, James Reed came to the front and motioned Bridger out of the way. "Mr. Foard has been trying to dissuade us from this obviously beneficial new route for some weeks now, and now he is contradicting even the local proprietor, who should know better than anyone," Reed said. "I wondered about Mr. Foard when he first impugned the reputation of the esteemed author, Mr. Hastings, in my presence. Well, I took it on myself to inquire to Mr. Hastings about Mr. Foard, by sending a letter addressed to Hastings at this place, by way of the party of trappers that passed us near Fort Laramie. When I arrived here, Bridger passed his reply on to me, and I would like to read the words of Lansford Hastings now."

Rebecca was looking at Eli, one hand over her mouth. A bolt of fear went through her. Immediately, she asked Judith Gagnon to take Cathy to play with the Gagnon children and to make sure she stayed there. She braced herself for what was to come, and Eli did the same.

" 'I met Eli Foard on August 16 of last year in Franklin, Missouri,' " Reed said, reading from the letter in his hands. " 'I know little about Mr. Foard, but I do know one thing – he is a murderer.' " The crowd stirred and there was a general commotion of voices. " 'Back in Missouri, Mr. Foard and I had a conversation after one of my speeches, and thereafter I engaged Mr. Foard in a friendly game of poker for money,' " Reed continued, the crowd quieting to listen. " 'During the course of this game, Mr. Foard became angry, threw his hat down on the floor, and accused me of cheating. He then stormed out of the saloon where we were playing. I followed him to Mr. Foard's home a block or two away, trying to reason with him. Upon entering the home, Mr. Foard found his wife in a compromising position with another man. Mr. Foard pulled out his gun and shot the man in the back, in cold blood.' "

The buzzing from the crowd was getting steadily noisier, and Reed had to quiet them so he could continue.

" 'Now I'm going to explain why Eli Foard resents me so much. I gave testimony at a hearing held before a judge a few days after this shooting, testimony that should have put Foard in jail. But the judge dismissed the murder charges, probably because the dead man was an outsider and Foard was well known in the town. So it's understandable why Foard would want to attack me. I give you this information so that you know why Mr. Eli Foard may have cause to put me in the most unfavorable light possible and to damage my reputation.' "

The crowd began to buzz again, and Eli, who had not moved from the log, waved to get their attention. Judith Gagnon had come up to put her arm around Rebecca, who sank down to sit on a stump. It was getting dark now, and the lanterns were glowing.

"This incident did occur – yes, it did," Eli said, calmly, but shouting to be heard. The crowd quieted. "But it was not quite as stated in Mr. Hastings' letter. Yes, I talked with Hastings, and in that talk I found that he has a lot to learn about the West – but that's a subject aside from what he's saying here. I did play poker with Hastings and I accused him of cheating, which he was, and then I left. I couldn't understand why Hastings was following me home because I wasn't threatening him. He was yelling at me. When we got home I found a man attacking my wife. He charged me and I shot him. Would you blame me for that?"

"And who, may I ask, can verify this story?" Reed asked Eli. All eyes were on Rebecca at this point, so she knew she had to speak.

"I can," Rebecca said, coming to the front. She knew what she had to say. "The dead man's name was Cole Carlin, and my husband didn't kill him – I did." There was a general murmur again. "My husband is trying to protect me but I don't need it – the truth is enough." She was in tears, and Judith tried to get her to sit down, but she stayed where she was, pushing Judith away.

"I can clear up a lot of things right here and now," Rebecca said.

"You don't have to do this, Rebecca," Eli said, but she waved him off and kept talking.

"I first met Cole Carlin in St. Louis, a few months before I met my husband. Carlin came to call on me a few times – enough for me to know he wasn't my type. He tried to get too familiar with me, and I told him not to come back.

"I didn't see Carlin for years, until that day, the one we're talking about. There was a knock at my door and there he was, standing there, smiling a crooked smile. I didn't invite him in but he barged in anyway, and I tried to reason with him, to make it clear I didn't want him there. He wouldn't take no for an answer. I tried to go for my husband but he grabbed me and tried to rape me. That's when Eli came in. Cole got up, and I saw Cole's gun in the holster on the floor. I picked it up. Eli had his gun out too, but when I saw Cole charging at Eli I shot him. Hastings was outside the door. He probably thought Eli did it.

"So that's what happened. Eli changed the story for the sheriff, to protect me, saying he killed Cole, gambling that a jury wouldn't convict him. As it turned out, he didn't even have to go to trial. I didn't plan to kill Cole Carlin, but I don't regret it."

The crowd erupted in jabbering and shouting at this point. Then Reed waved his hands and started to talk.

"Let's not get distracted here," Reed said, shouting above the commotion. It's understandable that Mrs. Foard would want to cover for her husband, but all of us must think of how all this taints Foard's opinion of Hastings. He obviously has a score to settle. Our purpose here is to decide on a route to California. Mr. Hastings has a wonderful reputation, and he and Bridger have presented us with this much shorter option. When there is a nearer route, it is of no use to take such a roundabout course as to go to Fort Hall."

"None of this business about what happened in Franklin really matters now," Eli said. "It did not change my opinion of Hastings. He is of a mind to promote this new route, and his reasons are his own. The same goes for Bridger. But I have made an independent judgment here, and I am telling you that you are taking a bad risk in traveling this untried route. You will get to California before the snows if you go through Fort Hall. The other way, you might not. I even think it might take a lot longer."

There was a loud buzz as dozens of conversations broke out. A few more men tried to speak, but it soon became apparent that each of the groups was going to settle the question of the route for itself. George Enderle came up to Eli and Rebecca and put his hand on Eli's shoulder. "Don't worry, Eli, we're with you. We know you're the most level-headed one here."

As the men debated, Tamsen Donner came over and put her arm around Rebecca. "You're brave to say what you did," she said. "I can tell you're saying the truth. You're strong and you wouldn't have said it if it weren't true. I know your husband must be a good man." By this time there were a dozen women around Rebecca, offering support.

Later that night, Eli was approached by several men led by Henry Forrester, the head of one of the six families still with Jack Benedict. "We have been talking, Eli, the families with Benedict," he said. "We still like Jack, but we feel he is wrong on this. Tonight decided us. We don't trust this fellow Reed. We don't like the way he handled this. He has never been out here, Donner has never been out here. Benedict has never been out here. You have, and

I don't know what arrangement Bridger may have with Hastings – maybe something, maybe nothing. But we've made our choice. We are inclined to go your way – all six families. We trust you and Dr. Enderle. Would you have us back in your group?"

Eli said he would be glad to have them.

That night, after Cathy had been put to bed, Eli and Rebecca sat silently, looking at the stars again.

"You didn't have to do what you did," Eli said quietly, when most of the noises of the camp had died down. "I could have answered that letter on my own."

"You could have, but I wouldn't feel as good about it as I do now. I feel like I've been carrying a great big ox on my back all these months. And what if they *hadn't* believed you? It was the women who convinced the men, you know, after they heard my story."

"You think?"

"I know. Women can tell when there's a ring of truth about something. They go with their heart, not their head."

"Well, yeah. But in this case I think logic would have won the day just as well. We had that on our side, too. Aren't you worried there will be talk?"

"Let them talk. It's better than me thinking I have something to hide."

"Well, it's only these few families anyway. We'll probably never see them after we split up at Sutter's Fort."

"And what if we did? It just doesn't matter to me. What happened, happened. Now that I've said it out loud, it just doesn't seem so monumental any more. I'm ready to start living in the present."

The Foard party left Fort Bridger the next morning, heading northwest toward Fort Hall in a long file of wagons that included everyone who had originally left Independence together except for the family of Jack Benedict, which had joined the Donner party. The rest of the Foards' journey was, by comparison, uneventful. They rationed provisions, the families cooperated and they all arrived safely at Sutter's Fort, California on October 10, a few days after the first snow flurries started to fall on the passes in the Sierra Nevada.

On the day the Foards arrived at Sutter's Fort, the Donner party was camped on the Humboldt River in present-day Nevada, with nearly 150 difficult miles to cover before even reaching the Sierra. Their delays had been caused mainly by difficulties on the Hastings Cutoff and in bypassing the Ruby Mountains. The party had set out from Fort Bridger only a day after the Foards, heading for the Salt Lake and hoping to find Lansford Hastings. They never did, and their hardships and tragedies, both on the cutoff and in the Sierra Nevada during a snowbound winter, are well documented. The Benedict family, along with George and Tamsen Donner, were counted among the thirty-nine dead, out of the eighty-seven pioneers in the stranded party.

The Foards did see James Reed again. They were still at Sutter's Fort on October 28 when Reed came in on horseback by himself, telling them he had been banished from his party after he killed a man in a fight before reaching the Sierra.

Through early November, Reed waited for his family at Sutter's Fort, but when the arrival of heavy snow in the mountains made it apparent that they were trapped there, he launched two valiant rescue efforts. On the second one, in February, Reed managed to bring his wife and four children out alive. Eventually the Reed family settled in San Jose, California.

LANSFORD HASTINGS SUCCESSFULLY led his 1846 wagon party to Sutter's Fort, well ahead of the Donner-Reed Party and beating the snow. He was hoping for a bloodless revolution in California, to establish a state independent of both Mexico and the United States. When that dream collapsed with the U.S. victory in the war with Mexico, Hastings became a delegate to the California Constitutional Convention in Monterey in 1849. Soon thereafter he moved his family to Yuma, Arizona.

Hastings sided with the South in the Civil War. He met with Confederate President Jefferson Davis in 1864, seeking support for separating California from the Union and joining it to the Confederacy. The so-called Hastings Plot ended with the South's defeat.

After the war, Hastings tried to establish colonies in Brazil and wrote *The Emigrant's Guide to Brazil* (1867) to attract potential colonists. He died in the Virgin Islands in 1870, possibly from yellow fever.

Eli, Rebecca and Catherine were at Sutter's Fort when the bedraggled James Reed arrived alone. Eli joined Reed's volunteers in February 1847 for their mission into the mountains to attempt to rescue the Donner group. After the full extent of the disaster became known, Reed and Eli never spoke of their conflict over the Hastings Cutoff. Reed had convinced himself that it was erroneous information, not his own judgment that was at fault, but Eli knew the truth and didn't forget Reed's attempt to discredit him at Fort Bridger.

Although the Donner disaster became a national legend, Reed salvaged his reputation through his rescue attempts and his success in saving his own family. He became a prominent citizen in San Jose, owned land in the center of the city and was instrumental in San Jose's temporary success as the state's capital city from 1849 to 1851.

The Foard family first settled in the area around Sutter's Fort, in what later became Sacramento. Eli opened a livery stable outside Sutter's Fort in 1847, and in 1848 he and Rebecca worked with John Sutter, Jr. to lay the groundwork for early Sacramento.

The discovery of gold in the Sierra foothills could not have come at a more propitious time for the Foards. Already established in the livery trade in Sacramento, and having extensive contacts with animal dealers throughout the northwest, Eli was in perfect position to profit from the influx of mining adventurers in 1849, and he did. He was tempted to join in the hunt and start prospecting for gold himself – it wouldn't have been human to ignore that possibility. But he was also smart enough to know a sure thing versus a chancy thing when he saw it. In his years of trapping, he had come across far more impoverished miners than successful ones. So, making a choice based on his savvy, he banked a profit of nearly $200,000 in two years supplying horses and mules to the gold prospectors.

But by the end of five years, having made this small fortune, Eli and Rebecca had grown to hate the heavy winter ground fogs and scorching summers of the Sacramento Valley. After a wave of cholera swept through the area in the winter of 1850/51, Eli decided to take an exploratory trip to San Jose to see the area and visit his old friend Elisha Stephens, who had settled on the west side of the Santa Clara Valley. Stephens had settled near there immediately after his pioneering 1844 trip over the Sierra. After only three days, Eli was convinced that was the place to be. Within a week he bought 240 acres on the valley's west side, next to Stephens' ranch, where Cupertino Creek wound from the Santa Cruz Mountains onto the valley floor, and he had plans for a new house underway. The Foards also purchased property in San Jose with an eye toward another livery operation. Six months later, they made the move.

It was no accident that Eli chose to live on the west side, miles away from Reed's holdings in San Jose's central area.

He avoided Reed when possible. When the two happened to pass on the street, they exchanged only polite nods.

Eli kept a half-interest in his livery and blacksmithing business in Sacramento, and a branch he had established in Stockton, but he released operational control to his associate. He took his capital and invested in more horses and mules – breeding stock for his Santa Clara Valley ranch. After a few years of getting re-established, he spent most of each week on the ranch, outdoors with his horses where he was always happiest. Once a week he rode into San Jose to check with the manager of his livery business there. And twice a year, he traveled to Stockton and Sacramento, mainly to see his Sacramento partner, Jordan Wills, and his other friends there. Sometimes he went hunting for big game in the Santa Cruz Mountains.

Catherine was thirteen when the Foards moved to Cupertino Creek. By 1854 she was sixteen and on the threshold of womanhood. And there was a new addition – Jeffrey, born in 1849. Rebecca was content to raise her family, secure now that her husband seemed to have settled down and proud of Eli's success. She often wore pants when she rode and was the first woman in the valley with a reputation as an excellent rider and horse trainer. In later years, it was also well known that wherever she went, she carried a loaded Colt .45 revolver.

Chapter 11

Monterey, California
August 1846

ON A FOGGY AFTERNOON, George Wheeler saddled his horse and began the ride out to the Amandillo hacienda with dread in the pit of his stomach. Guadalupe had been in his thoughts for weeks. Ending the relationship with Esperanza was for the best – he was sure of that now. Guadalupe was everything that Esperanza wasn't – steady, contented and perpetually sunny. Their married life would bring everything he wanted, Wheeler thought. And the more he was convinced of it, the more he feared saying what he had to say.

At the ranch, Guadalupe greeted him with her usual shy smile and warm embrace. The worry must have shown on his face.

"George, you're downcast," Guadalupe said. "What's wrong?" She took him by the arms and tried to read his expression.

"Oh, am I so transparent?" he said with a wry smile. "Let's go in and talk."

"What is it?" she persisted, but he just shook his head and sighed. They sat on the brown leather sofa in the rear parlor, where the sun kept it warm on sunny afternoons, but where today a cozy fire had been built to ward off the chill.

"I might as well just say it," Wheeler began, finally meeting Guadalupe's eyes. He hesitated, then decided to qualify the statement. "You're not going to understand what I'm going to say, but I have to say it because I love you so much, and I don't want anything unsaid between us." She was smiling a little now, wondering. "I've been in love before, with a woman in Singapore." Her expression was calm, attentive. "We had two children. I loved them all, but I was away for long periods, you understand. I had to be. There was another man, someone I trusted. He used his position to take Suyen and the children. I had no rights in his country. I tried to see them again, but it was too late. She had committed herself to him. I suppose it was unwise from the beginning, but I loved her. I was a long way away from home. I needed someone."

There was a long pause, and then he looked at Guadalupe closely, with a plea in his eyes. "Can you possibly understand?"

"Oh, George, my dear George," she said. "So that's what it was. How heartbreaking for you. And your children and your lady friend, are they all right?"

"I don't know. I think they are well taken care of, at least they seemed to be two years ago when I last saw them. Of course I can't know with certainty. If they were getting bad treatment I wouldn't have . . . well – I would have done more to . . ."

"Your children – how old?"

"Three and five now."

"Will you be going to see them again?"

"I don't know. Not soon. Perhaps someday, for a visit, if I'm wanted there."

"Of course."

"I know this must be shocking for you. Have I tarnished myself in your eyes? Could you possibly . . ."

Guadalupe took his hands in hers. "Oh, George, I know this must have been hard for you to say, but what a fool I would be to think a man like you would have never been with another woman. And what others have there been?"

"Very few, really."

"I'm disappointed." She giggled, looking at George's pained expression. "George, do you love me?"

"Oh, yes."

"And you're really going to quit the sea?"

"Yes."

"And is this where you want to settle down?"

"Yes, it is."

"Then what are you waiting for? Ask me."

Wheeler looked at her with amazement, then shook his head and stared some more, wiping away a tear. "Now I can't get the words out," he said, smiling at his own awkwardness and shaking his head again. "I love you. Can you see yourself married to me and having my children?"

"Oh, yes, George. Yes a thousand times." She kissed his moist cheek, and then gave him a long one, full on the lips. They stared at each other, both grinning and teary-eyed.

AFTER THAT DAY, Guadalupe began to put all her attention into preparing for the wedding, which was to be held in six months, on Christmas Eve. But no sooner had that matter been resolved than Wheeler gave Joaquin Amandillo another cause for concern. It was one day the following week when Amandillo, taking advantage of branding time on the ranch, invited Wheeler to observe and learn more of the cattle operations. Before they started out that morning, Wheeler pulled Amandillo aside and gave him some more troubling news.

"You know, it's going to be hard for me to say this, but I have to. From the way you talk, I'm starting to think that you expect me to begin taking on ranch duties after Guadalupe and I are married. Am I right?"

"Is that a problem? I have a very valuable piece of property here. I only hoped – expected – that my ranch would be perpetuated, would stay in the family. Esperanza is in no position … isn't this what you want?"

"Frankly, sir, it's not," Wheeler said. "Oh, I wouldn't betray your trust. I would keep the ranch running if there were no one else to do it. But my own plans – what I want to do most – is to stay in the import/export business to keep an income coming in while I develop a vineyard and a winery. I might want to make a little brandy, too. I have enough money and I have continuing income from the business and the ship. I don't think Guadalupe and I will need the ranch as a source of income."

Amandillo nodded his head slowly, sadly. "I can see I assumed too much," he said. "Well, where were you planning to develop this vineyard?"

"I haven't made any firm plans. Anywhere in the area – within 20 or 30 miles of Monterey – would seem to be ideal for it. As soon as I have my shipping business running I'll be looking into it."

Amandillo nodded again. "Well, it's good that you said something now. I'll need a good man to take over the ranch someday. I can see now that I'll have to find someone else." Amandillo was angry but not defeated. And later that day, as he began to rethink his long-term plans, he got a new idea, one that soon began to dominate his thoughts. But he would not tell anyone about it, not even Carmelita, because it was still something of a gamble. He would keep this plan to himself until the proper time. There was still a way, he thought, to achieve his goals and provide for everyone involved.

In November, a month before the wedding, Esperanza had her baby – a boy named Juan. The grandparents beamed. Joaquin especially seemed to have a fresh glow about him and a new quickness in his step. *Señora*

Amandillo fairly buzzed around the hacienda, full of energy and optimism. Guadalupe, her usual happy self, showed extra ebullience. The servants reflected this elevated household mood. As Christmas Eve approached, the wedding plans finalized, Wheeler was told to come for a pre-wedding party the night before the ceremony and stay the night in his old room on the far side of the patio. The next afternoon, the entire wedding party would be transported to the Church of San Carlos for the ceremony, and then would return to the hacienda for a grand reception extending into *La Nochebuena*. Decorations had been ordered and an elaborate menu planned.

Everyone in the family seemed to be riding a wave of euphoria – everyone, that is, except for Esperanza. In the seclusion of her room she nursed her son. But aside from that, aside from an almost perfunctory attention to her baby, she seemed distracted. She never came to the dining table for meals and seldom spoke to anyone in the family. When she was seen outside her room, she went for long, solitary walks along the paths that connected the hacienda to the pine forest on the farthest hill to the south, the one that overlooked the Bay of Monterey. She didn't understand why her father was so forgiving of Wheeler's transgressions and so intolerant of Costa's. Brooding, she wondered whether Wheeler's accent or his pale skin gave him some kind of special status. Guadalupe noticed Esperanza's odd behavior but was too busy with her wedding plans to think much about it. Joaquin also noticed, but he thought he had the answer – some news that would bring Esperanza back to her old vivacious self.

On the evening of December 23, Joaquin Amandillo gathered his family around him at the dinner table. On this occasion, he insisted that Esperanza join them at dinner, and so she left little Juan with a servant and sullenly took a chair at the far end of the table from her father and mother. Captain Wheeler also was present, seated with Guadalupe. Wheeler and Esperanza eyed each other solemnly and exchanged polite nods, but neither was comfortable enough for superficial conversation. At the end of the dinner, Joaquin stood.

"First, I want to wish everyone a *Feliz Navidad*, and also to say how happy *Señora* Amandillo and I are to be welcoming Captain George Wheeler into our family. Tomorrow will be one of the most joyous days in the history of the Amandillos. We will be wishing Guadalupe and George many happy years as husband and wife – but that's for tomorrow." He was beaming now, with the smile of someone who is about to bestow a wonderful surprise.

"As you all know, this ranch has provided great wealth and security for the Amandillo family," he began. "We have been fortunate that God has given us this land, and I hope it will provide well for generations of Amandillos to come." Everyone was listening now, even the servants, who had gathered at the edges of the room. "What you may not know is that I have been pondering the fate and the usefulness of the acreage the family has owned north of the Salinas River. This land has been essentially unused since I acquired title from Governor Alvarado 12 years ago. I have tried to lease it, but no one seemed to be interested. Recently, though, I have found someone – a horse breeder in the Carmel Valley who wants to expand his operation. This man happened to own 5,000 acres of beautiful, sunny property in the middle of that valley that I think would be ideal for a vineyard, and perhaps someday, a winery. I've thought for some time that this would be a wise expansion of the family enterprises. So I've made a choice. To make this story short, I have negotiated a trade – our useless acreage for this beautiful land. We now own it." He waved the title over his head, to applause all around.

"When do we start planting?" Wheeler inquired, grinning.

"Everyone may not be aware that George is an aspiring vintner," Joaquin continued. "As such, he will be a major part of our plans. In future years, I expect George and Guadalupe to be the primary custodians of this property and, at the proper time, I think we will see the Amandillo-Wheeler brand on the label of a bottle of the finest wine." Guadalupe and George looked at each other with big smiles.

"Now, you may be thinking that managing a ranch *and* a vineyard, separated by 20 miles, would be a big responsibility. Yes, I think so, too. That's why I have made arrangements that will keep both the ranch and the vineyard land in the family and yet ensure that both of my daughters are provided for." Esperanza then realized with a shock that this announcement concerned her. Her eyes widened and her mouth fell slightly open.

"We have a new grandson in the family," Joaquin continued. "A male heir at last. Well, he has a lot of growing up to do, but he's an Amandillo, so I know he has a rancher's blood. And he has a grandfather who is ready, willing and able to show him the ropes – when he's ready, of course. So my plan for the ranch is this: While I still have my health – and that should be a long time – I'll continue to run the ranch and teach Juan what he needs to know as he grows up. In the meantime, we will share joint title to the property with him, and with my daughter Esperanza as guardian. If anything should happen to me before Juan is 21, Esperanza and Carmelita would take custody until that time. Otherwise, title to the ranch will go to Juan on my death, with the stipulation that his mother and grandmother will always have a home here. The vineyard land will go to Guadalupe and George, and may they prosper with it. My lawyer, *Señor* Garcia, is on his way here now with all the appropriate papers to be signed tonight. I thought this would make a wonderful wedding present, and one that could be shared by everyone."

The whole family was now smiling and applauding – even the servants – except for Esperanza, who was still stunned and open-mouthed. As all eyes turned to her, looking for her to break out in a smile at last, she stood up, looking confused and horrified, as if she had been betrayed. She put her hands to her head, backing up as her chair fell behind her and her napkin dropped to the floor.

"What is it, daughter?" said the *señora*, rising herself and moving toward Esperanza.

Esperanza looked at her father again in amazement, shook her head slightly, then turned and ran to her room, shutting and latching the door. Her father followed, pounding on the door and shouting, "What is it – what's wrong?"

A few minutes later, with her baby crying and her parents pleading for an explanation, Esperanza yanked open the door, rushed past them and out of the house, running for the stable dressed in riding clothes. The entire family was after her now, but by the time they caught up, she had found Guapo, jumped on bareback and headed past them all, down the lane toward town.

"What could it be?" cried the *señora*, but Joaquin was already saddling his horse, ignoring the hubbub.

"I'll go too," Wheeler said, and began saddling his own horse. By the time they started out they were at least five minutes behind Esperanza.

The night was pitch-black. The sun had set hours ago. It was a mostly cloudy evening and at the new moon, so a few stars, blinking occasionally through gaps in the overcast, provided the only light. Esperanza rode hard, clinging to the horse's mane, eyes on the road ahead. But she had drunk a little too much wine, and her stomach was queasy. She had to find Costa, had to get there in time, had to put a stop to the whole thing. She just needed to go four miles, and she knew the road, but it was hard to see. The sound of the horse's hooves beating on the road mesmerized her. She started to pass out, then shook it off. Her head was beginning to pound inside. Then, at once, something loomed on her left – a buggy. The other horse reared with a piercing whinny of protest, and Guapo bolted off the road, reared when blocked by a huge oak tree and twisted with a jolt. Esperanza, with no chance to keep her mount, was tossed to the ground. Had it been ordinary soft ground, she might have fallen unharmed, or at the most broken a leg or an arm. But as fate dictated, she was thrown onto a huge granite bounder. Her head hit first, crushing the back of her skull and knocking her forward like a rag doll.

When Eusebio Garcia had his horse under control and his buggy stopped, he jumped out and ran to get hold of the other horse's reins, but then saw that there were no reins. He left the horse and looked around for the rider, finally locating Esperanza's body at the base of the huge rock. He checked for a pulse and then felt her chest for a heartbeat. She was not breathing. Then, with a shock, he realized who it was – his client's daughter, the daughter whose name was on the papers he had in his leather case, still in place on the seat of the buggy. He felt again for a heartbeat, but there was none.

In just a few minutes Esperanza had been transformed twice – first from depressed mother to terrified beneficiary, and then again, one final transition. As Joaquin and Wheeler rode up, Garcia recognized them and prepared himself to deliver the news. Instead of a welcome facilitator of good fortune, he was instead destined to be the bearer of tragic tidings.

But there was someone else at the scene of Esperanza's death – a figure unseen by the lawyer, unseen by Amandillo and Wheeler, and unseen even by Esperanza. As Garcia had struggled for control of his horse and then frantically caught his breath as he checked for Esperanza's pulse, a lone rider, on his way from Monterey at a gallop, heard the commotion and brought his horse up short at a distance. He dismounted and hid himself while he crept up behind a tree and listened to the voices. Then, as soon as he had ascertained what had happened, Antonio del Costa quietly backed away, remounted and returned the way he had come.

The next day, the body of Garson Jenkins was found on the road a half mile away, stabbed in the heart with a dagger.

The wedding of Guadalupe Amandillo and George Wheeler did not take place on Christmas Eve – the arrangements had to be put on hold to allow for a funeral on the day after Christmas. That was an uncelebrated Christmas for everyone in the Amandillo family.

But the wedding did happen – postponed until the end of February. Even then it was subdued, less joyous than originally planned. When the vows had been said, the congratulations given, the good luck wished, the food consumed and the thanks given, the bride and groom kissed again and spent their wedding night at the Amandillo hacienda, where they were to stay until their new home on the Carmel Valley land could be built. In the hacienda they shared a roof with young Juan Amandillo, who was under the care of his nanny and grandparents, unaware that he would grow up without a memory of his mother. His father was another story.

When the Amandillos buried Esperanza, they all felt remorse, wondering what they could have done to prevent this impetuous, inexplicable action that cost a young mother her life. What they did not know – what only one living person knew – was that Esperanza's action, by an odd twist, had prevented the death of her sister's fiancé and thus enabled the marriage.

On the night Esperanza died, Antonio del Costa had been in the Monterey cantina drinking whiskey by himself, wondering whether what he had planned would work, wondering if it was the best thing after all. The whole plan could backfire, he thought. Finally, he put his doubts to rest. Yes, it was the logical thing. It had to be done. No one would be able to prove he or Esperanza was involved – he would see to that.

At that moment – the moment when Eusebio Garcia was stepping up to his buggy for a quiet ride to the Amandillo hacienda, and the moment when Esperanza Amandillo was running to the stable in riding clothes – Garson Jenkins entered the cantina, spotted Costa and lurched his way to the bar where Costa sat.

"It's off," he said hoarsely. "I'm not doin' it."

It was one more twist in a plot gone horribly awry, one that ended in Esperanza's death. When Costa had first found Jenkins, he had felt extremely lucky. Expecting to have to convince someone to lie about George Wheeler, instead he had found a crew member who actually *knew* of a family that Wheeler had in Singapore – or at least he said he did, and that was enough. Costa felt he had hit the jackpot. Since Jenkins already had a grudge against Wheeler, Costa didn't even have to give him money to tell Amandillo the story – he bought him off with a bottle of whiskey.

But then things started to go wrong. First Joaquin Amandillo did not seem to care that Wheeler had fathered children out of wedlock with a Singapore woman, and then abandoned them. He also couldn't understand why Amandillo would accept Wheeler's flimsy excuse, a development relayed to him in Esperanza's messages, sent to him via Guadalupe's hand in sealed envelopes. What more could they try? Any further attempt to besmirch Wheeler probably would be brushed off. If Wheeler's real history could be so easily accepted, what good would it do to try a fictitious one that could be disproved?

After that, months went by and Esperanza's pregnancy advanced. After his son was born, Costa felt even more motivation to try to manipulate the future in his favor. If there was any justice in the world, he reasoned, he would be allowed to marry Esperanza, be welcomed into the Amandillo family, and would then be in a position to inherit a rich legacy, which he could pass on to his son. As it was, he had nothing – no lover, no access to his son, no security and no legacy. It wasn't right, and he had to do something – even something desperate.

From Esperanza, Costa learned about the plans for the wedding. He knew that on December 23 Wheeler would be staying, by himself, in a room at the back of the hacienda, separated from the rest of the house by the open patio. There, away from town and relatively unprotected, Costa thought Wheeler would be vulnerable. It would be easy for someone to sneak in at night, kill Wheeler in his bed, silently with a dagger, and escape. With no other male heir in line, the ranch would certainly go to Esperanza and Juan. And who knows – if Esperanza's father were somehow out of the way, then perhaps Costa could be reunited with her.

So Costa had another talk with Jenkins. When he told Jenkins his plan, the sailor turned him down. He had never killed a man for money. But a few days later, Costa asked him again, offering more money, and Jenkins agreed to do it. When he told Esperanza what he had planned, she sent back an urgent note telling him to stop, that it wouldn't work. But then, a day later, she sent another note. Go ahead, she said. She now hated Wheeler enough to kill him, so why not? But make sure that no clues were left, she told Costa, because she couldn't become a suspect in this crime.

On the night of December 23, Jenkins prepared his dagger. He put it on his candlelit dresser and stared at it. Breathing heavily, he took two quick drinks of whiskey and stared at it some more. Then he came to terms with himself and realized that he could not sneak into a man's bedroom at night and kill him while he slept. He would not do that, no matter how much he hated Wheeler. So he grabbed the dagger and left his room, found Costa in the cantina and threw the dagger on the bar in front of him. Then he threw down the money Costa had paid him.

"You want Wheeler dead? You kill 'im" Jenkins whispered. "I'm notcher man. I don't want no part of it."

"Fine. Go on, get out of here," Costa said in disgust. He scooped up the money, grabbed the dagger and stuck it into his belt.

"You're doin' it?" Jenkins blurted.

"Keep you voice down," Costa whispered. "Hell yes, I'm doing it. Go on, get out." He pushed past Jenkins and out to the street, where he swung up onto his horse and charged off. Jenkins, now thinking he needed to stop Costa to keep himself out of trouble, stole a horse from in front of the cantina and started after Costa, a few minutes behind him.

Costa never saw Garcia's buggy on the road ahead of him. He heard the commotion ahead caused by the near-collision of the buggy with Esperanza, who was riding to Monterey and desperately hoping to keep the murderer from carrying out his mission. When Costa advanced and saw what had happened, including the arrival of Joaquin Amandillo and Wheeler, he retreated, and on his way back toward Monterey met up with Jenkins. Enraged by the disastrous turn of events and somehow in the moment blaming Jenkins for what had happened, he wrestled Jenkins from his horse and when he had fallen to the ground, stabbed him with the dagger. The next day, he learned of Esperanza's death.

On the night of May 20, when Costa's son Juan was exactly six months old, Costa again took the lonely road from Monterey to the Amandillo hacienda. Waiting outside the house until everyone was surely asleep, he found an open window. He entered the house, quietly found the baby's room and gently put his son in a sling he had brought. The boy whimpered a little but did not cry out as they crawled out the window. Strapping his son onto the horse, Costa led his mount out of hearing range of the house and swung up to the saddle. Seconds later, father and son were on their way to Los Angeles.

PART TWO
GOLD IN THE HILLS

Chapter 1

Concord, Massachusetts
April 1854

THE GERM OF THE IDEA – the idea that would change his life – began to incubate in Charles Grayson's head one spring day in 1849, when he was an apprentice in his father's printing shop. Charles was 14 then. On Wednesdays the shop ran Concord's weekly broadsheet newspaper, the *Concord Freeman*, on its presses, and the job had just come off that evening. Charles washed his hands, still wearing his green printer's apron and smelling of ink, and picked up a copy as a quality check, especially to look for smearing. He noticed that the press work itself was fine but grimaced when he saw that the ink was still not drying properly. His father, Oliver Grayson, was shaking his head about it, too, but couldn't offer an immediate solution. Just then, as Charles scanned the page, a headline caught his eye: "California Gold Lures Young Men to Sail in Search of Wealth."

The story described the discovery of gold in the foothills of the Sierra Nevada, the sensation it was causing and the number of ships that were suddenly advertising passage to San Francisco via Cape Horn. Listed among the prospective voyagers, far down in the column, was one Gabriel Marbough of Concord. Charles knew the name. This could be none other than the older brother of his school friend, Jacob Marbough, who lived up on the Bedford Road.

Suddenly, Charles couldn't contain his curiosity. The next day he sought out the Marboughs and found out that Gabe was indeed sailing for San Francisco in two weeks' time. If there was gold in California, he would find it, Gabe told him. Charles was fascinated; Gabe was the first real adventurer he had ever met.

Well, not quite. There was the town's nature-lover, Henry Thoreau, an oddball writer who had a book out about his long hikes in the White Mountains and up to Mount Katahdin in Maine. Years before, while wandering out by Walden Pond, Charles had run into him a few times back when Thoreau was living there in a shack. At first Thoreau was a little scary to a 10-year-old, but he didn't seem to mind Charles's poking around. A few days later, Thoreau had made a friendly overture by steering Charles to a huckleberry thicket where the berries were just ripe. That might have been the end of their acquaintance, but Charles was curious about Thoreau, a loner living out in the woods. The next time he found himself at Walden Pond, he went up tentatively to the little house to see Thoreau, and they talked about some of Thoreau's hikes and river trips as they identified birds. Charles discovered that Thoreau really wasn't a hermit after all. But he was different.

The trouble was that Mr. Whitaker, the minister from town, saw Charles talking to Thoreau and stopped him on his way home.

"Say, Charles, I saw you with Henry Thoreau out at the pond," the minister said. "You aren't spending time with him, are you?"

Charles was taken aback – he had no idea he had done anything wrong, but he felt accusation in the minister's tone.

"No – I don't know him," Charles stammered. "He just wanted … we were just talking."

Whitaker frowned at him. "That's not a good place for you to be," he said.

Charles didn't go to Walden Pond again for a long time.

But as it turned out, a few days after Charles talked to Gabe Marbough about his California plans, it was Thoreau who showed Charles the answer to the ink-smearing problem – an odd coincidence, Charles thought. It happened this way: Gabe's trip started Charles thinking about Henry's adventure stories, the ones he had told years before. Charles remembered hearing that Henry was now working at his family's pencil-making factory in the upper story of their house on Main Street, where they used plumbago to make graphite. Charles thought there was a chance he might learn something from Henry about the ink they were using in the print shop. He knew that he himself would have to approach Henry because his parents thoroughly disapproved of the man. The Thoreaus attended First Church over on Lexington Road, the Unitarian congregation, along with the Grayson family. But it was well known in town that Henry Thoreau had turned his back on the church years ago – said he wanted nothing to do with it – and the Graysons snorted at that. They were zealously proud and protective of their church. Charles attended out of duty. That day, on his own, Charles decided to go over to the Thoreau pencil factory.

Well, Henry turned out to be just the man to deal with the ink problem. First, he showed Charles a mixing process he had figured out for the pencil lead, using clay to bind the plumbago and stop their pencils from smearing. Then he and Charles started tinkering with the mixture of linseed oil, alcohol and carbolic acid in the ink until it was drying pretty well. Charles told his father how he and Thoreau had solved the problem. Oliver scowled, but soon the Graysons started using that new formula in the shop. That should have been a feather in Charles's cap, but instead Charles sensed some resentment from his father that he, a 14-year-old, had succeeded where his father had not. And Charles was surprised that it didn't raise Oliver's opinion of Henry a bit.

"I don't want you associating with that man," Oliver Grayson told his son. "You know he worships false gods. And there was that fire he started a few years back. Nobody likes him."

"I don't know him very well," Charles said. He felt guilty for saying it. He didn't see anything wrong with Henry Thoreau. Charles also began to have an odd feeling about Concord. This town where he had grown up began to seem less like a home and more like a place he'd like to escape from.

From then on, Charles went out of his way to make a friend out of Thoreau, but quietly. At first he didn't tell his parents. He just said he was "walking in the woods." Soon the two of them were on a first-name basis. On weekends, Charles and Henry prowled the Concord River, along the railroad cut and through the woods outside of town to try to identify trees and look for seeds. Henry would record their findings in his thick notebook.

"The cycles of the forest are like the cycles of a person," Thoreau said one day. "Sometimes the oak tree takes over, but all the while, the oak is shading the little pine seedlings, so they can grow. Then when the oak dies, the pines can take over. The pines then yield to the hickory and the oaks again. In a person it's the same – you may have to end one phase in your life before the next one opens up, but it doesn't help to get impatient. Dr. Emerson said, 'For all nature is doing her best each moment to make us well. She exists for no other end.' You just need to stay of the way."

Over the next five years, Charles spent hours at a time with Henry. Concord was a small town, so the word soon got back to his parents. "Why are you with that man Thoreau so much?" Oliver said to Charles one evening. "What are you two doing out there in the woods?" It was the distrust and the unspoken accusation in his tone that offended Charles.

"I don't know what you're talking about," Charles said defensively. "He knows a lot about the outdoors, so he's teaching me. That's all."

Oliver challenged him: "Are you sure that's all?"

"What are you trying to say?" Charles answered. Charles had only a dim notion of why his father would be worried, but he caught the general drift, and it raised his hackles even more. "I don't even know him very well. Don't you believe me?"

Oliver stared at Charles, opened his mouth, hesitated, then said in a low tone, "Keep away from him."

In the months that followed, Charles relived that conversation a hundred times and pondered the meaning of it. He wondered what it was about a teenage boy's befriending a man in his early thirties that bothered people so much. He went inward with the friendship. He didn't even talk about it with friends like Jake Marbough. But he didn't stop his outings with Henry.

When fall came, Charles and Henry walked in the woods, Henry noting the exact day when each tree turned its back on summer and let go of its leaves in an elaborate color sequence. In the winter the two of them fished through the ice at Walden Pond. In the spring they went to the lakes and rivers every day to record the effects of warming on the ice. Always, Thoreau wrote in his journal.

During the five years that Charles was absorbing Thoreau's outlook on life and learning to be a keen observer of the natural world, the Marbough family shared with him their regular letters from Gabe, beginning with his three months as a gold miner. The mining was backbreaking work, and Gabe saw that most of the gold ended up in the hands of the saloonkeepers and store owners and builders. When he gave up gold digging and made his way back from the mining towns to San Francisco, he had intended to return to Concord. But when he crossed the bay to the city, he noticed something – a city that seemed to have grown up overnight. When he first arrived from the East, he had seen mostly ramshackle buildings and a lot of vacant land. This time he saw a city on the rise. Prosperous-looking men walked the streets looking busy. Everywhere, buildings were going up.

Gabe used the money he had saved for his return passage to buy a half interest in a hardware store. A year later, his partner decided to move on, and Gabe took out a loan to buy him out. Within another year the loan was paid off, and Gabe then built himself a house in the city. Now he had a wife and a young son. He invited his younger brother Jake to join him in the business and even said Charles, as a family friend, would be welcome as an employee until Charles could get his own printing business started.

Charles thought about what he should do. He was now a journeyman printer and already had the price of the voyage saved from his print shop earnings over the years. It was money intended for his education, but this seemed more important. Charles wanted out of Concord. He wanted to know what the rest of the world looked like. If this town was too narrow-minded to accept someone like Henry, it probably wouldn't accept Charles, either. It didn't. The prospect of California was too exciting to pass up.

Charles's parents shook their heads. They were against it, of course. To Charles, it seemed like the time for a heart-to-heart talk with Henry.

"What do you think you'll find in California that you can't find here?" Henry asked.

"It seems like a chance to start fresh," Charles said. "If I don't go, I feel like I'll never get out of my father's shop. I can't stand it there anymore."

"So you're miserable because of your father?"

"Because of him and this whole town. You're my only real friend. I'll miss you, by the way."

"What if you just told your father what's bothering you?"

"He wouldn't understand. I have to get out of here."

The two of them sat in silence for a minute or two. At last, Henry said, "It seems as if you're bound to leave. It may be good in a way. It takes courage to break free. But remember, it also takes courage to face the demons in yourself. Whatever it is that makes you hesitant to confront your father – to confront anyone in your life – that's what will hold you back in California, too. You have to find out what's true for you and then speak your truth. It's a choice. Someday you'll make that choice."

That was weeks ago. Now Charles was about to take the first step on his way west. Two days from now Jake and Charles, both nearly 19, would board a three-masted bark, headed on a journey of perhaps five months, around Cape Horn and then on to San Francisco, one of the most difficult journeys a paying passenger could undertake. It was possible that Charles would not see his parents and sisters again. He felt no regret. He had been packed for a week. There was just one more thing he had to do – he had to tell Henry good-bye.

In all their explorations together, Charles had never thought of the times in the outdoors with Henry as having a beginning or an end. Now, as he approached the Thoreau house, he suddenly realized that those times had been the happiest he had ever spent.

It was a warm day for April. Charles was told at the Thoreau house that Henry was over along the railroad cut, observing birds. Charles found him sitting there with his notebook, a pencil in hand. He nodded as Charles approached while giving most of his attention to a marsh hawk in the distance. Charles sat beside him. After a bit, they talked of some of their experiences together. Henry reached into his bag and handed Charles a thick notebook, like his own – a blank one.

"This is your journal," Henry said. "Remember me by keeping it. Every day, write down what you see. Write the color of the sky at sea, the feel of the wind, the character of the foam on the waves. Observe and write. When you get to California, you'll have a new home to explore and see. Notice the details and put them in your journal. Write your journal as a gift to your grandchildren."

Charles nodded, smiling. After a minute of silence, he asked, "What do you think California will be like?"

"First decide what you expect to find," Henry said. "Probably, that's what you'll find. But if you stay alert, you'll find other things, too, situations that will test your strength. When those times come, be true to yourself. Make that choice."

Charles nodded and turned to go. But Henry said, "Wait." He pulled another book out of his bag – a hardbound volume with a smell Charles knew, of a volume fresh off the press.

"Here," Henry said, handing it to him. "It's just in from Boston. Something to pass the time on the trip."

The spine read:

Walden

Life in the Woods

Thoreau

As Charles started back home along Main Street, he noticed Jake, walking a few paces behind him.

"Hey Charles," Jake said. "I won't ask if you're ready to go. I know you are. Say, did I just see you coming from the railroad cut?"

"Yeah," Charles said. "I like to walk through there sometimes."

"Haven't I seen you over there with Henry Thoreau before? You're fairly good friends with him, aren't you?"

"Oh, I don't know him very well," Charles said.

Inside, Charles cringed. Just then, from somewhere he couldn't see, a rooster started to crow.

Chapter 2

San Francisco, California
September 1854

WATCHING CAREFULLY ON THE STARBOARD side of the *James M. Glennon*, Charles and Jake stood for an hour before they could see anything that looked like land. A pilot had come aboard to take the ship carefully around the rocks that guarded San Francisco Bay. The barking of the seals on the rocks indicated they were close. But all they could see was fog and water.

"Look!" Jake said, grabbing Charles by the shoulder and pointing to port. Just ahead, a bare mountainside had appeared, the top in sunlight, jutting above the gray mist. Then a bit of forested hill emerged to the starboard side, and they realized that they were at the entrance to the great bay. Within minutes the ship was out of the mist and into full sun, and they could see the outlines of the bay and its islands. Their long voyage was over.

Except for the brief relief of a two-day visit to Rio de Janeiro, the 141 days on the ship had been nothing short of an ordeal. The ship was frequently pounded by the worst imaginable storms, some of which brought them frighteningly close to wrecking on desolate rocks. The carpentry work that converted the ship to passenger use had been slipshod, so the quarters constantly leaked rainwater, making sleep nearly impossible during a squall. Seasickness was a continuing problem in the early weeks, and Charles had been one of the most susceptible. The food was monotonous, partly wormy and, toward the end, almost inedible. A good part of the water was contaminated and sickening, and by the end of the voyage Charles had lost 20 pounds.

He had seen dolphins needlessly harpooned, crew members abused. He had endured no end of raunchy antics from some of the passengers. At one point, a near-riot had broken out when a group of passengers noisily broke into the captain's cabin to voice their grievances and had to be subdued by crew members. Ever since the ship had rounded Cape Horn on June 20 in a wintry blast, Charles's constant thoughts had been on the prospect of getting off the ship for good. As an outlet for his frustration, he turned to his journal.

Whatever California may turn out to be like, it cannot possibly be worse than the conditions aboard this ship. If I had the trip to do over, I would take my chances with the overland crossing. The river water would be preferable to the putrid supply we carry on board. As for food, I cannot imagine a worse menu than we have had to endure. The confinement, the monotony and the abominable manners of the entire company have been at times intolerable. – C.G.

Something else that Charles thought had suffered on the trip was his friendship with Jake. Or maybe they had never really been friends. It wasn't so much that they argued, but more that they had less and less to talk about. Sometimes Charles thought Jake's behavior crass – more like that of the raunchy crew members than he would have liked. When they saw the dolphins being killed, Jake cheered like the rest of them. Charles didn't know what to say to him after that. But he had *a lot* to say. What was holding him back?

A flock of little boats met the ship as it dropped anchor off San Francisco, just as they had in Rio de Janeiro, but here the boats were manned by a motley collection of scruffy, crude characters instead of Rio's black slaves and their masters. Some were trying to sell them liquor already and offering prostitutes. Jake and Charles chose a boat that gave them just transportation for 25 cents. After docking, they made for the post office, where they each collected a packet of letters, and then they headed for Kearny Street, where Gabe had said they would find Marbough & Co. Hardware.

They reveled in the feel of solid earth under their feet. It took all the will power the two of them could summon to walk past the doors of the restaurants with their smells of freshly baked bread and steaming fish and clam chowder, and the sights and sounds of people enjoying a good noonday meal of fresh food. After so many weeks of choking down greasy beans and putrid pork on a table constantly rolling this way and that, San Francisco seemed like a kind of heaven.

Their patience was soon rewarded. At the hardware store, Gabe gave them both a hearty welcome and soon had them unwinding in his wife's kitchen and tearing into a luncheon of tomatoes, filet of cod and fresh vegetables. After a good bath, they both visited a barber and then strolled the bustling streets of the city.

What happened next took Charles completely by surprise. As they turned onto Pacific Street, just as he was thinking that he could use some new clothes, and had said as much to Jake, his eyes latched on to a sight he had not seen since Rio – a colorfully dressed young woman with a certain build that he liked, eyeing them intently.

"Boys, you look like you've spent too much time at sea," she said. "Why don't you both come in here and have a whiskey?" Charles had rebuffed a come-on such as this in Rio, but then he was with a mixed group of six passengers. This time the woman seemed prettier and the constraints fewer.

Even on the sidewalk, the dark saloon reeked of beer and something exotic that Charles couldn't place. During his strict New England upbringing, he had never been inside a place that served alcohol. The stuff simply had not been allowed in the Grayson house. Suddenly, he felt like a man of the world, able to make his own decisions. He looked at Jake, who shrugged, and they went inside. It was midafternoon and the place was quiet, with one or two men at a corner table drinking.

"Set 'em up, Brad," the woman said. "These boys look thirsty."

A gray-bearded man in a plaid shirt, his eyelids heavy, put little glasses of brown liquid in front of them. Charles thought: What could it hurt? As he picked his glass up, he saw Jake eyeing his hesitantly. The woman put her arm around Jake as she sat next to them. "Relax, honey, you're among friends," she said. The liquor felt like cleaning fluid in Charles's throat as the first swallow went down. He coughed a little, then downed the rest, trying to look experienced.

"That's the way I like to see a man drink," she said. "You've been around, I can see. You're the kind of customer we like. Why don't you have another, on the house?"

The second drink was in front of him before he could answer. He drank half of it, then the woman said, "You know, I like you. You and I could have some fun upstairs, how about it? I'll bet you could show a girl a good time." She pulled her stool closer. She had her head close to his now, and her dress was pulled down at the neck so that Charles could see her entire left breast.

"I don't know," Charles said, weakly.

"We should go," Jake said.

"Oh, I've got a friend for *you*," she said to Jake. "You'll like her – her name's Liz. You can call me Kitty." She was purring in Charles's ear now. He was aroused and feeling warm inside – warm and confident. She had her arm around him and then down between his thighs, and he found himself standing up and putting his hand on her neck. He might have stumbled a little, and he felt slightly dizzy. She was guiding him toward the stairs.

Jake might have said, "Hey Charles, let's go," but Charles couldn't hear him very well. He had a sudden surge of euphoria. He kissed Kitty as she led him up the stairs. Then there was a dim little room, a mattress. Kitty helped him undress. He was excited now, and he pulled her dress off her arms, exposing her breasts. As he took them in his hands, he and Kitty sank to the mattress.

Later, Charles tried many times to remember what happened in the room after that, but he couldn't bring it back. The next thing in his memory was a pitch-black place and a huge ache extending from the back of his head to the front. His mouth was gagged, his hands and feet were tied, and he was cold, lying on a wooden floor. He seemed to be naked, except for being wrapped in a smelly blanket. He had no idea what time it was. He tried to call for Jake, but all he could get out was a guttural sound in his throat. The bindings were tight. If there were other people there, Charles couldn't see them – just blackness and the vague outlines of some walls and rafters. And somewhere, somewhere close, there was the sound of surf, gently hitting the shore. After a long while, he thought he heard muffled voices, but he couldn't make out the words. Then, some time later, a door opened and he could see the silhouettes of several men.

"Let's get 'em the fuck out there now – *move* your asses," someone was saying. There was enough light now for him to see that there were other shapes, maybe others like him in the large room, bound as he was – he could see three, maybe four bodies. Four or five men started carrying bodies out, but not toward the door where the men had come in. They were carrying them to the other end, but he couldn't see where that end was. He heard voices coming from that direction, and then, suddenly, he was being picked up and carried. He didn't try to resist, pretending to be asleep. He smelled the ocean clearly now. He was being lowered – into a boat! He could see lanterns reflected in the dark water. His head hit the side of the boat, and his headache pulsed hard against his temple.

"Careful, dumb ass, they want 'em alive," someone said. It was a long boat, perhaps 20 feet. He was at one end, still lying flat, straining to see. Then, suddenly, lights appeared everywhere, to his right, behind him, above him.

"Ahoy there, stop what you're doing," a man shouted.

"What's this?" came a voice close to Charles.

"We're taking over here, these men belong to us," the shouting man said.

"Bloody hell," came another voice, from the building. "What the fuck? Who are you?"

Charles could see the shouting man now. He was in another boat, and there were several other boats, all with lanterns, clustering around, casting a wavering light all over them. "Sheriff's deputy," he said.

A shot was fired, from where Charles couldn't tell. Then another shot, and a man in the doorway above fell onto the edge of the boat, his legs plunging into the water. Charles could hear pounding on the wooden floor above them, men scuffling or running inside the building. The boat suddenly listed to one side before the wounded man slid into the water. Then someone was pulling their boat away, towing it somewhere. All Charles could see were shadows of pilings, outlines of the ships in the harbor, some dim lanterns ashore. His headache was monstrous.

He must have passed out again, for how long he didn't know. There were men taking off his bindings in the gloom. His mouth was already ungagged, and he was lying propped up against a wall.

"Hey Charles, you're a sight," came a voice from somewhere. Jake emerged between two piles of rigging to stare him in the face. "You awake yet?"

"I've got a headache like I've never had. What in the world happened? Did they take you, too?"

"They tried to take me but they didn't drug me enough. I never drank all the whiskey. They had me bundled and ready to go, but before they tied me up, one of them left for a minute and I scrambled out of there. I didn't even have any clothes on. We couldn't find you when we got back. Gabe rounded up his friends. Lucky he's a local – he got the sheriff – hey, here he is. Thank God for my brother."

Gabe came over and knelt down, looking Charles closely in the face. "Well, you're not too worse for wear, it looks like," he said. "How does it feel to be shanghaied on your first day in San Francisco?"

Chapter 3

CHARLES GRAYSON MUST HAVE told his shanghaiing story hundreds of times over the decades. He left out some of the details when he told the grandkids, but he always gave Jake and Gabe credit for the rescue. After all, he owed them – probably his life. The drinks in the saloon had been spiked with enough laudanum to send a gorilla off to dreamland, so it took him a few days to start feeling like his regular self, and a week after that before the knot on his head went away. It was months before he could stand the sight of a saloon, and as for bordellos – well, he was more careful about his choices after that. A shanghai victim was lucky to make it back to his port of choice with his life and all the body parts God gave him. So Charles felt lucky that all he parted with that night was about $50 and the clothes off his back. The clothes were disposable, but the money was a good part of what he had left to get started in California. So he worked for Marbough & Co. a bit longer than he had planned – in fact, almost a year in all. During his months in San Francisco, he continued to live with the Marboughs on Telegraph Hill. Jean was a substitute mother to Charles whenever he began to despair, and he went to her for support as he would a member of his own family.

Charles's transition back to the printing trade might have been quicker, but Edward Malley, San Francisco's only printer at the time, turned out to be a miserly, cantankerous sort who did not want to hire Charles, despite his qualifications. And once Malley had relented and put him on half-time, the man proved impossible to work for. Charles quit after a week and went back to the hardware store. Then, in July, a newcomer named Humberto Rico set up a printing business in the city, and he hired Charles immediately. That was in the middle of 1855. Eleven months later, Rico decided that the pueblo of San Jose, 50 miles to the south, also needed a printing shop and that Charles should be the one to run it. Rico would set up the shop and give Charles a percentage of the profits.

It was obvious from the start why Rico needed Charles. Rico came up a bit on the short side in his printing skills, and he knew even less about the English language. When it came to assuring quality in the product, Rico relied on Charles to tend to those exacting details. But there was one thing Rico excelled at, and that was seizing an opportunity. If there was a printing need, Rico was going to fill it. He had relatives in San Jose who informed him that the town would prove a good source of revenue, and Rico was not going to let that go untapped. Charles grabbed the opportunity immediately. He had seen enough of San Francisco.

On the morning he left, the stagecoach was waiting in the fog at 7:45 a.m. as Gabe, Jake, Jean, Rico and Charles gathered at the stage stop in front of the Niantic Hotel at Clay and Sansome. The Niantic was one of those quirky buildings that was fashioned out of the hulls of abandoned ships, hauled up from the harbor during the Gold Rush and put to a new purpose. In those days, good lumber was too expensive to watch rot away. The coach driver was harnessing the last of the horses as Charles paid his six-dollar fare and handed his traveling bag up to be tied down on top. A few long hugs and handshakes later, they were off. Even though Charles was moving to a place just fifty miles away, he doubted he would be seeing much more of Jake, Jean and Gabe. But he knew he owed them a lot, so as he said goodbye he suddenly felt himself go teary-eyed – more than he had felt when he left his family in Concord. Once more, he was saying good-bye to his old life to go out into the unknown.

As the landscape outside the coach began to change, excitement took over as Charles's head filled with possibilities. His own printing shop in a town he had never seen! He had been told that San Jose was a growing community with high prospects, and he hoped it would be a bit sunnier than the hilly, chilly place he was leaving, squeezed between the cold ocean water and the huge bay. Charles knew all about cold weather, but the California seasons were still surprising him. Even in the summer the place hardly ever warmed up to his satisfaction.

The coach rattled over the dusty dirt track that was the shortest route south, close by the western shore of the bay. Seated opposite Charles was a well-dressed gentleman in his thirties who was with a young woman, nice looking but not stunning. On the bench with Charles were two preteen boys, both chatting away in French. The woman answered them in French. Charles wondered whether any of them spoke English.

This was his first trip farther than a few miles beyond the Marbough home and hardware store. He felt a surge of pleasure when the horse-drawn coach cleared the fog and the morning sun fell on his face. It was the first time he'd felt warm in weeks. He had gone walking with Jake to explore the western sand dunes and beaches of the Pacific on a gray day, but this territory to the south was new to him. He had never seen a place like this, especially the layers of mountains to the west of the bay, some partly covered with low trees and chaparral, some bare and tawny. Everywhere, he saw oaks and sycamores dotting the near landscape.

Charles decided to break the ice with his companions.

"Do you know much about San Jose?" he began, looking at the man in front of him.

"*Oui, monsieur*," the man said. "My brother and I own land up in the foothills, southeast of San Jose. My brother Louis has a nursery in town and we have a house there. It's a delightful place with a perfect climate."

"I've heard that," Charles said. "So you've been away then?"

"Three years and 9,200 miles away to be exact – in France. I'm Pierre Pellier, and this is my wife, Henriette. We were married at my family home in Agen just last fall. Actually, she is the reason I returned there."

"Well, congratulations. I'm Charles Grayson."

"*Merci*," Henriette said. "But I sometimes wonder if you didn't really return for those cuttings," she said, looking at her husband.

Pierre laughed. "As far as my brother is concerned, the cuttings are the *raison*," he said, "but growing is his life. He gives himself night and day to his work."

"So these cuttings – what do you expect to grow with them?" Charles asked.

"Peaches, plums, pears, cherries, apples," Pierre said. "We have vineyards, too. And I have several of a special variety of French prune – *la Pruneaux d'Agen*. These scions, some of them are from our plum trees, the *Prunier d'Ente*."

"So you must know a lot about orcharding, you and your brother."

"Oh, we are farm boys, as you say. My brother came here to mine gold, but that was a waste of time. Now we are doing what we need to do. And how about you, young fellow, you look like a man of purpose."

"I'm a printer," Charles said. "I'm starting a new shop in San Jose."

"Good for you," Henriette said. "A town needs a good printer. And may I introduce Delphin and Joseph Delmas. They have made this long trip from France with us, to join their father in San Jose."

"*Bonjour*," the boys said in unison, eyeing Charles shyly.

"*Bonjour*," he answered, suddenly feeling cosmopolitan.

It was after 1 o'clock by the time the coach pulled into the lunchtime stop, and Charles was sweating.

"Where are we?" he asked aloud to no one in particular as they stepped out of the coach. He looked over the two-story adobe in front of them, which stood alone in a flat expanse of tawny grassland. Its distinctive feature was a long, narrow second-floor balcony running the length of the building and overhanging the first floor, all topped by a two-foot-high façade of equal length. Compared with the handful of other adobe buildings he had seen on this trip, it was a palace of sorts.

"It's the *cantina* of Secundino Robles," Pierre said, smiling. He came close to Charles's ear and lowered his voice. "Secundino is a legend here, from a pure Castillian family and one of the old Californios from before the Gold Rush. My brother knows him well. His *vaqueros* run cattle, and he has a big family. The people you see around here are all his family members. I think he must own about 8,000 acres hereabouts that he bought from one of the Spanish land grantees. When my brother first came to the area, Secundino would give any traveler food and lodging without charging for it. To him at that time it would have been insulting to offer payment. Most of the Californios felt that way – it was part of their lifestyle. Now, there are so many people coming through that he has to charge, but he still would rather not."

It was surprisingly cool inside, and Charles's eyes had to adjust to the darkness as he sat at a table with the Pelliers and the Delmas boys. Some melon came, which was a welcome first course, and the tortillas and frijoles filled him up. Over the months, he had developed a partiality to the Mexican fare in the city.

"*Señor* Pellier, you have returned at last," came a voice from the dimness in the back of the room. A smiling, handsome, middle-aged vaquero was on his way to their table. "And look who you have brought with you."

"Secundino, your hospitality is unmatched, as always," Pierre said, getting up as the two men embraced. "May I introduce my wife, Henriette, Charles Grayson of San Francisco, our traveling companion, and the Delmas boys from France, Joseph and Delphin. Everyone, meet Don Secundino Robles."

"You are all welcome here, and I hope the meal is to your liking," Robles said, looking at Henriette. "And I congratulate the two of you. Señor Pellier, I can see you have chosen well. Now tell me, is our pueblo down the road going to see such an increase in population?"

"You've met Antoine Delmas, I think. These are his sons, come to live with him. Mr. Grayson is about to set up a printing business in San Jose."

"And what will you print, Señor Grayson? Not one of these *abominable* American news sheets, I hope. They offer nothing but gossip and lies, and they are only a tool of the lawyers. I have no use for them."

Robles' tone was suddenly incendiary. Momentarily taken aback, Charles mumbled, "Uh, well, I'm a commercial printer, really. But it's a shame if there's no proper newspaper here. Maybe you need one."

"The Americanos are in such a rush to know things," Robles said, shedding his momentary anger. "Everything

really worth knowing has already been written, hasn't it?"
He laughed heartily, and everyone within earshot joined
in. But Charles had the feeling that the comment was half
serious.

Later, when they were back in the coach, Pierre
leaned over to Charles. "You have to understand about
Secundino," he said. "He's a generous man – to a fault.
He's a wonderful host, but not really a hard-headed
businessman. According to my brother, he has run
into some trouble with the courts here over title to his
lands and has had some financial setbacks. The style of
the Californios is too casual for them to survive in the
American legal system. I suspect some of that is behind
his comment about the newspapers."

Hours later, as the coach rumbled on, they all were long
past being ready for the herky-jerky ride to end. Pellier
leaned his head out the coach window and pointed.

"There, look. There is the mission of Santa Clara,"
he said. "There's a college there now, run by the Jesuit
brothers. You boys might go to school there some day."

"I can't see," Delphin said as he scrambled to look past
Joseph. Craning his neck, Charles could see the outline
of a church tower against the perfect blue sky, oak trees
obscuring the rest of the mission. When the coach pulled
up to the front for a brief mail stop, he looked closely
at the church – a whitewashed adobe building with an
essentially flat front and an arched doorway, red-tiled
roof and a square tower on the left side, topped by a cross.
Another cross stood atop the front gable, and a third large
one was planted in the ground in front, on the opposite
side of the coach. Charles got out and looked around.
Farther back and to the left of the church was a connected
building, and some more small adobe structures stood
behind the church. The grounds were oak-shaded; the
place had a sense of peace about it.

As the horses pulled them away from the mission for the short final leg of their journey, they entered a wide avenue – The Alameda – lined on both sides by willow trees that went on for the final three miles to San Jose – the legacy of Father Catalá, Ynigo and Marcelo. For long stretches, a third and a fourth row of trees were visible to the sides, shading footpaths. This beautiful shady road impressed Charles, offering a nice respite from the warm afternoon – a good omen, Charles thought, as he approached his new home. At the time he didn't realize that he had already met two of the men who would help make his first two years in San Jose his most unforgettable. The next morning, sitting in a room in the Pellier home, he recorded his impressions:

> *For the first time in a week I have awakened to sunshine. I feel at this moment more hopeful than at any time since I left Concord. And I can say this knowing that I am a stranger here, in a land that is new to me, and yet comfortable. There is an open feeling about this place that I can sense already, without some of the crassness that I found in San Francisco. The air is clean and dry. I can hardly wait to start my work here. I have met a couple on the stage who are French, the Pelliers. They have proposed that I rent a room in the house they share with Mr. Pellier's brother. – C.G.*

FOR THE DRIVER WHO LEFT Charles, the Pelliers and the Delmas boys at the stage stop in San Jose, the end of a day's work was near. He drove to the livery, parked his stage behind the barn, then unhitched his team and guided the animals to their stalls. Antonio del Costa was then in his mid-thirties. Ten years before, he had taken his infant son to Los Angeles, where for three years, he hid out under the assumed name Jorge Villegas, while doing odd jobs and leaving the boy with a relative. At the end of three years, Antonio and the boy relocated to San Jose, where Antonio became a stage driver, still under the assumed name. He called his son Juan Villegas.

On this evening, Antonio walked the three blocks from the livery to the small house he rented on St. James Street. There Juan had laid out the beans, rice and bread for their evening meal, waiting for his father's return. When Antonio arrived, he took off his boots, washed his hands and face and prepared the food. Then they sat across the wooden table from each other and ate. This was the protocol they always followed.

"What did they teach you in school today?" Antonio asked.

"We read in our reading books. We practiced spelling. We made maps."

"What else?"

"Nothing." A long silence followed. "Papa?"

"What?"

"I was wondering ... about my mother."

"She died, I told you. It was an accident a long time ago, when you were a baby."

"But what happened? Did someone kill her?"

"Why would you ask something like that?"

"I was just wondering."

Antonio hesitated for a long minute, looking at his son's eyes, open wide, waiting.

"I guess I could tell you about it. You're old enough to know. We were living in Monterey, your mother and I. We were ready to get married. Your grandfather had a big ranch where we were going to live. There was a man, an evil gringo named Wheeler who came to town. He seduced your aunt Guadalupe, then lied about me to your grandfather so he could steal our rightful inheritance.

When you were born he wanted to kill you so he could have the ranch for himself. Your mother found out and was trying to get you away from Wheeler when she fell off a horse and died. Luckily for you, I was there, so I picked you up – you were just a baby – and finished the rescue. Otherwise Wheeler would have had you killed. So that's what happened."

After thinking for a minute, Juan asked, "Why didn't we ever go back to get the inheritance?"

"We couldn't. Your grandfather believed Wheeler, and he blamed me for your mother's death. And no telling what Wheeler would have done to you. I had to keep you safe."

"Is my grandfather still alive?"

"Yes. He's still on his ranch in Monterey. His name is Joaquin Amandillo. Someday we'll go there together and claim what should be ours. But not now. Not until you're older."

That was all Antonio told his son, and all he would ever tell him about his mother. Juan went to bed that night thinking of his grandfather and the scoundrel Wheeler on the Monterey ranch. He would think about them often in the years ahead.

Chapter 4

Foard Ranch, Santa Clara Valley, California
March 1856

IN THE SHADOW OF LATE AFTERNOON, Catherine Foard was finishing her grooming chores and putting the main stable in order. As she pulled apart a hay bale to divide over the last three stalls, a mouse scuttered out of it, and she swatted at it with the pitchfork before it disappeared around a corner. Maybe they needed another cat, she thought.

Catherine, eighteen, had been around horses all her life, responsible for their care for the last six years. The stable was home for her, its smell evoking everything she loved about her work – the energy and power of the animals, their unique personalities, the confidence that she could bond with a horse and make it her partner. On a horse, she felt in control of her life and her destiny. She finished spreading the straw and put away the grooming brushes and buckets.

"Don't forget we have a guest tonight," came her father's voice from the doorway. "Dinner's in an hour."

"Okay, Pop."

"How's that sore looking on Cory's leg?"

"Not any worse. I put some of the salve on it."

"Okay, then. I'll have a look at it."

IN THE WEST VALLEY, isolated as the Foard ranch was, it wasn't unusual to have a customer stay for dinner, or even overnight on occasion, especially important ones or repeat buyers. That spring evening the guest was Thomas Berkey, an entrepreneur from Sacramento who was about to begin laying rails for a horsecar line there.

The Foards bred mostly riding and trotting horses, those being the most in demand. But over the past four years Eli had been building his stock of a heavier, stronger type of horse, one highly in demand for farm work and one he believed would fill the coming need for farming and for pulling omnibuses and rail-tracked horsecars in the larger towns. The breed was the Percheron, originally from the Perche Valley in northern France. Catherine loved these gentle giants, some of whom stood seventeen hands and weighed around 1,900 pounds, the only draft horses currently being bred on the West Coast. Hercules and Josephine, the original pair of the Foards' Percheron line, were among the most carefully cared-for animals in Northern California.

"Mr. Berkey, could you tell us what future you see for horsecars with the coming of the railroad?" Catherine ventured when the table was cleared after dinner. Catherine had never been shy with strangers.

"The brightest," Berkey replied. "New York and other cities in the East already have several lines. You've heard that just last month we opened our steam railroad line, the first west of the Mississippi, between downtown Sacramento and Folsom. It's only 22 miles but there's more to come – much more. And you see, the railroad is just for inter-city transportation. We're going to have hundreds of thousands of people in our cities who will need a way to get around, and the horsecars on rails are the way they'll get there. The omnibus is on the way out. It can't compete with a railed system. The steam railroads are bringing us passengers – more and more people coming in who will need a way around town."

"I have to agree," Eli said. "A pair of my Percherons can easily pull a loaded horsecar on rails at six to eight miles per hour and not tire for six hours. Where will the rails be laid in Sacramento?"

"My first route will be down K Street starting at Front Street, near the railroad depot. We'll go out to Sutter's Fort and back, about two and a half miles each way."

"And you'll have enough paying customers?"

"I'm sure of it."

"How many pairs of horses do you think you'll need. You can't work them every day."

"No. I'm thinking six pairs will do to start. That way I can work two pairs over a twelve-hour day each direction and still have two pairs resting."

"That sounds about right," Eli said, "but you'll want a seventh pair so you'll be able to replace any that get sick. I have three pairs I can sell you tomorrow, more in the spring."

"Oh, it'll be a year or so before the tracks are ready. But I'll definitely be interested when we get closer to actually starting service."

"San Jose should be putting in horsecars soon, don't you think?" Catherine chimed in. Eli and Berkey both laughed, and Catherine blushed a little but set her jaw.

"Well, maybe someday," Eli said, trying to soothe his daughter's feelings. "It's a bit small just now."

"I don't think it's a funny idea at all," Catherine said, bristling. "The Alameda would be a perfect route for a horsecar line. People are always going back and forth to the mission."

"I'm sure it's an idea whose time will come," Berkey said. "When the railroads come to this valley, passengers will be everywhere. But that's in the future."

"Our Percherons are wonderful animals," Rebecca volunteered. "They're calm around people, friendly and don't scare easily. Even a gunshot will barely faze them. You'll be happy with them and they can pull all day without complaining."

"Mother's so good at changing the subject," Catherine said, refusing to be rebuffed. "I think San Jose needs horsecars now, just like the country needs a transcontinental railroad now. Someone should start planning for them. It's shortsighted to wait."

"My daughter never lets go of an idea once she takes hold of it," Rebecca said.

"It's not so far-fetched," Berkey said. "We have an engineer who came out here from New York to design the Sacramento Valley Railroad. Name's Theodore Judah. He won't stop talking about a transcontinental railroad. He's convinced the country needs it now that California is a state. But where is the money coming from? That's the sticking point. It's going to need the government's backing, and with what's going on in Washington, I don't know if we even have a united country."

That night Catherine took out a piece of paper and started to write.

"Plan for a horsecar line in San Jose," she wrote at the top. She mapped out a route starting at 10th Street and Santa Clara Street and proceeded west to the Alameda, then continued northwest to Mission Santa Clara. Under the maps she wrote:

1. *Three horsecars: Cost _____.*
2. *Laying track: Cost _____.*
3. *Six pairs of Percherons: Cost $2,100.*
4. *Cost to operate?*

Catherine knew that her father, with his West Coast monopoly, was asking $200 per horse, but she figured with her "in" she could negotiate a price of $175 each. As for the other costs, she had no idea – she would have to find the answers. Then there was the problem of securing the right to lay track on a public street. She had no experience with that, but her father was a county supervisor. That should count for something. For a start she thought an article in the local newspaper might get the ball rolling. She could write it if she had enough information. The next time she was in San Jose she would talk to that editor her father had introduced her to – Mr. Murdoch. Why not? Every new project had to start somewhere.

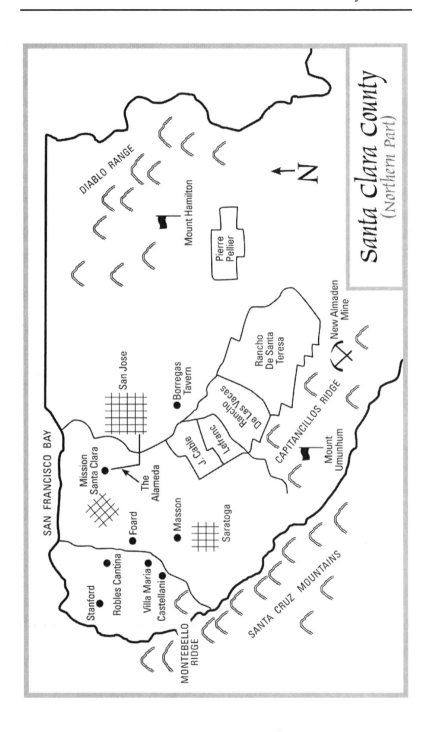

Chapter 5

San Jose, California
July 1856

AFTER A MONTH IN SAN JOSE, Charles was worried. Nothing was going according to plan. The equipment he needed to set up his shop had not arrived on time, and when it did come, some of it was missing. It was midsummer, and he was still getting his shop organized on North Market Street. Only within the past week had he been able to get everything in place for Rico Printing to conduct full-service operations.

Then there was the matter of customers. Humberto Rico was sending notes telling him to get out and sell their services to the town, but Charles had only vague ideas about how to do it. He printed up handbills and posted them on various street corners. He went into every shop, store, mill and factory in town to announce his opening and describe what his shop could provide. Some owners seemed interested, but few had jobs for him right away. Most had been taking their printing jobs to the *San Jose Telegraph,* the town's weekly newspaper, which did some commercial printing on the side.

In early August, Charles wrote a letter to Rico asking his approval to place an advertisement in the *San Jose*

Telegraph. It was a week before he got a response, and it was no. Rico was not going to pay some other printer to advertise his business. San Jose was small enough that Charles could get the word out himself, Rico said, and maybe they should think about starting their own newspaper. Well, Charles knew only the printing side of newspapers, so he wasn't eager to follow up on that suggestion. But fate intervened in mid-September when, just as business had started to trickle in, the office of the *San Jose Telegraph* burned to the ground. Early the next morning, Charles had a visit from Francis B. Murdoch, the newspaper's editor and proprietor. Murdoch wondered if Charles would be able to publish the next edition, which was due out in two days.

Six months later, Charles's print shop was thriving and he was still printing the *San Jose Telegraph*. Murdoch, who was not insured, had been unable to find financing to replace his newspaper office. One day in March, he proposed that they formalize their relationship. Rico Printing would get a contract to provide office space and printing services for the newspaper at a set price. In return, Murdoch would get a reduced rate and have the name of his newspaper on the front window. Humberto did not have to think twice – he endorsed the deal with a one-year commitment on both sides.

The new arrangement proved a godsend for Charles in several ways. For one, it sent his way all the printing business that had been going to the *Telegraph*. For another, Murdoch was a seasoned pro who knew everyone in town and could give Charles introductions in all the right places. He was a cornucopia of information about the area. And most important, Frank Murdoch eventually became Charles's best friend and advisor – but not without a few bumps in the road. Murdoch was about 50 years old, graying at the temples with piercing blue eyes – a crusty, impatient man who did not suffer fools gladly. When Charles seemed clueless in some area, Murdoch was merciless.

One day, when Charles overheard an extended dialog between Murdoch and a visitor to the shop, he waited until the visitor had left and then expressed admiration for the man's apparent store of information and experience.

"He's a fool and a bullshitter," Murdoch said. "Can't you recognize crap when you hear it? You're more naïve than I thought." Charles felt like a moron, and he thought twice before offering comments after that.

Another time, Charles arrived at the shop wearing a new suit, out of a box of stuff his mother had sent from Concord. Murdoch took one look and said, "Eastern clothes won't get you anywhere in this town. For God's sake, put on something practical. Or at least get that thing pressed." Charles went home and changed.

But over time, Charles thought Murdoch began to notice his work and develop more respect for him. After a few weeks Murdoch started giving him practical business tips that proved invaluable. He pointed out who made the real decisions in town and how to develop relationships with them. As Charles and his mentor began to share more about themselves, Murdoch seemed to mellow, and he often went out of his way to offer Charles a sounding board for problems. Charles began to think of him as a sort of fatherly partner but without the emotional undercurrent. At his best, Charles thought, Murdoch was generous and insightful.

Charles started doing small jobs for Murdoch when the editor was out of the office. At first, when people came in looking for Murdoch, Charles simply told them to leave a note and come back. After a few weeks, when he began to see what was needed, he would take information and leave the messages himself. This worked so well for

Murdoch that he offered to pay Charles on the side to act as an associate editor. Soon Charles was taking detailed orders for advertisements and even writing up short announcements. Of course, he checked with Rico first. His boss in San Francisco had no objections as long as the shop showed a nice profit each month – and it was doing pretty well now.

Even as Charles was forming a bond with Murdoch, he was also getting to know Louis and Pierre Pellier, who had a two-story frame house and a six-acre nursery on North San Pedro Street, just a few blocks from the printing office. The house and nursery – called City Gardens – actually belonged to Louis, but Pierre and Henriette lived there while Louis employed Pierre in the nursery. Charles had been staying in an extra room there since his arrival in San Jose. Every afternoon that first summer, after he closed the office and walked home, he would go first into the nursery to say hello to Louis and Pierre. Sometimes he would go there to eat his lunch. Louis, if he wasn't with a customer, would usually be busy with his fruit trees and his grapevines, but he was always eager to tell Charles about his plants.

Louis was more circumspect than his brother – not as gregarious, but still pleasant and supremely passionate about his work. He knew plants inside and out – the strengths, the vulnerabilities and the ideal growing environment for each one. He brimmed with information about what he had learned and with ideas for new varieties.

"A tree is the microcosm of all life," Louis would say. "She is born, she grows, she flowers, and then she reproduces. It is beautiful. Then, one day, she dies." Charles saw something of his old friend Thoreau in this man.

On Sundays, that fall and winter, Charles would usually be invited to an afternoon meal with Louis, Pierre and Henriette in their dining room. The Pelliers were good company, and Henriette's English was improving as Charles acquired a smattering of French. He always looked forward to sampling the Pelliers' peach brandy, which was made from their own fruit. One Sunday after they finished dinner, Louis hooked a horse to his delivery wagon and he and Charles drove out to Louis's property in the Evergreen area, a few miles southeast of town.

After they had gone a few miles and neared the foothills Louis said, "First I will take you up toward the ridge, so we can get a view."

It was a cool day in late February, and the winter rains had turned the nearly treeless eastern mountains a luxuriant green. A few cattle grazed on the hillsides. As the wagon left the wheat fields and ascended on the narrow road, Charles looked back. He could see the misty north-south ridgeline of the San Francisco Peninsula in the distance, the green foothills of Mount Hamilton directly in front of him, and between them, the sketchy outline of the San Francisco Bay. A few gulls circled overhead. The broad valley stretched out to the west, fields of yellow mustard covering large patches of the landscape.

In the lower reaches of these foothills, Louis Pellier was starting an orchard. The rows were defined and the small trees were taking hold, each row carefully labeled – pears, cherries, prunes, apples. Down the hill just to the north was a vineyard.

Louis took a bag of cuttings from his wagon, knelt by one small tree and motioned for Charles to come close. Charles watched as Louis carefully sliced the top off the little planted tree and cut a small notch in the main stem with his knife. Then Louis used the knife to shape the end of a cutting, forming it into a wedge-shaped tab. He inserted this tab into the notch, then took some string and carefully wound it around the tree at the graft and knotted it.

"Now I take some asphalt water emulsion," Pellier said. "It should be pliable but not runny. I shape it around the graft like this" – he used his fingers to form a thick coating of the emulsion around the graft point – "and it protects the joint." He stood up, admiring his work. "Now, with a little time – maybe two or three years – we will have a beautiful prune tree."

"Why do you do the grafting?" Charles asked. "Why not just plant a new tree?

"It's to make the tree strong. These local plums, they aren't the best, but they're resistant to disease. The top branch comes from France – *la Pruneaux d'Agen.* It's just a delicious fruit. So I've taken the scions Pierre brought with him and grafted them onto the local rootstock, to make them hardy and be sure they survive. It will be a wonderful thing to see the result. Here we have the ideal conditions – summers not too hot, winters not too cold, and just enough rain. The prunes and the pears, they don't seem to need to be watered all summer, once they get a start. The winter rains are enough."

"Where will you sell the fruit?"

"Oh, that *is* something to think about. California is attracting more people all the time. They come, and more in the future – many more. And the good thing about prunes is, they can be dried and transported. They are wonderful! I can see a valley filled with fruit trees some day." Louis smiled broadly. "And we have a vineyard maturing over here with the cuttings that Pierre brought from France. My friend Antoine Delmas is also doing some wonderful things with grapevines. A lot of his came from New England. They are not French, but he has produced some good wine. There is wonderful potential here. And it's not like France – the land is here almost for the taking, to be put to a good use."

"What about all the wheat?" Charles asked. "Are the wheat farmers and the cattle ranchers going to want to plant orchards?"

"There is plenty of land for wheat," Louis said. "If we can find ways to get the fruit to the people who want it, orchards are going to yield much more profit than grazing land or wheat fields. So economically speaking, the landowners are going to use their land in the way that gives them the greatest return. It's the way things work. And these changes do not happen overnight, either. I am thinking of the next generation."

Louis sees orchards going in to replace the wheat fields and grazing land in the future. I can't see how that will happen. Family orchards, maybe. But who is going to buy all the fruit? There aren't many people here, and the fruit is going to rot if it is transported very far. Maybe as San Francisco gets bigger the people there would buy fruit. Anyway, I hope Louis gets what he wants. – C.G.

Chapter 6

DAWN WAS BREAKING on the Foards' ranch house when Eli walked into the kitchen to get his first cup of coffee.

"Biscuits'll be out in a minute," Rebecca said. "Coffee's on."

Eli poured himself a cup as Rebecca cracked two eggs into a frying pan.

"Cathy up?" he asked.

"She's out to the stable, looking after Oscar. I just hope if I ever get sick, she'll take care o' me same as she does that horse."

"She'll have her own family to look after before long, I'm thinking."

"And how will that be happening? I haven't noticed any prospective suitors coming to the door, have you? Joe Parsons is the only man her age she's even talked to for weeks. And I don't think she's about to marry him."

"Joe's not the marryin' kind. But I knew that when I hired 'im. I wouldn't worry, though. She'll find somebody when she's ready."

"I'm not sure about that. I think she'd be happier riding Oscar up to Black Mountain than she would taking a walk down the aisle. Cathy's still a tomboy."

"Well, you would know all about that. Must run in the family is all I can say."

"Hmph. You must have seen some of the girl in me or we wouldn't be here talking about our daughter."

The screen door slammed and Catherine came through the back porch, running noisily in her boots. Immediately, Rebecca and Eli knew something was wrong.

"Dad, we've got two good saddle horses and two Percherons gone! I only checked one stable. There might be more."

"What, are you sure? Were they put away last night?"

"I know they were – I checked. They were in the stalls before dinner."

"Where's Joe?"

"I got him up. He's checking the other stable. Sparky's gone, Sally, C.J. and Dusty. Just gone."

Eli ran for his boots, pulled them on and hurried out to the stables. Just as Eli reached the first stable and confirmed for himself that the stalls were empty, Joe Parsons, the hired trainer and stable boy, came jogging through the rear stable door.

"None missing from the south stable," he said, out of breath. "Just the four gone, I guess."

"Didn't you hear anything in the night?" Eli demanded, staring at Joe, clearly looking for someone to blame.

"I didn't hear a thing, Eli," Joe said, shrugging. "I slept straight through. We don't lock the stables."

"Never thought we needed to. Until now."

San Jose
May 1857

It was shortly after the Foards' horses disappeared that Charles began to see the darker side of his new home.

During the last week in May San Jose was having a hot spell, over 100 by noontime for the third straight day. They were due for a break soon, everyone said. On Wednesday he was drinking lemonade while he read over a copy of the *Telegraph* that had just come off the press. In the Superior Court column he puzzled over a brief, obscure-looking report about a civil suit. It seemed that one A. Hamilton Cable was suing one Armando Contreras for possession of a piece of real estate. What caught his eye was the size of the property – 3,660 acres. It seemed to Charles like an enormous piece of land to be in dispute. Later that day, when Murdoch returned to the office, Charles asked him about the item.

"It got my curiosity up, too," Murdoch said. "The Contrerases have one of the largest Spanish land grants left in the valley where the title's been settled. Their *rancho* is out near the New Almaden quicksilver mine – called Rancho de Las Vacas. I think they have about 7,000 acres out there. And you must know who Hamilton Cable is."

"Uh, I've heard the name."

"You should have. He's a member of the county board of supervisors. Very well known, belongs to the First Methodist Church, a big man in town. I think he came from Georgia a few years back. Deals in mining equipment, and I'm pretty sure he owns a stake in the mine."

"So what do you think this suit is about?"

"Good question. You want to ask Cable?" Murdoch said, raising his eyebrows and flashing a mischievous grin.

"Me? Why me?"

"Might give you a chance to get your feet wet as a reporter. I'll pay you for the story if it's good."

"I'm just a printer, Frank," Charles said. "I don't mind helping you out here in the office, but I'll leave the important stuff to you."

"Suit yourself," Murdoch said. "But you noticed that little item, so it shows you've got a nose for news. You need to get out more and circulate. And aren't you going after that county printing contract? This would give you a good chance to meet a member of the board that's going to have to approve that. Never hurts to get acquainted around here. You want to approach him in a friendly way, though – maybe you can get him into a conversation after the meeting."

Charles thought a minute. "But I don't have a horse," he said. "Wouldn't I need one to go out and get all this information?"

"Oh, tarnation, go buy yourself a horse!" Murdoch yelled, then instantly cooled down. "Listen, this is your little shop and I know you don't have much money. I'll lend you what you need. Go get a horse – you're in the West now. Why not borrow one from Pellier for now if you need to go somewhere?"

As it happened, Charles learned the next day that he would have to be at the county board of supervisors' next meeting to answer questions about the printing contract. So he found himself walking into the board's chambers at the courthouse at 10 o'clock the following Tuesday. As he was choosing a seat in the nearly empty room, he noticed a well-dressed girl giving him a quick smile from her seat in the row just behind him. Just then, he wished he had worn a nicer shirt to the meeting. Automatically, he smoothed his hair.

A tall, rigidly erect man in a dark suit entered the room from the front, behind the long row of desks, and gazed around. After arranging his papers on the desk, he walked stiffly to where Charles was sitting. He had a long, thin face with a very prominent mole nearly covering one side of his nose. "You must be Mr. Grayson," he said with a distinct southern accent through a thin-lipped smile, showing flashy teeth. Charles nodded, extending his hand. "I'm Cable – I'll be chairing the meeting," Hamilton Cable said, offering Charles his limp, fleshy hand. "This seems to be a routine matter. I don't anticipate any discussion on it, but thank you for being present."

Then Cable nodded to the young woman on the bench. "Miss Foard, it's a pleasure," he said in his syrupy voice.

"Uh – Mr. Cable?" Charles said, wanting to get his attention back. Cable, who had already turned his back, stopped and glanced back at Charles with raised eyebrows, over his shoulder. "I was wondering – the item in the *Telegraph* about your suit against Contreras – would you have time to talk to me about it, for a story?"

Cable immediately wheeled and went ramrod straight again. "It's a private matter, Grayson. If the *Telegraph* wants information they can talk to my lawyer. And," – he paused with a quizzical look – "aren't you just the printer?"

"Sir, I'm doing some reporting for Mr. Murdoch on the side. Uh – could I get your lawyer's name?"

"Wallace. You want to talk to William Wallace. And why is the *Telegraph* interested, may I ask?"

"Just because of the size of the property involved. You being a prominent official and all."

"Yes. Well, as I said, it involves a contractual matter. Wallace can give you the details." He eyed Charles for a long second before his scowl relaxed. "Mr. Grayson, you're new in San Jose. Do you have a church affiliation?"

Whoa, Charles thought. *Where did that come from?* He hesitated. "Well, no, I'm not much of a churchgoer," he said.

"Mmm. Well, God judges everyone, churchgoer or not, Mr. Grayson. Come over to the First Presbyterian sometime. We're on North Second Street, you've seen our building. I believe you're single, am I right?"

"Yes, sir."

"We can correct that, you know." Cable gave Charles another flashy smile and walked back to his seat behind the desks.

As they waited for the board members to get settled, Catherine Foard leaned over towards him. "Do you have something before the board today?" She asked.

"Oh, uh, it's nothing important, just a printing contract. I, um, I don't think they're going to ask me anything, but I was supposed to be here just in case. How about you?"

"I came into town with my father. He's on the board – Eli Foard. We're going shopping later. So I'm just killing time here until he's free."

"I, uh, I'm Charles Grayson. I have a printing shop here," Charles said, turning around so he could get a better look at Catherine. He noticed the shine of her hair and her smile.

"Catherine Foard. My friends call me Cathy."

"Happy to make your acquaintance," Charles said. "Isn't this boring for you?"

"Horribly. If I could think of somewhere else to be, I would be there."

Just then Charles heard a gavel bang and he straightened around. The meeting was in session, so he figured he had better start paying attention. Cable began droning his way through a series of procedural matters. Suddenly, the printing contract came up, so quickly that Charles was startled.

"Mr. Grayson is here, I believe," Cable said. "Does anyone have questions for Mr. Grayson?" None of the other board members spoke; then there was sort of a mass grunt that apparently approved the contract, and Cable slammed the gavel down. "Thank you, Mr. Grayson," Cable said, nodding in Charles's direction. At that point, Charles wasn't sure what to do. The meeting went on, but he assumed he should probably leave. As he got up and left the room – maybe a little too quickly, he thought later – he nodded to Catherine Foard, who was grinning at him. Feeling a bit disoriented and useless, he wandered back to the printing shop wondering how he could ever get someone like Cable into a friendly conversation. He hoped he wouldn't have to go to the man's church.

The disorientation was slow to leave. For the first time since his arrival in San Jose, Charles felt pulled in several directions at once. There was plenty of work to be done at the shop that morning, so he knew that should get his first attention, but he had trouble focusing. He kept thinking of Murdoch's assignment – was it really an assignment? – to check out the Cable lawsuit. His curiosity was aroused. Instinctively, he thought he wanted to ask the Contreras family about it, to see what was what. Would they want to see him? There was Cable's lawyer to contact. And then too, there was the French garden party that the Pellier brothers had invited him to on Sunday afternoon. It would be fun, he thought – he liked the French people he had met at the nursery – and it would be a chance to get better acquainted in the town. But he fretted that he didn't have the proper clothes – the French dressed well. He was still struggling with his personal finances and couldn't afford a trip to San Francisco to improve his wardrobe. On top of all that, there was Catherine Foard. She was on his mind, for some reason. More than anything else just then, Charles thought it would be nice if she would come walking into his shop.

He didn't have to wait long. Just after noon, he looked out the window and noticed that Cathy and her father were crossing the street and heading for the front door. Hurrying, he grabbed a comb from his top desk drawer and gave his hair a few swipes. Checking his sleeves for ink stains, he cringed when he found one; he just managed to roll up his sleeves before they arrived. He decided to leave on his hopelessly blotchy apron. Eli and Catherine opened the door, setting off the bell attached to the top of it.

"Mr. Grayson," Eli began as soon as they were inside, "We wanted to congratulate you on your new contract with the county. Would you join my daughter and me for lunch?"

"Uh, well, thank you, I appreciate that," Charles said, feeling genuinely grateful. "Actually I, well, I do close up here at lunchtime. I usually go down to visit the Pellier nursery."

"We would like to take you to Clayton's – please come," Catherine said.

"Oh. Well, thank you, I would like that, but – well, I didn't wear a tie today."

"Your clothes are fine," Eli said. "Clayton's at lunchtime is very informal."

Charles took off his apron, turned the sign in the window to "Closed," and the three of them set off for Clayton's restaurant, which was just around the corner on Santa Clara Street near First. Charles had never eaten there, and suddenly he felt jittery: Here he was accompanied by a girl he had just met and her father, a county supervisor whom he didn't know at all.

"You do some nice printing work," Eli said as they were seated, apparently trying to put Charles at ease. "The *Telegraph* seems much easier to read now. We needed a good printer in San Jose."

"It's the ink, sir," Charles said. "I use a special formulation I learned from a friend in Massachusetts. Doesn't smear so easily." Eli nodded. "Do you folks live here in town?"

"We're out near West Side, at the base of the mountains," Catherine said. "It's a beautiful place. Are you new to the West, Mr. Grayson?"

"Is it so obvious?"

"Well, you do have that accent that's peculiar to those from New England. It suits you, though. You should ride out and see our place – we breed and sell horses. Have you had a chance to see our side of the valley?"

"Not really," Charles said. "I've been pretty busy setting up my business." He was ashamed to admit that he did not own a horse, sitting here talking to folks who were obviously horse people through and through.

"You don't still ride an English saddle, do you?" Catherine persisted.

"Well, no, no, strictly Western. I didn't even bring a saddle when I came west." He was becoming more uncomfortable by the moment, so he changed the subject. "You folks come West by wagon?"

"Yes, we did, ten years ago," Catherine said. "I still say they need a railroad across the country. And you, Mr. Grayson?"

"A ship around the horn. Not something I'd ever repeat."

"Why don't you ride out and see us a week from Sunday?" Eli asked. "We'll ride up into the hills. Nice views from up there. And we can show you our breeding stock. Say – by the way – has anyone been in the newspaper office talking about any horse thievery going on?"

"Not that I remember. You've had horses stolen?"

"Four, just a few days ago. I've told the sheriff, but he doesn't have a clue how to find those scoundrels. We might be needing a new sheriff soon."

Just then the food arrived, giving Charles a moment to think. He was pretty sure he could borrow a horse from the Pelliers to get out to the Foard ranch. By this time it seemed too late to back out by admitting he didn't own a horse, and that in fact he hadn't even mounted a horse since his arrival in San Francisco.

"Well, how about it?" Eli asked as the waiter left. "Will you pay us a visit?"

"That's very nice of you, sir. I would love to pay you a visit. Thank you."

"I've been told you're doing some writing for the *Telegraph* as well," Eli continued.

"Well, it's not much," Charles said, shaking his head. "Mr. Murdoch suggested that I work on a particular article, but I haven't really written anything important. I mainly help him out with, uh, you know, clerical things."

Now Eli leaned his head toward Charles and lowered his voice. "You want to talk to Secundino Robles. He'll give you a lot of background."

"The saloon keeper at the stage stop?" Charles asked, almost whispering. Immediately, he realized that Cathy had told her father about his short exchange with Cable.

"Oh, he's much more than a saloon keeper. Don Secundino is a legend around here. He's a cousin of the Contreras brothers. They're old Californio families, all of them. Since Mexico lost California to the United States, there's been a transition going on, and the Californios are getting the worst of it. Some of it's their fault, some of it's just the way our laws work. Some say they're getting swindled, and they may be right. Anyway, you ought to get to know Don Secundino."

It was a nice lunch, but Charles was kicking himself for not coming clean about his riding. The way things stood, besides having to borrow a horse, somehow he would have to brush up on his horsemanship, which had never been one of his priorities. He wanted to avoid embarrassing himself in front of Catherine. When he thought about it, he realized that whole lunch invitation must have been Catherine's idea. He smiled to himself.

I feel nervous about this new involvement with the Telegraph. I want to be sure I do a good job with the printing business, so I don't want to get distracted. Frank thinks doing some reporting for the paper will be a good way for me to become known in the valley. I can probably meet a lot of people that way. I'll have to be careful to keep it on a small scale. – C.G.

Chapter 7

The Robles cantina
June 5, 1857

CHARLES WAS THIRSTY and pretty hungry when he arrived at the Robles cantina just before 2 o'clock on Friday. It was another warm day. He hitched Louis Pellier's black stallion outside and went into the darkened adobe, which was lit inside only by oil lamps. He had forgotten how the smell of beer pervaded the place, and his mind flashed back to the day he was shanghaied. He didn't see Don Secundino, but there was a young vaquero sweeping the floor around a handful of patrons.

"You want some lunch, my friend, maybe some frijoles and tortillas?" the vaquero asked, coming over to him. "We got a little brisket left if you want that."

"Yes, all that," Charles said. "And a beer, please. Is Don Secundino here?"

"Oh, Don Secundino, he'll be back in about an hour. You want to talk to him? Sure, he'll be back. I'll get you some lunch and you can eat while you wait. He'll be back."

Charles had his lunch, and then ordered another beer. After he finished, he slouched in one of the high-backed seats that fitted up against the back wall of the cantina, and he dozed for a few minutes. When he awoke he was the only customer left in the saloon. He had been there

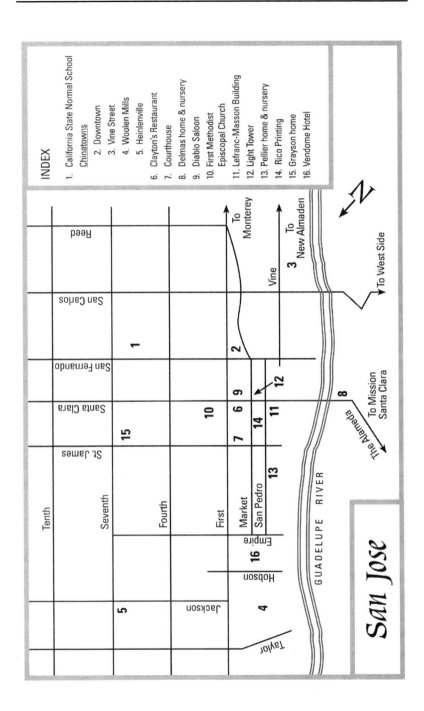

INDEX

1. California State Normal School
   Chinatowns
   2. Downtown
   3. Vine Street
   4. Woolen Mills
   5. Heinlenville
6. Clayton's Restaurant
7. Courthouse
8. Delmas home & nursery
9. Diablo Saloon
10. First Methodist
    Episcopal Church
11. Lefranc-Masson Building
12. Light Tower
13. Pellier home & nursery
14. Rico Printing
15. Grayson home
16. Vendome Hotel

San Jose

two hours before Robles appeared. Charles recognized him immediately and stood up.

"Don Secundino, hello. I'm …."

"Yes, Mr. Grayson, the printer," Robles interrupted. "And how is the printing business, and how is my friend Pierre? Are you here for business or pleasure?"

Charles was amazed at the man's memory. "Well, mostly business, but you do serve a good lunch. Do you have a few minutes to talk?"

"I would be glad to talk after I just take care of one or two things," Robles said. "Please excuse me." He went into the next room and returned after a minute or two. "Now, how are you, Mr. Grayson? You haven't been out this way to see us."

"I had to borrow a horse to get here."

"*Borrow* a horse? Oh, Mr. Grayson, a man must have a horse. Here in the West a man is nothing without a horse. My brothers and I were riding when we were three years old. We will have to get you a horse, that's for sure."

"Yes, I'm seeing the truth of that," Charles said. "But what I really came about was an item in the *San Jose Telegraph* last week. About this suit against the Contreras family by Hamilton Cable."

"Hamilton Cable," Robles said, grim-faced. "That snake. That vermin. Hamilton Cable and his gringo lawyers. Excuse my language. Hamilton Cable is a cheat, a worm, and he is getting his slime all over this valley." Robles pounded his fist on the table as he said it. "You want to know about Hamilton Cable? I'll tell you about Hamilton Cable. I needed a little money, just a little to get past a rough spot. I had a note with a lender in San Jose for 12 percent a month, and somehow Hamilton Cable bought this note – I don't know how he did it. I missed one payment, one payment! And Hamilton Cable got the court in San Jose to take my land from me – 50 acres! Fifty acres of mine Hamilton Cable got for buying a little $500 note. And I still had to pay him the $500! These gringo courts and gringo lawyers are ruining this wonderful land. They should all be put on a boat and shipped to *China!*" Now Robles' face was dark red.

"I'm sorry to hear that, sir," Charles said. "Do you know anything about this lawsuit against the Contreras family?"

"The Contrerases are my cousins, you know," Robles said, nodding his head. We are very close. We all grew up in Branciforte – you know, over on the San Lorenzo River near Santa Cruz, on the other side of the mountains. I know the Contreras brothers very well." He was calming down a little.

"We grew up, my brothers and the Contreras brothers, all of us riding and roping over there, on all the ranchos and in the rodeos, and sometimes over here in the valley. We would compete with each other, to see who could ride and rope the best, who could look the best in the saddle – to impress the ladies, you know. There were very interesting women over there when we were young." Robles paused for a breath, smiling a little and nodding his head again.

"Well, sometimes we got out of hand a little bit," he continued. He clasped his hands and looked at the floor, then looked up at Charles, his eyelids drooping a little. "We would have a little to drink, like all young men do, and we would start to play around a little, get a little wild. My brother had some aguardiente, some cactus whiskey, you know – very potent. This was long ago – in '39. He stole a horse and rode over here to make the rounds of the cantinas and the fandango halls. He got a little out of hand, and the proprietors, they kicked him out. He went down to Monterey then and got into the same kind of trouble. My father, he had to get him out of jail – my father was a very respected man, a respectable man, a member of the Mexican army. But that wasn't the end of it."

"Are you talking about your brother, Teodoro?"

"No, no, not Teodoro. This was my older brother, Nicholas. He got into some more of the same kind of trouble, and he was exiled to Santa Barbara. After he returned, there was a situation with him and a fifteen-year-old girl, a real delicious little package she was. Nicholas had to hightail it out of there, but he was pursued. My brother Avelino tried to help him, but they were both caught. They still would have made it out alive, but those people, they tried to humiliate them – I won't tell you how, it was so bad. They tried to escape, and Avelino was killed. Nicholas got away, but he died later."

"I'm sorry to hear that."

"Oh, it's all history now, and I don't harbor any grudges from those times; but it's all part of our story with the gringos, you see. My brother Fulgencio was the next, and his trouble was with a big, ugly Scotsman named Carmichael. My brother was trying to avenge an insult – he had to, you know. They were both drunk, and my brother was shot to death in a cantina. After that, my brother Teodoro and I, we calmed down a little bit. We used to be just like my other brothers, getting drunk and showing off. But we decided to settle down, so we came over here, to this valley. I became an official with the mission. That's when we came into good fortune."

"This is all interesting, sir, but I was wondering about this lawsuit."

"I'm getting to that. I just need to explain a few things. You see, when I was much younger – around 14 or 15 – I used to ride over here with Teodoro and we would explore around in the southern hills with the Contreras brothers, because the Contreras family owned land over there, including some around the Capitancillos ridge. We were very friendly with the Ohlones, the natives in the hills along the southwest edge of the valley, where it narrows.

They showed us how their ancestors painted themselves with red paint they made from grinding the red rock in those hills. That was their *mohetka*, they called it, and they used to trade it to the other tribes, you know. But they had to be careful because it could make you sick. I'm going to tell you their legend about this because we only realized what it meant years later. The legend was that some of their ancestors painted themselves all over with the red paint and became very sick. They were about to die before a female spirit in a black robe appeared to them. This spirit told them to go to a spring and to wash all the red paint completely off and to drink from the spring. They did this, and they recovered their health. You see, what we didn't know was that this sickness was quicksilver poisoning."

"From the mercury in the rock?"

"Yes. But we didn't know about the mercury then – we were looking for gold and silver. This was – oh, about 1824, when I was just a boy. We went to Don Antonio Sunol – me, my brother and Armando Contreras – because we were young boys and Sunol was a wealthy man and he owned a lot of land in this valley back then. He thought there was silver there, and he invested about $400 in a venture, but they didn't find any silver, so everything was forgotten. That is, until Castillero came."

"Castillero – who was that?"

"Well, you are new in the valley, so you wouldn't know Andres Castillero. We probably won't see him again because he went back to Spain. But he was an officer in the Mexican military when he came down here from Sutter's Fort in 1845, not long before the war started. And he is the reason we have this rich mercury mine now called New Almaden. It all got started one night in the Santa Clara Mission. My brother and I were there with Castillero and Father Real of the mission, who is our cousin, by the way, and Jacob Leese, a gringo, all of us talking around the fire, you know. Castillero was interested in the red rock because they had used it to paint the mission a few years before. We were showing him the rock, and he thought it might be silver with some gold alloy in it. But he was smart. He had training in geology and mineralogy, so he did some experiments with it. He put some hot coals inside an old roof tile and scattered some pulverized rock on it. After the rock got hot, he sprinkled water on the rock and put the empty tumbler upside down over the coals. After a few minutes, what do you think he found?"

"Mercury?"

"Yes. Little globs of it inside the tumbler. He filed a claim with the alcalde, the Mexican official in charge at that time, the claim that now some people are trying to steal from the rightful owners, and he formed a partnership with my brother and me and Armando Contreras, also Father Real, and Don Jose Castro, who owned some of the land, the Capitancillos Ridge. I made sure that Armando was included because he was there at the original discovery. Castillero was a fair man – he wasn't trying to claim it all for himself."

"But what does all this have to do with the lawsuit?"

"I'm getting there. We had a partnership with Castillero. He owned half and the rest of us owned half together. Castillero took a lot of ore out of the ground in the first part of 1846 and fired it up. Oh, it was a rich mine, Castillero knew that. But Castillero had a couple of problems. He needed capital to invest in mining and reduction equipment, which he didn't have. And just about then, the war started. While he was in Spain, looking for capital, he was called back to his military duty, so he decided to sell his interest to this English company, Barron, Forbes. And Castro sold, too, so the company had a controlling interest. My brother and I were offered $13,000 by the company for our interest, so we took it.

It was a lot of money for us. We were able to buy 8,500 acres – this land here, Rancho Rincon de San Francisquito. I don't have that much anymore, because, you know, I had gambling debts."

"So you don't have a share in the mine anymore. How about Mr. Contreras?" Charles asked.

"Armando wouldn't sell – he held out, but the company stalled and wouldn't pay him when they started making a profit. That's when this cockroach Cable got wind of the situation. He found out Armando still had a share of the mine, and he also knew Armando had gambling debts – big gambling debts. Armando was desperate – he was about to lose his land. So Cable paid the debt for him in exchange for his share of the mine, which wasn't paying off for him anyway. If you ask me, I think Cable and the mine owners were together in this thing – it was a swindle! But I can't prove it."

"Well, I'm confused. If Cable has Contreras's share of the mine, how can he sue to get his land away from him?"

"That's the devious part of it. It's one more swindle!" Robles pounded the table again. "Cable is going to use his slimy lawyers and his cronies in the court system to get the land, too, and Armando and his family will be left with nothing."

"But how can that happen?"

"Because they're all corrupt! I don't know the details. Armando has told me some things, but you need to talk to him to get everything straight. All I know is that he is being cheated, the way the gringos have been cheating us for years now. Nothing against you, young man, you are an honest man, I can tell. But your American authorities are corrupt!"

They sat at the table in silence for a few minutes as Charles thought about what Robles had said. The sun was angling through one of the adobe's narrow windows so that it was catching Don Secundino on the side of the face, accentuating his strong jaw. The tendons on his neck, which had been taut, began to relax. Don Secundino turned his clear blue eyes on Charles.

"So, why did you come all the way to my place to ask me about these things?" he asked.

"Well, Francis Murdoch sent me to investigate for the *Telegraph*, for an article."

Suddenly, Robles tensed again. "You are putting all this in your newspaper, what I told you?"

"Uh, well, um, I'm sorry if you misunderstood," Charles said, squirming a bit in his chair. "Yes, I'm here as a reporter. We would like to explain this lawsuit to the readers, so they'll understand what it's about."

Robles, hunched up, eyed Charles sternly for a few seconds, and then relaxed his shoulders. "Well, why not? Yes, tell it all. It needs to be told. But talk to Armando before you print any of it. You'll do that, won't you?"

"Oh, yes, of course."

"Good. You have to. Now, it's getting late. Will you have some supper with us and stay the night?"

"Thanks for the offer. It's tempting, but I should get back. I have to return the horse to Louis Pellier."

"I insist that you stay. You can return the horse in the morning. Louis will understand."

Charles hesitated, and then nodded. "Well, all right – thank you," he said. For the rest of the evening, Secundino and Charles talked about Old California and about life in New England, until Charles finally excused himself and shuffled to the little room in the back that Secundino had prepared. He fell into bed, exhausted.

In the morning, before Charles had a chance to finish dressing, Secundino came around to his room. "I am having one of my men ride with you down to see Armando Contreras this morning," he said, as if Charles already knew about this excursion. "I want to make sure you find your way down there."

"But ..." Charles hesitated. "I really have to return the horse to Louis."

"Don't worry – I've taken care of Pellier. He knows you'll be late. And I've left some food for you at the bar. Give my best to Armando." Obviously not one to take no for an answer, Secundino signaled good-bye and then vanished.

It was a long ride – over 20 miles, Charles was sure – from the cantina out to Rancho de Las Vacas. By the time Secundino's vaquero and Charles arrived it was close to noon. The tile-roofed ranch buildings were three – a long main house, what looked like a small guest house and a still-smaller one that might have been a kitchen or a smokehouse. In front by the horse corral, Charles was met by a lean young man about his own age dressed in immaculate Californio riding attire. "My father and my older brother have gone on a trip," he said when Charles asked for Armando Contreras. "They won't be back for a month."

"And you?"

"I'm Miguel."

"Is there someone else I can talk to?" Charles asked. He said he had spoken to Don Secundino and that he needed to explain Cable's lawsuit to the readers of the *Telegraph*.

"My father could tell you, or Mr. Soto – he's our lawyer. But no one else could," Miguel said. "You'll have to come back."

Charles nodded and turned slowly as if to leave. Then, looking at the half dozen horses in the Contreras corral, he had an inspiration. "Say," he said, "I'll bet you could ride any of those horses over there, couldn't you."

"Me, I'm the best there is."

"Do you think you could teach a gringo greenhorn?"

"What are you getting at?"

"I need lessons – just a few – to brush up on my skills and learn the western style. Could you show me a few things sometime?"

"You think you can just ride in here and order riding lessons?"

"Well, it was just a thought. Maybe you could recommend someone else."

Miguel shrugged and threw up his hands. "Oh, maybe I could, if you're a fast learner. You ever do any roping?"

Charles shook his head. Miguel rolled his eyes. "Well, how much time do you have right now?"

"All afternoon," Charles said.

Miguel went to the stable and brought out a beautiful palomino while Charles waited at the corral. Leading the horse from the stable, Miguel yelled, "Well, come get your gear. Do you want me to carry it for you?" Charles jogged over and picked up the saddle that Miguel pointed to, then listened as Miguel patiently explained how to saddle the horse. Miguel showed him the *jaquima*, the western bitless headgear, and the *mecate*, the reins made from horsehair that feel more natural to the horse than rope.

"You hold the reins loose and signal gently," Miguel said. "You won't learn this in a day – it's a communication between you and the horse. You need a lightning-quick response from your horse – it could mean life or death." He spent an hour teaching Charles to handle the sixty-foot *reata* of braided rawhide – something Charles never did get quite right. But he learned to twirl it a bit, and he tried unsuccessfully to rope a few hay bales from the saddle.

"You want to wrap the end around the saddle horn as soon as you've roped the calf," Miguel said. "But you have to be sure and get your thumb out quick. I've seen a vaquero lose his thumb when a steer suddenly pulls it tight." Charles winced.

The usual four o'clock breeze had started to whip through the valley before Charles realized he had spent nearly four hours with Miguel Contreras. Miguel spent most of the time teaching Charles to ride light in the saddle, erect but relaxed. Before Charles left for town he felt as if he had a new friend – and he had also bought himself a horse – a beautiful bay stallion named Cuesta. Charles didn't have the money with him, but Miguel took his promise to come back with it.

Charles returned to the Contreras ranch on Cuesta twice that week – once to practice his roping and again to make the payment for the horse. On his first trip back, he and Miguel rode up Guadalupe Creek toward the mountain peak that the Ohlone called Mount Umunhum, where Miguel showed him another huge oak tree standing alone in a meadow, bigger than the one near the ranch house. They stopped for lunch by the tree, and Charles talked about his boyhood in New England and his long ocean voyage. Miguel talked about ranch life.

"This right here is my favorite place." Miguel said. "This is where I always come when I don't have work to do."

On Charles's second trip back, Miguel's mother, Maria, gave them dinner, and they sat around the table, talking about the changes their family had seen in the valley.

"We have a tradition to uphold here, and we are not going to let someone like Cable trample all over us," Miguel said. "You haven't met my father, but he is very upset about this lawsuit," Miguel said. "We could lose our ranch. I can't explain the details – you'll have to wait for him to return. But I promise you one thing – we are going to defend our land." He stared at Charles unblinking, his eyes seeming to darken.

West Side
July 12, 1857

CHARLES COULD SEE the Foard ranch house from a mile away. It stood on a gentle slope where the valley floor connects with the foothills of the Santa Cruz range. To the west of the house, a narrow band of green forest marked where a creek ran down from the mountains to the southwest. On the east side of the residence stood three sizeable barns – stables, Charles assumed – one much larger than the other two. The outbuildings were dark in color, the house light, with a chimney on each end of the low, rambling building. Smoke poured out of one. Inside the fenced pastures, perhaps two dozen horses of different colors grazed lazily in the morning sun. Pines, madrone and low scrub formed a backdrop on the far slopes.

With butterflies in his stomach, Charles rode up the narrow access road that led to the house, trying to remember Miguel's lessons about riding light in the saddle. As he approached, Catherine signaled a greeting from her perch at the edge of a corral. She wore pants and a loose-fitting shirt.

"Beautiful place," Charles said, beginning to dismount, rather skillfully he thought.

"Thank you, Mr. Grayson," Catherine said. "We're very happy here. I hope you are also finding California to your liking."

"It's been a big change, but I like it. I especially like that people have new ideas here – that was one thing I came here for." Charles hitched the horse to a rail. He noticed how the pants Catherine wore emphasized the bend in her knee and the shape of her calf.

"Yes – I'm glad you brought up new ideas because I have one you might be interested in. I'll tell you about it later, but first I want to show you around."

She led Charles through the stables, showing off the Percherons and the saddle breeds. She showed him where the oats and hay were stored in the big barn.

"We have to bring in feed half the year at least," she said. "It's one thing about the climate that isn't so good, these dry months."

"Did your father say you came from … ?"

"Sacramento, about five years ago. Well, actually we came to California by wagon when I was eight. Pop thought this valley would be better for horses. Overall, it's a big improvement."

"I like these Percherons," Charles said, stroking the neck of a dappled-gray horse. "Can you ride them?"

"Oh yes, Percherons are fun to ride. They're gentle and easy to handle. Mainly they're workhorses, though. We're still looking for the four we lost."

"I used to see some Percherons around Concord. They were fairly new then – oh, about three or four years ago. And some shires, too."

"That's when we started our line. You know, I may as well tell you what I have in mind. We're breeding our Percherons for farm work but also for horsecars – you know, to pull the cars up … "

"Oh sure, I've heard of them. Boston put in a line like that – at least that's what I've heard."

"Well, don't you think San Jose should have a horsecar line too, and San Francisco?"

"I don't know. San Jose is just a little place, but maybe San Francisco."

"Well, San Jose is growing. I think your newspaper should have an article on horsecars. Don't you think?"

"I don't know."

"Yes, it's time. I know an expert in this subject who could write you an article."

"I'm not sure. It's really not my newspaper, and Frank doesn't usually like … "

"Why not? It's a growing trend. People should be informed. Don't you think?"

"Well, sure. I guess."

"Would you recommend it to Mr. Murdoch, then?"

"Who is this expert you mentioned?"

"Oh, he's a Sacramento businessman, well respected. He's researched this topic thoroughly."

"Frank would probably prefer someone local. But I'll, uh, I'll mention it to him, sure."

As they walked up toward the house to meet the rest of the family and have dinner, Charles began to wonder if he should have accepted the Foards' invitation. He liked them, but this Catherine was getting a little pushy.

July 12, 1857

I was nervous today going out to visit the Foards. I owe Miguel Contreras a lot for giving me confidence with Cuesta. Miguel is really my best friend out here, next to Frank. I felt pretty comfortable today riding up to Montebello Ridge with Cathy and her family – more like a real Californian than I have since I arrived. They have a neat-looking ranch over on the west side. Mr. Foard showed me a redwood grove – the first I have seen since coming here. These trees are spectacular. I wish Henry could come and see them. I am more and more comfortable here, but not really at home yet. I'm not sure what they expect from me. Catherine kept going on about horsecars. Are they just looking for free advertising? – C.G.

Chapter 8

San Jose
July 13, 1857

LATER IN LIFE, when Charles told about the events of July 1857, he shook his head. "I didn't come to California to fight with anybody or expose anybody or create a problem for anybody," he would say. "I just wanted to find a place that was better, where I could live the way I wanted and have the friends I wanted and earn an honest living. I wasn't even sure I wanted to have a family, but that's another subject."

After he returned from visiting the Foards, Charles started to worry that he was getting in over his head. It was obvious from listening to Don Secundino and Miguel that if he was going to write anything at all about the lawsuit, it would involve uncovering a lot of old wounds, serious ones, and also maybe crossing swords with one of the most important men in town. Some people weren't going to be happy about it. And Charles's instinct was to avoid confrontations. He was twenty-two years old, and he mainly liked to do things like walk through the woods. He couldn't understand why he was getting involved in this controversy.

So Charles told Murdoch the next time he saw him that he wanted to concentrate on his printing and that he couldn't write the story on the lawsuit.

"Are you afraid you can't get the story?" Murdoch asked.

"Oh, I'm pretty sure I can get some kind of a story," Charles said. "But these are strong accusations Robles is making. Contreras will feel the same way. If I put those in the story, Cable isn't going to like it. I don't feel like making enemies here when I'm just getting started in business."

"You're afraid of losing business, then – because you have to be nice to the people in power."

"Well, that is my job, to get as much business for my shop as possible."

"You're afraid you'll lose the county contract."

Charles felt a little chill go through him. He hadn't consciously thought about that, but he had to admit it was probably a factor.

"Why would I want to risk it?" he said. "Humberto might fire me."

"I understand," Murdoch said, nodding solemnly. They were silent for a few moments. Then he added, "You have to go along to get along, is that it?"

"Something like that."

Murdoch nodded again, putting his chin down on his chest. "Who do you like better, Robles or Cable?" he asked suddenly, wheeling in his chair and staring at Charles, leaning forward.

Charles hesitated, but he knew Murdoch expected an immediate answer. "Well, I like Don Secundino a lot – he has so much passion. Cable is a cold fish – almost a dead fish."

"Right. So whose opinion do you value more?"

"What do you mean?"

"I mean, if you were to write this story, and you had to offend someone, who would you rather offend – Cable or Robles and his cousin?"

"If I were to write it, I think I'd rather just tell the truth and let everyone think what they want to think."

"Then you're a real reporter," Murdoch said, finally leaning back in his chair. "You put the facts out there and let everyone else take from it what they want. Don't you think people have a right to know?"

"They have a right to know."

"Then who are you to hide it from them?"

Charles grimaced. "Why can't someone else tell it? Why can't you tell it?"

"Because for some reason, you're the one with the facts. Do you think it's an accident that you came to San Jose and got in the middle of this story?"

"What do you mean, 'an accident'? I chose to come here. You gave me the story."

"And you accepted it. You chose to print a newspaper and then to start writing for it, and then to go talk to Cable and Robles about what's going on. It's only fear that's holding you back now. You know what's right. You know you need to do the story. You just have to confront your fear. When you confront it and go ahead with what you know is right, you'll succeed. It can't be any other way."

Charles thought for a long while. He walked over to his desk and sat down. He slouched back in his chair. Murdoch was right, Charles thought. It was all about fear. It was like the time when Jake Marbough asked him if he was a friend of Henry Thoreau's, just before he left Concord. He was afraid to speak the truth – he always had been.

"All right," Charles said, finally. "I'll do the story. And, oh yeah, the Foards want us to run something on horsecars."

Murdoch nodded. "Pulled by Percherons, obviously," he muttered. "Free advertising."

CHARLES'S NEXT STEP was to do his best to find out about Alexander Hamilton Cable. But that was the toughest nut to crack. Cable himself wouldn't talk, and Cable's lawyer,

Wallace, kept putting him off. The story came together in bits and pieces over several weeks of digging and patient interviewing.

Charles's first stop, following a suggestion from Murdoch, was the home of Peter Burnett. California's first democratically elected governor, Burnett had led the state through its infancy for 13 months ending in 1851. During his tenure the state capitol was a two-story adobe building in the center of San Jose, and the fifty-year-old Burnett still lived in town, practicing law, so he wasn't difficult for Charles to find. Burnett was at home when Charles knocked in the door, finishing up a day's work in his study.

"I don't know the source of this litigation, only that my son-in-law, William Wallace, is representing Cable in court," Burnett said when Charles asked him about the suit. "But I do know Hamilton Cable, yes."

"How did you meet?" Charles asked.

"Let me think. Yes, Cable was in Sacramento then. He and his brother John were up in the gold mining country – I think it was sometime in 1850. They were trying to market elaborate, high-priced machinery to the miners for refining gold, but their timing was wrong. Back then it was a hard sell because the early miners didn't really have that much cash. What they wanted most were picks and shovels, blankets, whiskey … ."

"But how did you meet?"

"Oh, yes. Well, Hamilton Cable came to see me when I was governor – and the capital was here in San Jose at the time – and he wanted to know about the New Almaden mine. The owners were just beginning to turn the mine into a systematic operation back then. Cable knew mercury was useful for refining gold."

"What did he want to know?" Charles asked.

"About who owned the mine, how much it produced, what techniques and equipment they were using and so on. I couldn't give him all the details he wanted."

"Why do you think he was so interested?"

"He wasn't making the kind of success he expected selling the large equipment. I think maybe he saw mercury mining as possibly a better investment – I don't know. What do you know about gold mining?"

"Not very much."

"Well, it was all starting to change."

"How was that?"

"Oh, the first miners to go up to the mountains could pick nuggets up off the ground, pan dust out of the streams, make good money. But that gold was gone within a year or two. Even in 1850 you had a lot of men giving up and heading home when they found out how hard gold was to get out of the rock. The streams were still being worked, but in the newer claims, the miners knew they'd have to use different techniques for separating the gold from the rock and the gravel. If the Cable brothers had waited, they might have …. "

"What kind of techniques?"

"Well, they built dams, built flumes for bringing in water to blast the ore out of the ground. They were starting to put up mills and smelters – all that kind of thing. It was hard work, required quite an investment."

"So where does the mercury come in?"

"It helps get the gold separated from the rock. Someone else would have to give you the engineering details, but Cable knew about it," Burnett said.

"And he decided to move here because of the mine?"

"I suppose so. Anyway, he's a big investor now. Quite active in the mine, I think. You know, you probably should see Tom Fallon. He knows the Cable brothers better than I do. I can't tell you much more."

The next day, Charles found Thomas Fallon at the Diablo saloon downtown, campaigning for a seat on San Jose's newly created Board of Trustees. Charles already knew that Fallon was famous in town for raising the first American flag over the Mexican courthouse in San Jose in 1846, when Fallon was twenty-one. When Charles introduced himself, Fallon ordered a whiskey and sat down with him at a corner table, away from the hubbub at the bar.

"Not a whiskey drinker?" Fallon asked.

"Not much," Charles said.

"You're working for Frank Murdoch, then?"

"Yes, sort of," Charles said. "I run the print shop. Mr. Burnett said you could tell me about the Cable brothers."

"You probably should ask them. Why do you want to know?"

"There's a lawsuit against the Contreras family and I'm trying to understand it. No one will tell me much."

"I'm not a lawyer."

"I'm not looking for the legal points – I just need to understand the people involved. So you know the Cables?"

"I know John better than Ham. When John first came to town we used to play cards here at the Diablo a lot. He was fairly flush then – just inherited some money, I think."

"Weren't John and Hamilton in the same business?" Charles asked. He got his notebook out and began to write.

"Sort of. They were both interested in investing for profit, but Ham was more on the technical side – mining and such. John wanted to get into ranching. He was trying to find some land he could buy."

"Did he find it?"

"Oh, he found it. He married it, you might say, and bought some more. John's a major landowner in the valley now, southeast of town. He's related to the Bernal family."

Fallon was now on his second shot of whiskey. "Are you sure you want all this?"

"Oh, yeah," Charles assured him. "So how did John marry into the land?"

"You aren't quoting me on this, are you?"

"If that's the way you want it."

"Yeah, make sure you don't. I don't want my name in this." Fallon looked out the window, sipping his drink. "Well, it started with a purchase," he said, still looking out at the street. "He wanted me to introduce him to Antonio Sunol – you know about him, I guess." He looked at Charles.

"Didn't he have something to do with discovering the New Almaden mine?"

"Oh, I think so – early on. Sunol was the first postmaster here. He owned a lot of land south of town. So John ended up buying Sunol's holdings south of The Willows and built a house there. Then he expanded to the southwest. Bought a big piece adjacent to Etienne Thee, part of the Narvaez rancho. After that, he set his sights on Rancho de Santa Teresa."

"Where's that?"

"It's way south, just southeast of the Contreras ranch up against the hills." Charles's ears pricked up. "I think it was 10,000 acres in all. The Bernals own it."

"Are the Bernals related to the Contrerases?" Charles asked.

"Not related as such, but the families are all close down there. They're proud families, the Californios, and stubborn. They like their lifestyle, and it's been hard for them lately since we took over. Bruno Bernal inherited the land from his father. They're cattle ranchers, not about to change. Have their bull and bear fights the way they always have. Bruno wasn't about to sell any land."

"So did John give up that idea?"

Fallon shook his head. "He went at it a different way. He started going to the rodeos and the bull and bear fights on the Bernal ranch, just to get acquainted. He spotted Alicia Bernal, one of Bruno's daughters. Her brothers wouldn't let anybody near her. But John caught her eye."

"You mean he did all this just to acquire land?"

"I wouldn't go that far. But I don't doubt it was in the back of his mind, at least. He also became a Catholic, started attending Mass every Sunday at St. Joseph's. Of course, that's where the Bernals and all the other Californio families went to church. John was fairly taken with Alicia. And I understand that. My wife, Carmel, also comes from a Californio family."

"And she was the one John married?"

"Eventually, yes he did. He followed every courtship ritual the Bernals put in front of him – carried them all out to the letter. John must have impressed her or it wouldn't have worked."

"When did they marry?"

"Couple of years ago, I guess.

"And Bruno gave them a piece of land?"

"Oh, John had to pay for it, most of it. But that's the only way Bruno would have ever let that much land get out of his control. It had to be a family deal. Something like 3,000 acres, I believe."

"So how much does John have now?"

"How much land? Oh, I'd say well over 6,000 acres in all."

"And I assume he's on good terms with all the Bernals now."

"With most of them – not all."

"How's that?"

"Well – and you definitely can't say where you heard this – some say that Alicia's younger brother Ygnacio hates John, won't even talk to him."

"Why is that?"

"Who knows? Maybe he just doesn't like gringos. Anyway, it wasn't enough to keep John out of the family."

"How old is Ygnacio?"

"I think he's about sixteen now."

"So at the time of the wedding he would have been about fourteen?"

"That sounds right."

The two men sat at the table in silence for a minute or two while Charles caught up with his notes.

Finally, Charles looked up. "So what about Hamilton Cable and the Contreras family?" he asked. "How do they figure into this?"

Fallon shook his head. "That I don't know," he said. "But I'm sure land and money are at the bottom of it."

Charles went home that night feeling as if he'd just started to open an old can of rotting food. It stank, and he thought the worst might lie at the bottom.

ON THE MORNING MURDOCH challenged Charles to do the story, Hamilton Cable was hitching up his buggy at his home and office on South Third Street and starting on his way to New Almaden, twelve miles to the south, to see Henry Halleck at the Hacienda, the mining village. Cable was brooding over what he had to discuss with Halleck, business that he thought could lead to a substantial increase in his wealth.

Four years before, Ham and his brother John had come to the Santa Clara Valley with the aim of creating one of the largest landowning partnerships in the area. Now they were about to achieve their goal. It was land, the Cables believed, that was the key to wealth – Ham had learned that from his father and grandfather in Georgia. They taught him well, but their land dealings had also forced him out of his home state.

Before Ham even knew about San Jose, when he first heard of the discovery of gold in the Sierra, he hatched a plan. He would sell mining equipment to the gold miners – large-scale machinery for separating the gold from the rock and refining it – because that's where the big money would be, he thought. Then, when he had made enough money from the miners, he would buy land – as much as he could get in the choicest areas. That's where his brother John could help, because John wanted to become a rancher. Hamilton was interested in money and politics.

When the original plan fizzled, Ham and John refocused on the Santa Clara Valley. Here they had done well, but obtaining the Contreras ranch was the last piece of the puzzle. Ham's plan for claiming that land was the essence of simplicity: He would gain Armando Contreras's confidence, then draw up a contract whose inevitable result would be that Cable would take possession of the land. Then, somehow, he would have to persuade Contreras to sign it.

A few years back, Ham had bought a one-sixth share in the New Almaden Mine, the share previously held by General Jose Castro. At a shareholders' meeting, he had met and befriended Contreras. Then, through a lucky coincidence, he gained a further foothold. On arriving in California, Cable had taken the new name Alexander Hamilton Cable, keeping only his surname. As it happened, Henry Halleck, the mine supervisor, had married the granddaughter of the actual founding father, Alexander Hamilton. In the several meetings Cable held with Halleck, Ham had won Halleck's favor and had gotten himself appointed treasurer of the mining operation. These maneuvers were pivotal in his overall scheme. When he finally obtained Contreras's signature on the contract, he was sure he'd won. But one final detail needed ironing out.

Cable knew Armando Contreras's lawyer would mount a strong defense in the civil trail to save the Contreras ranch. Cable intended to call Henry Halleck as a witness, and he needed Halleck on his side, maybe to fib a little. What Cable was about to learn from Halleck would not make him happy.

Chapter 9

San Jose
July 18, 1857

THE FOLLOWING SATURDAY a man was hung in the county
jail yard on Market Street for killing a well-intentioned
fellow who tried to stop him from stealing a horse. It was
the fourth hanging in San Jose that summer by Sheriff
Phillip T. McTavish and the seventh since he took office in
October 1855 – a record for one sheriff's tenure. But instead
of giving McTavish credit for eliminating the bad guys,
influential townspeople began to say that McTavish was
letting crime get out of hand. The theft of the Foards' four
horses was still unsolved, and others in the county had
missing stock as well. A vigilance committee had formed,
meeting in homes around the area and formulating plans
to mete out quick justice to any known transgressors.

The next day, on Sunday afternoon, Louis Pellier
invited Charles to attend a gathering of local grape growers
at the City Gardens. Louis and Pierre were excited by
the increasing interest in cultivating the best varieties of
French wine grapes in the valley, because they both felt
the local climate provided great potential for vintners.
Charles, intrigued by Louis's passion for his nursery and
curious to meet his friends, eagerly accepted.

Eight growers, members of the Pioneer Horticultural
Society, were there, along with the daughter of a grower

and Antoine Delmas's two sons – the ones Charles had met on the stagecoach. Near the end of the meeting, Charles saw Louis Pellier stroking his chin as he and Delmas bent over the eighteen-inch piece of grapevine Delmas was holding in his hand, both focused on the part of the foliage that was turning purple.

"Hmmm," Pellier said at last. "Leaf curl, for sure. But how much of it have you got?"

"Just starting – maybe five or six vines in one spot now," Delmas said.

"Yeah? Well, you know, you need to get those out of there, and right away, Tony," Pellier said. "Go take them out today if you can. It's mealybugs doing it, you know. Most likely. But get them out before it spreads. You take all of those vines out, then keep an eye on the rest because some could be infected that don't show it yet. Keep a close eye now, Tony. You let me know if you see any more because we can't have that spreading around here. You burn everything you take out, burn it right away. Will you?"

"Yeah, sure," Delmas answered. "I hope that's all I lose."

"Well, I hope so too, but do any of the rest of you have this leaf curl, or anything like it? Have you all seen this sample here that Tony brought in?" Pellier inquired of the assembled group.

"Yeah, we saw it," said Charles Lefranc, who was there with his new wife, Marie Thee, and his father-in-law, Etienne Thee. "We have none of this in our plantings, but it's a good warning for all of us." Lefranc, thirty-three years old, had come to San Francisco during the Gold Rush, but quickly fell in love with the warm Santa Clara Valley. Now, as a member of Thee's extended family, he was the presumed heir to Thee's vast holdings south of the city along the Guadalupe River on the former rancho of Jose Narvaez.

All the growers at the party were cultivating vineyards in the valley. Earlier, Charles had been sitting beside Antoine Delmas, whose property and nursery lay just a few blocks south of City Gardens. Delmas had bought his land in 1851 from Antonio Sunol, the same long-time landowner who had sold property to John Cable. It was a closely-knit community, Charles was finding – just like Concord, Mass. – and everyone knew almost everyone else. Delmas said he had lately imported 10,000 cuttings from France, was now furiously planting those to add to the vines he already had from New England, and planned to have 350,000 vines and 105 varieties in place by the following year.

As the meeting was breaking up, Delmas explained his strategy to Charles. "What we have to do is get the better varieties established," Delmas said. "Just a few years ago it was only the Mission grape here, nearly all of those vines from cuttings at the Santa Clara Mission. That was what almost everyone grew here. It's really an inferior grape. Now we have all of these new varieties, and we will see what happens. This could be a wonderful area for good wine. Oh, and excuse our arrogance. You know, we Frenchmen think France has the best of everything. Because it does." Delmas had a twinkle in his eye, and Charles laughed.

"Mr. Lefranc here has sent home to France for vines, haven't you Charles?" Delmas continued. "When are they arriving?"

"Oh, this month – surely by the end of August, I'm told," Lefranc said. "We are hoping to have the vines established by next spring. But they won't be producing for a while."

"Tell about your prizes, Tony," said a fiftyish man wearing a black shirt and trousers. "Tony Delmas has won more prizes than anyone else."

"Prizes are nice, but the proof will be in how much people like the wine," Delmas said. "Charles, you've met Louis Prevost? He's been here since – when, Louis?"

"Since '49," Prevost said. "And I didn't come for gold. My land's to the west, the other side of the Guadalupe. But Tony's outdone me. He has nearly twice the varieties I have now."

As Charles listened to the growers talk about their grapes, he became aware of two mustachioed men wearing white suits, standing just inside the entrance to the gardens, under a trellis hung with wisteria. The older one, who appeared to be about fifty, glanced around the garden, his eyes finally falling on Charles. The younger man, speaking in the other's ear, was Miguel Contreras. Charles signaled a greeting to Miguel, but for some reason, Miguel didn't smile – he only nodded slightly. The older man, who Charles guessed was Armando Contreras, didn't smile, either, the two of them seeming to raise the tension level in the garden. He noticed now that they both bore a resemblance to Secundino Robles, but their expressions held none of Secundino's conviviality. Charles couldn't take his eyes off them as they walked slowly but purposefully toward him.

"My son says you're Charles Grayson," the older man said as all present finally turned their eyes on him. Miguel's face was blank.

"I'm Charles. You must be Armando Contreras, then." Charles eyed him cautiously.

"We were told you would be here. I heard you wanted to talk to me. Well, I'm here." He hesitated a few seconds. "So do you want to talk?"

"Um, well, it's Sunday and I don't have my notebook with me," Charles said. "We could walk over to the house and talk over there if you'd like."

Contreras nodded, again without smiling, and the three of them began to walk from the Pellier nursery toward the house, about 100 yards away.

"You have talked about me with my cousin, Secundino," Contreras said as they walked. "What did he tell you?"

"Well, uh, that he thinks you're being swindled," Charles said. "Do you think you are?"

"My attorney could explain these things better, you see – David Soto – but I will do my best. He doesn't even think I should talk to you. Secundino said you are an honest man and will do right by me in the newspaper. I hope he's right." Charles nodded as he studied Contreras's beleaguered expression. "Yes, they would *like* to swindle me – the Cables and all their fancy lawyers, but I am not going to *let* them," Contreras said with emphasis, his voice rising angrily. "They have schemed to get my land, but they are *not* going to get it. Not mine. I will die on my land fighting before I will let a gringo judge force me off of it." From his tone, Charles knew he was serious.

Charles had them wait in white wicker chairs on the front porch while he retrieved a notebook from his room. When he returned, they bore the same grim expressions. He sat down facing them.

Charles began: "Secundino said you used to own part of the New Almaden Mine."

"I was supposed to be part owner, but this English company, they never treated me that way," Contreras said. "I would go to these meetings they had, where they decided things. They would talk about things I knew nothing about. They would not explain anything to me. When I asked a question, they would answer in ways that didn't mean anything to me. It seemed like they had already decided things, and I didn't know enough to find out what was really going on."

"But you were getting a share of the profits?"

"They were supposed to pay me, and they gave me papers that showed I was getting my share, but it was just crumbs compared to what I heard the mine was making. I hired Soto to investigate, but they wouldn't tell him anything, either. And after that they treated me even worse. I got into an argument with Señor Halleck. He threw me out of his office. They didn't want to deal with me."

"So you sold your share to Hamilton Cable."

"That slimy lizard! He tricked me when I was drinking in the bar. I let him do it because I trusted him then. I owed some money, to pay off my gambling debts, you know, and Cable would pay me enough to pay them all off. I thought he was different from the other gringos – a kind man, a good man, I thought. He went to church – not a Catholic church, but at least a church. I thought he wanted to do me a favor by paying my debts and getting me out from under that burden. I was tired of dealing with the mine anyway – I didn't want to be part of it anymore."

"So what about this lawsuit?"

"That was the trick. I didn't see that little bit at the bottom. He had the contract translated into Spanish, which impressed me so much that I didn't read it all. He knew I wouldn't read it, and that's the way he planned it."

"What bit at the bottom?"

"That he could take my land if the mine didn't show a profit. I never saw that. It all looked like it belonged there, and since it was in Spanish, I didn't think of him trying to trick me. But he did. Now I have to go to court, and my lawyer is expensive. I don't know if the judge will see my side."

"If the mine didn't show a profit? You mean the mine isn't making a profit?"

"Oh, it makes a lot of money, but they have ways of hiding it. What my lawyer found out is that they spent a lot in the last few months on expanding. They spent all their profits for the quarter. That's something I didn't know, either. Cable, he planned this well – he planned it all. He knew I wouldn't know about these things, and he knew I wouldn't read the contract."

"Did you ever think about going to court to get your fair share of the mine's profits?" Charles asked.

"We almost did sue, but a question came up about whether this Barron, Forbes company really held proper title. And then I wondered what would happen if the demand for mercury went down. I thought my share might be worthless anyway. So when Cable made his offer, I signed. I was probably a little affected by whiskey."

Charles wrote furiously in his notebook for a while, then looked up at Armando and his son. He noticed that Miguel hadn't said a word. "Yes, it seems like you were swindled, all right," Charles said. "But what if the court decides against you?"

"Then I will appeal. But I will never be forced off my land."

Charles nodded. "How would you fight them?" he asked.

"I won't move, that's how," Contreras said hotly. "Are you going to put all this in your newspaper?"

"I'm doing an article – Secondino must have told you. That's why you came here, I thought."

"I know, but I don't want to tell you everything I have in my mind. You can't say this in the newspaper, but I will shoot anyone who tries to make me move, and I'll have a lot of people on my side."

Charles didn't say anything for a second, looking hard at Contreras. Then he said, "Okay, I'll pretend you didn't say that. But from now on, don't say anything to me you don't want in the newspaper, because I'll have to use it. I can only go so far to protect you, understand?"

Armando nodded. The two of them got up to go, and then for the first time Miguel Contreras spoke.

"My father, he is an honest man, a good man," Miguel said, his voice breaking slightly. "He didn't ask for this trouble, and he doesn't deserve to be cheated. I will defend him, and so will my brothers and my cousins."

Charles nodded. "Thank you for coming to see me," he said. "Your point of view will be a big part of my story."

July 19, 1857

I have thought a lot tonight about what the Contrerases told me. This is an important story, it seems to me. These Californios have their faults, but their way of life is being threatened, and sometimes unfairly. I think this story needs to get out soon. Cable's lawsuit is supposed to go to trial on Wednesday. William Wallace has not found the time to see me yet. I even sent written questions and he didn't respond. I'm going to write the story tonight from what I have. – C.G.

Chapter 10

San Jose
July 20, 1857

"WE HAVE TO RUN the story this week," Charles said to Murdoch when the editor entered the office Monday morning.

"Whoa – what story?" Murdoch asked, momentarily taken aback.

"The lawsuit! You know, the assignment you gave me, the one we just talked about. I have everything except Cable's side of it. His lawyer won't talk to me."

"Oh. You mean you think you've got the whole story? Cable's side has to be represented. Tell me what you have."

Charles quickly repeated what he had learned from Secundino Robles and Armando Contreras, and what little he had dug up about Cable. He showed Murdoch what he had written.

"It's a good story," Murdoch said after he read it. "I can tell you haven't written much for a newspaper before, but we can fix that. You've done well, but we need at least something from Cable's end, and you need to see Henry Halleck out at the mine, because these accusations implicate him. See if you can get out there today, and go to Wallace's office again."

Charles had several printing jobs to finish that morning, so he didn't get to Wallace's office until early afternoon. The lawyer was in court, his secretary said.

"That would be Superior Court?" Charles asked her.

"Yes, but you can't ... "

Charles was already on his way down the stairs, headed across First Street to the Superior Court building. There he found the courtroom and identified Wallace from listening to the proceedings for a few minutes. Wallace was a bespectacled young man of medium build with dark hair, clean-shaven, only a little older than Charles. When the judge called a recess, Charles approached the lawyer at his table.

"Mr. Wallace, I'm Charles Grayson, and I had ..."

"Oh yes, the printer," Wallace said. "Sorry, but I don't have time just now, why don't ..."

"You have to know that the story on the Contreras matter is going into print this week. We need Mr. Cable's side of the story."

Wallace snatched his glasses from his nose. "What? Well, why can't you wait until the trial starts? Everything will come out in court."

"Just tell me how a county supervisor can justify taking someone's land on a contract technicality, because that's all it is," Charles said, surprised at his own boldness.

"Mr. Grayson, it's more than a technicality. It's a provision of the contract. Contreras agreed to it, and we're insisting that it be complied with, that's all," Wallace said, his voice edgy. He put his glasses back on and started stuffing his briefcase with papers. "I don't have time to argue the case with you here. Come to the trial and you'll get everything you need. Now excuse me, I have business to do." Wallace strode toward the courtroom door, and Charles followed him.

"Armando Contreras feels he's being cheated," Charles said, matching Wallace's stride. "Does Mr. Cable have any response to that?"

"Mr. Grayson, you are being obnoxious. No one is being cheated. That's all I have to say to you!"

Charles let him go, then jotted in his notebook.

THE LONG, HOT RIDE Charles and Cuesta made that afternoon to see Henry Halleck in New Almaden turned out useful in more than one way. Halleck was gruff and businesslike, but he helped fill in several blanks in the story.

Charles decided to ease into the interview by asking Halleck about how the gold miners were using mercury.

"First, you have to understand that mercury is heavy and combines easily with gold to form an amalgam," Halleck said. "That's the basis of the two processes they're using. When they have solid rock ore containing gold, they put the ore through stamp mills. The stamp mills pound the rock to dust. Then they wash the debris over copper plates coated with mercury. The gold is heavier than the dirt, so it sinks to the bottom and combines with the mercury, and the rest of the debris washes away. Then they shut down the machine and scrape the mercury-gold amalgam off and cook it in furnaces. When the mercury vaporizes, all that's left is gold."

"I see," Charles said. "What's the other process?"

"That's the hydraulic placer mining that's just begun recently. They're blasting at the gravel in the hillsides with high-pressure water hoses. They have to have a good source of high-pressure water. They wash that debris through sluices containing mercury, and it separates out in the same way."

Charles nodded. "Okay, well, I can see why you're selling a lot of mercury. Can you tell me how you met Hamilton Cable?"

Halleck shifted in his chair and briefly put his hands to his temples while he stared into space. "I don't want to make myself a party to this lawsuit, you understand," he said. "It's bad business. And Hamilton Cable has served this mine well."

"Can you tell me how you met?" Charles repeated.

"Yes, he had some equipment we were interested in. The company was planning to expand the ore transport and reduction plant next to Los Alamitos Creek."

"That's just outside the village here?"

"Yes, at the base of Mine Hill. I became well acquainted with Mr. Cable as he was supplying us with this equipment."

"So you bought the equipment, and later he bought a share of the mine?"

"Yes."

"Okay. Now I'd like to ask you about Armando Contreras. He seems to think he wasn't getting enough information about the mine's operations or even getting his share of the profits."

"I have nothing to say about that. It's a business matter between the owners."

"Well, do you think Mr. Contreras is being treated fairly?"

"Nothing at all to say. Will that be all, Mr. Grayson?" He rose from his desk and walked to the door to show Charles the way out.

"Uh, sir, would you mind if I looked at the mine's production records?" Charles asked as he was about to leave.

"You want to see our production? Oh, I don't know why not. But you'll have to come back. I'm expected at home in a few minutes."

Despite Halleck's unwillingness to delve into the lawsuit, Charles thought he seemed to have no axe to grind. Charles got the impression Halleck regretted being involved in the controversy. But it was also apparent to Charles from what Halleck didn't say that he and Contreras weren't best friends.

By the time Charles rode away from the Hacienda, it was late afternoon, but the sun was still high in the sky. A little breeze had begun to penetrate the canyon, dissipating the heat just a bit. Before starting for San Jose, Charles decided to explore the area beyond the mine works, further up the canyon to the south, following the trickle that was Los Alamitos Creek. It was mostly open land, oaks here and there, lonely and apparently unused. After a half mile, as Charles paused to let Cuesta drink from the creek, he heard voices from somewhere off to his left – odd because no settlement or side road were visible. Then he noticed a small dust cloud rising just above the low ridge to the east. Curious, he hitched Cuesta to a tree and walked carefully up to the ridgetop to get a look past it. The voices became louder as Charles neared the top, and he thought of turning back, sensing trouble if he were discovered. Then, his curiosity winning, he fell to his knees, crawled the last few feet and peered over the ridge.

Spread out in front of him was a small side canyon seemingly filled with horses – perhaps forty or fifty of them split between two good-sized corrals. Some of the horses were galloping around the larger of the two corrals, throwing up dust, and a half-dozen men were gathered in a knot between the corrals, apparently arguing in Spanish. Charles couldn't understand their words, but as he looked at the horses more closely, he noticed two large, dappled-gray animals with huge chests and long hair around their hooves – undoubtedly Percherons. He studied their markings so he could describe them later, then quickly and silently backed away and returned to where he had left Cuesta.

Charles was sure he had just seen a gang of rustlers with their stolen horses. The only question in his mind was whether he should tell Eli Foard or go to the sheriff first. By the time he reached the turnoff for the West Valley, he had decided. He headed straight for the Foard ranch. He reached the ranch house just as the family was finishing dinner.

"Are you sure – do you remember the markings?" Eli responded when Charles told them what had happened. Charles gave them the details, which he had been going over in his head during his forty-five-minute ride. "Yeah, that's Sparky and C.J.," Eli said, his eyes ablaze. "And besides, no one else around here keeps Percherons."

"How did you find that place?" Catherine asked.

"I stumbled on it – pure chance," Charles said. "I had a little time and thought I'd explore."

"We'll have to tell the sheriff tomorrow – too late to do anything tonight," Eli said. "Stay with us tonight and we'll ride into town early in the morning."

"I'LL GET A POSSE TOGETHER and we'll go out there and surprise 'em tomorrow at daybreak," Sheriff McTavish said after Charles told his story in the sheriff's office in San Jose the next morning.

"What if they decide to move on today?" Eli asked.

"If they've got corrals, they're staying for a bit," McTavish said. "Besides, with a collection that large, they couldn't move more than two or three at a time. Attract too much attention." Then he looked at Charles. "You'll have to come, to show us the place. You know how to shoot?"

"I don't think he owns a gun, do you Charles?" Eli asked.

"No," Charles answered.

"Then you'll stay well out of the way when we move in – far back," the sheriff said. "I don't want you anywhere in sight. We'll take twenty men and let you know when things are under control."

Eli stayed in town that night. At five the next morning he and Charles met the posse at the sheriff's office and they all headed out toward the New Almaden mine. As they rode, Charles brooded for a while, and then asked Eli, "Sir, could you give me some lessons with a gun?"

Eli laughed. "Don't worry about it, Charles. We don't need you handling a gun today."

"No, I mean some other time. I feel like I should know how."

"Sure, I'll give you some lessons. Any time – especially after what you've done. You've earned it. And you're right – you should know how."

"Well, I hope the Percherons are still there."

"So do I."

By the time the posse had reached the south end of the Hacienda, some light was coming over the eastern horizon. They stopped and Charles went ahead with Eli and the sheriff to show them the ridge he had climbed and where he had seen the rustlers.

"Okay, I know where the entrance to that canyon is," McTavish whispered. "It's further to the southwest. We'll have to circle around. We'll take two riders down at a time, so we don't make a lot of noise. Eli, go get 'em and tell 'em to head toward the canyon entrance, each pair about a minute apart. I'll guide 'em from there." Eli and the sheriff rode off in opposite directions, leaving Charles by himself.

Although McTavish had told him to stay well out of sight, Charles was determined to see for himself what was happening. He moved quietly to the position he had taken two days before, at the top of the ridge. There he waited. As daylight just made the corrals and horses visible, the posse came galloping into the canyon in a pack. He saw some of the outlaws struggling out of their beds on the ground, then heard some yelling and shooting. He couldn't see who was firing, but the whole commotion lasted only five to ten minutes. As soon as he could hear the confident voices of Eli and Sheriff McTavish, and saw other members of the posse tying up a couple of prone bodies, Charles got up and started down from the ridgetop toward them. He had gone about halfway when he felt an arm grab him around the chest and hold him, a pistol barrel pressed into his right cheek.

The two of them, Charles and his captor, stood there, upright, for a few seconds before the man, catching his breath, yelled something in Spanish to the men below, perhaps 30 to 40 feet away. At that moment, acting on instinct, Charles freed his left arm and aimed a sharp elbow into the man's midsection. Charles jerked free and ran to his left towards a big oak tree. A volley of shots rang out. Charles dived to the ground, then rolled over and looked back. The body of the man who had just held him fell forward limply. Charles grabbed the man's pistol off the ground. He rolled the body over with his right foot. Part of the man's forehead was missing.

It took Eli a minute to walk up the hillside to where Charles and the dead man were. "You were supposed to keep out of sight," Eli said.

"Yeah," Charles said. He was still panting, his face was damp and his heart was racing.

The ride back to town calmed him down, but Charles had to endure a lecture from the sheriff. "You almost made a mess out of this thing," McTavish said. "You could've gotten killed and maybe got us shot, too. What in Sam Hill were you doing?"

"I thought it was over," Charles said sheepishly. "I shouldn't have come down so soon."

The sheriff just shook his head. "Well, someday you can tell your kids you helped bring in part of the old Anastacio

Garcia gang. Garcia was lynched back in February, but Tiburcio Vasquez may still be with them. We didn't find Vasquez, so he's probably away trying to find a buyer for those stolen horses. But we have three of their gang in custody and one more dead. That should slow them down for a while.

The Foards got back their two Percherons and their saddle horses as well, and Charles was a hero in town to everyone who had recovered a stolen horse. And, most important to Charles, his stock with Catherine rose sharply.

THE INCIDENT WITH THE RUSTLERS was Charles's first brush with violence in the West since he was shanghaied, but it would not be his last. Just three days later, he had to make another trip to the Hacienda to look at the mine records Halleck had promised to show him. On his way back, by the time he reached the southern end of San Jose, Cuesta was tired, and both of them were thirsty and well in need of a rest. It was nearly dark, and the Borregas tavern, lit from within, appeared ahead of them. Charles had never been inside the place, and it was a temptation he didn't want to resist just then. He pulled up to the little adobe building, let Cuesta get a long drink from a watering trough, and hitched him to a rail, again wondering if he should go in. The Borregas had a reputation.

The cantina was half full when he entered. A few shabbily dressed laborers and vaqueros stood at the bar while a handful of customers sat at tables, bent over drinks and plates of food. None of them seemed to notice Charles as he took a table by himself in the front corner farthest from the door. For a minute, he closed his eyes and took a deep breath of beery, smoky air, releasing the stress of the day. He could hear the muffled clatter of plates and pots. Then, when it seemed he wouldn't be served right away, he rose to go up to the bar. Only then did he glance to his left to see a familiar figure. Hamilton Cable sat at a dimly lit table in the back, apparently deep in conversation with a man Charles didn't know. He turned away, put in his order at the bar and returned to his table, deciding he was too tired to approach Cable just then.

But a few minutes later, as Charles sipped a beer, Cable and his companion came up to him, Cable nodding a greeting. Most of the light in the cantina was coming from the bar, and Charles had no lamp on his table, so he could barely see Cable's face.

"Grayson. You talked to Wallace the other day, he tells me," Cable said. Charles nodded. "Get what you needed?"

"He didn't want to answer all my questions," Charles said. "But I understand that. Will you be at the trial tomorrow?"

"Maybe, maybe not," Cable said. "By the way, this is my brother, John. John, this is Charles Grayson, who has the print shop on North Market Street."

"Mr. Grayson," John Cable said, not smiling. "Francis Murdoch tells me the *Telegraph* is planning to publicize this trial."

"We'll have something about it," Charles said, looking at Hamilton. "Your side may not be fully represented. You and Mr. Wallace haven't given us much."

Dimly in the background, Charles now became aware that another figure had approached and stood perhaps 10 feet away, facing them. As Charles craned his neck, trying to see around the two men in front of him, the Cables both twisted around to look.

"If it isn't the Cable brothers in person," said the voice of the man behind them, whom Charles still couldn't recognize in the darkness. It was a youngish voice, one he had heard before. He got up to see.

There stood Miguel Contreras. But instead of a white suit, Miguel was dressed in vaquero clothes, a black, straight-brimmed hat tilted back on his head and a holstered revolver around his hips. Charles felt his stomach crawl a little. He started to scoot to the right on the bench he was sitting on, so as not to be directly behind Hamilton Cable.

"Mr. Contreras, the younger," said Ham Cable. "What can I do for you?"

"You can drop your lawsuit against my father. You can stop trying to steal our land. You can go back to Georgia, or wherever you came from, and stop stealing from good, loyal California families."

"Your father had debts. That's unfortunate. I tried to help him out. But his mining share has been worthless, so I haven't been compensated."

"You're swindlers, both of you," Contreras said, his tone low and menacing. "You're interlopers and swindlers. You – he looked at John Cable – "you come here and marry into a good family and now suddenly you have land. Ygnacio Bernal is my friend. He doesn't trust you and I don't trust you. And now your brother is trying to cheat us out of our land. We'll never let you do that. Don't you know that?"

Contreras's right hand came to rest on his belt near the heel of his pistol. Charles flattened himself on the bench. There was a swish of movement in front of him, and then Contreras had his hand in Ham Cable's face, pushing him backwards over the table where Charles had been sitting. John reached over to pull Contreras off his brother, jerking him backwards onto the floor. Just then, Ham raised his head and Charles saw a single-shot derringer in his right hand. In an instant he fired it in Contreras's direction. But Contreras had seen him and rolled to his right on the floor, avoiding the shot. In a flash, he pulled his revolver and fired toward Ham Cable. But John had stepped between them, and he took the shot. He fell to the floor, clutching his chest.

For two seconds, everyone froze.

"You've shot my brother!" Hamilton yelled at Contreras. "You've killed my brother!" He knelt beside John, who was bleeding from the upper chest. For an instant, he made to reload his derringer, but stopped when Contreras cocked his revolver.

Contreras looked at them for a long time, motionless, still pointing his gun at Hamilton. "Why did you come to this valley?" he said, finally. "You don't belong here." He backed toward the door, glancing around the room, his pistol still in his hand. No one else moved as he took a quick look outside and then ran. Charles heard a horse galloping away.

Chapter 11

San Jose
July 21, 1857

THE NEWS OF JOHN CABLE's killing had spread before
Charles could get his bearings and ride into town on his
tired horse. He looked for the sheriff but was told McTavish
was already on his way to the Contreras ranch with two
deputies, so Charles went home and went to bed. By early
the next morning Miguel was still not in custody, and
the sheriff was not to be found. Word went around that
the vigilance committee was congregating at the Diablo
saloon downtown, determined to take quick action.

"You're right in the middle of this now," Murdoch told
Charles. "Better get over to the Diablo. But be careful."

The saloon was so noisy that it was impossible to
say anyone was in charge. Dozens of men from town
were there, most of whom Charles didn't know; but the
Bernal family, to whom John Cable had been an in-law,
was neither present nor heard from. With Alicia Bernal
now a widow, everybody seemed to realize that the
Bernals were in a painful position, seemingly forced into
a potentially bloody confrontation with their old friends,
the Contrerases. Also nowhere to be seen was Hamilton
Cable.

Amid the hubbub, Sheriff McTavish rode up outside,
walked in and confronted the group.

"You've all got no business getting involved in this," McTavish shouted, mounting a table so he could be seen. "I've been out to the Contreras place with my deputies, and Miguel isn't there. We searched real good. We're going to scour the county, and we'll find him. So all of you git on home now and mind your business."

"Yu'll never take 'im in," said a tall, mustachioed man, striding from the front of the room back toward McTavish as he talked in a gravelly voice. "The Contrerases'r still hidin' 'im down thur at thur place. He's got friends at the Bernals, too. Yer gonna need an army to roust 'im out. You and yer deputies don't have no chance. Wur goin' down thur now."

Men were shouting and pushing toward the door even before the man stopped talking, drowning out the shouts of the sheriff and pushing him roughly aside. But outside the Diablo, the mob was confronted again, this time by two of San Jose's most prominent citizens. Thomas Fallon and Peter Burnett had arrived in the street, and they held up their arms and shouted desperately for order. With them was William Wallace, Ham Cable's lawyer and Burnett's son-in-law. At the same time, Charles saw that Murdoch, alerted to the crisis, had come running from the print shop and was now stationed across the street to see what would happen.

The sight of these respected men in front of them brought everyone to a momentary halt.

"The law will deal with murderers in the proper way," Burnett shouted. "This group has no standing under law, and if you go hang a man without a trial, you're just as guilty as he is!"

"The law is too slow," someone yelled.

"We know what happened," someone else said. "We have witnesses. We don't need no trial." Amid shouts, the mob started to move again.

"Wait!" Fallon said, halting them again. "We have a sheriff and a jail and a court for criminals. Let 'em work."

"Our jail couldn' hold a jackrabbit," said the tall man, and the noisy crowd pushed past Fallon, this time not to be stopped. In seconds, two dozen men were mounted and riding south, toward the Contreras ranch. Sheriff McTavish chased desperately after them. His deputies were nowhere in sight.

"I'm going out there!" Charles yelled to Murdoch. "I need to see what happens."

"No," Murdoch yelled. "I don't want you putting yourself in danger. "We'll find out what happened later. There'll be plenty of witnesses."

Yes, Charles thought, *that's right. I'm just a businessman here. Why should I stick out my neck?* But wait. What had Murdoch just said about fear holding him back? Then, in his moment of decision, he thought of Henry Thoreau's last advice. "You'll find situations that will test your strength," Thoreau said. The incident with the rustlers had given him confidence. Charles knew he had to make his choice.

"But I have to try to stop it!" Charles said. "Miguel is my friend and he's not guilty. I can't just let them hang him!"

"No," Murdoch repeated. "You can't stop a mob, and if you're there you'll become complicit in a lynching. You're not cut out for this kind of thing."

But Charles knew what he had to do. The vigilantes had already mounted and headed out, so he ran as hard as he could the four or five blocks back to the Pellier barn where he still had Cuesta in a stall. By the time he had the horse saddled and headed down the New Almaden road, the dust from the gang of riders had already settled and he was at least ten minutes behind.

He rode Cuesta hard, but it still took half an hour to get down to the turnoff for Rancho de las Vacas, in the shadow of the Capitancillos Hills. He didn't know any shortcuts. The lather was flying off Cuesta's neck by then, so he knew he couldn't press any harder.

At the ranch house, all Charles could see at first was dust – the riders had cleared out already. Then he saw Maria Contreras leaning over the figure of her husband, who was lying in the dirt by the front steps. Charles swung off the horse and ran up.

"What happened?" he blurted.

"There were too many, all of a sudden," Maria said. "We didn't think they would come here after the sheriff searched. They burst in and ransacked the house."

"Is he OK? Where's Miguel?"

"They knocked my husband down, hit him on the head. I don't know where Miguel is."

"Didn't the sheriff get here? Are you going to be OK?"

Maria looked at Charles with desperate, panic-stricken eyes. "We haven't seen any sheriff. We haven't seen Miguel either. If I knew where he was, I wouldn't say. You want to help Miguel?

"That's why I came! Which way did they go?"

"I think they are riding to the Bernals' place. They think he might be hiding there. Please try to help him."

Charles already had his foot in the stirrup and hit the saddle as she spoke. He headed out the gate and then southeast, on road he thought led to the Bernal ranch. Charles had passed that way once but had never been on the ranch itself. It took another ten or fifteen minutes of hard riding to get there, following what he thought was a cloud of dust in the distance. He made a wrong turn once, finding only an abandoned shack. By the time he found Rancho de Santa Teresa, he could see that he might be too late. A phalanx of men, their backs turned Charles's direction, hid his view, but clearly all their eyes were focused on something else.

As he pulled around them and dismounted, he saw what it was. Two men held a third on the ground while two others were tying his arms and legs. Another man held a handgun over him. Moving closer, Charles saw that they had Miguel.

For a minute he stood and watched, dazed and out of breath, as they knotted the ropes and dragged him past, to an old wagon standing beneath a giant oak tree. They lifted him up to the bed of the wagon. Where was the sheriff? Charles felt desperate.

Just then the whole wretched scene froze before his eyes. He stepped outside himself and saw it all clearly, like a tableau. In that moment of clarity, he knew that it didn't have to be that way. He knew that he could change it. All the pain, the meanness, the hate bore into him, searing him like a hot iron.

"Stop!" Charles yelled with all the voice he had. Every head seemed to turn. He jumped onto the wagon where the men held Miguel. "Don't do it. He's not guilty, believe me, I was there. He fired in self-defense."

"Who are you, his friend or something?" someone shouted.

"You're goddamn right I'm his friend," he yelled. "He's a good man. He's only trying to protect his land – his family's land, the same as any of you would do if you were in his place. He's not a murderer and he deserves a fair trial. I was there and I saw it. You don't have the right to do this."

For a second, maybe two or three, there wasn't a sound. Then came a single cry: "Hang 'im!"

Immediately the mob had its momentum back and the shouting took over. Charles felt himself being shoved out of the way, off the wagon and into the dirt. He got up and tried to shout over them, but he could barely even hear himself.

Again someone took hold of him and shoved him away, this time into the hands of two men who held him fast. He turned his head and saw Miguel's panic-stricken face and the noose being tightened around his neck. The rope, already over the limb, was pulled tight and then tighter still, and anchored, lifting Miguel slightly off the wagon bed. A few men grabbed the wagon tongue and pulled it away.

Charles stared at the scene. He wanted to remember it. He wanted to have every detail in his head. He stared, heartsick, for a few seconds, a minute, two minutes. Then they let him go. He put his head in his hands, sick at heart. Later, he couldn't remember how long he stayed in that spot. Before he mounted to leave, he turned back again to look at the faces. He wanted to remember them. He wanted to remember every face. He hated them. He hated them all.

Something important happened today. It had to do with what Henry told me years ago – about having to end one phase of your life before the next one can open up. I couldn't keep them from hanging Miguel but at least I didn't stand by and watch. Today I stepped out of my old skin, the skin of the old me that needed to please people. I don't have to please anyone anymore. I'm not sure what the next part will look like, but I do know what it won't look like. – C.G.

THE NEXT DAY, SHERIFF McTAVISH claimed he had been waylaid and held hostage at gunpoint by parties unknown on his way out to intercept the vigilantes. Charles's opinion was that without his deputies, McTavish didn't have what it took to confront a frenzied mob of armed men. Charles went to the sheriff's office and told him all he knew about what had happened, including the five or six names of the men he knew by sight. The sheriff later claimed that he questioned them and that they all had alibis. That was the end of the sheriff's investigation.

It was rumored that Miguel had learned of the Cables' presence at the Borregas from his closest friend, Ygnacio Bernal, who was John Cable's brother-in-law, so the vigilantes suspected Ygnacio might be hiding him. They had found Miguel hiding on the Bernal property. Persuaded by Ygnacio, the Bernals had taken in the killer of Alicia's husband, preferring to deal with him in their own way rather than surrender him to a mob of gringos. But the vigilantes were too powerful. They found poor Miguel in a woodshed and dragged him out. The oak where they hanged him for the shooting of John Cable was the one where Cable, the Contrerases and the Bernals had watched many a bull and bear fight together.

Charles had to work all night Wednesday to print the weekly edition of the *Telegraph* because he had spent all day writing the story of his life – the story of a Californio family caught up in the Americanization of a beautiful valley, a family once happy and prosperous but now the tragic victims of greed, ignorance, chicanery, vengeance and an inevitable cultural clash. His account covered it all – from Armando Contreras and Secundino Robles's first discovery of red rock in the Capitancillos Hills to the hanging of Miguel. Murdoch had added two extra pages so Charles could write the story to its full length. Two hundred extra copies were printed, and they were gone by midmorning.

At 10 o'clock on Thursday, Charles was in court for the beginning of the civil suit of Hamilton Cable vs. Armando Contreras. An empty chair next to William Wallace at the plaintiff's table confirmed Cable's continued absence from public view. At first, Charles thought Contreras would also fail to appear, but at the last minute Miguel's father walked in, looking distracted and ashen-faced, to sit next to his attorney, David Soto.

The judge gaveled court into session, and Wallace rose immediately.

"Your honor, due to circumstances of which everyone is aware, my client is currently indisposed, so I request … "

He was interrupted by a voice from the back of the courtroom.

"I can shed some light on this matter, your honor," said a man wearing a dark suit. Charles didn't recognize him, but on the vest under his coat he seemed to have some kind of badge. Just then Charles noticed that another man in the back wore an identical badge.

"Approach the bench please, Mr. Davenport," the judge said. "Is the gentleman with you also a law officer?"

"U.S. Marshal Harvey Davenport from San Francisco," the man said, nodding to the judge. "I am here with U.S. Marshal Gordon Hecht from Atlanta, Georgia, to report to you that we have taken Alexander Hamilton Cable into custody this morning. There was no time to notify anyone until now. Mr. Cable is to be extradited to Georgia to face federal charges there of land fraud in interstate commerce. He is in the county jail now."

"Your honor, I had no knowledge … ," Wallace stammered. "This is extraordinary … . If this is true, this proceeding will have to be continued, I would assume … indefinitely."

"Yes, I would think so," the judge said.

"This outrageous lawsuit should be thrown out," Soto said. "I move for dismissal."

"Mr. Soto, and Mr. Wallace, I will continue the case for one month. If these facts are borne out, I will be inclined to dismiss. Understood?" Wallace nodded. "So ordered."

In the confusion that followed, Charles rushed toward Davenport as he walked out, but couldn't get his attention until they had gone into the street.

"Marshal, I'm Grayson from the *San Jose Telegraph*. Can you tell me more about these charges against Cable?" Charles blurted out. But he was interrupted by Soto, who had come running up.

"Why wasn't I notified of this?" Soto asked angrily. "Didn't you know about the situation here? Two men have been killed here this week!"

"We didn't know any of this until we arrived last night," Davenport said. "There was no time to notify anyone, so we're doing it now."

"Marshal ... ," Charles interrupted.

"I can tell you much more, but not right now," Davenport said, continuing to walk and turning to Charles. "Mr. Cable has been on the run for quite a while. I have to go to the telegraph office to make a report to San Francisco, and then I have to attend to my prisoner. Why don't you tell me where your office is and I'll come by this afternoon?"

After giving Davenport the location, Charles looked for Armando Contreras but couldn't find him.

That afternoon, Charles and Murdoch got an earful from the two marshals in a two-hour interview. What they learned formed the basis of another story in the following week's newspaper that became the new talk of the town.

"You good folks here in California have had just a taste of what happens when the Cable family gets involved in something," Hecht began in his Georgia drawl. The two marshals had settled themselves in the printing office with the two newsmen. "The Cables have been perpetrating frauds for three generations in Georgia. You might say it's become a family tradition. It began with the Yazoo Land Fraud – you might have heard of it. Happened around the turn of the century. At that time the land under Georgia's control extended to the Mississippi River, taking in what we now call the states of Alabama and Mississippi. Our good elected officials looked at all that unused land and decided they could make an easy profit out of it. So a lot of state legislators and a few of their friends formed some private companies with names like the Virginia Yazoo Company. Then in 1794 those companies quietly and conveniently convinced the state assembly – consisting mainly of the company owners – to sell 40 million acres to themselves for a little over a penny an acre. One of the primary owners was a friend of Governor George Matthews named Hap Cable. He whispered in the governor's ear and got him to sign off on it. When the scandal came out, it was denounced by President Washington and the U.S. Congress, most of the sales were nullified and Georgia lost jurisdiction over the land. But Hap Cable managed to come out of it with a nice wad of cash in his pocket. That was Alexander Hamilton Cable's grandfather."

The marshal had their full attention. But he was just getting warmed up.

"Then you might also know about the removal of the Cherokee nation from the land they rightfully owned in Georgia, Tennessee and North Carolina. When the Indians were finally forcibly removed to Oklahoma in 1838, a few thousand died making the trip. They call it the Trail of Tears now. That all got started during the Georgia Gold Rush in North Georgia in 1829. The Cherokee by then were living peacefully and had even adopted a lot of European customs. But when the white folks saw that so much land in North Georgia was owned by the Cherokees, they began to covet that land and resent the Cherokee just for being there. So a bunch of them got together and sent Jasper Cable to Washington to talk President Andrew Jackson into signing the Indian Removal Act, which got through Congress and was signed by Jackson in 1830. Jasper Cable was Hap Cable's son, as you might have guessed. Jackson was only too happy to sign it, since he didn't like Indians.

"Well, that worked so well that Jasper decided he could put some more cash in his pocket by becoming an agent of the Georgia Railroad. This is a 137-mile line that runs between Atlanta and Chattanooga, Tennessee, through a lot of the land that the Cherokee used to occupy. The state started acquiring land for the road around 1840, and Jasper's sons by now were old enough to help him perpetrate his scheme. Jasper got together with one of our later Georgia governors and decided where the station stops should be for the railroad. But before any announcement had been made, Jasper sent his sons in to buy up substantial property in those locations, knowing towns would soon be springing up. Then later, after the stations were under construction and the land value had gone through the roof, the Cables conspired to sell the land for a huge profit, seeing that the governor collected his share of the loot. We have been working on this investigation for ten years or so, and we have a conviction in U.S. court against Jasper."

"And Jasper's sons would be ...?" Charles interjected.

"That's right, the ones you know as Alexander Hamilton Cable, and the late John Cable. Oh, and Alexander Hamilton's not his real name, by the way. His real name is Andrew Jackson Cable, and he changed it when he came to California. Chose another famous name thinking he'd throw us off the trail. But we know who he is. Fortunately, I met Andrew Jackson Cable about ten years ago when he was still in Georgia, so I knew I could recognize him. We didn't know he was in California until three months ago. That's when we got a message from David Soto. When he asked for background on this man Cable, described the lawsuit against his client, the deception and so forth, I knew it was A.J. Cable. It took me almost ten weeks to get here coming through Panama, but it's been worth it. I only wish I had made it two days earlier. I might have prevented a murder and a lynching. Maybe some day soon we'll have a transcontinental telegraph line. But at least we have A.J. now."

"But how could you be sure he was the Cable you wanted?" Murdoch asked. "It's a long trip from Georgia."

"That was the lucky part," Hecht said. "Soto was thoughtful enough to include a detailed description of this Cable, including that peculiar mole on his nose. That's what convinced me."

July 25, 1857

Someone threw a rock through the office window Thursday night. I've been getting a lot of stares as I go around town. But Burnett and Fallon came into the office on Friday to thank me for what I had done, and we now have a new sheriff. A number of people, especially women, have come up to me on the street and said I did the right thing.

It was one of the longest rides of my life going from town out to the Contreras house today. It was only an eight-mile trip out there but I didn't want to face the Contreras family after such a tragedy. I talked to Frank about it, and he was right – I had to do it. I found Maria and Armando Contreras at home. Maria didn't say much. It was clear she was having trouble speaking about the whole situation anyway – she was too emotional. Miguel's two older brothers had arrived from Monterey, and learned of their brother's death. They were cursing themselves for lingering too long at a cantina.

Armando seemed drained. His face was gray and slack. But he didn't seem defeated. "I still have two sons and a daughter," he told me. "We will go on." But he was a bitter man, and I don't blame him for that. Soto had already given him all the information on Cable, and he seemed thankful that at least his ranch would be safe. As an Easterner still new in California, I felt some guilt about what had happened — as if we, the gringos, were perpetrating an injustice on the old families here. Then I had to tell them what I saw in the Borregas Tavern: "I was there in the Borregas that night, you know, and I'm pretty sure Ham Cable fired first." It didn't seem to matter much to Armando. He just gave me a long look and then slowly nodded.

On the ride home, I thought some more about it. What the vigilantes did was despicable. But during that ride, I realized I wanted to do the same thing to Hamilton Cable. What does that make me? — C.G.

Part Three

Strong Medicine

Chapter 1

Changtsu village, Kwangtung province, China
August 1859

"DO YOU WANT TO COME OR NOT?"

Lee Hwang Dung, 15, looked back over his shoulder to see if his younger brother was going to answer him or ignore him – Hwang never knew which it would be. Ming Tao was twelve and had lately turned rebellious – not as quick to follow Hwang's lead as he once was. It was nothing personal – the brothers were as close as always – but a byproduct of Ming's twelveness. He had started to question everything.

"How do you know we'll find fish today?" was the first query out of Ming's mouth.

"How do you ever know? We go after it rains. That's when the fish get up into the ditches."

"It rained yesterday. Why didn't we go then?"

"I was working for Zhou Lin yesterday, as you know already. Why do you ask stupid questions?"

"I could have gone."

"Then why didn't you?"

"Because you haven't taught me how to catch the fish."

"Then you've answered your own question. If you want to come, then come. I'm leaving."

Hwang started off on the northern path out of the village of Changtsu. Ming snatched his basket from beside the family's rude hut and jogged after his brother to catch up. They found the path that followed their district's particular arm of the Pearl River, where it begins to broaden out into the delta. They walked for a mile or two, through undergrowth and past rice paddies, until they came to a place where several irrigation ditches merged, out of sight of any settlements. Here, Hwang knew from experience, he could fish for a while without being chased away.

Hwang put down his basket and knelt on the very edge of the largest ditch where a tree shaded it, so his own shadow wouldn't distract the fish. He put his good arm, the right one, slowly into the water while he held his left arm just above the surface. Then he waited.

It was the left arm that made Hwang unusual. It was deformed, a birth defect, the forearm shriveled and the hand just an inflexible claw.

"Watch," Hwang said.

"What are you doing?"

"Just watch."

For three, perhaps four minutes, they waited in silence. Then a dark form appeared below the surface. In a flash and with a great splash, Hwang had the carp in his grasp, speared on his claw and held fast with his good right hand. In two more seconds it was safely in the basket.

"I couldn't see what you did," Ming said.

"You have to try it yourself before you know," Hwang said. "Just put one hand in the water and wait till you see one. If I can do it with what I have, you can do it."

Ming tried to imitate his brother, but time after time he failed to get the fish in his grasp. At last, after two hours of trying, he snagged one, and it was big.

"Wow," Ming said.

"It's a nice one. You've done it. We have enough – let's go home."

Hwang and Ming had learned to do what they could to keep the family – themselves, their mother and two younger sisters – from having to depend totally on relatives, since they had no father at home. Zhou Lin, an old herbalist in the village, taught the boys how to go into the countryside and scavenge herbs for him – ginseng, wolfberry and horny goat weed, hawthorn and chrysanthemum leaves. They would sell these to the herbalist for a little bag of rice, some lychee nuts or maybe some green tea. Sometimes the herbalist would let them help make the tonics he prescribed for people with various common maladies. Zhou Lin also had a few pigs, and he would let Hwang and Ming collect the manure, which they would put into a bag and sell to the farmers in the countryside. The income wasn't much, but they had learned to live on it.

Their father, Lee Dung Kwan, had been a wounded survivor of an early battle in the Taiping Rebellion against the Manchus. After that, according to the family stories Ming heard, their father did his best to avoid political entanglements and became a storekeeper in the village, struggling to eke out a living. A few years after Ming's birth, his father made a business arrangement with a man from Canton. Ming never learned the details, but the family's situation only worsened. His father began making visits to the city, and those visits became longer and more frequent, each time leaving the store for his mother to run by herself. When Ming was 10, his father said that his business in Canton had soured and he would have to find new work in the city to recoup the loss of his investment. That was the last the family ever saw of him. Without money or other resources, Ming's mother had to close and sell the store. Relatives would sometimes give them food, but they had nothing else. They managed to keep the household going in their little one-room hut, but often they ran out of basic items.

After Ming learned to fish, life was a little better. Over a five-year span, the two brothers together were able to increase their knowledge of herbs enough that Zhou Lin was ready to call them herbalists in training. While one of them was gathering herbs and trading for rice, the other could go fishing. But with their sisters growing, the family still just scraped by.

Then, one day, they had a stroke of good fortune. Seven years after their father left, when Ming was 17, they were visited by an uncle from Canton, one of their many relatives who were thought to be involved in the opium trade. That was in August of 1864, by the Western calendar. By then, the Manchus had crushed the Taiping Rebellion, which ended one of the bloodiest episodes in human history. Ming did not know the full extent of this tragedy at the time, but he saw the results – subjugation and poverty. The farmland in their district was devastated. Villages such as Changtsu were left to get along as they could, and most of the people had little hope for their future. Their government could not help.

They had all heard of *Gum San* (Gold Mountain), the faraway place of great riches and opportunities across the ocean. Hwang and Ming's uncle, Chow Bing Shew, sat down with his mother and the rest of the family. He talked for a while of their plight, and then he announced that he had saved money to pay for the long voyage to *Gum San*. He said he also had enough to take a nephew. Their mother, Song Shee, then looked at Ming and smiled, which was the signal that there was already an agreement that Ming would make the trip. Hwang, then 20 years old, stared at the rest of them, comprehending, realizing that his handicap was going to hold him back and that his younger brother was to have this great opportunity. His face darkened, and he ran from the house.

It was hard for Ming to sort out his feelings. The thought of this great adventure, in a place he had often imagined, filled him with excitement. He wanted to celebrate his happiness, but he could not share it with his brother. Ming hated being the object of Hwang's jealousy. As for his mother and sisters, he didn't care if they saw he was happy, since it was obvious that he would be more useful to them in a place where he could earn money. And his prospects would be far better than Hwang's. At first he would have to use some of his earnings to repay his uncle for the cost of the trip. But as he grew older, he could earn more and one day return to the village a wealthy man, by local standards. That was what his uncle said could happen. Clearly, that was what Ming's mother expected of him. He would have to take the chance, and of course he wanted to. But he barely knew his uncle. If he had known him better, he would have been more suspicious.

Hwang pouted and did not speak to Ming for three days. On the fourth day, a week before Ming's trip, Hwang sourly suggested that they go out in the morning to collect herbs before the heat set in. After they had walked a mile, Hwang grabbed Ming by the arm and said, fiercely, "You have to send us letters and money. You can never stop sending us letters. Our mother is depending on you, and you have to send us all the money you can."

Ming said, "What do you think? That I would forget my family? My family is giving me this chance to succeed, and I am going to do it for you. You will still be my brother. My mother is still my mother."

"If you do well for yourself, I will find a way to get there," Hwang said, calming down but still serious. "But first, our mother has to have enough money to get by." Ming nodded, and they were silent for several minutes as they walked. Finally, Hwang said, "And at least we won't have to feed you anymore."

"What, that pig slop we have? I'm eating nothing but roasted duck and rice pudding from now on." They both laughed, and the tension seemed to be gone.

The night before Ming was to leave, he laid out his clothes – his trousers, his *changshan*, the outer shirt, and his shoes of woven straw. He packed a straw bag with a few extra garments, dried fish and rice snacks and a small amount of money. The next morning, he was the first one awake. He dressed and took a few steps outside the hut in the darkness, excited but knowing he had only a dim idea of what was ahead. He made mental notes of their little lane – the dank odor of the rotting vegetation around the rice paddies, the smoke from early morning cook fires, the rooster crowing, the dim lights from the houses. Ming painted a mental picture of it to remember in the times ahead, because he knew that he might never come back. Over the coming years, he recreated that scene hundreds of times in his mind.

Ming felt the heat starting to rise from the river. It always seemed hot in the Pearl River Delta. About midmorning Bing Shew arrived, they said good-byes, and the two of them prepared to leave. As they walked down the lane, Ming burst into tears. He turned to run back to the hut, but his uncle grabbed him. "We have to go now," he said. As Ming looked back, he saw his brother and sisters standing by the hut in a row. His mother had gone inside. As they walked, he cried for a little while longer.

At the river, one of the tributaries that led into the Pearl River and then to Canton, they waited at the little dock as the heat and humidity bore in on them. They boarded a small boat with about a dozen other passengers. A heavy thunderstorm hit them a few miles down the river; everyone was soaked, and they all worked to bail the rainwater out of the boat. They were miserable, but Ming was too excited by then to care much. He had never traveled as far as Canton, even though they lived only thirty-five miles away.

By the time they arrived in Canton that evening it was nearly dark, but the sights and sounds and smells of the city pressed in on them, like nothing Ming had ever imagined. Everywhere he looked, people were busy – men docking their fishing boats, throwing lines and shouting, groups of travelers arriving, arguing and crowding the docks. The air was heavy with the smell of fish and garbage being hauled in baskets, while barkers offered lodging, gambling and prostitutes. The buildings were higher, the ships at the dock much bigger than any he had ever seen.

Ming and his uncle bought snacks of rice noodles and fried river snails from a street vendor. Somehow, as they ate, his uncle threaded his way through the chaotic dock area, and soon they came to a lane where beds were advertised. Upstairs, in a room filled with perhaps thirty straw mats, the proprietor found them two that had not been taken, and his uncle handed him some money. But as soon as they had settled on their mats, and Ming began to take off his still-damp clothes, his uncle announced that he was going out.

"I'm going to gamble," he said. "You don't want to do that since you don't have any money to lose. I'll be back in a few hours. Get some rest."

The room became noisy with men coming in and out, complaining about this or that, arguing. Ming watched for a while in the stifling heat, sitting with his arms around his bent legs. Then he lay back and tried to sleep. In a dream, he found himself floating on a wide river at night, alone in a small boat. Huge ships went by on both sides, brushing the sides of his little boat until he thought he would be crushed between them.

He didn't think much time had passed, but suddenly he was aware that the room was full and yet quieter and very dark, and there was snoring all around him. Then he was shocked to realize that his uncle had not returned. He thought Bing Shew was probably still gambling, but after a bit he began to worry. He got up and went down to the street. People were still milling about, and it didn't seem too much calmer there than it had earlier in the day. He walked down the street, soon found a noisy store where men out front were arguing excitedly about money, and he went in. In the back, at various tables, men were bent over, playing *pai gow* and *fan-tan*. He edged through the crowd, looking at every face.

"Boy, what are you doing? Do you want to gamble or not?" said a gravelly voice from behind him. He turned around. An old man was glaring at him.

"I need to find my uncle," he said. "Do you know Chow Bing Shew?"

The man continued to glare. At last, in a low, steady voice, he said, "Yes, I know Chow Bing Shew. He is your uncle?"

"Yes, yes, I told you. Is he here?"

"Calm down. He was here. He is a good customer, but he got into an argument tonight and I had to throw him out. He and one of his friends got into it. They were bothering everyone else."

Just then a loud voice from the front of the store interrupted them. "Stop what you are doing," a man said. Ming edged toward the front and saw that three policemen were standing near the front door.

"Quiet down," one of them said. "Who has seen a man of about 40 years of age, wearing a dark blue *changshan*, with a black and white sash around his waist?"

"Yes, we know him," said the old man, the proprietor. "I threw him out earlier. Is he in trouble?"

Suddenly recognizing the description, Ming yelled out, "He is my uncle. Do you know where he is?"

"Come up here," the policeman said, and Ming went forward. "All of you, we are shutting down this place tonight, but you cannot leave yet. You will all have to answer some questions that these officers will ask you.

Then you can go." He took Ming by the arm and said, "Come with me."

They went out into the street and stopped, still in front of the store. "Where are you from?" the policeman asked him.

"Changtsu," he said. "Where is my uncle?"

"What are you doing in Canton?"

"We're leaving tomorrow on a ship, the *Shining Eagle*. We're going to Gum San."

"Just you and your uncle?"

"Yes, they have reserved the ship just for us. What's this about?" Feeling he was in a tight spot, Ming was trying to joke his way out of it. He knew right away it was a mistake.

"Think you're very bright, don't you?" the policeman said. "How would you like to go to jail?"

"Sorry," Ming mumbled.

"Did you know your uncle was in the opium trade?"

"No, I don't know anything about it," he answered, which was an honest answer because Bing Shew had not said anything to him about that.

The policeman looked at him silently for a few seconds. "Come with me," he said. He led Ming down the street. They had walked a hundred yards or so before they turned into an alleyway. Ahead of them, a couple of policemen were holding lanterns, and one was bent down. As they approached, Ming saw a man lying in the dirt, and then he recognized the sash the man was wearing and knew that it was his uncle.

"What happened to him?" Ming asked. He was breathing hard and his stomach felt queasy.

"He's been murdered," the policeman said.

Chapter 2

THREE DAYS LATER, back in Changtsu, Ming had not recovered from his misfortune. He was sorry his uncle was dead, but that was mostly because his plans for going to Gum San had been crushed. The police had questioned him for several hours, and when they released him he managed to talk his way back to Changtsu by telling his hard-luck story. There was no chance of trying to get onto the ship alone because Bing Shew had all the money for their passage, and it was gone by the time the police had found his body, stabbed several times in the back and chest. At least, that's what the police said. Bing Shew's killer had also killed Ming's dream.

Ming's world had never looked blacker. He began to curse his uncle. Before Bing Shew came, Ming could not see beyond his village, and it didn't seem so bad there. Now he had glimpsed the world beyond, and he wanted to be part of it. He was deep in misery. In a matter of days, his life had been transformed from routine poverty to high adventure and back again. When his family heard the story, they were deflated more than Ming had ever seen, and the reaction of his mother and sisters, their high hopes dashed, made Ming even more depressed. He began to hate his dead uncle and to think of him as a betrayer for going off that night and getting into trouble. Even his mother did not seem too upset that her brother was dead, only angry that he had let them down.

Bing Shew had been little but a name to Ming before he appeared so suddenly two weeks before. Now Ming began to wonder just what his uncle was up to before he died. Was it all really about opium? Was his real plan to go to Gum San at all? Was he smuggling? Or did he have something even more sinister in mind? Was his death the result of a simple argument or did someone plot to have him killed? Was Ming the only pawn in the plan? These questions persisted, like an annoying tune Ming couldn't forget. He didn't know how to answer them, and he thought they might never be answered. In his despair, he almost didn't care.

Then a new idea came to him, a kind of premonition – that maybe there was another way to get to Gum San. He didn't know it then, but a new stroke of luck was already on its way. A few days after Ming arrived back home, he and his brother stopped by Zhou Lin's store to see what items the herbalist might need, and they began to talk about what had happened in Canton. The little herb shop seemed more cramped than ever, the air heavy with the scents of herbs in hundreds of boxes and jars. The old man listened attentively as Ming described his uncle's proposition, the preparations for the journey and the events on the night his uncle was killed.

"And so, what will you do now?" Zhou Lin asked when Ming had finished.

"What can I do now? I will do what I was doing before. We will have to get along. But somehow, I have to get the money to get to Gum San. I'll find another way. It will take longer now, but I have to go. For my family, for our future."

"And what will you do when you get to Gum San?"

"I will work hard and send money to my mother and brother and sisters so they can have a better life. I can't let them have this kind of life forever." He said it sincerely, with the best of intentions.

"And for yourself? What kind of life will you have?"

"I will have enough. People are rich in Gum San. I will have enough for me and my family, too."

Zhou Lin nodded as Ming and Hwang stared at him. The dim light accentuated the old man's wispy beard and the wrinkles around his eyes. But the eyes, as always, were bright and full of curiosity. "Tell your mother I will stop by tonight, for a visit," he said. "We will talk some more about your plans."

Zhou Lin came to the house that night as he promised. As they all sipped tea, he said, looking at Ming's mother, "Ming has told me of his misfortune in Canton. Do you still wish for him to make this journey?"

"I wanted him to make the journey with my brother, so he would have someone to protect him and give him a start over there," she said. "Now we don't have the money; and if we could get the money, he would have to go alone. I'm afraid of what might happen. Even in Canton, we know that murderers lurk about. I would worry for his safety."

"Perhaps your brother invited this misfortune," Zhou Lin said. "We do not know what his intentions were. But as for Ming here, I believe his intentions are good. He would find a smoother path if he tried this journey on his own, I believe. In other words, I would have no fears for your son. He will find success."

"He is young."

"And able. I have known your son for several years now. He and his brother have been of great service to me. He will be able to do what he wants to do in his new home because his judgment is good. In fact, I have such confidence in him that I want to buy his ticket to this Gum San. California, it's called. I have read the stories."

Ming was stunned. He had not expected this. He couldn't believe it at first.

"But it might take a long time for him to repay you," Song Shee said.

"There is no need to worry about repayment. This is a gift. Ming will repay his village many times over with his success in his new country. We will all benefit. And you should be proud that this exceptional young man is willing to take on this venture on your behalf. I'm sure he is ready. In fact, I have examined the schedule of departures and know of a ship departing from Hong Kong in four days. If he takes this ship, it will allow him to bypass Canton, in case of any possible fears you may have because of the incident with your brother. I would advise that he leave for Hong Kong in the morning since it will take longer to get there."

The arrangements were made. The next morning, Zhou Lin handed Ming the money he needed for the trip, plus some extra to keep him going after he arrived. "May the gods protect you as you go in search of your fortune, young Lee Ming Tao," he said.

"Kwan Gung will smile on you for what you have done, and you will be honored in this house," Song Shee said, bowing to Zhou Lin.

Ming couldn't find the words to say anything until the herbalist was out the door. But then he ran to him, bowed and blurted out, "I will not forget you." Zhou Lin smiled and nodded, and then went on his way.

Four days later Ming boarded the three-masted *Caroline Marie* in Hong Kong harbor, bound for San Francisco, his new life ahead of him.

Chapter 3

San Francisco, Calif.
October 1864

MING TOOK A DEEP BREATH as he waited to disembark. The docks had a familiar smell, as if he were still in Canton or Hong Kong – the stench of rotting fish mingled with smoke from morning fires and oil lamps. His legs wobbled as he shuffled down the narrow plank, following the others onto the dock. He was not used to the footing of dry land, but the freedom he felt from finally leaving the ship behind overwhelmed his other sensations. Shouts came from a distance out of the morning gloom.

" … the men from Sze Yup district … "

"I seek men from Heungsan … "

"All who come from Sam Yup … "

The crowd of men just off the boat, all in a hurry in their fresh changshans and loose trousers, jostled Ming as he tried to move toward the calling voices. He listened desperately for his familiar dialect. What would he do if he couldn't …

In an instant, Ming felt himself fall, hitting his left hip on a post and slamming to the deck. A foot stepped on his arm. He struggled up, was knocked again in the back and then jerked himself to his feet, breathing heavily. Where was his traveling bag? Panicked, he scanned the ground, but it was gone. He fell against a wall for support, trying to get his bearings.

Then he heard it.

"I am from the district of Pang Chuan. I am looking for all strong men who come from that area."

Giving up on his bag, Ming clawed his way through the throng until he located the voice, the one voice he had been looking for.

"Pang Chuan!" he blurted out.

"Pang Chuan! Good man! Join with this group over here."

"Pang Chuan," Ming said again, vigorously nodding his head as he smiled at the men who were gathered under a white- and purple-striped banner. "Pang Chuan!"

"Pang Chuan, yes," said another man. "You have found us. Welcome to San Francisco."

AFTER AN HOUR OR SO, the men were told they would be taken to the headquarters of their district association in Chinatown, the *tong*, where their dialect would be spoken and where they would find temporary housing for immigrants in transition – and, perhaps, work.

As they made their way, single file, through the dusty street, it began to sprinkle. Just then Ming started to feel lucky – that he was off the stinking, cramped ship where he had somehow avoided disease and death, that he was finally on land again and in a place where he could stretch his legs and walk for a distance, where he might finally have a chance to do something with his life. It really didn't matter that he had lost his bag since he had little of value in it anyway. What money he had was tucked away inside his shirt. He began to feel a new hope rising, shock evaporating, a confidence that good things would now be possible.

The place looked nothing like Ming had imagined. It was noisy, people were hurrying this way and that, and it all looked so haphazard and confusing and crude. He couldn't imagine from the sight of it how all those fabulous stories of the Gold Mountain had come from such a place. But in spite of this oddness, he somehow knew that he was going to like it here. After the squalor of the ship, the place gave him a comforting feeling of relief – as if he were in a strange new land of opportunity.

He decided to say something to the man in front of him, who was the one who had spoken to him on the dock, so he tapped him on the shoulder.

"Do you have a relative here?" Ming asked.

"I have a cousin," the man said, twisting his head around to look at Ming. "Are you looking for a place to work?"

"I just need some place to get started."

"The tongs have people who just organize work crews. You can probably get on a work crew of some kind. But if you want, you could come with me to San Jose – south of here, two or three days' walk. My cousin has a laundry there. Perhaps he'll hire you."

"How will we get there?"

"I told you – walk. The letter my cousin sent said a great steam train will soon be running to San Jose, but tracks are still being built."

Ming could not imagine what this steam train would look like, or how it would work. The idea seemed fantastic. Since this man seemed to know something about the place, Ming decided to stay with him and see what he could learn.

"How long will it take to get to this San Jose?" Ming asked him.

"I told you – two days, maybe three. If we walk fast, might get there in two days, my cousin said. I am Wong Han-shee. Your name?"

"I am Lee Ming Tao from Changtsu village."

"OK. But you should call me by my new name, Charlie Wong. My cousin said it's better if you make your name sound more American."

"Charlie Wong? OK. Maybe I should have an American name too, you think? What would a good American name be?"

"I got my name from my cousin – he sent it to me. He said I could be Charlie or Jack. Maybe you want Jack."

"Jack Lee? Does that seem right?"

"Jack Lee is good. It sounds very American." Just that quickly, Ming had the name he would use in America until his old age.

They walked some more in silence, the rain now beginning to make a mess of the street. By the time they reached the communal hotel – actually a kind of converted warehouse – Ming was already feeling better. He had a new name, a friend and a place to go. The future held promise, and China already seemed far away.

Chapter 4

IN BLISTERING INDIAN SUMMER HEAT, Jack and Charlie made their exhausting walk to San Jose in two and a half days. By the time they finished, they were a party of three.

As they walked, Jack stared in amazement. This was land of a kind he had not imagined – open, empty and largely dry to a native of the Pearl River Delta. Except for the great bay that was sometimes visible to the east, Jack saw water only in little streams, but there were enough of those to keep the two of them supplied, even in the hot sun. They spent their first night out in the open and were chased out of that first campsite by two young vaqueros on horseback. The second night they chose a location where they couldn't easily be seen.

Late on the first day, they overtook a small person walking their direction whom they first took for an American boy, but who proved to be a young Chinese traveler, probably in his mid-teens, in American western dress. He was alone and apparently friendless, but not too depressed about it, and so they walked with him while he told his story. He had attempted to hide with the baggage aboard the stagecoach bound from San Francisco to San Jose, but he was discovered and dumped halfway there. He gave them the name Ah Bing, which is what Jack and Charlie always called him thereafter. He told them he had no money and no idea where he would eat next, or how.

Ah Bing was fifteen. He said he was one of three brothers making the voyage from Canton – it turned out, on the *Shining Eagle*, the same ship that Jack and his uncle had been booked on. The ship had been plagued with cholera, and Ah Bing's two older brothers died of the disease during the voyage. In San Francisco, he lost his money and was booted from the tong headquarters in Chinatown. Thinking it best to start over in a new town, he shoplifted some clothes, and, as the stagecoach pulled away from the hotel, scrambled aboard. Ah Bing seemed ill-equipped to survive in this strange new world without help, young as he was. On hearing his story, Jack and Charlie looked at each other – a look Jack took to mean that the two of them should adopt him – at least temporarily. Later Jack learned that Charlie had no such idea.

"You should go back to China," Charlie said, still using his native dialect.

"Why?" Ah Bing said. "If I go back, my family would be angry I didn't try to make it. Besides, I have no prospects there. I'm one of a large family. No inheritance for me."

"What happened with the tong?" Jack asked.

"The boss there collected part of our wages for putting people on work crews. I said I wouldn't pay. He started to push me around and I made him trip. Everyone laughed at him, and he threw me out."

"You should learn not to cross people like that," Charlie said. "You could get hurt."

Ah Bing glared at Charlie. "You think I should kiss his butt?"

"Smart asses usually get sat on," Charlie said, smirking.

Once in San Jose, they found the laundry with no difficulty. San Jose was not very big then, and the Chinatown looked small too, after San Francisco. Charlie's cousin Ching Ghu, who ran the laundry, had no encouragement for them.

"I give Charlie job," Ching Ghu said in English. "Business slow. No work for three. You other two have to go somewhere else."

"Sorry, no jobs for you two," Charlie said in Chinese, to make sure they understood. It was a disappointing result after walking sixty miles. Jack thought Charlie had misled him into thinking it would be easy to get a job with his cousin. On top of that, he thought Charlie seemed callous about their situation. From that day on Jack never trusted Charlie.

"Be seeing you around," Charlie said with a shrug.

The next morning Jack took Ah Bing and they went looking for jobs, to no avail at first. Toward the end of the second day, Ah Bing accepted an offer of bed and board plus 15 cents a day from a man named Ah Chong to keep his store and gambling room clean. Jack was glad to see Ah Bing find a place, but he could not accept such a low wage. Besides, Ah Chong was said to be a tyrant. Jack continued to sleep in the woods by the Guadalupe River at night, and his food money had nearly run out. Finally, after three days, he got a tip from Ching Ghu. A family in town, customers of his cousin, wanted a houseboy. If Jack went there right away he might be the first applicant.

By that time Charles and Catherine Grayson had been married seven years and had two children. They had a fine new house on St. James Street east of the central area. Jack, who spoke almost no English then, had to memorize his opening lines, with help from Ching Ghu: "Come here for job. Be houseboy." He practiced on his way to the house, but when Catherine came to the door, the speech came out wrong – something like, "Come houseboy. Be job for here." She smiled and invited Jack in. He didn't understand most of her questions, but when she seemed doubtful and about to send him away, he managed to blurt out, "Here three days. Want … learn English. Do good job, you see." She smiled again and nodded. She gave him a meal and told to come back the next morning.

Before Jack met the Graysons, the only Westerners he had met were the hands on his ship, so he had a very bad opinion of them in general. But Catherine and Charles were different. Since they were the first Westerners he really came to know, he was lucky that they were so generous. They gave him a job with room and board and a decent wage – more money than he had ever seen. Over the next few months, they taught him English and advised him on the customs and culture of his new country, so that he could make his way in the world of white people.

Most Chinese, in those days, kept to their own, and with good reason. Westerners looked down on them and treated them as a lower class, unfit to join their society and institutions. The schools were closed to Asians, and later there were even laws that kept them from owning property or testifying in court against a white man. Crimes could be perpetrated against them with impunity. They could not even go into the same places where white people socialized. Their customs and manners were disdained. The Chinese had developed Chinatowns as a way to survive and to function with their beliefs and customs as a kind of island in a larger society where they were unwelcome and even in danger. Many Chinese, it's true, did not want to learn English or to adapt in any way. But Jack was always more curious and adventurous than that. He wanted to know about the wider world, and he wanted to be part of it. The Graysons showed him that he could do both, and that some white people were worth knowing as friends.

In return, Jack worked hard for the Graysons. Catherine showed him around her house, a house that seemed grand and luxurious, almost like a palace, to a Chinese such as Jack from a poor village. He learned how to keep things clean and in working order, and where everything belonged. He shopped for food and ran errands, which taught him the geography and customs of his new town.

The Grayson children, five-year-old Lucille and two-year-old Lincoln, added their own kind of joy and curiosity to the mixture, and they all spent time together talking of Chinese traditions, and the Graysons of their Western ones. It was a time of learning for Jack. Once he even overheard Lucy defending him to her friends, who spoke disparagingly of "that Chinaman that lives with you." He smiled when he heard that, for he knew that Lucy was now his friend.

Nearly every evening, Catherine would sit down with Jack and give him an English lesson. Soon he had a functional knowledge of the language and had learned to write his name and address. Charles, who was busy with his printing and newspaper business, was not home as often as the others. But Charles always treated Jack with respect. After Jack had learned to write, Charles even asked him two or three times to fill in for his office receptionist, taking information and relaying messages. It was an important step and gave Jack confidence in dealing with the townspeople.

As time went on, Jack got to know the Graysons' neighbor, Dr. George Enderle, the physician who had come west with the Foard family. A few times, Dr. Enderle asked Jack to help out in his office, too. Jack tried to get Enderle interested in herbal medicine, but the doctor was not ready to accept practices that ran counter to his scientific training, so Jack got the hint and left the subject alone. Many years later, Enderle had reason to change his mind.

After Jack had worked for the Graysons long enough to feel secure there, he sought out the only herbalist in town, who also operated a general store in Chinatown and dispensed herbs as part of his business. This man, Wong Choi, was not a talented healer such as Zhou Lin in Changtsu, but Jack never tried to correct him or embarrass him. Jack merely kept in touch with Wong Choi and cultivated his friendship, since he knew that someday he would want to be more than a houseboy, and that this man might be useful. Wong Choi taught him about the sources he used for obtaining Chinese herbs in California, which were entirely different from the sources in China. This information proved useful to him later. On his day off, which was Sunday, Jack would spend a few hours helping Wong Choi tend his store, at first for no wage, and in doing so he learned more of the practicalities of being an herbalist and a businessman.

During the eight months that Jack worked for the Graysons, he also tried to keep in contact with Ah Bing, and when the two of them met Ah Bing insisted on inviting Charlie Wong, who was still at the laundry. The more Jack learned about Charlie, the more he disliked him. Charlie was a braggart, he talked too loudly, and Jack thought Charlie often went out of his way to insult him or Ah Bing. Charlie did not wear well on Jack.

Then one day Jack learned that Charlie had started to deal *pai gow* games at night at the Ah Chong store, after his laundry job was over. *Pai gow* was one of several games that went on in the back of that store at night. Jack sensed that Charlie, being so close to Ah Bing in Chinatown, was leading him in the wrong direction. The way Charlie began to talk, Jack wasn't even sure that all of Charlie's activities were honest, and he didn't want Ah Bing getting into trouble.

So Jack tried his best to counteract Charlie's bad influence. When he could, he dropped in on Ah Bing at the store and sometimes gave him some money. Jack thought Ah Bing was being treated so badly there that he tried to get him to leave, but Ah Bing was determined to stick it out until he could think of a better plan.

Chinese did not often venture into the white part of town together because Chinese in groups were viewed with suspicion. But one afternoon Ah Bing and Jack were on their way from Chinatown to a quiet place a few blocks away along the Guadalupe River where they sometimes went to talk and speculate on their future. Usually they saw only individuals or couples who paid them no attention. On this day they noticed four or five boys talking and hanging out on a vacant corner lot. As they passed, the boys stared at them and their conversation stopped.

"Just keep walking," Jack whispered to Ah Bing. Jack could see the white boys out of the corner of his eye, felt them beginning to move in their direction.

"Hey, Brownie," one said. "Hey, Chinks, where you goin'?" Again Jack and Ah Bing quickened their pace just a little, until a rock hit Jack in the leg.

"Let's go," Jack said, and they took off at top speed toward the river. A shower of rocks started landing around them, but they weren't hit any more. Jack could hear the boys yelling, but he couldn't tell what they were saying. They ran down along the river for a little way and then doubled back through the brush toward town, so they lost them. When they were in the clear Jack, out of breath, put his hand on Ah Bing's shoulder, and they stopped. "You OK?" Jack asked between pants.

"I'm OK," Ah Bing said, not even winded, and with a smile on his face. "We are pretty fast."

"We're fast, sure, but what's this?" Jack wiped some blood off Ah Bing's neck with his fingers and showed him.

"Oh – I got scraped by a branch down there by the river," Ah Bing said, still grinning. "Now I have a battle scar."

Jack always stood in awe of Ah Bing's resilience. He had some power in him that Jack had never known. And even while Jack constantly felt protective of him, in every telling situation Ah Bing would prove the braver of the two.

As Jack and Ah Bing had fled from the white boys and made their retreat down the riverbank, a solitary, unseen figure sat on the opposite bank, eyeing them closely. He was a grizzled Indian, seventy-nine years old, dressed in an assortment of Native American and western garb. His name was Marcelo, and 65 years before, he had helped Father Magin de Catala lug willow saplings from this riverbank and plant them along the thoroughfare connecting the Santa Clara Mission with San Jose, the road now known as The Alameda. Eight years before, Charles Grayson had made his first entry into San Jose along the tree-shaded Alameda, in a stagecoach driven by Antonio del Costa, known as Jorge Villegas. Marcelo was a ubiquitous, recognizable figure in the area with a reputation for ferocity in a fight, the survivor of five marriages. At one time he had owned land north of town, by the bay. He knew the Grayson family, and he also knew that one of the Chinese boys he had just seen was a houseboy employed by the Graysons.

After seeing the boys, Marcelo thought for a few minutes, then slowly made his way to the Foard livery stable on Second Street, the one where Jorge Villegas boarded his horses and the one where Villegas's son, Juan Villegas, now eighteen, was employed as a stable boy. Marcelo stood in front of the stable awhile, as if he had nothing better to do, waiting. Soon, the stable boy emerged, preparing to go home for the day.

"Hello, boy," Marcelo said, giving Juan a nod.

"Marcelo, what are you up to?" Juan said.

"I just saw something you need to know about. You know that Chinese boy been hired by the Graysons?"

"Yeah, I've seen him. He brings their horses over here. Why?"

"He and another boy were down by the river. Clayton Phaneuf and his gang chasing them. Throwing rocks."

"What for?"

"Nothing. Just Phaneuf making trouble again. You see that Chinese boy, you should tell him about Phaneuf."

"Tell him what?"

"You know, just give him a warning. They could get into trouble."

"Sure, OK. Listen, I got to get home. My dad's due home soon."

Two days later, Jack Lee rode Cuesta, Charles Grayson's old horse, to the stable to get a shoe put on. Juan, unloading hay at the back of the building, waited until Jack had left the horse with the blacksmith and then jogged after him as he left.

"Hey you, Chinaman," he called. Jack turned.

"Listen, I don't know why I'm telling you this, but there's a thing you need to know."

"Thing I need to know?"

"Listen, what's your name anyway?"

"Jack Lee."

"Okay, well listen, Jack. See, there's a mean gang here, some kids. You know what I'm talking about?"

"Mean? Bad people?"

"Yeah, bad. People saw you, you and some other kid, these guys were chasing you, throwing some rocks?"

Jack looked at him but said nothing.

"Well, anyway. This guy Clayton Phaneuf, he's the one. He and his gang, they're bad eggs. You're new around here. They could make trouble for somebody like you. If I was you I'd stay out of his way. You know what I mean?"

"Out of way? Not go there?"

"Yeah, just stay out of that place by the river. That's where they hang out. Especially in the afternoons around four or five, that's when they meet up. Stay up here in town and you'll be all right."

"Stay in town?"

"Yeah. That's all. Okay, I've said it. Now I got to get back to work. See you around."

Jack looked at Juan's back as he walked back through the stable, wondering who had seen them by the river and what this trouble might be. But he understood the message.

Jack soon learned that such a warning was no deterrent to Ah Bing. Of course, Jack told him what the stable boy said. But in answer, Ah Bing's eyes glistened.

"So now we know when they meet – around four or five in the afternoon, where we saw them before by the river. We're going to make trouble for them, not them for us."

"Wait, Ah Bing, we better listen to this boy."

"We're smarter than that stable boy. I have a plan – come with me."

By a circuitous route, Ah Bing took Jack down by the river. There he showed Jack his plan for revenge – a trip wire across one of the paths they used and a big pool of mud just beyond. When Jack first heard this plan he laughed because it sounded childish, but then he thought it might be simple enough to work. Jack did not want to seem timid in Ah Bing's eyes. And after all, Phaneuf was just another kid like them.

A few days later, about 4:30 in the afternoon, Ah Bing and Jack made another sojourn toward the river, making sure Phaneuf was around and could see them. When Phaneuf caught sight of Jack and Ah Bing, he set out after them at the head of his little band of tough guys. Knowing the location of the trip wire, Jack and Ah Bing sailed over it and stepped to the side of the mud hole. A few seconds later, they had the pleasure of seeing Phaneuf himself go flying into the mud.

Just as Ah Bing and Jack were enjoying their laugh, Jack turned around and nearly jumped out of his skin. The largest man he had ever seen close up was now towering over him no more than three feet away. He was an old man with hundreds of wrinkles on his dark face, with a white, grizzled beard, wearing boots, cowboy pants and a shirt decorated with ribbons. As the man stood there in silence, Jack and Ah Bing backed away.

"Who … who are you?" Ah Bing managed to get out in English.

"You boys better watch out," the big man said. "You'll get yourselves into trouble."

"Okay," Jack said. "We watch out. We go now."

"Not so fast. Stay here a minute." He turned and yelled at Phaneuf, "You boys, you get out of here." The mud-soaked Phaneuf and his friends sauntered off, yelling insults, and Marcelo watched them go.

"You might need someone on your side if you have to answer for this later," Marcelo said, turning to Jack. "You tell them Marcelo will back you up. They'll know who you mean."

"Marcelo," Jack said.

"That's right, Marcelo. Everybody knows me around here." He turned and disappeared. Jack wasn't sure, but it looked as if this Marcelo was a good man to know.

Apparently, word of the incident got around to Charles, because he took Jack aside a few days later.

"I hear you have been having some adventures down by the river," he began. Jack nodded, ready for a reprimand.

"Well, that's fine," Charles said. "Just make sure you don't get hurt. I want to keep my houseboy. And just as a piece of advice, I would keep clear of that area for awhile. I think you're smart enough to do that." And he winked.

THREE DAYS AFTER JACK and Ah Bing had their encounter with Marcelo, Jorge Villegas drove his regular stage route from San Jose to San Francisco. When he had unloaded the stage, he boarded his horses as usual and went to the bar where he usually had a few drinks and played some poker before heading to a nearby boardinghouse.

After about an hour, one of the men in the poker game began to get angry. He argued with Villegas, then accused him of cheating. Villegas stood up, a fight ensued, and soon several drunken men were tearing up the saloon. Sheriff's deputies came and hauled Villegas and two others off to jail.

That night, Villegas and the other two were served plates of food containing a beef stew. Although the jailers were unaware of it, this beef stew had been made two days before and had not been kept cold. The other two men smelled the food and didn't eat it, but Villegas did. During the night, Villegas began to vomit. He threw up blood and lay on his cell floor, sick and dehydrated. By morning Jorge Villegas, formerly Antonio del Costa, was dead.

Chapter 5

AH BING DETESTED HIS BOSS, Ah Chong, who never relented in his tyrannical treatment of the underlings who worked in his store. But Ah Bing had grit. Abuse that would have reduced most boys to quivering jelly fell off him like so much confetti. He worked for that man for three months without complaining. And then something happened that changed the direction of both their lives.

One day when they were having lunch in Chinatown, Ah Bing told Jack he had learned from one of the *pai gow* dealers that Charlie Wong was running a cheating scheme at the store. Certain players were favored in the dealing of tiles and were guaranteed to be the "big winners." Charlie was rotating these players in and out of the games so as not to arouse suspicion. The dealers had to cooperate by keeping certain favorable tiles to pass to the right player during the deal. The big winners were expected to kick back part of their winnings to Charlie, and also to Ah Chong, who was in on it.

"Don't say anything to Charlie about it," Ah Bing said.

Somehow – Jack never knew exactly how – Ah Bing and the other dealer had come up with a plan for exposing Charlie's scheme while the pai gow game was going on. That way Ah Bing could get his revenge on Ah Chong. When Ah Bing went to Jack the next night and told him about the plan, Jack advised him against it. "It's too risky,"

Jack said. "If one of the gamblers gets very mad, he could become violent. Someone could get hurt, even you. And you don't know what Ah Chong might do to you, or what Charlie would do."

"Are we going to let them keep cheating people?" Ah Bing said. "Don't you want to stop what's going on?"

Immediately Jack thought he smelled a rat. "Who put you up to this?" he asked. "Are you sure Charlie doesn't know what you're up to? Charlie's dangerous." Ah Bing denied it.

"You're too set on revenge," Jack said. "You need to get out of there before you get into trouble. Just leave." Jack knew instinctively that it would be useless for two Chinese boys to go to the police, who never involved themselves with matters inside Chinatown unless they affected the white community. As Ah Bing turned to leave in a dejected mood, Jack grabbed him and turned him around. "Watch out for Charlie Wong," he said. "He can do you harm."

Jack heard nothing from Ah Bing for a few days. But a week later Jack got word that one of Ah Chong's dealers had not been quite deceptive enough and was exposed right in Ah Chong's store. There was a fight. Jack knew Ah Bing was in the store when it happened, but he had disappeared, so Jack went to the laundry to find Charlie and grabbed him by the shirt collar.

"What happened to Ah Bing?" Jack yelled. "What did you do to him?"

"Calm down," Charlie said, "Ah Bing didn't get hurt."

"How do you know? Where is he?"

"I don't know where he is, but he got out. He doesn't need protection from you. What are you, his keeper?"

Jack pushed him away and left, sure now that Charlie had set up this situation to get back at Ah Bing for trying to expose him. And if that wasn't the case, Jack didn't want to put Ah Bing in any more danger by telling what he knew.

The store never opened again. The disgraced Ah Chong packed up and cleared out of town the next day, and Ah Bing did not resurface. Jack hoped that maybe, as on his disease-plagued ship, Ah Bing had escaped another dangerous situation unscathed.

A tense month went by for Jack, who now thought of Ah Bing as his younger brother in Gum San, until a letter from Ah Bing addressed to Jack finally arrived at the Grayson house. The boy was working on a crew building the Transcontinental Railroad in the mountains east of Sacramento. A recruiter had come through San Jose the day after the incident in the store, and Ah Bing, now sixteen, had signed on that very day for a wage several times what he made at the store. "There was no time to tell anyone," he explained. As he read the letter, Jack felt a huge weight lifted from his shoulders. Without knowing it, he had become closer to Ah Bing than to his real brother thousands of miles away.

A month later, Jack got another letter from Ah Bing, who wrote that he had heard the Central Pacific was looking to hire a Chinese herbalist. By then, about 12,000 of the 13,500 workers on the railroad crews were Chinese, none of them comfortable with Western doctors. Some were leaving the crews so that they could go back to the cities and obtain the herbal remedies they depended on. Ah Bing had told the railroad men that Jack was a competent herbalist and might be available. Would he meet with a Central Pacific man to discuss it?

Jack was intrigued, and he thought about the idea for awhile. In no way did he consider himself a fully competent herbalist. But he certainly knew more than Wong Choi, who was providing services for a growing population in San Jose. He now knew where to obtain the herbs he would need, so he could probably serve the men building the railroad well enough – certainly better than a Western doctor who refused to be educated in Chinese ways. With Catherine Grayson's help, he wrote to the address Ah Bing had given him. Jack's rudimentary English must have been good enough for the railroad people; within a month, in June 1865, he was on his way to the Central Pacific's construction site in the Sierra Nevada.

As the stagecoach carried him away from San Jose, Jack started to feel sorrow and loss in his heart for leaving the Graysons – a deeper loss, in a way, than he felt about his own family in China. The Graysons had made it possible for him to take this new step. He had an investment in them, and they in him. He thought of Lucy and Lincoln, who had run to him and put their arms around him when he left, while Catherine held her newborn, John Sutter. Jack knew that his nervous laugh concealed his feelings. He told Lucy and Linc he would be back to see them, and it was true – he was to return. They all understood that he could not stay with them forever. It made perfect sense for Jack to be with his people, doing the thing he seemed destined to do. But in his heart, Jack knew that the possibility of seeing Ah Bing again played a large part in his decision.

It was a warm August day when Jack made his trip to the Sierra Nevada. In Stockton, the stage picked up a middle-aged woman impeccably outfitted in a long, dark green dress and a matching hat, traveling by herself, who took the seat opposite Jack. When the stage had barely started again, she began – without introduction – to question him.

"Where are you going, young man?"

"Be ... herb doctor ... railroad," Jack said hesitantly.

"You're going to be a doctor? Administering medical treatment for the Central Pacific Railroad?"

"Y-yes."

"You're very young. Where did you receive your training?"

"T-training? Sorry ... my English."

"What medical school did you attend?"

"School? No ... I learn about herbs ... in China, from doctor there."

"Humph. Well, I suppose the railroad people know what they're doing. Charles Crocker is a personal friend of mine. He had to talk to the other investors at great length to them to hire Chinese workers, you know." Jack smiled. "They wouldn't have done it if enough American workers had been available. I hope your people are up to the job." Jack smiled again and nodded. "Charles told me, 'After all, they built the Great Wall, didn't they?' The other men had to agree."

"Chinese work ... hard," Jack said.

The stage took them to the rail head in Sacramento, and then Jack caught a crew train to the end of the line east of Auburn, where the construction crews were blasting, picking and shoveling their way into the mountains.

The crews had reached Auburn with tracks on May 13, 1865, and were working their way towards Colfax, 19 miles further along. There, as the cooler fall weather set in, the crews began in earnest the treacherous task of blasting a route through the heart of the great mountains, up the American River Canyon to the summit and down to Nevada along the Truckee River Canyon. The route had been chosen because it offered a single summit, near where the Donner party had been stranded nine years before – not a double summit as in most of the range. But the danger from avalanches and from cave-ins and blasting could not be avoided.

At a place called Cape Horn Promontory, a few miles east of Colfax, a rail bed had to be blasted out of a thousand vertical feet of solid rock. Workers were being lowered over the face of the promontory in wicker baskets to a point 1,330 feet above the canyon floor, to first chisel out holes for the blasting powder, then place a fuse, light it and scramble up the ropes so as not to be blasted to pieces.

The change in scene refreshed Jack. These mountains held a beauty like none he had seen, a land full of deep canyons and rocky, tree-covered slopes extending ever higher. At the canyon bottoms, water ran swiftly past the boulders in the rocky streambeds, offering both life support and a quick death to those who didn't respect its power.

When Jack first saw Ah Bing at the Cape Horn encampment, he wanted to know immediately about the incident at Ah Chong's. "It was Charlie, wasn't it?" Jack asked him.

"It was nothing," Ah Bing said. "I just pulled one of the players aside and showed him how he was being cheated. He was the one who started the fight. I got out of there fast and never went back. I hope you didn't tell anyone where I am." Jack said he hadn't. But he thought that Ah Bing must be covering up for Charlie.

Ah Bing, true to form, sought out the riskiest and most glamorous of the railroad jobs. He would climb into one of the baskets with a supply of blasting powder and fuses, then let himself be lowered by ropes over the cliff at Cape Horn so that he could plant the explosives in the rock wall. After lighting the fuse, he had to jump out of the basket and scamper up the narrow rock ledges to get out of the way of the explosion. He was small and good at scrambling, so he was a natural for the job. Later that fall, the workers on the cliff above began swinging the baskets to the side after the fuse was lit, which Ah Bing considered safer than having to scramble out of the way. But the timing had to be exact.

"We have to watch out for ourselves," Ah Bing said. "The white bosses don't care if one of us dies. We're like animals to them. If we step out of line an inch they hit us, call us names. We don't eat the bad American food they give to the white workers, but they still only pay us a dollar a month more for buying our own food. It stinks. Still, nobody else is going to pay us this much. I can send $15 a month home to China."

"I'll bet they won't get any American to work for that pay and work as hard," Jack said.

"Ha. You got that right."

As an herbalist, Jack had a lot to learn. In Sacramento, he had been lucky to find another herbalist, who gave him a temporary supply of cinnamon, hawthorn, gardenia, clove, licorice and chrysanthemum leaves. Through him Jack also found a source for blossoms, roots, rhizomes and pods and put in an order for ginseng, wolfberry and horny goat weed. With these essential items he began his career. Later, he expanded his repertoire by ordering a book on acupressure and teaching himself how to employ that ancient Chinese art.

The maladies of the Chinese railroad workers were mostly chills, fever, coughs and colds, nausea and stomach trouble. Jack had already learned how to make tonics for these symptoms from Zhou Lin back home in China. For cuts and scrapes, he would concoct a poultice as he had seen Zhou Lin do at home and Wong Choi do in San Jose. At first, he couldn't treat complaints such as a lack of sexual potency, but he made inquiries and eventually obtained a source for dried sea lion genitalia and some other exotic items. The mail was slow, but the workers were patient; and after a few successful treatments, Jack's prestige rose. They knew he was their only hope.

At the end of the day, Ah Bing would come back to camp tired but exhilarated. He thrived on risk, and when Jack looked in his eyes he finally understood. Ah Bing had escaped the denigration of Ah Chong and his gambling den and had found something that paid him five or six times the money he might have made in China.

It was around this time that Jack began to think he should contact his family. He wanted to help them out and fully intended to, but he wanted to be sure he had what he needed to get established in his business. That way he would be of more help to them in the long run, he reasoned. He thought there was still plenty of time.

On Sunday, their day off, the Chinese workers would have a huge feast, consisting of steamed fish, dried oysters and fruit, mushrooms and seaweed, perhaps pork, chicken or abalone. It was an elaborate banquet, especially by contrast with the poverty all of them had known in China, where deprivation and even starvation were common. While some chose to gamble on Sunday, Ah Bing and Jack would busy themselves preparing the food. They soon had so many friends coming to dinner that they had to turn some away. After the meal they would relax and talk of their families and home villages. It was a happy time for Jack and Ah Bing.

Then there came a day that was the blackest Jack had ever experienced, even worse than the murder of his uncle in Canton. One sunny, cool afternoon in November, word came down to the camp that there had been an accident at the cliff – a fuse setter in a basket had been swung away from the powder, and then, somehow, back into the explosion. Either the fuse was too long or the swing too short, and the worker was dead. As Jack probed the faces of the others, he realized the worst – it was Ah Bing.

Jack wanted to blame someone. He could have blamed the railroad, which knew full well the dangers involved in what it asked the workers to do, but pushed ahead anyway. He could have blamed the supervisors of the work crew. He could have blamed Ah Bing himself. But somehow Jack settled on Charlie Wong as the ultimate culprit. He couldn't shake his resentment of what Charlie had done to Ah Bing in San Jose. If it hadn't been for Charlie's scheming, maybe Ah Bing would have found a better job in San Jose and would still be alive.

As it happened, one of Jack's extra duties to the railroad was to serve as a stand-in mortician for Chinese workers who met their demise in the mountains. So it was up to him to take the broken, partially charred body of his friend and prepare it for burial. He chose a special place near a waterfall where the two of them used to go sometimes. Jack marked it and made a careful notation of the position, for he knew that eventually Ah Bing's bones would need to be recovered and returned to his home village in China. Then he gathered up his friend's belongings and sent off a note to his family. That night, and for many nights to come, Jack woke up often, each time shaking, with moist cheeks, thinking first of that joy he had seen in Ah Bing's eyes, and then of his burial. In the coming years he would have other friends, some that he would call close. But never was there one he loved as much.

Chapter 6

By the fall of 1868 Jack had worked for the railroad three years. He had watched the work crews complete the costly task of laying rails through the Sierra, and trains from Sacramento were now arriving daily at the work sites in Nevada to deliver increasing quantities of rails, ties and spikes. A race was on to see which company could lay more miles of track over the next six months or so – the Central Pacific, Jack's company, or the Union Pacific, which was building from the east. By all reports, the two would meet sometime next spring, probably in Utah. Then the Transcontinental Railroad would be complete.

Charles Crocker's argument for using Chinese workers had been validated. Not only had Chinese workers proved as good as the white crews; they were cleaner, their diet tended to prevent the dysentery that plagued others, and they fought less and generally caused less trouble.

During those three years Jack had built up a nice nest egg, both from the railroad's paycheck and from treating Chinese passing through. The bigger it got, the more secure he felt, and the money was addictive. He did not forget his family in China – they came to mind every day. He knew he should be sending them money as the other workers did, but month after month he postponed it. He became fascinated with the increase of his nest egg. Each time the work crews moved their camp, Jack found a new hiding place for his stash. He carefully counted it daily and made notes of its growth. He had earned this, he said to himself, and it would help him start a nice business in San Jose when the railroad was finished. Then he would be in a perfect position to help his family.

When Jack saw the workers coming back to camp exhausted every day, he knew he had a cushy job and should be grateful, but he began to hate the barren Nevada landscape. He had seen California's coastal valleys and the great Sierra, and this Nevada life was not for him. He was ready for a change. He gave his notice a week after they had finished building across the forty-mile desert, and by August he was back in San Jose with his accumulated savings, ready to set up his herb shop.

The city he returned to in 1868 was visibly changed. Three years before, it had seemed raw and largely populated by single men seeking money and adventure. Now it had more stores, more bustle and a more settled feeling. With the American Civil War in the past, Jack saw more white couples and families – people who looked as if they meant to make a home here. Even among the Chinese, where single men still predominated, there were some families with children. New schools and churches had popped up.

Jack's first goal was to get his shop started, so he could bring in some income again. He thought he would begin sending money to his mother as soon as he was established in his own shop. While he was setting up the shop in Chinatown, in the block southeast of Market and San Fernando streets, he stayed again with the Grayson family, renting space above their carriage house.

About this time the tracks were being finished for the first horsecar route of the San Jose and Santa Clara Railroad Co., running from downtown San Jose along

The Alameda to Franklin and Main streets in Santa Clara. Samuel Addison Bishop, a 300-pound, opera-loving former Indian-fighter, had bought the Percherons he needed for his line from Eli Foard, in a sale handled by Catherine Grayson for her father. On the day of the inaugural forty-five-minute run, the entire Grayson family, decked out in their best clothing, was to be on hand, and Catherine insisted that Jack go along.

When Jack and the Graysons arrived downtown, Rebecca and Eli were already seated on the shiny red and black horsecar as it sat poised for the four-mile trip. As Charles prepared to board and Catherine began to help the children up, a camera flash scared the horses. When the car lurched, nine-year-old Lucy lost her grip and slipped off the step. Immediately, Rebecca flashed back to the incident she had witnessed on the wagon with the Gagnon boy twenty-two years before. But this time Jack was there, watching over the children, and he grabbed Lucy before she hit the ground. It was not really as close a call as it might have been, but the family had a scare, and Jack got a profuse round of thanks. From Lucy's point of view, Jack was a hero. As Jack finally swung aboard, he caught sight of the old Indian Marcelo standing to the side of the road, giving him a wave and a nod.

It was around this time that Jack met the Reverend Thomas S. Dunn, who was pastor of the First Methodist Episcopal Church at Second and Santa Clara streets. This was where Dr. Enderle and his family worshipped, and where they and Tom Dunn had set up a Sunday school attended by 166 Chinese. This school was a revelation to Jack for a couple of reasons. For one, most white people's churches were frowning on the increase in Chinese population, calling them heathens and "the yellow peril." Jack didn't understand why this church was different. And he couldn't fathom why these Chinese would be interested in this white church.

Jack was mostly indifferent towards religion. Of course he knew the gods of the old country. There was Kwan Gung, the most popular god of the Chinese temples, really a historical figure of the Three Kingdoms period. Kwan Yin was a favorite deity, an immortal regarded as the goddess of mercy, and Tien Ho was another immortal, called the queen of heaven and ruler of the seas. But to Jack these were more traditions than matters of belief.

When Jack met Tom Dunn, he liked him immediately. Tom looked Jack in the eye and gripped his hand as if to pull him in, to save him from whatever trouble might be engulfing him. Dunn seemed interested in Jack right away and took time to find out where he had been and what role he played building the railroad. After one meeting Jack began to see Dunn as a new friend. Then he discovered that the minister had been speaking out against unfair taxation and laws that discriminated against the Chinese. Jack saw the Chinese in San Jose gravitate toward Dunn, whom they saw as a kind of lifeline to the Western world.

After that first meeting with Dunn, answering the pastor's questions about his family in China, Jack had to do some soul-searching. Finally, Dunn made Jack face his failure to provide for them as he had promised. He knew the other workers on the railroad sent money home with regularity. He could delay no longer. So he composed a letter to his mother with the help of a letter-writer in Chinatown – Jack had forgotten what little he once knew of Chinese writing – and sent it off. He begged her forgiveness for his long silence and lack of support. He sent her enough money for the family to subsist for a year – it was only a small part of what he had saved – and promised to send more. He briefly summarized his story in Gum San and sent the letter off, not knowing when he might get an answer.

Soon Jack was attending the Sunday school at Dunn's church, partly to get reacquainted with the Chinese community, in which he now had only a few friends. To become a successful herbalist, he was going to need lots of contacts. He was beginning to feel like a part of the community again when, in the middle of the night on Feb. 22, 1869, Dunn's church at Second and Santa Clara was set on fire and destroyed. A group of anti-Chinese agitators sent out word that they were responsible. It was a scary time for Jack, and he began to worry that coming back to San Jose had been a poor choice. What other violence might these people do to the Chinese?

The smoke had not cleared from the fire when Dunn received a letter marked with a skull and crossbones, threatening him with death if he didn't leave town. But the pastor would not be bullied. He read the letter to his congregation the following Sunday as they met in a field and posted it prominently, using the threat as a tool to build support for rebuilding the church. He raised $25,000, completed a new church five months after the fire, and redoubled his support for the Chinese community. Jack admired his tenacity and loved him, but the yellow peril idea continued to gain strength. And for Jack, there was worse to come.

Toward the spring of that year Jack received a letter from his home village, with devastating news. The letter was not from his mother but from Zhou Lin, the village herbalist who had paid for Jack's trip. In translation, it read as follows:

Your mother, brother and sisters waited two years for word from you but heard nothing. You sent no money or even any indication of whether you had arrived safely. They thought probably you were dead because otherwise you would have contacted them. Finally, your mother insisted that your brother attempt to find you. He borrowed money to make the trip to San Francisco. There he searched for you for weeks, all in vain. Unable to support himself any longer, he posted a letter to your mother and boarded a ship to return. At least we know he was placed on the ship's registry, but he never made it back to China. Either he died of some disease or he fell overboard – we don't know. When your mother realized what had happened, she fell ill and died shortly thereafter. Your sisters found other families and are now married. I have given the money you sent to them. Since they refused to write to you, I am doing so in their place, with the hope that this news will have some beneficial impact on your life.

As Jack read these words he wept, realizing that his family was no more and that he was responsible. When he changed his name to Jack Lee, he had not intended to hide from his family, but that was the result. He had abandoned his family just as his father had, and now his mother and brother were dead. Jack never imagined that such tragic things could happen, but they did. For several days he did nothing at all – only sat alone. He thought of the years he had saved his money while working for the railroad, and done nothing for his family, and he became obsessed with the knowledge of this selfishness. During this time he thought of ending his life; the guilt seemed too much for him to live with. He was only 22 years old and now he did not know if he wanted to go on. Finally he told Catherine, and she told him to talk to Tom Dunn.

"Tom is a good man and he can help you understand this, if anyone can," she said.

So Jack went to see the minister and told him his story. He told him about life in China, and about the hope his family had placed in him. He told him about his uncle's murder and about Zhou Lin's faith and trust. He told Dunn about his selfish hoarding and about his remorse. Finally, he began to sob uncontrollably.

When Jack had regained his composure, Dunn said, "You have had a very painful lesson. What do you think it is?"

Jack thought awhile, and then he said, "That I am a worthless person. I have given back nothing for all I have been given."

"Is that so? Didn't you help support your family during the years you were in China?"

"Yes."

"And didn't you provide good service for the Grayson family?"

"Yes."

"And during your years as an herbalist for the railroad, did none of those workers benefit from the remedies you gave them?"

"I helped some of them."

"And didn't I hear that you saved Lucy Grayson from a dangerous fall off the horsecar?"

"I was just in the right place at the right time."

"And what if you hadn't been there? Don't you think God had a plan, that he wanted you to be there?"

"I don't know."

"Listen, Jack. You are responsible for your own life from this time forward. Despite what has happened, you can make it a good life. Do you have any ideas about how to do that?"

"I don't know. I'm an herbalist. I could help people."

"Yes, and you can help your community. You have a lot of skills, and you speak English better than most. You can't bring back your mother and brother, but it's not too late for you. You have a choice now – either waste your life or make it a useful one. You should find yourself a wife and start a new family here. You're not a bad person, you're a good person who has made a mistake. Now that you've looked at your mistake and grieved over it, you can go ahead and contribute to your new community. That's your job."

After thinking about what Tom said, Jack gradually regained some of his spirit. With Tom's help, he composed a letter to Zhou Lin expressing his remorse, and then asking him another favor. He knew it took a lot of nerve, but Jack asked if he could arrange to have a wife sent to him from the village, someone who would be willing to relocate to Gum San. Again he went to a letter-writer to have this written in Chinese. He never received an answer from Zhou Lin, so it wasn't clear whether he ever received the letter. But as it turned out, Jack didn't need his help this time.

Chapter 7

In January 1870, another calamity befell the Chinese in San Jose. A fire of mysterious origin swept through Chinatown and destroyed it, taking Jack's new herb shop and living quarters. After the fire, everyone – about 500 Chinese – had to move a few blocks, over to Vine Street next to the Guadalupe River. Because Jack now had friends in the white community, he took a lead role in this move and helped find the new location. It didn't take long for most of the old businesses to reappear – the restaurants, gambling houses and brothels. Chinatown had a butcher, a baker and all the other elements of a little town. Jack even found that his undertaking experience was in demand, so he added that to the services he offered as an herbalist.

As soon as the move to Vine Street was finished, the businessmen in Chinatown started to talk about moving back to Market and San Fernando, which was more central to the city. On Vine Street, the storekeepers could see that they were too isolated, and it was affecting business. So Jack gathered some other Chinese businessmen together and they sent a message to a man named Ng Fook, who was a wealthy San Francisco merchant. Ng Fook arranged for the financing of several new brick buildings, and by 1872 San Jose's Chinatown was functioning again at its former location. This time there were a dozen grocery stores, a large theater and even a temple where Chinese could practice their traditional faith. If the anti-Chinese movement had been as organized then as it became later, the white leaders of San Jose would have prevented such a move.

In the early 1870s Jack was still attending Tom Dunn's church and had regular contact with a lot of people in the white community. He wore mostly western dress and spoke decent English. He also still saw a lot of the Grayson family, who remained his closest white friends even though they were not members of the church. This relationship led to something nobody was expecting, especially Jack.

CATHERINE GRAYSON KEPT a close watch on her children. By mid-1871 John Sutter Grayson was six years old, Lincoln was nine and Lucy twelve. They were healthy children, mostly happy with their daily lives and secure in their close-knit family. Weekly trips to the West Side ranch to see the grandparents, Eli and Rebecca, gave the children a strong outdoor outlet and a relationship with horses. Lucy and Lincoln were already competent riders. Lincoln was the most curious, taking strongly after his mother. Lucy was the most emotional, John the most self-contained.

One spring day Lucy came home from school complaining of a sore throat. The next morning, a Saturday, she still had it. Catherine called off the weekly visit to the ranch, over Linc's protests, and made Lucy stay in bed. By that afternoon a rash of tiny red dots had appeared on Lucy's neck and chest. Catherine called Charles into the bedroom to look.

"I'll get Dr. Enderle," Charles said as soon as he saw it.

The rash seemed to be spreading fast. By the time Dr. Enderle came to the house, the redness covered Lucy's upper chest and was beginning to appear on her arms. The doctor pressed the skin and felt its texture, then examined Lucy's throat. Enderle took Charles and Catherine into the adjoining room.

"It's scarlet fever, no doubt about it," he said. "The skin is rough, like sandpaper, and whitens when I press it. The rash is spreading."

Charles felt the immediate sting of fear. He and Catherine could name four children who had been friends of their kids and died of the disease. They both looked desperately at Enderle.

"What can we do?" Charles asked.

"First, burn anything she's touched in the last few days – clothing, any personal belongings. I'll need to start bleeding her right away. That will give her the best chance of recovery. I'll get towels and some water."

Charles went into action, gathering up the items to be burned – dresses, pajamas, socks, underclothing, a few toys – while Catherine made sure the two boys were occupied and kept away from Lucy.

Seeing the worry on her mother's face, Lucy said, "Don't be afraid, mommy. I'll be fine."

"I know you will, honey," Catherine said. "Why don't you drink some water?"

"Mommy?"

"Yes, honey?"

"Would you tell Jack? I want to see Jack."

"Sure sweetie, I'll let him know."

Enderle returned to the room, took out his lancet and made incisions in Lucy's arms, starting a flow of blood from each. Catherine, unable to watch, paced a few feet from the bedside, glancing over Enderle's shoulder to keep Lucy's face in sight as it became paler and paler.

"Isn't it time to stop now?" Catherine said, tension in her voice, after a few minutes had gone by.

"She can go longer," the doctor said. More minutes went by before he announced, "She's fainted." Catherine looked at Lucy's white face and grayish lips, and she wrung her hands. Enderle carefully wiped the incisions and wrapped them up with cotton gauze, compressing his hand over the bandage, and Catherine took the bloody towels away.

"Burn those, too," Enderle said. He stayed by Lucy's side another 20 minutes, until she was conscious again and able to talk. He reassured her and gave her some water.

"The disease has to run its course – I can only lessen the effects," Enderle said to Catherine and Charles at the door as he was leaving. "You'll have to keep a close watch over the next few days. I'll check back tomorrow morning, but let me know if there's any change."

Lucy slept fitfully; so did Catherine, by her side. Lincoln was sent to inform Jack, who came to look in during the evening when mother and daughter were both asleep, but Charles was still awake.

"Lucy is weak," Jack said to Charles. "I see her body trying to survive. Dr. Enderle good doctor. I won't stay, but let me know if I can help."

By Sunday afternoon the rash covered most of Lucy's upper body and arms. Two days and another bleeding later, she was no better. Dr. Enderle stopped by on Tuesday evening and recommended to Charles and Catherine that he induce vomiting with syrup of ipecac.

"Purging is indicated when symptoms persist," Enderle told them. "It cleans the system, getting rid of whatever's making her sick."

Weak as she was, Lucy had no power to resist the ipecac syrup, but she had trouble swallowing it. When she did, she gagged immediately and regurgitated what was in her stomach, which wasn't much. When the nausea subsided, she took a few deep breaths and then fainted. She was revived but seemed on the verge of death as Catherine anxiously watched over her during the night.

Jack Lee made his second visit to Lucy's bedside the next morning. After seeing her desperate condition, he spoke to Charles and Catherine in the Grayson kitchen.

"Please excuse me for … for my saying anything against Dr. Enderle, because Dr. Enderle is good doctor. If you would allow me to suggest, I think … certain herb remedies would do no harm and … could help, I think."

Charles and Catherine looked at each other but said nothing. Jack took this as an encouraging sign.

"Also," he went on, "I think no more bleeding or purging. Lucy needs to regain her strength to resist this sickness." When the Graysons did not argue, Jack gave them a package of herb powder for Lucy. "This is … I can't explain in English … *Sheng Ma Ge Gen Tang*. It is an herb concoction for such cases. You mix with food or water. Also, if I may suggest, cold towels. Lucy very hot – needs to cool down her body. And I have something else." He pulled out another small package. "I have old Indian friend – Marcelo. He gives me this American herb, which is purple cornflower. I think it helps immunity. You give it to Lucy."

Catherine accepted the packages with a nod of thanks. Then, with a bow, Jack left.

Catherine and Charles did not know what to think at first, but they were desperate. "She's not getting better," Catherine said. "I want to try it."

"We don't want to make her worse," Charles said. "Dr. Enderle is our doctor."

"I still want to try it. I don't like this bleeding and purging."

So Catherine prevailed. She mixed the herbs with water and a little applesauce and gave the mixture to Lucy, telling her, "This is from Jack." Then she applied the cold towels at intervals throughout the day. By Wednesday evening the high fever had subsided. By the next morning Lucy was feeling better. Dr. Enderle came by and pronounced the patient improved. Catherine wasn't brave enough to tell him what she had done or why. Lucy's skin had begun to peel, but the doctor said it was a normal stage of the illness. Over the next few days Lucy continued to feel better and stronger.

When ten days had passed, Lucy was well enough to get out of bed. Her skin was still peeling, but she was obviously on her way to recovery. Dr. Enderle thought he had saved the patient. Charles wasn't sure. It was years later when the doctor learned what had happened, and even then he was slow to give Jack any credit. But in Catherine's eyes there was never any doubt – Jack's remedies had been the turning point for Lucy.

The final verdict was given by Lucy herself. "Jack saved me," she said. "I was dying before I took the herbs. Then I started to feel better, and the cold towels felt so good. And this is the second time. Remember when I fell off the horsecar?" It was one more link forged in the bond being formed between Lucy and the former houseboy.

If Jack had been almost part of the Grayson family before Lucy's illness, he was a full-fledged one after it. Holidays, family outings and almost any other occasion, special or not, always included Jack. His friendship with Lucy blossomed. By the time Lucy turned 17, five years later, Jack was 29 and still looking for a wife. One day Lucy went to Catherine with an announcement.

"Jack and I love each other," she said. "We want to be married."

"Yes, I thought so," Catherine said, for she had always been Lucy's confidante and had been prepared for this eventuality. Charles, however, had been slow to see it coming. He knew Jack well by this time and respected him, but he was not prepared for any Chinese man to marry his daughter. Both he and Catherine were afraid that their grandchildren would be badly treated by a society where hatred toward Chinese was mounting and where interracial marriage was frowned upon. Before they would consent, Jack had to promise that he would provide a proper house for his family in a good neighborhood, not in the back of a store as many Chinese did. By then Jack had put aside enough money to do it, so he could make that promise. Lucy and Jack were married in June of 1876.

JACK'S HERB BUSINESS GREW, as did his family. Lucy and Jack had two sons and then a daughter – Hang Wah (later called Hank) in 1877, Robert in 1878 and Helen in 1880. After Hang Wah, the couple decided to give the children English names to help them become Americans. By the time Hang Wah was born Jack began to increase his income by paying regular visits to the small farms and orchards that surrounded San Jose and were beginning to take the place of the old wheat fields and grazing land. Out on these farms, Chinese workers were living at least part of the year to plant and harvest strawberries and vegetables, and to prune and graft and pick fruit in the orchards. Sometimes they had no convenient way to get to town, so by making visits, Jack doubled his total business over a three-year period. The farmers and orchard owners liked to see him come because he made their workers happier and healthier. He also attended to the needs of railroad workers again as the Southern Pacific Co. extended its tracks up and down the Santa Clara Valley.

On the farms and in the railroad work camps, where the Chinese were known as dedicated and skillful workers, there were few problems with harassment. But in the town, where out-of-work white men, especially Irishmen, tended to congregate in saloons and look for someone to blame, it was another matter. There, anti-Chinese feeling began to foment. In July 1877 there was a bad incident in San

Francisco: A white mob of thousands rampaged through Chinatown shooting Chinese bystanders and even tried to burn the docks and ships that had been bringing Chinese into the country.

Late one night a few weeks later, Jack was riding home in his buggy from visiting a farm when he saw in the distance what looked like a torchlight parade headed south on First Street. Fearing the worst, he turned onto Second Street so as to avoid running straight into them. As he passed San Antonio Street and stopped to look west, his heart froze. "Chinese Out" signs declared the purpose of the march. Jack gave the horse a sharp flick with the reins and got home as quickly as he could. He was glad his children were too young to see this demonstration of fear directed at them.

More such parades and rallies would follow. Then in 1879 California passed a law forbidding any corporation to hire a Chinese person. Many left the state after that, either returning to China or migrating to the eastern United States.

In the midst of all this anti-Chinese sentiment, something happened that buoyed Jack's spirits. One day in 1880 his neighbor, Dr. Enderle, sent Jack a patient he had been unable to treat successfully. This was a first for Dr. Enderle, and it showed that after knowing Jack for 15 years, and finally acknowledging Jack's role in Lucy's recovery from scarlet fever, he was willing to give herbal medicine some credibility.

The patient he referred was a man named Charles McKiernan, known to nearly everyone in the valley as Mountain Charley. Charley had been suffering from persistent severe headaches. Dr. Enderle was pretty sure that these pains stemmed from a serious incident years before, but his note of referral was cryptic:

I treated Charley at the time of his bear encounter and again about a year later, when he was having intolerable headaches. I successfully treated an abscess in his head at that time. Now the headaches have come back, and nothing I try seems to work. Maybe you can help.

"Don't get scared when I take off my hat," Charley said when he walked into Jack's store. His forehead was kind of pushed in, a horrible-looking depression about four inches in diameter. His left eye was missing. Jack didn't see how anyone could have survived such a wound, but there Charley was walking around twenty-six years later.

"What in the world happened?" Jack asked, aghast.

"Enderle didn't tell you? Oh, me and a friend was out hunting near my property – you know, up in the Santa Cruz Mountains. We come upon a big female grizzly bear with two cubs. I seen this bear several times before. We tried to sneak up on the bear, but she got 'round behind us and got me in a hug. I guess I wasn't so smart about it."

Jack had him lie down and got him relaxed on his couch. Then he found some good pressure points around his head and neck and gave him about a half-hour treatment. When he was through, he gave Charley some breathing techniques to use and told him to start drinking tea made from a rosemary sprig and three leaves of betony.

Two weeks later, Charley came into the store and said Jack had greatly relieved his headaches. He visited several times a year after that for an acupressure treatment, and every winter thereafter Jack and Lucy got a nice gift of venison from him around Christmastime.

DURING ALL THIS TIME, Jack's best friend among the white businessmen was John Heinlen. John had brought his family to San Jose in the early 1850s, when he was thirty-seven years old. He had bought farmland and grazing land in Coyote, south of town, and more in Kings and Fresno counties, and he had been successful in ranching and real estate. But he and his wife Jane never joined the usual social networks in town – they kept their family life private.

Jack first met Heinlen in 1869 after the Methodist Episcopal Church burned downtown. He was one of the first to contribute to the rebuilding, and he asked others to contribute and to reaffirm the church's statement of support for the Chinese. Jack admired that and decided to cultivate his friendship. Heinlen had a dour, stoic look about him, with gray hair and big ears. He was not an easy man to get close to, but no one Jack ever knew was as straight with him, or a better man of his word. If John Heinlen promised something, you could take it to the bank. Soon after they met, Heinlen gave Jack some useful advice and references that helped relocate Chinatown to Vine Street after the fire.

Angelo Heinlen, John and Jane's first California-born son, was in the first graduating class of San Jose High School in 1870, and Jack attended his graduation ceremony. Soon after that, Angelo invited Jack to visit the family's farm in Coyote, where they had built a bunkhouse of Chinese design to accommodate their Chinese workers. That visit got Jack started on his "herbalist circuit" trips, which eventually included dozens of farms and orchards, so he owed much of his business success to the Heinlens.

For a few years Jack often saw Angelo or one of his brothers on the family's Coyote property. When he was finished tending to the needs of the workers, Jack would look for Angelo and spend a little time with him talking about how the Heinlens were managing the ranch and how the Chinese workers were contributing.

Jack held the Heinlens in high regard for two reasons. First, it was such people as John Heinlen and Pastor Dunn and the Graysons who stood like bedrock when public opinion mounted against the Chinese, demonstrating that the hysterical mobs did not represent everybody in white America. The other reason was that in the late 1880s, John Heinlen, a German by birth, personally saved the Chinese community from annihilation. It was Jack Lee who persuaded him to do it.

Heinlen's involvement started one morning in late 1880 after another torchlight meeting downtown that included some vitriolic anti-Chinese rhetoric. Jack saw Heinlen walking along Santa Clara Street, and they stopped to chat for a moment. Out of the blue, Heinlen asked Jack to come to his house that afternoon. This invitation was so unexpected – rarely had Jack been invited alone as a guest to a white family's house – that he could do nothing but accept.

Heinlen was not usually a man for small talk. But when Jack sat down with him in his house on North First Street later that day, Heinlen began telling Jack about his childhood in Ohio.

"My parents sacrificed to bring us to America," he said. "In the old country it was hard to move out of your native town. But we were starving, so they had to leave. My father's idea was that in America, everyone was accepted. But there was no welcome mat laid out for us. We prospered because we worked; but as Germans, we weren't considered 'real Americans.' There were anti-German rallies in Ohio and Indiana. I even saw German effigies hanged. They broke up German church services.

"I brought my family west partly because the weather's nicer, but also the society seemed more open to newcomers here. So we've worked hard and done well, but we're still seen as 'those Germans.' I can feel it. We don't get into the social registry. Not that I care about that."

"You're lucky," Jack said. "You look just like the rest of them. I'll always be an outsider here because of the way I look. I can only hope things will get better for my children."

"I know, but that's why I asked you here," John said. "I've been following what's been happening back East, and also here in San Jose. I think there's going to be a new restriction on Chinese immigration to this country, and if that happens, there's bound to be a local effect. Powerful people here in town are already saying Chinatown has to be wiped out – that it's a blight on the community. They want to modernize the city, give it a face-lift; and besides, the Chinese don't look like 'real Americans' to them. If enough people get that idea, you might not be able to stop them."

"You're saying we might be forced out? How could they do that?"

"They could do it. It just takes political will. But you could push back. My son Goethe is a lawyer in San Francisco. He might be able to help you."

"I'm afraid we don't have money for lawyers, Mr. Heinlen. And if we had to move, I don't know where we would go. We don't even have the rights of citizens."

"There's another possibility," Heinlen said. "You could move Chinatown again. The City Council wants the land at Market and San Fernando because it's right in the middle of downtown. But they might not object to your moving somewhere else. I'm not telling you this because it's going to happen right away, but just because you need to be prepared. And to let you know that I'm on your side. Understood?"

Jack nodded and thanked him. His news was troubling. Jack was gratified that a white man had chosen to give him this kind of information and support. But he had no idea what to do about it.

Chapter 8

To CELEBRATE AMERICAN INDEPENDENCE DAY in 1881, Eli and Rebecca Foard gathered their growing extended family at the West Side ranch for a midsummer feast. It became an annual tradition. Catherine and Charles always came, along with Jeffrey Foard and his family, John and Lincoln Grayson, and, of course, Jack and Lucy Lee and their children. Sometimes a few neighbors would be invited as well, bringing with them pies and vegetable dishes, and thick cuts of beef were roasted in the stone fireplace in back of the house. Eli and Rebecca reveled in the conviviality.

At the first such gathering, the teenaged Grayson boys had a fine time demonstrating horsemanship to their young nephews. Santa Clara Valley wines were served. But late in the day, while the kids raced around the yard trying to prolong the last light of day, the talk on the Foards' front porch about freedom and independence inevitably led to the continued threats of repression against the Chinese population.

"The *Mercury* never has anything good to say about the Chinese," Catherine complained. "Anything to do with Chinatown or a Chinese person is always put in a negative light. J.J. Owen definitely has it in for Chinatown."

"What about the light tower?" Eli asked. "It's supposed to be the only one of its kind. Should be a great addition to that part of town."

"It's Owen's idea, and if he's for it, it can't be good for us," Jack said. "I think he's just trying to show us up. Chinatown will never be good enough for those people."

"You're probably right about that, Jack," Charles said. "Owen's trying to make it look like a promotion for San Jose, but I think he knows full well what's going to happen. With that big light shining on everything, Chinatown is going to look even shabbier, and then he can start saying that Chinatown needs to go."

"That's what John Heinlen warned me about," Jack said. "But where could we go?"

"I don't know," Charles said, "but I'm just saying that's the way the wind is blowing. It wouldn't hurt to make a plan."

It wasn't long before Jack began to see the effects of the modernization ideas that John Heinlen had described. And sure enough, the light tower played a central role. The city finally yielded to the pressure of Owen's campaign and put aside $4,000 for the tower. Its foundation was laid a month later at Santa Clara and Market streets, just a block or two north of Chinatown. On December 13, 1881, the lights were lit for the first time. It was spectacular – the whole town turned out. Atop a 237-foot tower glared six carbon arc lights providing 24,000 candlepower, powered by something called George's Dynamo, a generator at the San Jose Brush Co. a few blocks away. By later standards it wasn't all that bright, but for the time it was impressive enough and could be seen from miles away. People began calling San Jose the first electrified city west of the Rockies. Whether this was true or not, that huge tower started to give people the idea that San Jose was going big-time and that downtown needed to be improved. The rickety, ramshackle buildings in Chinatown did not figure into their plans.

Then came the Chinese Exclusion Act that Heinlen had warned about. President Chester Arthur signed it in

May 1882. It stopped new Chinese workers from coming into the United States for years thereafter. And, as Heinlen had predicted, instead of resolving the issue it tended to inflame people further. Violence cropped up in cities across the West over the next few years, and Chinese communities were repeatedly terrorized by those bent on expelling the remaining Chinese.

In San Jose, the move to force the Chinese out of downtown Chinatown began in earnest. A short time after the Exclusion Act was signed, the Rinaldo Bros. cigar factory put the word out that it would employ only "first class white labor." Other factories and canneries followed suit. Then a new City Hall site was chosen just across Market Street from Chinatown. In addition, the parishioners at St. Joseph's Church, just to the north, began to get vocal in their complaints about being so close to the "smells and sin." In 1886, with the City Hall set for completion the following year, the City Council started its clampdown by passing an ordinance that condemned laundries in wooden buildings – a law aimed squarely at the laundries in Chinatown. Every article about the Chinese in Owen's *Daily Mercury* tended to have negative connotations. Articles called them "little brown men" and "John Chinaman," tending to depersonalize what was happening. In essence, the Chinese were considered fair game.

It was inevitable that Charles Grayson would have to become involved to counteract these anti-Chinese activities. As editor of the *San Jose Weekly Journal*, the mostly widely read daily newspaper in town, Charles had been widely criticized when he editorialized against the Chinese Exclusion Act before it was passed. He never changed his stand, but in subsequent years he had tried not to take deliberately inflammatory positions on his editorial page. At the same time, he would not allow the defamatory rhetoric that appeared in his rival papers masquerading as news.

When the anti-laundry law was passed, Catherine confronted him. "We have half-Chinese grandchildren and a Chinese son-in-law," she said. "Are you going to stay silent and let this go on?"

Charles had no answer. He had been putting off a decision that would put him in direct opposition to widely held public sentiment, but now it seemed he would have to. He thought of Frank Murdoch, his mentor from nearly 30 years before. Murdoch had sold his *San Jose Telegraph* to J.J. Owen in 1861 but later returned to newspapering when he established the *San Jose Weekly Patriot* as a pro-Union, anti-slavery paper. Murdoch had been dead for five years, but Charles knew what he would say if her were alive: "Be true to yourself. Do what you know is right."

The day after the anti-laundry ordinance was passed, Charles rode out to the West Valley to see his father-in-law, Eli. Now 77, Eli Foard spent most of his days sitting with Rebecca on their front porch, reading and receiving occasional visitors while their 37-year-old son, Jeffrey, ran the horse ranch with the help of several hired hands. Eli still took an occasional ride around his property or up into the mountains.

Sitting down for coffee with Eli, Charles laid out the problem he was facing. "I have to think this could ruin my business," Charles told Eli. "If just a few advertisers desert, or a few good printing customers ... I don't know."

"I don't know why you're *hesitating*," Rebecca said, bringing a pot of tea out to the porch. "Everybody knows about Jack and Lucy. If you don't stand up for them, nobody's going to have any respect for you."

"Rebecca has a knack for boiling things down," Eli said with a crooked grin, his raspy voice growing faint. He cleared his throat, took another sip of coffee and set the cup down. "But I think she's right, as usual. You might make a few folks unhappy, but in the long run it's your integrity that'll see you through. You have a lot of friends in the county, people who know you and what you stand for. They'll support you." He squinted at Charles, the wrinkles framing his clear blue eyes, and nodded, winking.

The night after Charles published his editorial against the laundry ordinance, he spent the night in his shop with his sons Lincoln and John, all three of them armed with shotguns. Just after midnight a gang of four riders galloped past, hurling rocks at the windows. They broke three panes and a small fire started when a lamp overturned, but the Graysons ran the gang off with two shotgun blasts in the air. Within a week, four advertisers withdrew their business, but circulation grew. The newspaper got a few angry letters, but the lost revenue was soon recouped through higher circulation.

The push to get Chinatown out of the way came to a head in 1887. Mayor C.W. Breyfogle and the City Council issued an order on March 25 declaring Chinatown a public nuisance. The *San Jose Daily Mercury* kept up the onslaught with stories of crime and debauchery committed by Chinese, while Charles's *Journal* took the opposite view. It was evident by then that the city wanted to use public sentiment to wipe Chinatown off the map. The only question was how long it would take.

ON THE MORNING OF MAY 4, Clayton Phaneuf sat in a dark corner of the dingy saloon on South First Street where he sometimes worked. The place wasn't open yet, so the front doors were locked; and Phaneuf, thirty-nine, sat there alone, drinking whisky. It was not odd behavior for Phaneuf, who often started drinking by 11 a.m., but today was a special day. Along with most of the town, Phaneuf had been following the growing pressure being put on Chinese workers. He was well aware of the Chinese Exclusion Act and had been at some of the torchlight rallies that had led to San Jose's anti-laundry ordinance. It was high time, he thought. The doom of Chinatown was overdue. Everyone wanted it gone. He could smell the place even from here. When it was gone, the Chinese would have to move out. He wanted them out.

In the little storage shed in back of the saloon, Phaneuf had put the things he would need. It wasn't complicated – just some matches, a bottle of kerosene and a few rags to help the blaze along. These were what he had used 18 years before, when he set the fire that burned down the Methodist church. Those Chinese-loving do-gooders deserved it. What business did pagan Chinese have in a good Christian American town?

As an hour ticked by and then another, Phaneuf finished most of his bottle. He knew that just before 3 p.m. most of Chinatown would desert Ah Toy Alley and gather at the Chew Kee gambling house for the regular announcement of weekly lottery winners. Finally, about a quarter to three, he put a cork in the bottle and set out.

When everyone else went to hear the lottery announcement, Jack Lee usually locked his herb shop and took a half-hour nap in the back. His children were in school and he knew Lucy was busy at home. It was a good time to get refreshed for the busy evening hours when he went out to the farms. By the time the flames started to lick at the sides of his building, he was sound asleep. He didn't even hear the shouts in the street.

Charlie Wong heard them. He was in his laundry and stepped outside to see fire and smoke at the opposite end of Chinatown. The Chinese had their own volunteer firefighters with ladders and buckets, and several turned out; but the flames were spreading too fast through the wooden buildings. The city firemen also came but could barely keep the fire contained to Chinatown. The water was coming out of their hoses in a pitifully thin stream.

Charlie was pretty sure his wife and kids were either at home or in school, but he checked a few stores to make sure. Then, in the midst of the fire, he thought of Jack Lee. Jack had not spoken to him for the last twenty-two years, since Jack and Ah Bing left to work for the railroad. He didn't know why. At first he thought it probably had something to do with Ah Bing's death up in the mountains, but after a few years he stopped thinking about it. As he looked at the flames starting to consume the north end, he found himself running toward Jack's shop. When he got there, the building was burning and there was a lot of smoke around the entrance. Charlie pulled up his shirt to protect his nose and mouth and went in, shouting to anyone who might be inside.

A few moments later, he found Jack alone in a small back room and trapped by a collapsed wall. By then Jack was awake, saw Charlie and yelled for help. Charlie knew he couldn't move the fallen timbers by himself, so he went back into the alley and pulled another man in to help. Together, they moved enough debris aside to clear a space for Jack to climb out.

As the two men lifted Jack through the narrow opening they had created, another burning timber fell against Jack, knocking him down and pinning his right leg. They were all choking on the smoke.

"Get out," Jack said. "You'll die in here." But Charlie wedged himself against a wall and used both his legs to shove the timber off Jack's leg. They helped Jack up again and staggered toward the front door, barely getting into the street before the front wall caved in.

The three of them were pretty scraped up, bruised and sooty, but Jack only had one burn, on his left arm. All of them still coughing, Charlie took Jack by the other arm and led him out of Ah Toy Alley toward Market Street, away from the fire.

Jack and Charlie were breathing hard, struggling to clear their lungs of the smoke. "I was taking a nap," Jack gasped, speaking in Chinese. "Then I woke up in a fire."

Charlie and Jack stared at each other, and then they just stood and watched Chinatown go up in flames. After he had his breath back, Jack said, still in Chinese, "Thanks for getting me out, Charlie. You saved my life. You were the last one I ever expected to come."

Charlie nodded sadly and said nothing for a minute or two. Then, his face blackened with soot and tears starting down his cheeks, Charlie said, "Why did you cut me off?"

Jack stared at him, amazed. "Don't you know?" he said. "It was Ah Bing. Your *pai gow* cheating at Ah Chong's made trouble for him. If it wasn't for that, Ah Bing would still be alive. You knew he was going to get hurt. Why did you do it?"

"Wait, you got it completely wrong. Didn't he ever tell you?"

"Tell me what?"

"He was ashamed to tell you, I think. He looked up to you like a big brother. I wasn't cheating, and neither was Ah Chong. Ah Chong was a mean guy, but Ah Bing and his friend had the cheating scheme. They were skimming off people right and left."

"You're lying," Jack said. "That doesn't make any sense at all. Why would he make up a big lie about it just for me?"

"Don't you see?" Charlie asked. "He was setting up a defense because he knew they were going to get caught sooner or later. He told me they would. But he had an escape plan for when it happened. Ah Bing was smart. He had plenty of money stashed somewhere. And when he escaped, he didn't want you to think he was a cheater – he had too much respect for you. So he made up a cover story, so you would think he was a good guy."

Jack stared at him, finally comprehending. "Why didn't you tell me this when he first left town?" he said at last.

"Oh, well. You two were such close friends. It was a good thing to see. I didn't want to tell you something bad about him you wouldn't believe anyway. And I thought he'd tell you about it someday."

After a while, it all made sense to Jack. How could he have been so wrong? Maybe Ah Bing had planned to tell him the truth someday; but then he died, so he never did. For a long time, Jack just stood with Charlie and watched vacantly as Chinatown burned.

Downtown Chinatown died in that fire and never rose again. So the white merchants, the real estate people and the City Council that served them got what they wanted. But San Jose's Chinese were not going away, and as their old neighborhood lay in rubble, the fight for a new one was already getting started.

Chapter 9

JACK'S FIRST SURPRISE after the fire came in an envelope that arrived at his house from Mountain Charley McKiernan. It contained $785 that Charley had collected from mountain people, with an instruction from Charley to "Give it to the people who need it." Jack split it among the benevolent associations that had been trying to find homes for displaced people in the Woolen Mills Chinatown.

Then, three days after the fire, Jack went out to John Heinlen's house on First Street to get his advice on what to do next.

Over the years since Jack first met John, they had grown closer. Four years ago, Heinlen's son Angelo, by then a leading citizen of Kings County and Jack's friend for 14 years, had died in an accident while driving cattle. John had called on Jack to give him the news personally and to ask him to take care of Angelo's body. Jack had gone with John and Jane to Oak Hill Cemetery when they buried their son.

"I've been expecting you," John said when he answered the door, inviting Jack to sit in his parlor furnished with Irish cut glass, oriental carpets and Italian paintings. "You need a new Chinatown. I have land and money. So I have a proposal for you and a question."

He described how some years before he had bought land between Fifth and Seventh streets north of Jackson Street, land that was currently under an informal lease for pastureland. He had a plan to spend $30,000 to build and lease to the Chinese a collection of buildings – perhaps 20 or so to start – built of brick to be fire-resistant and designed to provide a long-term home and business center for the Chinese of San Jose. He would need to have lease agreements signed before starting construction, and he would take on the burden of getting the city's approval.

"My question is this: Will the Chinatown businessmen do business with me?" Heinlen asked, looking at Jack with raised eyebrows.

Jack stared at him for a few minutes, nodding and considering the idea. "You're right – we need a new Chinatown," he said finally. "I think all of us know they won't let us build again downtown. I think the Chinese would do business with anyone who presented a good offer. This would make a lot of money for you. What do we get?"

"You get your Chinatown built, and I talk the city into approving it. That's not going to be easy." Jack nodded again.

"But there's another part of this, and I need your help with that, too," Heinlen went on. "I want in on the downtown redevelopment too, where Chinatown used to be. The land belongs to the Reed brothers. As it stands now, the political pressure on Mayor Breyfogle and the council would be strong enough to keep the Reeds from doing business with me. Folks are dead set against any new Chinatown, and the Reeds wouldn't want to be connected with that."

"So what do you want me to do?"

"Talk to your wife's grandfather."

"You mean Eli?"

"Eli Foard came West in a wagon party. It's pretty well known that he was acquainted with James Reed and that they arrived about the same time. Reed's dead, but Eli might be able to influence his sons."

Jack was shaking his head before Heinlen finished. "I don't think you understand," he said. "Eli doesn't have anything to say to the Reed family, ever. He never wants to talk about all that stuff with the Donner disaster."

"Just talk to him," Heinlen countered. "If he says no, then fine. But try to get him to understand that having a new Chinatown may depend on this. It's going to affect his great-grandchildren. Without Eli, I think Breyfogle will be an obstacle for both developments."

Jack was quite aware that John Heinlen would reap a tidy profit from these arrangements, so he was under no illusion that Heinlen's motives were entirely altruistic. Still, it was clear to both of them that no other landowner in town would dream of opposing community sentiment by cooperating with the Chinese population in such a way. The Heinlen family's reclusiveness left them free to act as they wished, since they had no social standing to lose. Jack told Heinlen he would give the new Chinatown his full endorsement with the other Chinese merchants. As for convincing Eli to speak to the Reed brothers, he made no promises.

CHARLES C. REED WAS THIRTY-NINE at the time of the downtown Chinatown fire. He was married with two children, ten and fourteen. His brother Thomas was thirty-four and single. Both had grown up in San Jose and done well, confident in their business abilities and well provided for from their father's estate. Together they owned and managed extensive real estate holdings in and around San Jose. Although Charles and Thomas had nothing against the Chinese, having done business with them for years, once it was clear that Chinatown was gone, they were eager to see that newly vacant land start to turn a profit again.

When Eli Foard wrote requesting a meeting, Charles Reed was shocked. Neither he nor his brothers had ever met Foard, and they never expected to. They knew there was bad blood between Foard and their father. They had no desire to renew any old animosities between their family and the former county supervisor. Neither Charles Reed nor his brother could imagine what Eli would want to see them about.

Spring rain clouds were bringing a heavy mist down on San Jose on May 12 when Charles and Thomas Reed sat inside their glass-fronted business office on Second Street and waited for Eli Foard's arrival. They watched as he pulled up in his buggy, eased his seventy-eight-year-old body out onto the muddy street and hitched his horse to a post, then shook the water off his hat and entered the building.

A secretary showed Eli into the inner office where Charles and Thomas both rose to shake hands with the old man, who was still brushing raindrops off his jacket.

"Eli Foard," Eli said, nodding gravely.

"Charles Reed," Charles said. "My brother Tom. Sit down, Mr. Foard."

An uncomfortable silence followed as Eli found a straight chair and slowly placed himself in it, leaning heavily on a walking stick as he did so.

"Do you know what I came here about?" Eli asked. Charles and Thomas shook their heads. Eli looked at the floor, letting a few more awkward seconds go by. "You have some land, over at Market and San Fernando. Mr. Heinlen would like to use his money to develop that land. And yet he finds that you are reluctant to accept his proposition. Do I have my facts straight?"

"Are you part of Mr. Heinlen's business proposition, Mr. Foard?" Thomas asked.

"Let me be straight with you," Eli said. "I'm only interested for the sake of my family. I have no financial interest in this. I don't even know Heinlen very well – only by reputation, really. But my granddaughter is married to a Chinese man – you may know Lucy's husband, Jack Lee. He's a fine, upstanding businessman. He and the other people in Chinatown need a place to do business – a place to live, a lot of them. Heinlen wants to provide that. Some people are against it. I don't know how you feel about it, but I think people, citizens of this town, deserve a place to live."

"We're not standing in the way of the Chinese, Mr. Foard," Charles said. "Heinlen is free to deal with the Chinese any way he wants."

"But you're afraid of what will happen if you make Heinlen part of this downtown development. You're afraid people will connect you with the new Chinatown."

"You've got to understand, we're only looking at it from a business point of view," Thomas said. "We want to get our land back into productive use – that's all – and as fast as possible. We're not making any money while it sits with burned-out buildings on it."

"I know, I know," Eli said. "But whatever you do over there, you're going to need city approval. I can help with that."

"How?" Charles asked.

"I can talk to Breyfogle. He has strong influence over the council. Once he sees that this downtown plan can go hand-in-hand with the new Chinatown, I think he'll come down in favor of both. He's as interested as you are in getting that downtown block rebuilt soon. Those burned-out shacks don't look good right now sitting next to his new city hall."

"But why would he go against the town that way? Most people are against a new Chinatown."

"The public is fickle," Eli said. "They'll be riled up about something one day and not care a whit the next. Breyfogle knows that. Leaders can be a powerful influence over opinion. I think he'll make the right decision."

Charles and Thomas looked at each other, then out the window for a few moments, then back at Eli. "Would you like some whisky, Mr. Foard?" Thomas asked.

"Not just now. But there's something else I need to ask. Did you know your father and I came west at the same time?"

"He mentioned it a time or two," Charles said, fidgeting.

"Nothing good to say about me, I assume."

"Actually it was the opposite," Thomas said. "I never knew he knew you at all until I was grown up. Then a few weeks before he passed on I was asking him about the wagon party and all, about the reason all the people died. I was up there in the mountains with the rest of them but just little at the time, so I barely remember it at all. But one of the things he said was that if he and Donner had listened to you, they wouldn't have taken the southern route. That was the only time I ever heard him tell anyone he made the wrong decision. I think he felt bad about it, but had a hard time saying it."

Eli nodded slowly. "Humph," he said finally. "Well that's really something. Humph. Say, if you've still got that whisky, I think I'll have some."

THE SUN WAS SINKING low when Eli pulled his buggy into the barn at his West Side ranch that evening. Rebecca came off the front porch, calling Jeff to help Eli get his horse unhitched and put away.

"I can still unhitch a horse, for God's sake," Eli shouted.

"I know you can, but why do it when you can have your son do it for you?" Rebecca answered.

When Jeff arrived to take charge of the horse, Eli and Rebecca joined hands and walked slowly up to the house.

"Well, did you get things straightened out?" Rebecca asked.

"I hope so."

"Did you talk to the Reeds?"

"Yeah."

"Are they agreeable?"

"I guess they are."

"Did you talk to Breyfogle?"

"Yeah."

"Well, what did he say?"

"He'll go along, eventually. But he's got to let the uproar die down first."

"What uproar?"

"The uproar over the new Chinatown. Heinlenville, they're calling it now. People are upset. He's going to wait for it to simmer down before he lets it go through." Eli sat back into his easy chair. "Can you get me a drink, 'Becca?" She was still standing.

"How did you talk him into it?"

"I just took Heinlen's downtown plan over to him and laid it out. I said it already had the Reeds' approval and they could go right into construction. I said if it didn't get approved, months might go by with nothing done, and no tax revenue coming from it. And I said Heinlen would only go ahead if he got the approval for new Chinatown as well. And as a capper, I implied Charles would endorse him for another term in the *Journal*."

"You did *what*? How could you promise a thing like that?"

"I didn't promise. I just implied. Charles knows the right decision to make. And when the times come, if he endorses somebody else, maybe I'll be dead anyway."

Rebecca shook her head. "You men," she said in disgust.

AFTER HIS MEETING WITH HEINLEN, Jack tracked down as many Chinatown merchants as he could. He found eleven who were willing to do business with Heinlen, and on June 20 they all went to see him together. Heinlen told them he had already filed official paperwork with the city to build the new buildings at Fifth and Jackson. They all agreed that Heinlen would build thirteen one-story brick buildings as dwellings and four one-story buildings for lease as stores, each of these to be divided into six rooms. Also, he would build several two-story brick buildings to be leased as stores and restaurants with living quarters on the second floors. The storekeepers all signed long-term leases.

Everyone expected a fight to get the new Chinatown built, but nothing like what actually happened. The citizens of San Jose threw a collective fit. Two thousand people massed on June 8 at Fifth and Jackson, the building site, to protest. The project was denounced in a petition as "injurious to private property adjacent thereto, dangerous to the health and welfare of all citizens who live and have homes in its vicinity and a standing menace to both public and private morals, peace, quiet and good order ...." The protesters decided to form the San Jose Home Protection Association to fight the plan. More boisterous meetings were held featuring bonfires and a brass band playing patriotic numbers.

Again, the *Mercury*, now owned by Charles Shortridge, and Charles Grayson's *Journal* took opposite positions, the *Mercury* opposing Heinlen and the *Journal* supporting him.

Public outrage focused on John Heinlen himself. After the first big demonstration, seven city officials visited his home to emphasize to him that he would be the most unpopular man in town if he went ahead with his new Chinatown. This was surely the weakest argument to make to John, stubborn and indifferent to popularity as he was. During the weeks after this visit, anti-Chinatown demonstrators repeatedly massed in the street in front of his house to denounce him.

Heinlen's son Goethe, a lawyer, left his San Francisco practice to help his family deal with the crisis. He argued at council meetings that property values would not suffer if Chinatown were built. When someone asked him if he would like to live next to a Chinese person, Goethe answered, 'Yes, rather than next door to many Irish.' " Predictably, this remark sparked even more outrage. The City Council voted to allow no materials in the building of their new city hall unless they were made by white labor.

But the Heinlens' patience paid off. Although a judge ordered a temporary injunction preventing any building on the property because of the previous lease, he eventually had to rescind the injunction because the lease had never been put in writing. A crew of white and Chinese workers began laying bricks at Fifth and Jackson late that summer. About the same time, new commercial buildings started to go up downtown, across from City Hall, where old Chinatown had been. Early the following year Jack became the first merchant to move into the new Chinatown. Most white people called it Heinlenville, but the Chinese called it *San-Doy-Say Tong Yun Fow*, or San Jose Chinatown. Jack leased one of the buildings and re-established his herb shop and undertaking parlor there, at 32 Cleveland Avenue, next to the Quong Wo Chan store. The entire neighborhood was fenced, mainly to protect the Chinese.

Several hundred Chinese followed the lead of the eleven businessmen, most of them merchants with families, as well as district associations such as those of the Yeung Wo, Sui Hing and Sze Yup. They moved from the run-down Woolen Mills Chinatown a few blocks away that had served as a temporary neighborhood after the fire downtown. In 1888 the Chinese in Heinlenville built a large temple with $2,000 in donations to the district associations. The *Ng Shing Gung* temple was furnished with carvings and fixtures ordered from China. They had a place where they felt comfortable and reasonably safe. But not until decades had passed did the residents finally feel secure enough to leave the gate to Heinlenville open at night.

The Yellow Peril movement was far from over. In Jack Lee's lifetime he never saw full acceptance of the Chinese as equal to whites. But in the decades after the last fire, he saw Heinlenville prosper and he saw a generation of children, including his own, grow to adulthood there, get proper schooling and go out into the larger world to start their own families. It was a beginning that Jack thought developed in small ways – the individual courage of people like the Heinlen family and the Reverend Tom Dunn, and the relationship some in Chinatown worked to develop with them.

In his old age, Jack still thought often about his family in China and how he had neglected them. He never purged that sorrow from his heart. But in the end, he consoled himself with the thought that maybe at least Zhou Lin, the old herbalist, would think that his life had served a good purpose.

Epilogue to Part Three

THE CHILDREN OF JACK AND LUCY, who grew up during the era of most fervent anti-Chinese activity, continued to feel its effect all their lives. During their early years they were prevented by law from obtaining a public education in California. Later, they were allowed to attend public schools, but for years Jack and Lucy preferred to educate them at home and in the Chinese school in Heinlenville rather than subject them to the social stress of attending a white school during that era.

Jack Lee continued to provide herbal remedies, acupressure and undertaking for the Chinese community, in Heinlenville and in the orchards and fields, for 50 years, witnessing dozens of New Year celebrations, Moon Festivals every September and the *Da Jui*, a four-day festival celebrated in June during cherry season. He also saw prostitution and racketeering perpetuated by the tongs, the Chinese secret societies. He was in his store several times when Cleveland Avenue buildings would be shuttered for a tong war and gangsters would come through driving Buicks, spraying the street with gunfire.

Despite the adversities, the Lee children felt happy and safe growing up in San Jose. While they absorbed the Chinese traditions, even the gods of the *Ng Shing Gung*, the Temple of Five Deities, they considered themselves

Americans and continued to attend the Methodist Episcopal Church with Jack and Lucy. They especially loved the holiday celebrations in Heinlenville, because those always involved special food, costumes and strings of firecrackers set off during the parades.

After the fire of May 1887, Jack reestablished and cultivated his friendship with Charlie Wong. Their families often visited each other, and the children of the two families became best friends.

In June 1890, after contacting Ah Bing's relatives in China, Jack made a special trip, accompanied by his two sons, Charlie Wong and Charlie's son Chuen. The five of them boarded a train in San Jose and got off at the Colfax depot. They then walked to the waterfall near Cape Horn, to find Ah Bing's burial place. When Jack had found the spot, under two heavy rocks he had placed there, the five of them carefully unearthed Ah Bing's bones. After Jack had said prayers in Chinese and English, they placed the bones in a box, which was sealed up. Back in San Jose, Jack addressed the box to Ah Bing's family and mailed it, knowing that soon his friend would be resting peacefully with his ancestors.

PART FOUR
BITTER GRAPES

Chapter 1

MARCO CASTELLANI WOKE to the smell of baking rolls, the sounds of his mother working in the kitchen and the sun's early rays already warm on his orange-striped bedcovers. He was content and untroubled – his last happy morning for years to come. Later he relived that day in his mind a thousand times – a cruel day that would change his life forever, in ways he could not imagine.

Marco was eight years old then. He lived in the fertile, rolling hills of Italy's Abruzzo region, a few miles inland from the Adriatic coast, near the village of Controguerra, where the undulating land starts its gradual climb to the jagged crest of the Apennines, some 30 miles to the west. In a few minutes he could walk or run as he pleased from the vineyards by his family's little farmhouse to the top of a bald hill and see the sometimes snow-capped Gran Sasso d'Italia, the highest peaks on the Italian peninsula, on a ridge that separated and isolated Abruzzo from Rome on the western side. Then, standing about 700 feet above the sea, he could turn to the east and feast on the fine view of the blue Adriatic, its waters stretching far to the north, towards Marche, and to Molise to the south. On a warm day like this one, he would lie on that hill, bathing in the ocean air and staring at the sky, at the massive mountain range and then at the distant horizon, thinking of worlds beyond, of places far and strange.

The family's twenty acres of vineyards surrounded their house, a half-mile from the village, off the Via San Rocco. Soon his father would be taking the harvest of Montepulciano grapes to sell to one of three winery owners in the area. The grapes produced a ruby red, light-bodied wine that was coveted far beyond Controguerra. Marco's father always said that someday he would build a winery on the little knoll behind the house. There he would make his own Montepulciano D'Abruzzo, the finest to be had, and maybe a white wine as well. When Marco was old enough, he would become a winemaker himself. Until that time, the family would survive on the sale of the grapes, supplemented by what little Marco's mother could make from selling vegetables from her garden.

Marco loved his home. There was nothing better than a day in the vineyards, playing or helping his father prune the vines or harvest the grapes. Sometimes Marco would daydream and his father would remind him to get on with his chores. But he loved having a job to do, and he tried to do it well. When he worried about something, he kept it to himself. He usually found a solution on his own, even if it didn't always work as he hoped. He didn't much trust people outside the family. Most of all he trusted his father, Carlo Castellani, who was an optimistic and gregarious man, especially with his family. When Marco made a little joke, his father would laugh, and Marco confided in him. For Carlo, if the sun was shining, it was a beautiful day. If it was raining, then God had answered his prayers and was watering the vines.

As for Marco's mother, she often found fault with Marco when she was unhappy, and lately she was unhappy more often than not. Marco wanted her approval and thought he deserved it, but she rarely gave it.

As Marco dressed and then ate his breakfast – rolls and coffee-flavored milk – he thought of his plans for the day. Later on, he would help his father prepare the baskets for the grape harvest that would be coming soon. Today his father was already in the vineyards fussing over the grapes, gauging how soon they would be at their peak for harvesting.

Carlo Castellani inherited the twenty acres they lived on from his father, who had divvied up a larger parcel that came down from Marco's great-grandfather. Carlo, as the youngest of three sons, had received a little less than his two older brothers, but he was content. He spoke of the land as a trust, as the foundation on which he would build a future for the family. Someday, he said, it would be Marco's, and he must always treasure it, cultivate it, and use it for its highest purpose, which was to produce Abruzzo's best wine grapes. As long as Marco looked after his family and protected the land, God would always smile on him, his father said.

When Marco was seven, there had been a financial setback. His father had saved a little money, enough to carefully guard but not yet enough to build the winery. Apparently, in trying make the nest egg grow faster and get the winery built sooner, Carlo decided to put the money into an investment – something a few of the other winegrowers had heard about that had done well for some of their friends. A group of them went to a nearby city to see a man known as "the Spaniard," who was known to be a shrewd investor. Soon the money was gone. This man had disappeared, never to be seen again. These things Marco heard late at night when he crawled from his bed to listen by the kitchen door to the furtive, anguished conversations his parents had after the children had gone to bed. The incident lodged firmly in his mind, oozing to the surface every time he met a man who looked Spanish.

Since then a year had gone by. Marco's sister Sophia was five and his brother, Carlo Santino, was three. Their life was simple. On Sundays the family would go to mass at the little Church of the Conception in the village, where Marco had taken his first communion the year before. If he could, Marco would find Father Dorian after mass and tug on his cassock, just to get a genial reaction from the old priest. Father Dorian was Marco's favorite person outside the family. Sometimes, when he was allowed, Marco would walk into the village and then up to the Benedictine monastery on the hillside beyond the church. He might find Father Dorian there among the vines owned by the brothers, or in the winery itself, looking after the barrels or the fermentation vats. While Marco tagged along, Father Dorian would tell stories of Daniel in the lion's den, of David and Goliath, or maybe of Leonardo or Michelangelo and the popes.

After Marco's confirmation, it was Father Dorian who gave him the crucifix. It was a little bronze cross on a chain with the figure of the crucified Christ on the front like other crucifixes. Unlike some of the others he had seen, it was smooth and shiny on the back. Marco liked to take it out of his pocket and dangle it in the sun and let the reflected sun's rays wash over his face.

At home, at an age when his cousins were still spending most of their time playing, Marco liked to help his father in the vineyards, with the harvest in the fall and with the pruning in the winter. There was an art to it, his father said. Every vine had its own destiny, every branch its best pruning point. You should look for the vine to tell you how it should be trained and how it should be cut. The vine would know. Then when the leaves began to turn and the grapes were ready, again it was time to listen. In their own way, the grapes would say when their time had come. Carlo said over and over that Marco should stay alert for the signs God gave.

Always, there was music in the Castellani house. What voices his parents had. Lusty and brash, they would carry far out into the vineyards. Opera and folk songs, melodies of Carmella and Lolita, all of them in the air almost any time of day. On Sundays, Marco's uncles and aunts would come, bringing violins, clarinets and accordions. A long meal in the afternoon would be followed by naps and then music into the evening. Marco would sing along on the songs he knew. When the day was over and the relatives had gone, he would lie in bed, remembering the songs, wondering who had first sung them and where.

That day, the terrible day Marco would never forget, as he ran to the top of the nearby hill, nothing seemed amiss. The sky was blue except for a tight little mass of cumulus clouds far to the north. It was a normal warm September morning, and he could see the fat grapes ripening quickly on the vines as he skipped along between the rows. In a week or two, his father and uncles and cousins would all be out among the vines, filling their baskets with the heavy clusters. Then there would be money for the family, enough to get through another season and maybe a little left to start another fund for the new winery.

But something else was happening that day. Marco didn't understand it then, but later he read about it, trying to imagine why God would play such a mean trick on his family. High in the skies above the Apennines to the north, subfreezing air was advancing, moving steadily southward toward Abruzzo. At the same time, the warm air around Controguerra was becoming saturated with moisture from the ground. The two air masses were about to meet. Just after the family had finished the midday meal, Carlo stepped outside, looked up and stroked his chin. "It's going to blow," he said, looking at Marco. "Don't go running off."

Marco looked up and saw more puffy, white clouds accumulating high above. For miles around, hot, moist air was rising high, meeting the much colder air above and condensing, forming huge, water-filled thunderheads. Within an hour, the sun had gone and the sky had grown dark and everything outside had taken on a blue-green cast. A rumble of thunder told them what was happening aloft. At 20,000 feet the winds were already fierce as the cold, dense upper air relentlessly pulled the warmer currents upwards. As the moisture hit the freezing air, the first ice began to crystallize around tiny bits of salt and dust brought up from ground level. Caught by the wind, the crystals were whisked to 40,000 feet and then pushed violently downward, picking up more moisture as they plunged towards the surface. Then more rising air turned the ice clusters around, catapulting them back into the freezing heights. As the cycle repeated itself, the hailstones grew layer by layer each time they hit the upper air. And as the winds grew ever stronger with the violent collision of warm and cold, the black clouds of wind-blown ice grew to an enormous height, at the same time moving closer and closer to the ground. The winds aloft were now gusting to ninety miles per hour, carrying ice balls the size of lemons.

On the porch of the house, Marco stood beside his sisters and his father, watching the sky in silence. His mother busied herself covering her garden as the gusts increased. She shouted at them not to venture out. As for the vineyards, there was nothing to do but pray. Marco stood holding his crucifix, the little bronze one that Father Dorian had given him that he kept in his pocket, asking – pleading – for God to help.

For several minutes, a smattering of rain disturbed the dust on the ground, a few enormous drops leaving tiny puddles in the dirt. Marco held out his hand, smelling the pungent ozone and feeling the plops of a few heavy drops on his forearm. Then, when the clouds had fallen to within 200 feet of ground level, the first hail began to hit. Everyone retreated into the house, all of them left to stare through the one front window. At first the ice just rattled on the wooden porch roof, small pieces tapping harmlessly. Then the bigger stones came, blown in waves by the now-raging gale. For three, then four, then five, then six full minutes the deluge of ice thundered down in a deafening onslaught. As his brother and sister cringed, clinging to their mother, Marco just stared, nearly mesmerized.

In the vineyards the virgin clusters of grapes, first washed clean by the rain, took the full fury of the ice. The marble-size hailstones bruised the fruit. Then the larger, heavy balls began to fall, most of them tearing at the vines at seventy to ninety miles per hour. They crushed and ripped and tore until hardly a cluster was left intact. Then, as the hail subsided, the winds picked up, gusting to over 100 miles per hour, tearing the vines from their trellises and flattening them on the ground. When it was over, the grapes lay devastated.

When the gale died, Marco broke from his trance and looked for his father. Somehow, while Marco was still staring into the storm, his father had left the house and gone out into the rain. Running outside through the ice and into the vineyard, Marco saw him, his tall, white-shirted figure outlined clearly against the dark sky, which was now beginning to lighten at the horizon. Very slowly, he was working his way down the rows, stooping now and then to examine the grapes, taking the clusters in his hand, staring.

Marco ran to him, looking for reassurance. But Carlo's eyes were vacant, seeming not to notice Marco for several minutes as rain dripped from his hat. Then he stopped, looked at his son and suddenly stooped to grab him into a crushing embrace. He kissed Marco on his wet forehead, then on his cheek, his tears merging with the light raindrops.

After holding Marco for a minute, his father finally said, "It's all gone. We have nothing." Then he stood up, looked to the sky for several seconds and said, his voice breaking, "I'll have to get the pruning shears, up in the barn. We need to clean up." Then, as he started to walk slowly to the barn, he said a terrible thing, something that Marco had never heard from his father's mouth: "God has forsaken us."

Those were the last words he ever heard his father speak. A few minutes later there was a sound from the barn. Marco, still standing among the rows of ruined vines, saw his mother run to the barn, and then heard a terrifying shriek. He ran as hard as he could to the big barn door.

"He's fallen," his mother said. "Help me, Marco, help me carry him." His father lay unconscious, his figure draped oddly over the rungs of the tall ladder, now also fallen, the ladder that had led to the loft. With effort they lifted the ends of his father's slack body and carried him, haltingly, into the house. Marco would always remember the blood, pulsing in a small, steady stream from his father's head. Before they had him on the bed, his mother stooped and grabbed his shoulders. "Run to the doctor's house," she said. "Do you know where it is?"

"The little one with the fence by the church."

"Yes, that's it. Go, go now! Tell him to come!"

Marco found the house, but the doctor was gone. He would not be back until evening. By the time Marco returned to the house, his father was dead.

Chapter 2

"Marco, get your things. It's time to go." His mother was calling from the front porch.

"I'm coming."

Marco was sitting on the side of his bed. The mattress was stripped bare. Everything he owned was in a little canvass bag beside him. Nothing that the family valued was left inside the house. Outside, his brother and sister waited in a wagon as their uncle loaded their things onto the back and tied them down.

"Marco!"

Desperate and acting on impulse, Marco did what he had done hundreds of times before. Leaving his bag on the bed, he dashed for the back door. He ran out through the garden and vaulted the wall into the next vineyard. He ran through the rows as fast as he could go, over another wall and down a dirt path that led to a side road. Within two minutes he was headed down the main road that led to the village. He didn't stop. His lungs ached, but he didn't stop. He ran hard until finally he came to the outskirts of Controguerra. Only then, sweating and panting, did he stop to walk and look back. No one had followed him. He walked as fast as he could and then ran again, up the road to the Benedictine monastery that sat on the hillside near the church.

"Where's Father Dorian?" Marco, panting, asked the first monk he saw.

"Whoa, slow down, boy. What's the trouble, now?" They were standing outside the big door to the aging cellar, Marco panting.

"Father Dorian! I need to see Father Dorian!"

"Okay, let's just catch our breath a little. You're Marco?" Marco nodded. "Father Dorian is busy now. Can you tell me what's wrong?" Marco shook his head. The monk waited, looking at him, but Marco was silent. "All right. I'll go try to find Father Dorian. Here, sit down here and wait." He pointed to a chair hewn from a stump beside the door.

As the monk went off toward the church, Marco sat down and began to cry. After a few minutes, Father Dorian came striding over from the church. "Marco, Marco," he said, shaking his head as he approached. What's happened? I thought you would be on your way to Rome."

"I don't want to go to Rome," Marco said, the tears flowing faster now. "I won't go to Rome!" he sobbed, hardly able to get the words out. "I want to stay here! I want to stay here with you. I want to become a monk. I want to be a monk and work in the vineyard. Please, can't I stay here? Can't I be a monk? I'll be a good monk. I'll do anything you say. I know all about how to grow the vines. I can help. I want to stay here with you." He sobbed, wiping his tears away but unable to stop them.

Father Dorian knelt down in front of Marco and took him gently by the shoulders. "Marco, I think you would be an outstanding monk – one of the best," he said.

"Really?"

"Yes, really. But there are some other things we have to talk over first. Let's go inside."

The two of them went up the stairs and into the monastery. It was cool and dark inside, and Father Dorian led Marco into the kitchen and gave him a chair. He brought cups of water for both of them and sat down at the table next to Marco.

"Let's talk about this, you and I, just man to man," Father Dorian said. "If I were to take you as a monk here, what do you think your mother would say?"

"You could explain it to her."

"No, I don't think I could. I think that would be too hard to explain, even for me. Your mother has a plan for you, and right now, being a monk isn't in the plan. Do you know how old you have to be to become a monk?"

"No."

"A lot older than you are now. So even though I know you would make a fine monk, I wouldn't be able to have you here right now. Later on, in a few years, if you still want to be a monk, we could talk some more about it, okay?"

"No, I won't like it in Rome. I can't be a winegrower in Rome."

"I know, but that doesn't mean you won't be, someday. In a few years you'll be able to make your own decisions, but right now your mother needs you. You know what you are, don't you?"

"What?"

"You're the man of the house now. Your mother's going to need your help with a lot of things."

"Like what?"

"Like taking care of your brother and your sister. Like helping around the house. If you ask her, she'll tell you. You'll be a big help to her, I know. That's what a man does. Will you do that for me?"

Marco looked at him, the tears drying now, and nodded silently.

"Good. Now, I want you to do something else. Do you still have the crucifix I gave you?" Marco nodded. "That's good. Now every night when you say your prayers, I want you to hold that crucifix and remember the promise you made me. Will you do that?"

"Yes."

"All right, that's what I want to hear. Now let's get you back home before everyone gets too worried. I hope they haven't left for Rome without you."

Marco went along silently. But in his heart, that's exactly what he hoped his family had done.

FOR A WHILE MARCO TRIED, but he did not thrive in Rome. Shoehorned into the corner of a room in the cramped house of his great-uncle and great-aunt, he longed for the open hills where he had room to roam. Here the streets were narrow and dirty and there were no open fields. The place was crowded with bustling, shouting people who had no time for him. He seemed to be in people's way, with no haven to escape to. His mother, Maria, and the three children occupied a single room in the shabby house, and Marco couldn't find a good place to be alone. There was never any music. The sons of his great aunt, his much older cousins, were constantly coming and going. They seemed to barely tolerate Marco's presence. And the worst of it was that he had no friends. The neighborhood kids regarded him as a bumpkin and taunted him without mercy. He retreated to whatever private places he could find, venturing out only when he thought the nearby streets would be empty. He began leaving the neighborhood during the day, risking his mother's anger, just to escape to the public areas where he could get lost amid the crowds of people. He sought out places where music could be heard coming from the windows of houses. For hours he hung around piazzas and fountains and marketplaces, quietly watching the street scenes, returning home only at nightfall.

At night he lay, alone with his thoughts, wondering how things could have gone so wrong. He would never have another father. He would never again tend the vines that his father and grandfather had owned. He would never become a winemaker. His mother could not provide these things for him. He seemed to have no future.

In the midst of Marco's depression, he decided he could not trust God. He hated his life and he hated God for giving him such a life, for taking his father and leaving his mother. Why couldn't he have taken *her*? Why did it have to be *him*? One day, when Marco was sulking as he wandered through the Piazza Navona, he impulsively grabbed the crucifix in his pocket, the little bronze one Father Dorian had given him, the thing he had once treasured most, and threw it with all his strength into the Fontana del Moro and left it. He wanted nothing more to do with God.

His mother enrolled him in a school, but there it was even worse. Marco's mind wandered constantly, and he clashed with the teacher. Bullies ridiculed him. Soon he stopped going and walked the city instead, moving on whenever he felt he was being noticed. He came to know the avenues and alleyways of the city, becoming expert at keeping out of people's way. Since there was never enough food at home, he began to steal from the carts in the crowded markets. He argued often with his mother, and after a few weeks he refused outright to attend school and dared her to force him. Finally, exasperated, she relented.

When spring came, Marco was invited to return to Abruzzo to work on his uncle's dairy farm. He jumped at this chance and plunged himself into the work of the farm. Back in the country, where he had been happy, his mood brightened as he worked with his cousins and his uncles. But as the summer wore on, he felt a swelling sense of loss. At night, before he went to sleep, he wanted his father. He wanted back the times when they worked in the vineyards together. Often, he would softly cry himself to sleep. Sometimes he thought of his mother and felt bad for hating her, but not enough to want to return to Rome. When September came he begged to stay, to be part of the grape harvest, but his mother came for him and took him back to Rome with her. She had found a new school.

Before Marco started at the Santa Lucia school, his mother sat down with him at the table of the tiny kitchen in the house where they lived. "You are my oldest son," she said, taking him by the hands and fixing her eyes on him. "Look at me. Someday you will be the man of the house. You have to start getting ready now. We will depend on you for our living. You will have to find out how to get along in the world. I can't do it for you. You need to make friends and you need to learn the things that will help you later on."

The man of the house. That was what Father Dorian had said he was. But it was clear he wasn't – not the man of this house, anyway. He didn't want to hear any more, so he just nodded and told himself he wouldn't worry about it now.

In spite of his resentful mood, at the new school he began to feel more comfortable. The teacher took an interest in him and encouraged him in the areas where he fell short. And soon he found a friend – Antonio Fanelli. Antonio shared his love of the outdoors, and on their days off from school they ventured into the countryside, where Antonio had an older brother, Rodolfo, who owned an orchard. They would play all day in the orchard, eating good meals in Rodolfo's kitchen and making up outlandish new games. Sometimes Antonio's younger sister, Louisa, would come with them. Louisa was a fountain of energy and would bring her friend, Renata, and perhaps Antonio's youngest sister, Sara. By spring the five of them had become fast friends.

Over the next few years, Marco's life fell into a pattern. In the summer he would return to Abruzzo to work in the dairy and to learn the business of vineyards and winemaking. He would work hours for his Uncle Beppe, also stealing a visit to Brother Dorian in Controguerra whenever he had a day off to learn about the art of winemaking. Brother Dorian was always glad to tell Marco what he knew. When Marco finally told him that he had rejected God, Brother Dorian did not get angry. He just took his hands, looked into his eyes and said, "It's all right. You can reject God. But remember – he has not rejected you."

Marco began to confide in his uncles. As soon as he had matured enough to do a full day of man's work, when he was fourteen or so, he decided to learn everything he could about the growing of grapes. During the day he would think over everything he knew about some aspect, such as testing ripeness. Then at night he would corner Beppe and get him to fill in the gaps in his knowledge. Late at night he would write what he had learned in a journal.

In the fall Marco would return to school in Rome. At last his mother had found the family a small apartment where they had more room for themselves and where Maria could earn money selling home-baked goods. Marco would renew his friendship with Antonio and Louisa, they would all tell about their summer adventures, and they would find new places to explore around Rome.

Louisa Fanelli was bright and shrewd, and Marco was a little in awe of her even though he was a bit older. At thirteen she was already handling much of the housework for her mother and could shop wisely for food and prepare a full dinner for the family. She had less and less time to spend with Antonio and Marco. But when they did venture out together, Marco thought she was beginning to notice more things about him. When Antonio and Marco found a sturdy tree branch they could climb on, Marco saw Louisa eyeing their gymnastics. It was about this time that he started to pick his clothes more carefully, choosing shirts that showed off the new muscles in his arms.

Through these years, Marco never stopped thinking of the times he had spent with his father and the loss of that legacy. But he began to come to terms with it and to figure out his future. As he tried to envision the course his life would take – someday he could probably return to Abruzzo and work for one of his uncles – he never forgot his father's dream, the winery. If he could somehow, someday build a winery, he would feel that he had helped make up for the family's misfortune. Then his mother, sister and brother would once more have a decent place to live – a place all their own. But they had no land, their money was running out, and Marco's only prospect seemed to be as a hired hand. Something had to change.

Chapter 3

"Do you think Marco is – you know – normal?" Louisa Fanelli was addressing her brother, who happened to be in the kitchen when Louisa was cutting up a chicken for their evening meal.

"What are you talking about?" Antonio was absorbed in a newspaper.

"Do you think he, well, likes girls?"

"I know he likes you."

"He hardly even looks my way. If he likes me, why is he ignoring me?"

"Hey, he's sixteen. We're not going to fawn over anybody. He likes you."

"How do you know?"

"Guys know this stuff."

"You'd think he would be a little more personal."

"He's shy. He's a little afraid of you, too." Antonio was still reading his newspaper.

"What, does he think I have claws?"

"You could be friendlier. Sometimes you come on a little strong for a fifteen-year-old. Act a little more girlish. He probably wants to know you're interested first."

"I didn't say I was interested." Louisa washed the last piece of chicken and added it to the pot.

"If you weren't interested you wouldn't have brought it up. Just make the first move and see what happens."

"Girls want boys to do that."

"Like I said, he's sixteen. How long do you want to wait?"

Sometimes Louisa would lie in her bed, thinking of the last time she and Marco were together, wondering what it would feel like to be alone with him, to take his face in her hands and smooth back his hair, to feel his body beside hers. Late at night, she would write her feelings down in a journal that she kept squirreled away in her underwear drawer. A few days after her exchange with Antonio, Louisa concocted a scheme. On a day when she knew her mother would be away for the day, she casually arranged for Antonio to invite Marco to come by. Immediately, Antonio sensed what she was up to.

"You finally decided to make the first move," Antonio said. She met his gaze.

"So?" she said. "You think I'm too young, I suppose."

"You're too young to have dates. Mama would never let you, and I won't either. You have to be more subtle about it."

"And how long do you think you can stop me? You said I had to make a move."

Antonio mulled this for a minute. "You're serious? You'd sneak around behind our backs to see Marco?" he asked, eyebrows arching.

"I'll do what I like," she said, her nose in the air. "Today, or next week, or next month. Is something wrong with him? Maybe you'd rather have me going with that ugly *allocco* next door who keeps making a fool of himself when he thinks I'm looking." Antonio snorted, staring at her. "Look," she said. "Just give us an afternoon alone. Give us a chance to talk. Okay? Take Sara to the market. I'll take Marco to the Spanish Steps and be back by sundown."

Louisa was surprised by how quickly Antonio acquiesced. Getting Marco to the Spanish Steps was even easier. She thought he even seemed to brighten when he arrived at the house and realized he and Louisa would be going alone.

"But won't your mother …," he began.

"She's out," Louisa said, giggling. "We'll have some fun today, okay?" Marco nodded and grinned at her in a way she hadn't seen before.

Extending east from the Piazza di Spagna, about a mile from the Fanelli house, the 138 wide Spanish Steps led up to a small plaza in front of the twin-towered Trinita dei Monti church, which had one of Rome's best views. That day, in the warmth of the afternoon and standing with Louisa, looking over the plaza's balustrade toward the Via Condotti, Marco began to feel something else new – a sense of possibility. As the sun edged toward the horizon, Louisa and Marco looked out on the crowded piazza and talked about their families, their hopes and their dreams.

"What do you think you'll do – you know, with your life," Louisa said.

Marco looked at her, seeing just now the sheen of the sun on her black hair and feeling at once the sadness that had dominated his life and just a fleeting glimpse of what might lie ahead. "I want to make a new start – maybe somewhere new, where there's land I can buy," Marco said. "What about you?"

"I want a happy family," she said. "I want to be with someone who will want a family, too, and provide for us. Just simple things. I want a good life." Louisa's cheeks took on a rosy color as she looked at Marco and smiled.

A rush of emotion enveloped Marco. He put his arms around Louisa and pulled her close. Her cheeks flushed again, and he looked closely into her brown eyes. She kissed him, and they stayed there, feeling the dying warmth of the sun, holding each other for a long time.

In 1870, WHEN MARCO was nearly eighteen, a cousin of Antonio's came from America for a visit. Giovanni Castagnolo had gone to America in the 1850s, had seen New York City and then worked his way to Nevada to work in the silver mines. He told fabulous stories of the American West, and he spoke for hours about the opportunities in California, where he planned to move on his return to America. It was an exciting place, he said, where there was land and money and work for everyone.

Marco listened to these things and thought about them for a week. Why had he met Giovanni Castagnolo? It must be a sign of some kind, he thought. Before Giovanni was to leave, Marco went to the Castagnolo house, found Giovanni, and they talked again.

"I'll be in San Francisco at the Joseph Reger Co., on the waterfront," Giovanni said. "If you come, I'll help you out." Although Marco didn't know it at the time, he had already made the decision of his life.

He dropped out of school, and for a year he worked at a cordage mill, saving everything he could but saying nothing of his plans to anyone. The following June he could take a ship from Civitaveccia for New York. From there, he could take the three-year-old transcontinental railroad to San Francisco. But he needed money. By the end of May, Marco found that he had only half the amount he would need. So one day he hitched a ride to Controguerra to talk to his Uncle Beppe. If Beppe would lend him the money, Marco said, he would promise to repay it from his earnings in California.

"You've been a wonderful help to me, Marco," Beppe said. "Your father was my little brother. He would want this chance for you. I'll give you the money, and you'll pay me when you can. Don't forget us when you get to your new country." The two men stood on the front porch of Beppe's house, looking at the vineyards. Before Marco left, his uncle, now two inches shorter than Marco, took him by the shoulders and embraced him.

Two days later, when Marco told his mother about his plans, the blood drained from her face. She shook her head and looked down, then riveted her eyes to his. "I would stop you if I could," she said. "You could do well for yourself here – find a good job. You have friends who would help you. What do you really know about this place?"

"The chances are better in California, Mamma," Marco said. "I'll be able to help you better from there. And you have Carlo, he's thirteen now. You won't be alone."

They argued some more, then and on the days that followed, but they both knew the decision had been made.

Louisa, however, was another matter. Marco had kept his plans to himself, afraid to bring up the subject with her. She and Marco had been in love for nearly four years. When she heard, she could not be consoled. "Why didn't you tell me what you wanted to do?" she said. "Do you trust me so little? Do you care so little for my feelings?"

"I only just decided," he said, lying. "I didn't want to get you upset unnecessarily."

"Well that didn't work, did it?" she retorted. "You could have made plans to take me with you. You are thoughtless!"

"The life will be hard at first," he said, "and I couldn't get enough money for both of us. I couldn't ask Beppe to pay double. I want you to come, but I want to have a proper place for you. I'll come back for you when everything is ready."

"And I'm supposed to wait, who knows how long?" she shot back. "You'll have found someone new. You won't wait."

"I will wait," he said. "There's only you, Louisa. I'm doing this for us, for the family we want to have."

"Well, that's all nice for you. But I didn't have any say in it, did I? Maybe you could have asked just once what I wanted." She stalked away and slammed the door on him. When he called after her, she yelled back, "Just go!" He could hear her sobbing in the other room.

Five days later Marco stood alone on the dock in Civitaveccia where the SS *Letitia* was ready to sail for New York. He had said his good-byes to his mother, brother and sister the day before in Rome. Antonio had also said farewell, but Louisa refused to see him. "She won't talk about it," Antonio told him. "You should have told her sooner."

On the dock Marco searched the crowd of people for a familiar face, but in vain. On board the ship, he gazed down at the dock, still expecting to see Louisa in the crowd. Even as the ship moved out over the water and the dock receded into the distance, he looked, but she wasn't there.

Chapter 4

MARCO CASTELLANI FIRST ARRIVED in Sacramento, California, by train in early October of 1872. Immediately, he took a steamboat that went down the Sacramento River into San Pablo Bay and then docked in San Francisco. It was a glorious Indian summer day, sunny and warm when the boat left Sacramento but 15 degrees cooler by the time they reached San Francisco Bay. He found the Joseph Reger Co., an import-export firm, housed in a warehouse on the waterfront, jammed between several other buildings. When he went in and asked for Giovanni, he had a major disappointment. Giovanni had left, and no one knew where to find him. But there was another Italian man there, and he told Marco about James Lick.

"We're not hiring here," the man said in Italian. "Go over to the Lick House at Montgomery and Sutter. They usually need people to work in the kitchen. But be careful to avoid running into Mr. Lick. He is not such a nice man."

The Lick House was the most opulent hotel Marco had ever seen. Rome had old, classic buildings but nothing that resembled this. Inside, the hotel looked like a palace. When Marco asked about a job at the desk in his halting English, the clerk had to find someone to translate – Marco could not yet understand Americans well, even though he had practiced some during his two weeks riding the train across the country. There were no jobs open at the hotel, he learned, but there might be one in San Jose.

"Mr. Lick needs a gardener at his home near the flour mill," Marco was told. "If you go there tomorrow, you could apply."

"But I've heard Mr. Lick is difficult," Marco said in Italian.

"Ha!" the clerk responded, and then whispered, "You'll be lucky to keep the job more than a day, even if you get it. But if you do exactly what he says, you might. You know, he's the richest man in California."

"What about this San Jose – can you grow grapes there?"

"You can grow anything down there, I've heard."

Marco went to San Jose on the Southern Pacific train the next day and found the Lick flour mill a few miles north of the city. The mill, in its own way, was as magnificent as the hotel – mahogany and cedar on the inside and red brick on the exterior. Adjacent to it was a round, brick warehouse. Marco was told he could find Mr. Lick at his home nearby. When he approached the magnificent house, he almost left without knocking, he was shaking so much at the prospect of meeting such a man.

Lick was not at all what Marco expected. He was dressed in an old suit and without a tie. It seemed he had been sleeping in the suit. He had a stern face and a bushy, dark gray beard, no mustache. He seemed to be perhaps in his mid-seventies. Marco thought right away that he was quite odd for a rich man, but that wasn't the half of it.

"Wait here," Lick said, motioning with his hands to a spot, and left Marco alone in his house. That was the first test. After making him wait for half an hour, Lick took Marco to an open field where he was building a garden shed, with a large pile of bricks to one side.

"Take 500 bricks from this pile" – he motioned to the pile and spelled out the number with his fingers – "and stack them up in that corner," Lick said, motioning to the opposite side of the building's foundation.

"You want bricks ... there," Marco said haltingly, pointing to clarify. Lick nodded.

Marco went to work, moving the bricks as fast as he could, using a hod that happened to be lying around. When he had finished, Lick looked over the stack he had created, and then gave Marco the strangest order he had ever heard.

"Now move these bricks back to where you got them," Lick said, his face as serious as ever.

"Bricks ... back over ... there," Marco said, pointing and staring at him. Lick nodded. Then Marco remembered what the clerk in San Francisco had said about following his orders. He nodded and started piling the bricks in the hod and moving them back. That's when he realized he was being tested. Lick wanted to see if he could follow directions unquestioningly, he thought. While Marco was moving the stack, he prepared himself mentally for the next order. "He's odd but he's not crazy," Marco thought. "Nobody that rich could be crazy. He's probably going to make me move the stack of bricks again." He was right.

"Now move the bricks over here," Lick said, pointing to a third location. Marco nodded and did it. By this time over an hour had passed and Marco was getting a little tired.

"Congratulations, you are hired," Lick said when Marco had finished the third move. "Be at work at 8 a.m. tomorrow morning."

MARCO WORKED FOR JAMES LICK for nearly two years while he lived cheaply in a room provided for him by the brothers at the Santa Clara Mission. That was a little ironic because while Marco took advantage of the generosity of the Jesuit fathers toward new Catholic immigrants, he worked for a man known to be an atheist. But he actually felt more in common with Lick than he did with the fathers at the mission. Marco was not an atheist, but he still hated God for what he had done to his family in Abruzzo. The brothers at the mission knew Marco was faithless, and they were determined to bring him back into the fold. It was a challenge for them because Marco was a hard case.

From talking to people in town, Marco learned that Lick had also been extremely generous at times. He was known to have helped build an orphanage and an old age home. Marco respected that. During those two years he never questioned any direction Lick gave him, and there were some strange ones. One time he was planting cherry trees and Lick came by to check on his progress.

"Put that next tree in branches down," he said.

"You like branches in the ground, roots in the air," Marco said, looking at Lick with a straight face. He nodded, and Marco did it. The man was odd, all right, but it was his cherry tree, Marco thought. The next day Lick had him turn the tree around and plant it correctly, but it died. Another time he had Marco dig a hole ten feet in diameter and fill it with water. Lick never did anything else with that hole, and eventually Marco had to fill it in. But the cruelest thing Lick ever did was with the six ladies from the horticultural society when they came to visit his gardens. When Marco overheard one of the ladies say she had seen prettier flowers elsewhere, he cringed because he knew Lick didn't take criticism well. Sure enough, Lick took the poor ladies to the far corner of the twenty-acre orchard and left them there. When Marco realized what had happened, he had to run out and escort the lost, flustered women back to their buggies.

Marco saved all the money he could while he was working for Lick, and he felt he was always paid fairly. One day, about halfway into Marco's second year working for him, Lick invited Marco into his home to have lunch. That surprised Marco – Lick had often come out to eat with him and the other gardeners but Marco had not been inside the home since the day he arrived. He had begun to feel sorry for Lick because he seemed to be such a lonely man. He knew that Lick had fallen out with his son several years previously. At lunch Lick started telling him about some of his history – he had been a piano builder in Argentina, and then he had come to San Francisco just before the Gold Rush and made wise investments in land. He had used some of that land to build his plush hotel.

Marco asked him about all the glass paneling and metal framing he had seen stored in crates in one of the outbuildings. Lick told him that he had bought a replica of a conservatory at Kew Gardens in London that he ordered shipped to San Jose and had intended to build on his land off Willow Street.

"I'm not going to do it now," he said.

"Why not?"

"There was an item in the newspaper about me," he said. "They made fun of the way I dress. As if anyone around here would know what it means to dress well. These San Jose people don't deserve to have my gardens. If they want to call me a shabby dresser, to hell with them."

A few months after Marco began working for Lick, he happened to make friends with Father Aloysius Varsi, who at the time was president of Santa Clara College. He bumped into Father Varsi one day in the vineyards at the mission when Varsi heard him in conversation with the Italian monk who was tending the vines.

"Where are you from, young man?" Father Varsi asked him in Italian. Marco told him about Controguerra village in Abruzzo.

"I myself grew up in Sardinia," Varsi said. He told Marco he was a physicist who had been sent to California to teach in 1865. They talked for awhile, and several times thereafter Marco would see Father Varsi on the mission grounds and they would talk about wine, about Marco's passion for growing grapes and about the old country. Then one day in 1874 Varsi sought him out with a proposition. The Jesuits had purchased 160 acres in the foothills on the west side of the Santa Clara Valley and were developing a vineyard and winery for the production of sacramental wine. Would Marco be interested in a job there?

That was the opportunity Marco had been looking for. He could work a vineyard again, be part of a winery and get a start on his dream of producing wine of his own. From that point on it would be only a matter of timing. In July Father Varsi and Marco rode out to the place they called Villa Maria, on Montebello Ridge, to meet the brothers there. A few days after that, Marco began to work weekends at the vineyard and to make plans for a permanent move in the fall.

That move came sooner than he expected. One morning in August James Lick told Marco he had learned that he had found other employment, and Marco told him about his plans.

"So you have decided to move on, then," Lick said. "Well, fine. But you cannot serve two masters. Come by and pick up your last wages from me at the end of the day."

Marco was offended by Lick's abruptness because he had worked hard for Lick. Still, he wasn't too disappointed. After all, he was already planning to quit. But when he came in from the orchard and went to Lick's house to get his wages that afternoon, he had a shock. Lick did not answer the door. Instead, Marco found the mill foreman, who informed him that Lick had suffered a stroke that day just after lunch. He was being attended by a doctor and would probably be transported to San Francisco the next day.

As it turned out, that was the last day James Lick would ever spend in Santa Clara County. He never fully recovered from the stroke, and two years later he died.

Chapter 5

"So Marco, when are we going to see this girl of yours, this Louisa?" Brother Michael was tying some of the newer shoots of the vines, the mission grapes, to the trellis, being careful not to break any. Marco, in the next row, was repairing one of the trellis sections that had fallen in a windstorm.

"Someday," Marco said.

"You better send for her or she's going to find herself another boyfriend."

"Not Louisa. She's not that type."

"When did you say you left Italy?"

"A year and a half, or two years ago."

"She's probably married by now. You better look for someone around here. Girls don't wait forever, you know."

"It won't be forever. And how would you know?"

"Does she send you letters?"

"No. But I write her. I'll get a letter soon. She's just making me pay for leaving."

"Making you pay, huh? Oh, girls are good at that," Brother Michael said with a loud laugh. "Girls know how to make you pay. Me and the other brothers, we don't worry about that anymore."

"I don't know how you do it."

"We make love to the vines. The vines never talk back to us, see. The vines don't keep us awake at night. We can walk away from the vines any time we like and they don't say a word. And whenever we go back to them, they're glad to see us. Vines are the perfect companion. They never complain. They just grow and keep bearing grapes, and we keep picking them, and soon we'll be drinking the wine." Brother Michael laughed again. "It's a beautiful arrangement," he said. "The only one we have to please is Brother Linus."

"I think I'd rather have a girl than Brother Linus."

"Oh, but you've got him, too. And you're his assistant, so you've got to really watch your step." He was whispering now. "Brother Linus isn't going to let you get out of line. You might as well be one of us. We've got it good. We just do our work and he can't fire us. You, your job is always on the line."

"I'm not worried about it."

"Okay, fine, but just remember what I said. Brother Linus expects the best. And find yourself a wife. Is Louisa a good Catholic?"

"Sure, I guess so."

"Good. You need a wife to bring you back to God."

The monks continued to work on Marco's faith. He would not attend church because God was still his enemy, but he had affection for these men, who for some reason had devoted their lives to serving this detestable God. The brothers patiently prodded Marco and waited for him to find his faith again.

But Brother Michael had a point about Brother Linus, Marco said to himself. The prior at Villa Maria, Linus was a big man with a large, bald head and a commanding presence. No one spoke out of turn when Brother Linus was around, and he met any transgression with an icy stare. A monk would not want to be on his bad side. But Brother

Linus would go to great lengths to make sure that good performance was rewarded. When Marco was eventually able to double the usual yield from the Burgundy vines – this after two years or so – Brother Linus recognized him at the September harvest dinner and arranged for him to have a nice bonus. Marco was always deferential to Brother Linus, but he never really got to know him, and he had the feeling Brother Linus preferred it that way.

Brother Michael, on the other hand, was the jokester of the monks. He had a slim build, always-tousled, thinning blond hair and a ready response to any situation. He was good company and kept a group in high spirits, but his wit bordered on the caustic; occasionally he would offend someone. Then he would go out of his way to smooth things over, which he did with ease and grace. No one could stay mad at him for long. Brother Michael took the trouble to make Marco feel welcome when he first arrived at Villa Maria, and over time Marco grew as close to him as he had ever been to Antonio in Rome. He remained Marco's special friend for life.

That day they finished their morning work and were headed to the refectory for their noonday meal.

"What do you think Brother Raul will make for us?" Marco asked.

"Some really good tamales or enchiladas. I know Brother Raul. He'll stew up a chicken and season it just so. Brother Raul is a perfectionist, and thank God for that."

"I wish he would make some pasta just once. He could make us a little pasta if he wanted."

"Brother Raul isn't going to make pasta. If you want pasta you have to get Louisa to come and make it for you. You better write again and ask her to come. Have you asked her?"

"I'm not ready."

"You're going to wait too long. You won't get any pasta out of Brother Raul."

Marco had made friends with nearly all of the monks at Villa Maria, but not with Brother Raul. Marco stayed out of Brother Raul's circle. He didn't feel like getting close to Brother Raul, the one brother of Mexican descent, whether because of his father's lost investment to the Spaniard or some other latent prejudice one couldn't be sure. Brother Raul's culinary skills were great, but he was also stubborn and very partial to the Mexican tradition. He would never cook plain, unseasoned food as a few of the brothers kept begging him to do. He would throw in an extra flavoring or an unexpected sauce or marinade, even if the menu called for simple meat and vegetables. Although Marco didn't really like Brother Raul, he had to admire his cooking ability. The only time Marco saw him upset was when a dish he made did not meet his own expectations. The other brothers thought he was one of Villa Maria's best assets – not just for his food but because he was jovial and full of stories – and Marco never heard him say anything mean.

WHEN MARCO FIRST ARRIVED at Villa Maria he was still only 22 years old, five feet nine inches tall, 148 pounds. His black hair and darkish skin told of his Mediterranean origin, and his sharply chiseled, clean-shaven face and blue eyes made him handsome to many women. He had learned how to work hard. He had also learned how to depend on himself. And he was good enough with English that he could converse with anybody. After his first day at Villa Maria he made his plan. He would work there for five years and then, using what money he had saved, he would strike out on his own, send for Louisa and start a family. So far, his letters to Louisa had gone unanswered; but he was sure Louisa was still thinking of him.

One day, Marco began to think that Brother Michael had a point about Louisa. So he put his plan in another letter to Louisa and waited hopefully. Three months later he got this reply:

> *FIVE YEARS!* [underlined three times] *You expect me to wait FIVE YEARS while you make sure everything is perfect? I am coming NOW! I am coming as soon as I can get the money for passage, whether you are ready or not. And when I get there, you will marry me. That's the end of it, and that's how it will be. I don't care how poor you are – we will get by somehow.*

Marco thought he had better soothe her a little, so he wrote back that of course he would be overjoyed to see her any time, but that he did not have enough to pay for her trip just now, or a decent place for them to stay. As it turned out, it took two more years for Louisa to get enough money together for her boat ticket, which gave Marco a chance to get more established in the Valley and to develop some relationships in the wine-growing community.

His closest working relationships were with the brothers at Villa Maria, the ones he lived with, dined with and worked alongside every day. About 20 brothers at a time lived at the vineyard – 15 working with the vines and five or six in the winery. Everyone had a job, and Marco was the only non-Jesuit. When he first arrived, the winery was still under construction, but it was completed in a few months and produced wine by Marco's second year. He soon realized that Father Varsi was only telling him half the story when he said the winery would produce sacramental wine. Yes, some of the wine supplied the churches in the area, but most of it was sold and shipped out to stores, eventually bringing in thousands of dollars a year to the brotherhood. And, of course, a lot of the wine found its way onto the brothers' own dining tables.

A few months after Marco arrived at Villa Maria, he and Brother Linus took a wagon into San Jose to attend a meeting of the Santa Clara Valley Horticultural Society at a place called The Lake House downtown. Most of the members, Marco learned, were French in origin – many of them the same nurserymen, orchardists and winegrowers Charles Grayson had met as a young printer – although a bit older now and not all of them French. Brother Linus was from Swiss-American stock and Marco, of course, was Italian, so they hoped they would not feel out of place. As it turned out, they had nothing to fear. When they arrived, a few of the members were having conversations in French, but the proceedings, fortunately, were in English.

They had gone to the meeting because at Villa Maria they were still planting vines – only 50 acres or so had been planted – and they heard that some of the winegrowers had cuttings they would sell or give away from their varietals brought over from France. Until very recently the predominant grape in the valley had been the Mission, which had its start in the old vineyard at the Santa Clara Mission. But all the new European arrivals recognized that the Mission would never produce the quality of wine they knew was possible in the valley. In particular, Marco had learned from making inquiries over the last year or so that Charles Lefranc's extensive New Almaden Vineyard south along the Guadalupe River had won prizes for best claret and best sherry. Lefranc was also making excellent Rieslings that had been praised by experts, and he had a large plantation of red Bordeaux vines, a variety Marco especially coveted. He had rehearsed a conversation he wanted to have with Lefranc, with the aim of getting some cuttings from him.

However, the first person Marco noticed at the meeting was not a winegrower or a vintner or even an orchardist but a pretty girl whose name was Henriette Pellier. To his disappointment, he learned Henriette was only fourteen years old. She was there with her father, Pierre Pellier,

Charles Grayson's old friend, who turned out to be one of the nicest men Marco ever met. Pierre Pellier had extensive vineyards on the east side in the Evergreen district. Pierre's brother Louis, the nurseryman, had died shortly after Marco's arrival in the valley. Marco went out of his way to meet Pierre, who introduced him to his daughter and his sixteen-year-old son, Louis. That was fortunate because through Louis, Marco met another teenager, Louis's friend Henry Lefranc, whose father was Charles Lefranc, the man Marco most wanted to talk to.

After the meeting, Marco managed to get the elder Lefranc's ear for an hour to talk business, and Lefranc invited him out to see his vineyards and winery. Marco was thrilled.

"You should see my Malbec and Mataro vines," Lefranc told him. "I've done well with those. I'll give you some Riesling cuttings, too, because, you know, the more of us that produce good quality wine, the better it will be for this valley. We need to establish a name for ourselves if we want to do well." Marco thought this a sensible attitude.

That evening he told Brother Linus he thought they had achieved everything they had hoped for from the meeting. But privately, Marco couldn't stop thinking of Henriette Pellier. It bothered him that he had barely been able to keep from staring at her, and he hoped that no one had noticed his eyes wandering in her direction. Attractive as she was, she was definitely too young for him.

Chapter 6

Montebello Ridge
June 1876

BY THE TIME MARCO had been at Villa Maria two years, his routine began to fill him with the kind of joy he hadn't felt for years. On those sunlit mornings he would get up early, sit with the brothers while they prayed, and then eat. It was a reassuring ritual to start the day with. He felt some of his zest for life returning, living with these monks. He didn't want to *be* a monk, as he once told Father Dorian he did, and he couldn't embrace the monks' unquestioning faith, but he felt reassured in their shared daily rituals. The warmth of summer on California's Central Coast was already filtering into the rows of vines by the time he walked out with his shovel and hoe. They were planting and grafting then, putting in the rooted cuttings of Black St. Peters they had acquired from Antoine Delmas, the ones Marco had seen doing so well in some of the Santa Clara vineyards. Marco had Brother Michael on his planting crew, and they would work their way up and down the rows together, mostly in silence, with an occasional Brother Michael wisecrack, all of them soaking in the morning sun and the dry, refreshing air as they dug, planted and staked, until they had sweated enough to take a break.

It was around this time that Marco started to plan how he would boost his income. He liked his job at Villa

Maria, and he had saved a little nest egg, but he knew he would need to earn more if he expected to support Louisa and raise a family. It had been known for several months that Leland Stanford, the former governor and railroad tycoon, had acquired extensive property in the northwest section of the county, around Mayfield, and was starting a vineyard there. Marco knew that Stanford already had a vineyard and winery on the east side of San Francisco Bay at Warm Springs. So, thinking Stanford's new vineyard might need a foreman, Marco arranged to see him. It took several attempts – Stanford was a difficult man to track down, and after dealing with James Lick, Marco was a little afraid of eminent men. On his third trip to Stanford's Mayfield property, Marco found him with some horses he was bringing in to occupy a new barn. He approached tentatively.

"Mr. Stanford, I wanted to see you about . . .," Marco began, but was interrupted by a colt creating a ruckus with his handler.

"Hold on there . . . Whoa!" Stanford said, backing away awkwardly. Stanford was a big man, and he jerked back into Marco, nearly knocking him down. "All right now, easy does it."

For a few moments Stanford seemed to have forgotten Marco's presence. Then, with another jerk, he turned around to face him.

"Oh yes, the vineyard man, am I right? I was told you were coming. We have a tremendous opportunity here to create a wine that will be known throughout the West – maybe all over the world. I'm investing a lot of money. You know, I've bought 650 acres here – hope to buy more. I'm going to train horses — these are the first. And then I'm building a winery, right over there." He pointed to a field nearby. "My brother Josiah is in charge, but he'll need help here at the farm because he lives in Warm Springs. So your coming is fortuitous. Some other vineyard men have been recommended to me, but only one has come around." By now the handler had taken the colt away and Stanford was standing, looking straight at Marco.

"I could do a good job," Marco said.

"Well, why don't you tell me about yourself?"

Marco stammered a little and then he started to describe his experience with winegrowing, beginning with Italy and going on to tell him about Villa Maria.

"Italy – yes, I've heard the wines there are wonderful. I want to see for myself some day. My wife is interested in traveling but I like it here. Weather suits me. She puts great store in . . . Oh, confound it, I nearly forgot I have to meet a man at the house. I've got to go, but come back in two days and I'll have my brother here to talk to you." He hoisted his big frame into his buggy and was off, his horse trotting away at a good clip.

Marco returned as Stanford had asked, two days later, and had a meeting with Stanford and his brother. Somehow, they had managed to get information from Brother Linus about Marco's work – or maybe from Father Varsi, Marco thought. At any rate, Marco was offered the job of assistant foreman at the Stanford vineyard in Mayfield at a salary that tripled what he was making at Villa Maria. The vineyard would consist of 168 acres but would not be ready to plant before next spring, so he could start then. He accepted eagerly.

Marco decided not to tell Brother Linus about his new job right away, since he needed to work at Villa Maria for several more months. But something happened that moved his timetable up.

Marco had been seeing more of Henriette Pellier lately – she was sixteen now – and he found himself seeking out occasions when she might be present and making conversation with her. One of those occasions was a funeral. Sixteen-year-old Louis O. Pellier had contracted typhoid fever and died in 1874, soon after Marco met him, leaving Pierre without a male heir. Since then, Pierre had been grooming Henriette to take over the family business, schooling her intensively in winemaking. Marco knew she would be a good catch, and he hoped her father might see him as someone who could be a good custodian of the property he would be handing down. He knew Louisa would be coming to America some day, but he didn't think it would hurt to keep up friendly relations with Henriette. After all, things might not work out with Louisa after such a long separation, and he still didn't know exactly when she would be coming. His rationalization turned out to have painful consequences.

For one, he nearly lost Louisa. One day in midsummer 1876, on one of those idyllic days with the vines and when Marco was least expecting it, a letter arrived from Italy. Brother Raul delivered it to his hands when he was out in the vineyards. That kind of letter rarely came, and Marco noticed two things about it right away – it was addressed in Louisa's unmistakable handwriting and it was postmarked two months previous. He wondered what had taken it so long to reach him. When he read it, he was aghast – Louisa would be embarking for New York immediately, and if all went well, she would arrive by train in Sacramento around August 5. To his horror, he realized she had been due two days ago and might be there even now, waiting for him.

He immediately made plans to leave for Sacramento, but while he prepared, a telegram came from New York. Louisa was now expected in Sacramento on August 9, the day after tomorrow. So he breathed a sigh of relief and went ahead and made his trip, without the added worry of being late. But as he braced for meeting Louisa, his anxiety grew. He realized that his growing interest in Henriette Pellier was now common knowledge in the valley. Louisa was bound to learn about it soon after her arrival. He cringed inside, knowing he had not thought everything through. He wondered how seriously the Pelliers had taken his advances.

Louisa's train was delayed, arriving in Sacramento on August 12. Marco was bowled over when he saw her – radiant, full of life and more desirable than ever. Almost instantly he forgot about Henriette for the rest of the day. Once they had arrived back in the valley, he helped get Louisa settled in her room – she would be staying with the Lefrancs in the Almaden Valley. Marco was so glad to see her, and they had so much to catch up on, that he pushed Henriette to the back of his mind. They talked excitedly all the way back to San Jose. But before going to the Lefrancs, Marco knew he had to explain what had happened.

He softened the news as much as he could. He told Louisa she might hear about a girl he had paid some attention to – it wasn't a serious thing, and they had not spent any time together unaccompanied. He was lying – those moments in the shadows at the evening dances were unforgettable. But he told himself he hadn't been unfaithful.

Louisa took this revelation harder than he had expected. "What were you thinking, and what about the love and adulation in your letters?" she asked, her voice rising. "How could you have meant any of that? Were you just trying to make me feel good? You must not have thought I would ever come. You were going to cut me off, weren't you? You were going to marry this girl and then cut me off and tell me to stay home!" She pouted, and then, when they arrived at the Lefrancs, she sent him home, retreating to her room. Marco went back to Villa Maria feeling as low as he had since his first days in Rome.

He went to see Louisa the next evening, but she refused to see him. On the third day after her arrival, she came out of her room solemnly. He walked with her around the Lefranc gardens and apologized with all the self-incriminating words he knew. With complete sincerity, he promised undying fidelity for the rest of his days. He told her he loved her and promised to treasure her forever.

"What will you tell Henriette?" she asked seriously.

"I'll apologize and break it off." he said. "She will have to accept it."

"She has accepted it," Louisa said, to Marco's shock. "I went to seen Henriette and we have worked it out. You will ride over to their ranch now and give your apology to her and her father. If they don't shoot you on the spot, come back tomorrow and we will arrange our wedding."

"But ... how did you ...?"

"Agostino, the Italian stable boy here, knows English. He and Mrs. Lefranc helped me get over to the Pellier ranch. I know how to get things done – you should know that."

Marco did as he was told, and he survived. Pierre did a good job at feigning indignation, but Marco suspected he wasn't at all unhappy about losing a poor Italian boy as a possible future son-in-law. As for Henriette, she was stone-faced.

"I couldn't marry you now in any case," she said. "It was horribly dishonest of you to make me think you might. So go to your future wife, and learn to treat her with respect." She wheeled and left the room. Marco was both heartsick and relieved, and never again did he have two such starkly conflicting emotions.

The second consequence of Marco's lapse in judgment involved a wine tasting, a newspaper article, a libel suit and the loss of his job. It all started one Saturday just before Louisa's arrival, when Marco had been talking to Henriette and Pierre at a vintners meeting. Pierre had mentioned that a wine judging would take place in September at the county fair, and by the way, would Marco like to be a judge? Blind to the red flags, Marco thought this would be another chance to get his name in the front of the valley's wine-growing elite, and would probably impress Henriette as well. So, of course, he accepted. After Louisa arrived, he felt he couldn't back out of this commitment without offending the Pelliers even more. Maybe, he thought, he could mend relations with the Pelliers if they happened to win a few prizes.

Although the tasting would be blind, Marco had already sampled enough wine in the valley that he thought he could distinguish the major labels. For example, the Lefranc reds had a fruitier taste than the others, and the Pellier whites were definitely drier. He didn't want to be deliberately partial, but he was not going to damage his reputation with the Pelliers any further if he could help it. By the time of the judging he saw clearly what a tight spot he had put himself in and dreaded the choices he would have to make.

Unfortunately, the tasting would be public, under a tent on the fairgrounds, and so would the votes. The other two judges were from elsewhere in the state; Marco had been picked because the Villa Maria wine was not ready for consumption, so he would not be tasting any of his own wine. But he finally understood that, by being forced to take sides, he was going to damage his relationship with someone. Unfortunately, it was too late to back out.

The brandies were not a problem because one maker stood head and shoulders above the others and everyone knew it. Henry Naglee was a retired Mexican War and Civil War general who had studied brandy making in France. On his property on the east side of San Jose he had regrafted his vines and was now producing a kind of brandy that no one had tasted outside France. Marco had seen his distillery and knew that he was using white

Riesling, Charbono and Pinot Noir grapes to produce a crystal clear brandy with a tinge of each grape in the final product. It was really fine stuff, so the judging was no contest. Naglee's brandies won the top prize.

The reds and whites were another matter. In previous years, Charles Lefranc had won most of the honors at the fair, and Lefranc was clearly expecting that trend to continue. But Pellier and others were definitely at the same quality level. The Napa and Sonoma judges were split on most categories, so Marco had the deciding ballot. He was dreading an offense to Henriette so was relieved to see the Pellier Riesling win in that category. He knew that Antoine Delmas had been one of the first grafters and promoters of Black St. Peters, but still he was surprised to see him win over Lefranc in that category. Since the judges couldn't see the labels they were trying, Marco attempted to pick LeFranc's by taste alone – but chose what turned out to be Delmas's product instead.

After seven prizes had been awarded, they came to the last category, the clarets. Marco desperately wanted Lefranc to win at least one category, so he voted for what he thought was the New Almaden Vineyard entry. He was shocked when it turned out to be Pellier's, and Pellier took the blue ribbon. When the vote was announced Marco was eyeing Charles Lefranc in the crowd. Lefranc turned his back and left the tent in a hurry, not to be seen again that day. But from the report Marco got from Louisa, he let his displeasure be known at home, although he was careful not to mention Marco's name when she was present.

At the time, Marco thought all this would blow over. He and Louisa went ahead with their wedding plans and said their vows at the Mission Church in Santa Clara on November 18, 1876. It was hard to find a home they could afford just then, but Marco did locate a small living space behind a farmhouse on Stevens Creek Road a few miles from Villa Maria. He thought that would serve until his Stanford job started, but as it turned out they needed the place a bit longer. That house happened to be on the ranch of Rebecca and Eli Foard.

In January Marco attended another meeting of the horticulture society where, unknown to him, a newspaper reporter was present. He was there to get some information on production during the past year or to learn of any new developments in wine-growing. But Marco waded into a discussion about which wineries were producing the highest quality product. Someone – Marco forgot who – remembered he had been a judge at the fair and, thinking he was in a position to judge impartially, put him on the spot. What was his view overall? Not expecting this sudden interrogation, he did not have the presence of mind to just refuse to speculate. Never did he expect his statement to be repeated outside the room. But something came out of his mouth to the effect that the New Almaden label could no longer be automatically considered dominant and that those wines were not necessarily better than a number of others.

Well, this statement turned out to be the lead of an account by editor Charles Grayson in the *San Jose Weekly Journal* two days later under the headline "Vineyard Man Downgrades Lefranc's Wines." Charles Lefranc went on a tirade when he read this story. He went to his lawyer, and a week later Marco was served with papers charging him, the *San Jose Weekly Journal* and Charles Grayson himself with libel. In subsequent issues, the newspaper began to print articles on its front page explaining the libel suit, which seemed to compound the offense.

To deal with the lawsuit, Marco had to ask for time off from Brother Linus, who was reluctant but gave him the two days he needed. Marco first went to see Grayson to vent his anger.

"How could you print this article when you did not announce yourself at the meeting and I didn't know my words would be reported this way?" Marco demanded to know. Charles said he had been introduced at the meeting, and that Marco must have arrived late or he would have heard. Marco admitted that he had been late.

"But you should have checked with me anyway, to see if I wanted to be part of your article," Marco said.

"Did you say these things?" Charles asked. Marco admitted he had. "Then you have no complaint with me," Charles said. "You were at a meeting where the public was invited and where a reporter was known to be present, so your statement was something I had a right to report."

Marco could see he was getting nowhere, but he still thought he was right, and he was about to walk out when Charles stopped him.

"Do you have an attorney?" he asked. Marco said he didn't.

"Get in touch with Delphin Delmas," Charles said. "He's the son of Antoine Delmas, the winegrower. Delmas is one of the most prominent defense attorneys in the state. He will be representing the newspaper and might agree to represent you as well." Marco nodded to Charles and left.

Then, just when it seemed Marco's life could not get any more complicated, it did. Brother Linus grew impatient with the attention he was giving to his personal problems at the expense of his duties at Villa Maria vineyards. He called Marco in one day and told him he would have to hire a new foreman.

"But this is temporary," Marco pleaded. "I won't be this busy for long."

"You have a trial coming up, so you'll have to go to court," Brother Linus said. "And also, you are now married. We have a monastic order here, and we hired you because you were single and would fit in here. I happen to know that you have agreed to take a job working for

Leland Stanford in the spring, and you've tried to keep that a secret from me."

Marco's stomach turned a little. He knew he'd been nailed on that count.

Then Brother Linus's tone turned softer. "You have a lot of ability and you should be using it wisely," he said. "You know, there's a piece of land just above us here on the Montebello Ridge. I heard about a year ago that it was for sale. I advise you to buy it. Plant your own vineyard and build a house for your family. That's your future."

And with that encouraging note, Brother Linus fired him.

It was now mid-December, and Marco's job with Stanford wouldn't start until spring. He was out of work, he had a new wife who was brand new in the country and knew little English, he had ruined his relationship with two of the area's most important winegrowers, and now he had to defend himself in a libel suit. It was not an auspicious beginning for the marriage.

Marco had made some poor decisions, but he had made at least one good one – he had been thrifty and saved his money. In his first job, James Lick had advised him to look for land that was priced low and positioned well for appreciation, and to buy it. So the year before, when 160 acres adjacent to Villa Maria came up for sale on Montebello Ridge, Marco had negotiated a good price with the owners and bought the land. That was the property Brother Linus had said he should buy – the land he didn't know Marco already owned – and that's why Marco wasn't too worried about being fired.

Marco had saved enough so he and Louisa could get by until the Stanford job started, so he decided to use the winter months to start building a house on the land they owned. It would be *their* house – the first of his own Marco had known since Controguerra, and the place where Marco and Louisa intended to raise their family.

Chapter 7

San Jose
January 1877

DELPHIN DELMAS HAD COME a long way since Charles Grayson first met him as a 12-year-old on Delphin's arrival from France. He had graduated from Santa Clara College, then from the law school at Yale University. He had been admitted to the bar, joined a law firm and served two years as Santa Clara County District Attorney. He was now in practice alone, ensconced in a building he owned on South First Street, had been married eight years and had a growing family. On the day Marco and Louisa went to his office, Delmas was thirty-two years old.

"So you are in the same trouble as my friend Charles," Delmas said as they took seats in the walnut-paneled room. "Charles and I first met on a stagecoach, he probably mentioned. But our conversation was limited because he didn't speak French and I didn't speak English. Now, what's all this about Mr. Lefranc's wines?"

"It was just a casual comment I made at a meeting," Marco said. "Someone asked me. I didn't know so much could come out of a little thing like that. Please, I hope you can help me. I'm still fairly new in this country and I'm an immigrant, like you. I'm unemployed and I won't have another job until April. I'll be wiped out by this. We might even lose our land. I don't even know how I'm going to pay you." Marco looked at the floor and shook his head, putting his right hand up to smooth back his hair.

"Don't get upset. Legal filings can seem overwhelming sometimes, I know, but it's usually less devastating than it seems. There are solutions to these problems."

"Mr. Delmas," Louisa said haltingly, in her primitive English. "We are just now married, starting out, you know. I am … we have a baby coming later this year." She blushed slightly. "Marco has work hard and I save money for two years to come here. We need help."

"I completely understand. My own father came here and started a nursery. He's a vintner as well. I've worked the vines, so we have that in common. It's satisfying work. How are your wines coming along out at Villa Maria?"

"Well, I'm … I'm not working for Villa Maria any more …"

"Oh yes, you said. But you must have been part of the last vintage out there."

"The wines are coming out very well. I think the reds are going to be good, but it's really just basic sacramental wine, you know. Not as good as better vines would produce."

"My father pioneered the Black St. Peter's variety here fifteen years ago. He's very partial to it. I love wine myself, and if you're going to have your own vineyard …"

"Oh yes, yes, that's going to be our life, our future," Marco said.

"Well, what I mean is, I understand where you are in life and I want to help you get through this. And don't worry about payment right now. I know we can work something out. And I think I can help you get out of your predicament."

"Thank you, Mr. Delmas," Louisa said, with genuine gratitude. "But will there be a trial and a jury? Mr. Lefranc is so … such an important man. We're new here. Could we win?"

"I want to avoid a trial at all cost, and I think Lefranc will, too, once he thinks about it. Actually, Lefranc and my father are old friends. I know the family well. If I talk to him, I think I can convince him to settle."

"What do you mean, settle?" Louisa asked.

"You know, to come to an agreement. He may want something – a retraction or some such. It's common in these matters."

"But what I said was true," Marco said, banging his fist on the arm of his chair.

"Well, yes, I'm sure it was from your perspective. It comes under the heading of fair comment and criticism, and theoretically that argument might win in court. But you can't depend on a jury to understand that. It would be foolish to risk it. And, frankly, I don't want to oppose Lefranc in court. It wouldn't be good politics, and it would put you folks at an unnecessary risk. Even if you win, you might later wish you hadn't."

Marco nodded slowly. "Yes, I think I understand. It's political. We need to get out of this the easiest way we can."

"Exactly," Delmas said. "Well, suppose I go see Mr. Lefranc and see what we can work out."

"Thank you, sir," Louisa said. "We're depending on you."

Louisa went away from the meeting with Delmas feeling worse than she had before. Was Delmas saying they didn't stand a chance of winning if the case went to trial? What if Lefranc wouldn't drop his suit? Would they lose everything?

"We don't have $5,000 or even close to it," Marco said morosely, speaking to Louisa in Italian. "Even if we sold the land we wouldn't have enough."

"We just have to find a solution to this, somehow," she said. "I hope Mr. Delmas is the right lawyer. I wonder if he's really on our side and not Lefranc's." The last comment elicited an uneasy glance from Marco.

Two weeks later, when they heard from Delmas, the news wasn't good. Lefranc had refused a settlement, and Delmas was preparing for trial. Marco put his head in his hands, but Louisa just nodded. She had a plan.

WHILE THEY WAITED for the libel trial to start, Marco worked on their future homestead. Every day he and Louisa rode from the tiny house on the Foard ranch up to their property on Montebello Ridge, about three miles, and walked the land, staking out their future vineyards, the footprints for the barns and their house – and, of course, the winery. They knew it would be a few years before they would see their way clear to actually make commercial wine. But now the house was the priority. Through Eli Foard, Marco managed to obtain plans for it – a two-story frame structure with a gabled roof whose front porch looked out toward the valley. A magnificent stand of California redwoods dominated the view from the back. He also arranged for the use of one of Eli's wagons and began hauling building materials to the site. Painstakingly, he graded the site, poured the foundation for the house and began putting the first upright members in place.

One evening after an especially long, exhausting day of building, Marco returned from Montebello as Louisa was preparing dinner and collapsed into a chair. "I've had it," he said. "I don't know how I can do this and still hold a job. This is enormous, what we're trying to do."

"It's too much for you to do alone," Louisa said.

"I need a partner, somebody who can share the work. This is 160 acres I'm trying to manage, and I haven't even started growing grapes yet."

Immediately they both thought of Carlo, Marco's younger brother in Italy. He had not married yet, as far as they knew. He might welcome the chance to come to America. While they pondered this possibility over the next few days, Louisa received a letter from her sister, Sara. To their surprise, Sara said she would love to visit them when their house was complete. Then they started to reassess their plans for the house. The two extra bedrooms now seemed inadequate. When they had sons and daughters, plus an uncle and an aunt living there or visiting for extended periods, they were going to need more space. Marco took out the house plans and began sketching in an addition to one side. None of this was going to be easy or cheap, he realized.

As they contemplated the expenses they would have coming up, Marco couldn't avoid worrying about the libel suit, knowing a good outcome was imperative. He couldn't bring himself to pray about it, but he knew Louisa did. A bad ending could cripple them for years. Seeing the concern in Louisa's eyes, he said, "Don't worry. I start the job with Stanford next week. Then we'll have money coming in." They decided that, whatever happened, they would invite Carlo to America and Sara as well, for as long as either of them wanted to stay. Louisa and Marco would both be glad to have family members there to help with the work and for company as well. Although they knew other Italians in the valley, there was still no one they could talk to from the "old days" in Abruzzo and Rome. Still in their early twenties, both of them were homesick.

After Marco began supervising the planting of the Stanford vineyard in Mayfield, he was too busy to work on the house every day, so progress stalled. That discouraged them, but soon a letter from Carlo confirmed his enthusiastic acceptance of their offer. However, it would be late summer before he could manage to leave his current employment, and he would be another month or two in transit. In the meantime, work on the house inched along.

Then in early June, a week before the libel trial was scheduled to start, Delphin Delmas sent an urgent message: Would Marco meet with him in San Jose the next day? There might be a settlement.

Louisa didn't go into town with Marco, but before he left she admonished, "Whatever Lefranc wants, give it to him. We have to get this over with." Marco only shook his head.

"Promise me," she said, urgency in her voice as she took his hands in hers. Finally, he agreed, but she could tell he had reservations.

"It's what I've been hoping for," Delmas said when Marco entered his office. "Lefranc will drop the suit if you will apologize publicly and have it printed in Grayson's newspaper."

"Apologize?"

"You have to say his wines are really fine and your previous judgments were wrong. Something of that kind. We'll get the wording approved before you publish it."

"But I was right. His wines aren't the best anymore."

Delmas grimaced. "Oh, Marco, don't you see this is just a game? We're beyond what's right and wrong here. You're a young man who's been put over a barrel by an old, established family. Your future is at stake here. The solution is to take your medicine and get on with your life. No one's going to think less of you. You just got in a little over your head and now you have a chance to escape. Take it."

Marco nodded slowly, thinking of his promise to Louisa and of their dreams. After hesitating for a minute and taking a deep breath, he gave his answer: "All right, I'll do it."

The following week, a square, gray-bordered advertisement appeared in the lower left corner of the *Journal*'s third page:

> **To Whom It May Concern:** I have the highest opinion of wines made by the New Almaden Winery and by the Lefranc family. I believe them to be the best available, any previous statements of mine notwithstanding. – Marco Castellani

Charles Grayson did not charge Marco for placing the advertisement.

That night, when Marco and Louisa were looking at the paper, Marco said (in Italian), "I still can't figure out what made Charles Lefranc finally agree to this. Did he just want to make me squirm for a while?"

"You haven't figured it out?" Louisa said, amused. "No, he wanted to make you squirm all right, but he also wanted a trial."

"How do you know that?"

"Because I talked to Marie. We became good friends when I first arrived here, when I was staying at their ranch – remember? I went out there a couple of weeks ago, after you started your job. We had a long talk about it. Marie talked to Charles. That's when Charles went to Mr. Delmas and suggested this settlement. Now do you get it?"

Marco grinned and chuckled. "And you thought if you told me, I wouldn't go along?"

"Well?"

"No, you're right, probably not."

They looked at each other for a minute and then hugged.

"It's all over now," Marco said. "A tempest in a teapot, as they say in English."

"In a wine bottle, you mean."

Chapter 8

DURING THE TWO YEARS that Marco Castellani worked as
Governor Stanford's vineyard foreman, he put money
aside for getting his vineyards plowed and planted. After
he resigned as foreman, he continued to consult with
Stanford and advise when he was needed. For starting
his own vines on Montebello Ridge, he had to go ask
Antoine Delmas for most of his cuttings and rootstock –
he no longer felt comfortable asking Lefranc or Pellier –
and he later got cuttings from Stanford after the Mayfield
vines became established. Carlo and Marco planted the
Montebello vineyards themselves with the help of Chinese
that they hired through a labor contractor in San Jose's
Chinatown. Row by row, acre by acre the land was cleared
and plowed, and by 1882 most of the 160 acres was either
producing wine grapes or well on the way.

As they worked together, the Castellani brothers grew
close – closer than they had ever been while growing up
in Italy.

The string of highland vineyards that stretched from
Montebello on the south to Woodside on the northwest
became the home of some of the greatest wines in America.
There, in the so-called *Chaine d'Or*, the grapes thrived in
cool, wet winters and long, warm, dry summers. Marco's
vineyards anchored the southern end of the chain.

Marco resisted the temptation to try any Italian varietals that hadn't been proven in Santa Clara and so he planted the vines of Bordeaux's Médoc area: Cabernet Sauvignon, Cabernet Franc and Merlot. He also took hundreds of Delmas's Zinfandel cuttings, the grape Delmas established from its beginnings in California under the name Black St. Peters. After Carlo arrived, he and Marco tripled their rate of progress and essentially completed their initial planting by 1881. Marco thought then that a winery of his own could not be far off.

His was the vision of thousands of growers and producers before him – to create a bountiful crop, to produce a valued product, to make his family secure and to pass along a rich, productive estate to his heirs. But his story came with added incentive: His father had been cut off in his prime, prevented from fulfilling his dream, and Marco had to make up for that. He *had* to succeed, and no adversity was going to block his way.

As soon as Marco's vineyards began to produce a marketable vintage, he and Carlo worked full time on producing the highest-quality crops and finding the best market for the grapes. It wasn't difficult to sell them – by the late 1870s the demand for California wines had grown, and the local wineries could sell all they produced. The Castellanis began to turn a nice profit. By the mid-1880s even New Almaden Vineyard began to buy some of his crop, influenced by Charles Lefranc's son, Henry, who by then had taken an active role in managing the business. Henry was closer to Marco in age than his father was and had no interest in perpetuating old grudges.

Then came further good fortune. One Sunday in early 1884, Sara and Louisa were getting dinner ready while Marco and the children sang Italian folksongs in the parlor accompanied by Carlo on his German concertina.

Up to the front gate, unannounced, pulled a buggy driven by Delphin Delmas, who had his son Paul beside him in the front seat. Delmas and son stayed for the meal, and afterwards the lawyer took Marco aside.

"My law practice is doing well," Delmas said. "You might not be aware that I have been acquiring land along El Camino Real near the old Robles cantina."

"I heard something about it from Governor Stanford," Marco said.

"Well, anyway, I have about 300 acres now, and what I'm planning is a vineyard and a winery. It seems to be a good spot."

"That's good. The more wineries, the better known we'll become, I think. When are you going to plant?"

"That's what I came about. I need someone to supervise, and I immediately thought of you. My father likes you, and so do I. We know you'd do the job right. Would you want the work?"

Marco thought for a minute and stroked his chin. "Well, Mr. Delmas, as you can see, I have all the work I can handle here on my own property. My brother and I can barely keep up with it. I had to quit my job with Stanford because I just didn't have time for all of it."

"Yes, I know. But here's my offer. I'll pay you as much as you were making from Stanford, and you wouldn't have to work full time – only enough to hire the right workers and foremen and supervise them, perhaps half time. I need to know someone is in charge who will make sure the job is done right – that's all."

"I see."

"It would give you the money you need to build that winery you've been wanting."

"You lawyers know how to make a convincing case. Let me talk it over with Louisa and Carlo and let you know."

Three days later, Marco accepted Delmas' offer. It was a lot to take on, but Marco knew that once he hired the right workers and foremen, he could supervise Delmas' vineyard by only showing up there occasionally. He couldn't turn down the extra money.

FOR SARA FANELLI, the visit to America was going to be a lark. She loved outings – she lived for them. This trip would be another outing, just a bit longer than the others she had taken. Ten kilometers, a hundred kilometers, a few thousand kilometers – she didn't make a sharp distinction in her mind. She never had a plan to stay in America. Planning wasn't her forte. She lived for the moment. She would enjoy the trip, stay with Louisa and Marco a few weeks or a few months, then go on with her life, wherever it might take her.

By the time Sara arrived at Montebello Ridge in mid-1878, Carlo Castellani had been there for seven months, working hard to help his brother finish the two-story house. Carlo was putting on the last coat of yellow paint as the wagon carrying Sara and her trunk pulled up the road to the front door. Mario was ten months old and Louisa was pregnant again. Marco was at work getting Stanford's Mayfield vineyard established.

Sara, adapting easily to California life, happily helped around the house – with the cooking, the gardening, with the care of Mario. After Paulo arrived later that year, Louisa began to find Sara indispensable. But it took time before Sara realized what a fixture she had become in the household. By the time she did, she found it too awkward to leave.

The bond between the sisters was as strong as their personalities were different. Louisa had always been the assertive one, the capable one, the responsible one. Sara was easygoing, the picker of wildflowers, the family charmer. Her capabilities were many, but she had developed them more by default than by intent. Enjoyment was her state of mind as much as purpose was Louisa's. But when Sara needed a friend, Louisa was always there. When Louisa needed to let her hair down, Sara listened. They talked and laughed incessantly, from morning until night.

For Sara, it was a good life. She would go with the family to picnics held by the Italian-American Club, to socials at St. Joseph's Church, to holiday gatherings at the Foard ranch three miles down the road along Cupertino Creek. Rebecca Foard, now in her mid-sixties, became like a second mother to Sara and Louisa. Any time either needed a shoulder to cry on or some sage advice, Rebecca was there. Soon the sisters began to feel like extensions of the Foard-Grayson family.

Sara first met Lincoln Grayson when he was in high school, but it wasn't until his graduation from Santa Clara College that Linc began to pay special attention to Sara. He was six years her junior, and until then he had been too absorbed in his engineering studies to socialize much. At Linc's graduation party at his grandparents' ranch, the two began to have a real conversation. Linc, usually on the quiet site, was thrilled to find someone who would sit still for his long discourses on the science of electricity; he talked a blue streak. Sara was genuinely fascinated – she wasn't used to boys like Linc. He had plans, hopes and dreams beyond her experience – wild, even fantastic ideas about how the world should work, would work. He opened new worlds for her.

Soon, Linc found more reasons to make his way up to Montebello Ridge. His visits from San Jose to his grandparents' ranch now nearly always included a side trip to the Castellani house. By 1884, the year of his graduation, Marco and Louisa had three children. Camilla was the youngest at four, Paulo was six and Mario seven. Linc came to know them all well.

Marco was making firm plans for his winery now and had engaged Hamden McIntyre, California's best winery architect, to help him with the plans. McIntyre had designed a three-level stone building with gravity powering the flow from one level to another. To this plan, Lincoln wanted to add his engineering expertise. Electric lights would facilitate evening operation, Linc said, and he was fairly certain he could get a dynamo working that would take the labor out of turning the wine presses. Marco was skeptical.

As part of these visits, Linc would be invited to supper. An evening of games might follow, or Linc and Sara would find a quiet place to talk long into the night.

Linc was far from the first California man to take an interest in Sara, but he was the first to pass Louisa's stern scrutiny. One after another, each potential suitor had been found wanting. This one was too poor, that one too frivolous, the other too coarse. For a time, Sara casually deferred to her sister's judgment. But when Linc came along, she stiffened. Here, finally, was someone she really liked who was substantial enough to withstand Louisa's critical judgments.

Sara was lighthearted, but she wasn't stupid. She could see clearly that Louisa had come to depend on her and that she would have to exercise some independence if she was ever going to break free of Louisa and have a life of her own. She was not going to let the world pass her by – not Sara.

When Linc first proposed to Sara, he had just secured his first full-time paying position as an engineer. But Sara sensed that this alone would not meet Louisa's high standards for the man who would marry her sister. So Sara devised a plan.

One morning she said to Louisa, "Lincoln won't marry me."

"What? What do you mean?"

"He promised he would, but now he says he's too busy, that marriage will have to wait."

"You didn't tell me about this. How long have you been planning this?"

"Oh, he asked me a couple of months ago …"

"What? Why didn't you say anything?"

"We were going to announce it together, at the Christmas party." Her eyes were red.

"Oh, Sara, you must be heartbroken. How could he do this to you? The little cad! What are you going to do?"

"I don't know. He says he'll marry me someday, but I feel so let down."

"Oh, honey. Do you still love him?"

"Oh, Louisa, I do, I do." She began to cry.

"Oh, honey, here," Louisa said, putting her arms around her sister and stroking her hair as Sara buried her face in Louisa's shoulder, sobbing. "I'm going to find out what happened. Don't' worry. We'll get it straightened out."

That afternoon Louisa rode down to the Foard ranch to see Rebecca.

"Becky, that grandson of yours has broken my sister's heart. What was he thinking?"

"Louisa, I don't know what you're talking about."

"Linc Grayson! He reneged on his promise to Sara. You didn't know?"

"I know nothing at all about it. What promise?"

"To marry her! You didn't even know your grandson was engaged?"

"I certainly did not. What in the world makes you think that?"

"They're engaged – Sara and Linc. You must have known, and why didn't you tell me?"

"Calm down, Louisa. First we have to find out what happened. There's bound to be a good explanation. Why are you so upset about it?"

"Because he's backing out! Sara's heartbroken. You have to have a talk with him. He can't go around playing with girls' feelings like this! Not with *my* sister's."

That evening, Rebecca sent word up to Montebello Ridge that Lincoln would be around the next day at noon. Right on time, Linc pulled up in front of the Castellanis' big yellow house in a buggy and Sara went out to meet him at the gate before Louisa could say anything. She took Linc by the arm and led him slowly back to the buggy.

"It's working," she whispered. "All we have to do is walk down the road a little ways and then walk back, go in the house and tell her we've worked it out."

"I don't know why we have to go through this charade at all," Linc said. "You could just tell her you're getting married and that's it. You're not under her thumb."

"Just do this my way. If it's more like it's her idea, she'll feel better about it."

They were all in on the ruse – even Rebecca. It worked to perfection, and no one ever let on to Louisa. Sara and Linc said their vows in the garden of the Castellani house in March of 1887.

Chapter 9

LINCOLN GRAYSON WAS TWO years old on January 16, 1864, when his mother and father took him to see the first steam-powered locomotive arrive at the San Pedro Street terminal in San Jose. The train, carrying a passel of bigwigs from San Francisco, was an hour late, but Linc didn't know the difference. He was entranced by the station, the switching equipment, the tracks themselves. The enormous black machine with its driving rods churning, smoke belching, its whistle drowning out all the cheering voices, became his first lasting memory. It changed his life. From then on he wanted nothing to do with baby toys. "Train" was the word he uttered most frequently, and from that day on, it seemed his future was clear. He would always be somewhere near big machines.

Catherine and Charles did nothing to discourage this mechanical inclination in their son. When he was six, Linc was one of the first children to ride on Samuel Bishop's new horsecar that towed passengers up and down The Alameda, behind horses bred and raised by his grandparents. Soon thereafter he began to build forts and castles in the yard, which he put together using spare wooden parts from sketches he had drawn. At eighteen he entered Santa Clara College, ready for the mathematics and physics courses instituted by the former president, Father Aloysius Varsi.

Linc had his choice of professions. He could easily have become a printer – Charles would have liked that. Or he might have chosen ranching and worked with horses on the West Side ranch with his uncle Jeff. At different times, growing up, he held jobs at both the print shop and the ranch, but he always gravitated toward the mechanics of a process, often shrugging off the business consequences. Twice, to his father's annoyance, he caused print deadlines to be missed while he figured better ways to feed the paper through the press. On the ranch he devised a chute that would refill the feed troughs in half the time, which made the horses bloated.

The startling advancements in the fields of electric power and transportation came at a propitious time for Linc. When he was eleven his parents took him to San Francisco to see the world's first transportation system powered by a moving underground cable; the cars latched onto it like skiers going up a rope tow. Running up and down Nob Hill on Clay Street from Kearney to Leavenworth, the cable cars were already a raging success. They were literally a lifesaver for the city's horses, which had been so severely taxed trying to pull heavily loaded cars up San Francisco's steep hills that some had dropped dead trying.

When Linc was sixteen he heard that Leland Stanford had built a cable car line parallel to the Clay Street line two blocks away on California Street. That year, he got a job as a telegraph operator at the Western Union office in San Jose, and it was then that he first learned about Thomas Edison. Over the next four years Linc read the reports coming from New Jersey as Edison announced his invention of the phonograph and then a useful version of an electric light bulb. By the time San Jose's electric light tower went up in 1881, this new power source had everyone's attention, especially Linc's.

In that same year, Linc learned about something that, to him, was even more spectacular – the installation of an electric-powered tram system in Berlin, Germany, using a powered third rail to transmit the current. The obvious difficulties with such a system – innocent passersby and curious children getting shocked by the rail and interrupting service – did not keep Linc from imagining the possibilities. What if the "third rail" could be a wire housed just *below* the surface, he thought, where accidental contact with it would less likely? He made a sketch of his plan, then put it away.

Three years later, on the day of Linc's graduation from Santa Clara, he and his family rode Samuel Bishop's horsecar from the college back to San Jose. Linc thought again of his theory for an electric railway. None had yet appeared in California, and he told his parents he thought it was time.

"Why don't you go see Samuel Bishop?" Catherine suggested. "Remind him who sold him on the idea of horsecars."

The next day Linc took drawings of his old plan in hand and sought Bishop out. Finding the gregarious businessman in his office at the San Jose Savings Bank, the young engineer laid out the proposal: an electric-propelled trolley with an underground power line between the rails.

It was just the sort of innovation that intrigued Bishop, who saw something of himself in this fresh-faced young man. "Has it worked anywhere else?" Bishop asked.

"They did experiments in Berlin about three years ago. But nowhere else that I've heard of. We'd be the first in the country."

"Then it's probably got a lot of problems connected with it. It's interesting that you come to me with this just now because I've been thinking about a trolley. There's a lot of new money coming in from the East. Real estate's booming. This could be just the thing to make San Jose the hottest town of the West. But it has to work right. I've been thinking about an overhead-wired system myself. Some people are talking about cable cars, but that's more than we need."

"Overhead would work, but it's an eyesore, and then what if one of the wires falls? It could electrocute somebody."

"Hmm," Bishop growled. "Well, son, you have some ideas, but not much experience, it seems. Why don't you investigate some more, find out what could go wrong with this underground plan of yours and then come see me again? I need to know all the pitfalls."

"Sir, I have more experience than you might think. I've built dynamos and set up a steam-powered generator on my grandfather's ranch. I could design a system for you."

"That's good, but we're going to need to convince investors that this thing will work, so I'm going to need to see something more than that – some solid record of success. It's a business, son, transportation is. Nobody wants to throw their money at something that hasn't been proven."

"My mother said to remind you that horsecars were once a novelty."

Bishop laughed. "That was a good sales job she did on me, all right," he said. "Apparently it runs in the family."

After that meeting, Linc did what Bishop suggested – he investigated. It turned out that several men were imagining new ways of powering trolley cars. One of them was a budding inventor only three years Linc's senior named Frank E. Fisher. Fisher was the manager of the Detroit Electrical Works. He was working on a full-scale demonstration version of a system for Highland Park, Michigan, very like the one Linc had imagined. Fisher wouldn't divulge the details – it was a proprietary invention – but several months after Linc wrote to him about the possibility of designing a system for San Jose and Santa Clara, Fisher finally gave out enough information so that Linc could take a proposal back to Bishop.

"It's going to be a working system," Linc said. "This line will save 60 percent over horsecars and 25 percent over a cable system in operational costs. Fisher says it would cut the travel time from San Jose to Santa Clara from 45 minutes on the horsecar to 20 minutes on the trolley. He thinks his system will be working in Highland Park within a year."

Bishop was intrigued. "You know, we might have something here," he said cautiously. "The majority of the county supervisors and the city councilmen are now opposing my overhead system. They think it's going to be unsightly and possibly dangerous. But they might buy into this plan you're talking about. If it actually works – if I could see it in operation ...."

"I'm sure I could arrange a visit to Highland Park, when it's working, that is," Linc said. "But there's something else I need to talk to you about."

"What's that, son."

"I need a job, sir. I've been out of school over a year now and can't depend on my family forever. You're going to need a chief engineer if you go ahead with setting up a trolley system here. You wouldn't have to pay me a lot to start."

Bishop chuckled. "I see what you're getting at," he said. "You're right – I can't pay you much now. But I could put you on a small retainer – say $40 a month? Then when this thing gets going, you'd be in position to step up to a higher level. How does that sound?"

Linc eagerly agreed, and with that agreement began one of the oddest episodes in the Santa Clara Valley's transportation history.

The first disappointment came when Bishop and Grayson went to Michigan to see Frank Fisher's demonstration system. It was working, all right, but it was not what they wanted. The electrified third rail, instead of being underground, as Grayson had described it to Bishop, was mounted above ground where it could be contacted by any random passerby. Could the rail be buried, they asked Fisher? That was the only design that Bishop thought would satisfy the San Jose and Santa Clara officials.

Fisher's curiosity was piqued. After some thinking and figuring, he agreed that such a system could be designed by enclosing a 5/8-inch copper electrical wire attached to an iron bar in a concrete culvert built just beneath street level. The bar could be mounted using glass insulators, with some means of cleaning out the culvert when it became clogged with debris. The cars could draw power through a slot in the street similar to the slot used by the cable car lines. A 250-horsepower dynamo, one of the largest ever built, would supply the power.

Fisher told them he could build a complete system for roughly $500,000 at the Detroit Electrical Works. That was a lot of money, Bishop said, but it was only half what he knew it would cost to install a comparable cable-driven system. He thought he could sell the idea in Santa Clara County.

Although the project had its skeptics back home, Bishop managed to reorganize his company, expand its capital and obtain the approval of the appropriate boards and commissions. As soon as the financing was in place, Lincoln Grayson became the railroad company's chief engineer – at a comfortable new salary – and Fisher's main contact point in San Jose. The project was under way.

Opponents of the proposal, mainly those supporting overhead or cable, did not go away. Many residents were incensed when crews began to tear out the middle row of willows on The Alameda – ones that had shaded the road for decades and were thought to have been planted by Father Catala in 1799 – to make way for the double tracks.

Construction started October 5, 1887. Twelve cars were ordered from the Pullman company in Chicago. By March of the following year the system was ready for testing. At 12:20 a.m. on March 16, a time chosen to minimize the number of witnesses, a car left the stables headed for the Santa Clara town line. Just short of The Alameda's sharp bend at the Agricultural Park, the forty-three passengers – including Fisher, Bishop, Linc Grayson and his new wife, Sara – were jolted to a halt when the car's contact carriage hit an insulator's metal cap. It was a disappointing initiation, but just a sample of the difficulties to come.

A number of operating problems pushed the beginning of regular service back to July 28, and still the trolley was allowed to go only as far as the Santa Clara line while that town's trustees debated whether they should admit the electric cars. By September the cars were running with some regularity, and some 40,000 passengers paid a nickel each to ride the area's latest novelty from downtown San Jose to the Agricultural Park during county fair week. Fisher and Grayson sat down to a celebratory dinner with Bishop and his investors. Unfortunately, the toasting was premature.

Just when it seemed the newfangled contraption was safe for ordinary folks to ride, a gaggle of society ladies got together for an afternoon excursion one Sunday. As reported in the *Mercury*, the trip ended suddenly at Cinnabar Street and The Alameda with a shower of sparks and a scary blue flame. "We had to get off right there in front of the Fredericksburg Brewery," Lida May Gillette, a dedicated member of the Women's Christian Temperance Union, told a reporter. "I was never so mortified in all my life."

The electrical system shorted out at the drop of a hat, it turned out, which shut down the line every time it happened. Then a boy fell into a construction trench on Santa Clara Street and died. Wires burned and broke, sometimes charging cars with electricity. Motormen and passengers were shocked – literally. Temperature changes caused the underground rails to expand and contract, separating them from the glass insulators. Then the next car along would tear out the rails, breaking the undercarriage. The third rail proved inadequate to carry the necessary load of electricity, which necessitated the addition of copper wires throughout the system. Then the main dynamo failed and three smaller generators had to be brought in to replace it.

Those problems alone might have doomed the project, but there was more. Mischief makers piled rocks on the tracks. Random passersby started poking their metal umbrella tips into the conduit slot so they could see the sparks fly, bringing the system to a halt.

As the problems mounted, Bishop put increasing pressure on Linc to make Fisher get the system up and working. Linc never shirked his responsibility, but he and Fisher, using their combined ingenuity, could not keep pace with the failures. No sooner would one problem be fixed than two more would come up. The town officials lost their patience, and investors, facing huge losses, turned their backs and refused to contribute another cent. Bishop was finally forced to admit defeat and go back to his horsecar railroad.

That was not the end of electric trolleys in San Jose – far from it. Under new ownership, the San Jose and Santa Clara Railroad ripped up the underground wires and went into full service with an overhead-wired trolley by August 1890. Eventually a number of trolley lines served the valley. But 1888 did mark the end of Linc Grayson's foray into transportation. Disgraced, he resigned and went back to work on the Foard breeding ranch. In truth, poor design by Fisher doomed the system, but in the public's mind Bishop and Grayson got the blame.

The humiliation was bitter, but it was only a temporary setback in Linc Grayson's career as an inventor. Encouraged by Sara, Linc continued to tinker with machines. Before a decade was out he would produce one that eventually made him a founder of one of the valley's largest industrial companies.

Chapter 10

Montebello Ridge
February 1884

THE IDEA FOR A SCHOOL came first from Louisa, but it took a team effort and a benefactor to finally make it happen. It all started the year Mario was seven, Paulo was six and Camilla was four.

"I have to drive the wagon three-and-a-half miles to get the boys down to Lincoln School," Louisa said.

"Not every day," was Marco's first thought, but he decided to rephrase it. "It's good that the Daffins and the Nicolettis up the road share the driving," he said.

"When the children get older they can walk home, but now it's twice a day," Louisa went on, ignoring him. "We need a school up here on the ridge. We have twenty-three kids right now that I could name who need it."

"I'm not sure we have the money up here to pay for a school," Marco said. "Some of the families are just getting started."

"Eli Foard could tell us how to do it. Why don't you talk to him?"

Marco thought for a minute, trying to gauge how much work he'd be getting into. "Sure, I'll ask Eli," he said. "At least I could find out what we have to do. It would be nice to have our own school."

Six months later, Marco and a few neighbors had a proposition on the ballot to create the Montebello School District. Unfortunately, Marco had not gained sufficient grass-roots support. The financing was too murky. Two of the larger childless landowners on the ridge decided that a higher tax rate was to their disadvantage and lobbied enough of their friends to defeat the proposition. The Castellanis were disappointed, and so were the Foards, but they did not give up.

A YEAR AFTER MARCO and Louisa had their first discussion about a school, Charles Grayson found himself taking a horse and covered buggy, in a drizzling rain, northwest along El Camino Real, the main road between San Jose and San Francisco, toward Leland and Jane Stanford's Palo Alto Stock Farm. It was a muddy trek. Stanford had recently arranged for his own appointment to the U.S. Senate by the state legislature and was about to begin his begin his term. So Charles was off to interview the former governor, who was spending a few days away from his San Francisco office, to get his thoughts about representing the state in Washington, D.C. Although the Stanfords maintained three separate mansions, Charles knew that Santa Clara County readers of his *San Jose Weekly Journal* liked to think of him as one of their neighbors, so the Stanford article would be well read. One subject he did not plan to open was the death a year ago of the Stanfords' only child, fifteen-year-old Leland Stanford, Jr. He felt it would be far too personal.

By the time the interview was over, the rain had subsided, so Stanford invited Charles to look over some of the 600 trotting horses he was training on his private tracks. As they walked toward the barns, the rotund Stanford in his herky-jerky style, he suddenly stopped and turned to Charles.

"You know, I hadn't planned on making an announcement just yet, but I'm going to let you in on a secret."

"Wait, senator," Charles said. "You know a newsman can't keep secrets."

"It's all right. Jennie and I are ready to let the world know. I wish she were here with us, but she's a bit under the weather today." His voice turned somber. "Um, you know, I'm sure, that we lost our son last year. Typhoid fever."

"I was so sorry to hear it, sir. The whole community mourned with you."

"Well, we talked about what we could do – to do something for the young people of California and the country. We came up with the idea of a university. We're going to give a substantial part of our personal resources to found a university right here on this farm. The president of Harvard told us it could be done for $25 million, but we're giving $40 million."

"That's ... that's amazingly generous, sir."

"Next month we'll get the founding documents endorsed by the state legislature. Then we'll have the job of appointing a board of trustees. I expect the board to have its first meeting in November, to get things rolling."

"That's quite an announcement, sir. May I ask why you chose to tell me now?"

"Because I need your advice. We'll have twenty-four members on the board, but so far I only have the names of judges and lawyers and businessmen – mainly people I've known in Sacramento and San Francisco. I'd like to have one local person, from this area, to keep a tie to the community here. Could you recommend a name?"

Charles thought for a few seconds. "I can think of someone. Perhaps you already know him – my father-in-law, Eli Foard."

"Oh yes, Foard. I bought some Standardbreds from him two or three years ago – good man. He seems like a sensible type. Do you think he would like to serve on my board?"

"I don't know, but I'm sure he'd take the job seriously. He's got good judgment and he's served on boards before."

And so it was that Charles's newspaper had the first local public announcement of the founding of the Leland Stanford Junior University, named in honor of the Stanfords' late son.

Eli was prepared for Stanford's invitation to visit him at his farm, having been alerted by Charles, so he had a few days to think about what he would say when he got there – and whom he would bring with him. Stanford was a bit nonplussed when Eli, Charles and Marco all appeared on his doorstep.

But Stanford's face lit up when he saw Marco. "My vineyard man come back to see me! Marco, how have you been?"

"Well, Governor Stanford, the family is doing well. Louisa and I have three children, a fourth on the way, and the vines are producing better and better crops. As are yours, I've heard."

"They are, thanks in part to you. And the newspaperman, too? How are you, Grayson?"

"I'm fine, sir."

They were inside and seated in Stanford's plush parlor before the senator finally asked, "And what may I conclude from the arrival of this obvious delegation? Surely not just interest in a pending appointment to my board of trustees."

"Yeah, about that, senator," Eli answered, "I'm honored to be considered, I'm sure, but I'm hardly qualified to be connected to a fine university. I'm an old horse trader and mountain man. My manners might be somewhat lacking."

"Your manners are fine, and it's your good sense that I value."

"Well, I do appreciate the offer, but I'm also seventy-six years old, sir. I believe you would be better off with someone a little bit younger. I know a superior court judge in San Jose, Francis Spencer. He's been in the State Assembly, too. I took the liberty of sounding him out on this and he's willing."

"I see. Well, if you really feel that way, then I will get in touch with Spencer. I owe you thanks for making that overture for me."

"Not at all."

The room was silent for a few moments. Finally, Stanford spoke. "Well, gentlemen, I sense that you have come about something else."

"It's about a school, gov ... uh, senator," Marco answered, wanting to break the ice. "I mean, another school, not the university you're starting. Up on Montebello Ridge, we have a lot of children who have to go down to West Side to go to school. It's three to four miles each way for those kids, including mine. It's down the mountainside and back up again. Those kids would be a lot better off if they could walk to a local school on the ridge."

"We tried to form a school district last year," Eli said. "We didn't really have all our ducks in a row. Some folks were worried it would cost too much, so we were defeated. What we really need is a nest egg, to get things started."

"Yes," Stanford said. "How many students would be attending?"

"Twenty-five or more," Marco said.

"And what do you think you would need to build this school?"

"Sir, I'm contributing the land myself," Marco continued, "Half an acre. I'm also putting up $250 to get a building fund started."

"If we could raise $1,000, I think we could put up the building with contributed labor and pay a teacher for a year," Eli said. "That should satisfy everybody. If we had that, I think the school district would be voted in."

"The ongoing funding would come from taxes, then?" Stanford asked.

"Yes, sir," Charles said. "Do you think you could help us?"

"How could I turn down such a well-intentioned request from friends? Of course. I'll write you a check for $1,000 right now, and you can add that to your $250. Let me know when the school gets built so Jennie and I can go up and see it."

STANFORD ALMOST DID NOT live to see Montebello School's opening day. Despite his contribution, the voters of Montebello Ridge continued to vote against forming a school district for five more years. Finally, in 1891, they gave their approval, and in September 1892, the little red schoolhouse opened its doors, with Leland Stanford personally serving punch to the students and parents gathered outside. A few days later, at a newly constructed sandstone and tile-roofed quadrangle on his property, Senator and Mrs. Stanford and more than 2,000 spectators welcomed Stanford University's first class, one that included a young engineering student named Herbert Hoover. Less than two years after that, Leland Stanford died on his Palo Alto farm.

A few months after Stanford's death, in early 1894, Charles Grayson received a visit to his newspaper office by Judge Spencer, the Stanford trustee from San Jose, who had bothersome news to report.

"The university is in trouble," he said. "The U.S. government has filed a $15 million lawsuit against the Stanford estate, and we're crippled, financially. We made a mistake by not insisting from the start that the university have separate accounts."

"You mean ..."

"I mean the Stanfords were paying the bills out of their own accounts. It's a confounded mess. Those accounts are now frozen, and Mrs. Stanford is trying to keep the university going out of her household funds. She's even tried selling her jewelry."

"What's the suit about?"

"Stanford owed money on some government loans he got while building the transcontinental railroad. Now the government wants those loans repaid immediately, out of the estate. So we don't get any money until it's settled."

"What are you going to do?"

"Well, the board has recommended closing the university until this is all worked out. Personally, I think that's a mistake – the faculty would disband and that would kill us, academically. We have to find another solution. Can you do anything?"

Charles thought for a minute. "Let me see about it," he said. "Stanford helped start Montebello School. I think some of the folks out there might contribute to a loan fund, as long as they thought it was a temporary thing – you know, that the university would eventually get out of this mess. I'll see what I can do."

When Charles told Eli and Marco about the problem, they got a group of their friends together and pooled their resources to collect a $10,000 loan fund for Stanford University. Jane Stanford was overcome when they presented the money.

"You're all angels," she said, tearfully. "I can't thank you enough. We will get through this. My husband would have scrubbed the floors himself to save this university."

The government dropped its lawsuit the following year. The loan was repaid and a university holiday was declared.

Chapter 11

GROWING UP IN A WINE-GROWING family, Mario and Paulo would have been drawn to work with the grapes even without encouragement. But their father, obsessed as he was with the need to provide a legacy, took great care to point them in that direction. At seven and six, respectively, he took the two boys by the hand and led them through the vineyards close to harvest, pointing out each variety and its characteristics. He gave them a detailed lesson on each implement in the barn and how it should be used and maintained. Mario began helping with the grape harvest when he was eight, and by his tenth year he and Paulo were pitching in with the pruning shears, the harvest and whatever odd tasks might pop up. Marco's heart warmed when he saw how naturally Mario took to the vineyard. Now all Marco's work was paying off. He would be able to give his family the things his father had not lived to give – the tutelage, the careful nurturing, the land and the vines – the culture. It was in their blood, and now Mario and Paulo would carry it on.

At that age, Mario was on the shy side, but ever curious. He willingly pitched in on the vineyard work, but his real passion was always, somewhat oddly, for the tools. He kept a nail and screw collection. When Marco put him in charge of the pruning and harvesting implements, Mario meticulously cleaned each one and hung them in the barn by order of size. Paulo made fun of his zeal, but when Marco heard of it, he was quick with his praise.

For a few months after that, Marco was spending so much of his time establishing the Delphin Delmas vineyard and helping with the construction of a winery on the Delmas property that the supervision of the Castellani vineyards fell largely into the hands of the boys' uncle Carlo. Mario and Paulo spent little time with their father. Louisa was busy with their youngest sons, Michael and Adamo, who arrived two years apart, so she gave less attention to Mario and Paulo as they became more independent. Camilla and her mother remained close.

With his father often away from the homestead, Mario began to go his own way. When the Chinese workers came at harvest time, Mario would observe their every move, these odd little men with their pajama-like clothing. They gave Mario a sense of the exotic. He stared curiously at their wide, umbrella-shaped hats made of split bamboo, concealing a braided queue coiled under the top for the day's labor.

The dozen or so Chinese workers camped in a far corner of the ten-acre vineyard nearest the barn. In the evening, when the Castellani family ate at their kitchen table, the workers would build a cooking fire at their camp. Mario would see the smoke rising as he finished his chores. He had seldom spoken to them, wondering if they could understand him given the primitive form of English they used when speaking to his father or uncle.

One day, about halfway through the harvest, Mario posed a question to one of the friendlier Chinese, who was called Bai: "What do you eat at night?" he asked tentatively, hoping he wasn't being too intrusive.

"Eat? We eat food, like you. Chinese food."

"What, linguini?"

The man laughed. "Not your food. We have rice, pork, cucumbers. We steam. You like to try?"

"You mean eat with you?"

"Your mother have to say okay. You ask her."

"Is your name Bai?"

"Huang Bai. You ask mother."

Mario got Louisa's reluctant acceptance for dining with the workers that night. "Don't be a pest, Mario, be polite and come home when supper's over."

In the camp that night, Mario was astonished at how quickly the Chinese were able to get an efficient fire going with small twigs and get their food cooked, all of it in a single black iron pot.

"Here – you use these," Mario's new friend said, handing him a pair of chopsticks. Soon he was dexterously feeding rice into his mouth, to the delight of his hosts. He took note of how clean the workers kept their campsite. The cooking implements were immaculate, as was each serving bowl. Strong tea was served in little cups with no handles. The rice and squash with small chunks of dried fish was superbly cooked, each grain of rice fluffy and separate.

When Mario brought out a small bag of sugar to add to the rice, the Chinese laughed, but they all cheered when he announced he was converting to chopsticks for all his meals. They seemed fascinated by Mario and treated him like a visiting potentate. At the end of the meal, they presented him with a gift of ginger and lychee nuts. They jabbered for a few minutes in their native tongue until Mario asked, suddenly, "Why do you always walk single file?"

"Tradition," Huang Bai said. "We follow custom of ancestors. When Chinese do this we show respect for them. We honor traditional ways."

Every day or two, a man named Chen Lok drove out to the ranch in a somewhat dilapidated wagon dispensing spiny cucumbers, rice, tea, dried fish, tobacco and – never discussed openly – opium. Chen Lok, who was also the labor contractor, had the payment for these items deducted from the workers' wages.

That harvest season, Mario worked every day next to Huang Bai as they went up and down the rows with their grape razors, carefully but quickly cutting the grape clusters and depositing them in big baskets. Mario would happily listen to Bai chatter about life in China, about his family, the shortage of food and Chinese traditions. Mario would interject a question here and there, but mainly it was Bai who supplied the talk. At the noontime break, Bai would get out his snack of rice cakes and fried seaweed while Marco opened a container of panini, cheese and fruit, which he gamely tried to eat with chopsticks to show how well he could use them.

"Your father work hard to make … success," Bai said to Mario one day. "He push you up – high hopes."

"High hopes? You mean when I grow up?" Mario asked.

"Grow up, yes. Some day you be top man here, yes?"

"I don't know. I'm just a kid. Maybe someday."

"Oh, kid grow up fast. Learn now, be better boss later."

"Do you think I'm learning?"

"You good learner, Mario. Good with razor, good with chopsticks." They both laughed.

That fall, Marco decided to keep three Chinese workers through the off-season to help Carlo excavate a cave in the hillside where wine would be stored once their future winery was in operation. Mario was glad when he heard that Bai was one of the men staying on. Mario was in school by then, and the cave work was too hard for him anyway, but every day after school he would ask his mother for a jug of tea and take it up the hill to the excavation to give the workers a break on those hot Indian summer afternoons.

"Here come rescue man," Bai would say when he saw Mario approach with the jug of tea, patting him on the shoulder. "Save diggers from hot stroke."

When the Castellanis' favorite cat, a calico named Goldie, died that winter, it was Bai who helped arrange the burial and supplied perforated, curled papers inscribed with Chinese characters as a final tribute.

One evening, after Mario told about a conversation he had with Huang Bai, Louisa said, "You shouldn't spend so much time with him. It's not healthy for you. He's a pagan, not like us." Inwardly, Mario cringed. He said nothing, but now he hated his mother for saying that about his friend.

One day in the spring, Mario came home from school to the news that Huang Bai was sick. "Don't go out there – you'll be in the way," his mother said, but Mario snuck out and went down to the camp anyway. The other workers had sent for the herbalist from San Jose, Jack Lee, and Jack was in Bai's hut treating him with an herbal remedy.

"What's wrong with him?" Mario asked Chen Lok, who was sitting on the ground outside the door.

"Pain in stomach," Chen Lok said. "Long time – come this morning at work. Have to carry back here."

Mario sat and waited until Jack Lee emerged from the hut, solemn-faced.

"Is he getting any better, Mr. Lee?" Mario asked.

"No better," Jack said. "He should be improving soon, though, if …." He shook his head instead of finishing the thought. "It might be more serious."

"What's more serious? You mean you … You'll make him well, won't you?"

"I'll do all I can do," Jack said.

"Can I talk to him?"

Just then Marco came walking down the dirt path. "What can I do?" Marco asked Jack. "I just heard. Should we get a doctor?"

"Chinese method will work if he's not too sick," Jack said. "We'll see."

"Okay. Well, you come back to the house with me, Mario. You shouldn't be out here."

Mario wanted to object, but he knew he shouldn't argue, so he went with his father. He didn't eat much supper and had a hard time falling asleep that night. In the morning his mother told him that Huang Bai had died.

Mario's face fell. He couldn't think of a thing to say that would express his feelings.

"Did they get a doctor?" he asked, finally, as he sat at the kitchen table with a glass of coffee-flavored milk.

"There wasn't time," Louisa said. "He went fast. They sent for the doctor but it was too late. Listen Mario, I know this is a hard thing for you. It's hard for everybody. Just remember, he's in a better place now."

"That's not what you think." All his pent-up anger came bursting out. "You think he's a pagan." His voice seethed with disgust for her. Both of them were shocked at the outburst. Open-mouthed, Louisa watched as Mario stood, his eyes red, and ran out of the house. He ran up the road toward Black Mountain until he couldn't run any more, and then he walked to a log where he sat, sobbing. Leaning his body on top of the log, wet already with morning mist, he stayed there, limp, his body heaving great long sobs that shook his every fiber.

When all the sobs had passed and he was too tired to cry any more, Mario slowly propped himself up on the log, realized he was wet and cold, and started to walk back to the house. His father met him near the edge of the vineyards.

"You're late for school," Marco said. "Your mother's worried."

Mario looked at him, forlorn, and suddenly, with a rush of emotion, ran to him and hugged his waist, his head on his father's chest.

"Bai's not a pagan," he sobbed. "I know he's not. Bai's good. Bai will go to heaven."

"Oh, Mario, you shouldn't worry about Bai. God will be good to Bai, I'm sure. It's all okay. Here, look at me."

Mario lifted his head and looked, still red-eyed, into his father's face.

"You've lost a friend, I know. A hard thing. But you still have your family, and a home. So think good thoughts. Bai's where he's supposed to be now. Remember him well."

There was a funeral procession for Huang Bai that started in San Jose's downtown Chinatown and went out to the Chinese section of Oak Hill cemetery. Marco took Mario and Paulo and they watched, fascinated, as the mourners scattered papers with perforations and Chinese characters, like the ones Bai had made for Goldie's funeral. All the Chinese weaved and moaned and beat their chests to the rhythm of a drummer and two hired trumpet players. At the cemetery gate, clashing gongs and cymbals met them, along with a volley of firecrackers.

"Scare devils away," a Chinese man told them as Mario looked on.

Mario always thought of the funeral as the most bittersweet moment of his young life. Bai was gone, but when Mario left the cemetery to ride back to Montebello Ridge with his father and brother, he knew that all was well between God and his friend.

A week later, Mario heard that downtown Chinatown had been destroyed by a fire.

Chapter 12

DOWN IN THE HEART of the Mississippi Valley, where underground caverns send up springs that make the vegetation green and thick, a tiny yellow louse thrives. It chews on fleshy leaves in the summer, and when winter comes the louse goes underground, where the grubs gnaw at tender roots.

The yellow louse, called phylloxera, has a favorite food: grapevines. In North America, by the mid-eighteenth century, the native grape varieties had long since developed a strong resistance to phylloxera by evolving into forms that could fight off natural enemies. But in the vineyards of France and the other wine-growing regions of Europe, where phylloxera was unknown, the vines had developed no such defense. They didn't need it – that is, before 1850.

It was around then that French vineyardists became interested in American vines for resistance to mildew, and so they imported a wide range of species to investigate their suitability for winemaking. When the vines in Missouri were dug up, the diggers unwittingly collected a huge population of phylloxera. The insects – each less than a millimeter long – easily escaped detection as they clung to the roots of the plants. Steamships carried them to France quickly – so fast that the phylloxera didn't die. Then, firmly planted in French soil, the American vines began to thrive, and so did the phylloxera. Soon the root lice, sometimes in their winged form, were migrating to the French vines, which were caught without warning, defenseless.

In 1866 a thirteen-acre section of grapevines in the lower Rhone Valley turned yellow and died. No one knew why or suspected that it was the beginning of a cataclysm. By 1890, most of the wine-growing vineyards in Europe had been destroyed while confused scientists and desperate growers spent years looking for a cause and a solution. By the time they found both, thousands of winegrowers had been driven out of business or forced to start over.

It happened that around the same time, new settlers in the Sonoma Valley and other wine-growing areas of California brought with them some vines from the Eastern United States of a variety called Catawba. These Catawba vines also carried the phylloxera louse. By this time, the Mission grape – the type planted by the Spanish when they established the California missions – was well established, as were dozens of French varieties. Because these grapevines were all European in origin and had never encountered phylloxera, they, like the vines in Europe, had no defense. The Castellanis would see the consequences of this chain of events.

In 1860, the same year Marco Castellani lost his father and his vineyard legacy in Abruzzo, a few dying vines were noticed in a vineyard two miles from the town of Sonoma, north of San Francisco. By 1868, three acres had to be dug up and replaced. It took another five years before the yellow louse was first noticed on the roots of still-healthy vines. Only then did the winegrowers begin to make a connection and try to think of what to do. By that time, more of California's wine-growing regions had been infected. The root louse was spreading slowly – much more slowly than it did in Europe – but it had a foothold and would not be stopped.

In 1894, WHEN MARIO CASTELLANI was 17, his brother Paulo 16, their father made them a proposition: Clear, plow and plant a five-acre hillside parcel at Montebello that had never been cultivated, make it produce chardonnay grapes with vines Marco would provide, and reap the profits. Once the vines were yielding on a par with the rest of the Castellani vineyards, the land would be theirs, along with twenty additional acres to cultivate as they wished.

To Marco, this was a stroke of genius – a perfect way to help insure the continuation of the Castellani wine legacy while giving his sons valuable lessons in both grape-growing and economics. It was also an offer Mario and Paulo couldn't refuse. Mario knew his future was in wine and had been looking for a chance to shine. Paulo had not thought much about his future, but he could work hard when challenged, and he was more than willing to follow his brother's lead. After six months of pulling up oak trees and moving rocks to get the land ready, Mario and Paulo went down the rows, planting their new vineyard with the chardonnay vines their father gave them.

Shortly after the brothers cast their first satisfied gaze on the completely planted acreage, the Castellanis had dinner guests – Mr. and Mrs. Paul Masson. It was far from the first time Louisa and Marco had dined with Paul and his wife, the former Louise Lefranc. Because of Louisa's long-standing friendship with the Lefranc family, and Marco's connections with the valley's French winemakers, Paul and Marco knew each other well. But it was the first time Mario and Paulo had heard Masson talk – and talking was one of the things Masson did best.

A French immigrant in 1878, Masson had run out of money and gone back to his native Burgundy two years later, then returned to the Santa Clara Valley for good in 1885. For several years he managed the Lefranc properties, but he had been producing champagne under his own label since the early '90s.

"You've had good notices on your champagne, Paul," Marco said as they sat down to dinner.

"We're doing well," Masson said. "The quality is good, and that's my main goal. If I make a superior product, people will drink it. But what about you? I thought I'd see a Castellani label by now."

"It's coming. Next year we'll build the winery. I have plans."

"It's long overdue. You have a nice family here. A winery will give them all a place to work."

"Mario and Paulo are in the growing business now," Marco said, looking at his sons with pride. "They've just finished planting five acres in chardonnay. You should see it."

"Wonderful. I hope you have planted louse-resistant vines."

"Phylloxera? Nobody seems to agree which rootstocks are resistant."

Mario looked puzzled. "Excuse me, but do we really have to worry about phylloxera here? I thought it was mainly a problem up north."

Masson shook his head. "It's been showing up on the east side of the valley. I also know of one grower just a few miles north of here who has lost half an acre."

"I didn't know about this," Mario said. "Why haven't we talked about it?" He was looking straight at Marco.

"What's the use?" Marco said. "As I said, no one knows exactly what to do."

"You have to graft your vines to native American rootstocks," Masson said. "The *vitis rupestris* or *vitis riparia* seem to work best. But you have to match the right variety to the right rootstock. The French have finally learned this lesson. Phylloxera was why I came to America, after all. The plague killed wine-making in Burgundy for a generation. We had no jobs."

"Pop, you did buy resistant rootstocks, didn't you?" Mario asked.

Marco's lips pressed into a tight grimace, and his voice showed his annoyance. "Of course, but I still say it's anyone's guess whether it will work. We've planted *vitis californica*."

"It may work," Masson said. "But you'd be well advised to get the latest reports from France on the best matches. I can share them with you."

Mario and Paulo looked at their father questioningly, but Marco just nodded silently. For the first time, Mario began to doubt his father's judgment on a matter related to the growing of grapes.

"Are your vines healthy, Mr. Masson?" Mario asked.

"Yes, thank God," Masson replied. "I've left no stone unturned to prevent phylloxera. It would destroy everything I've worked for."

Nine-year-old Michael had been listening. "Can't you just kill the phylloxera?" he asked.

"Unfortunately, no," Masson said. "The French found that out the hard way. You can't get rid of it. They've tried flooding and other things that work for a time, but it always comes back. You can only plant the right rootstocks, the ones that can fight the little buggers off."

FOR THE NEXT TWO YEARS, Mario and Paulo watched their vineyard grow, tending it carefully, training the tender vines onto the trellises, looking for any sign of disease. For two years, the vines grew. Then, in the spring of 1897, Mario noticed a vine that looked yellowish. A few weeks later, several more vines seemed to be faltering. Worried, he asked his father to have a look. When he saw the vines, Marco shook his head. "I don't know," he said. "I've never had phylloxera. But this might be it. I hope not."

Mario didn't sleep well that night. The next day he took a horse and rode to San Jose to see Paul Masson. Since their phylloxera discussion at dinner, the two had talked several times at winegrowers' meetings.

When Masson looked at the vine sample Mario brought, he grimaced. "I don't want to alarm you, but it doesn't look good. Do you want me to come out to your vineyard? I'll need to look at the roots."

"Please, I wish you would," Mario said.

When Masson arrived at Montebello and went out with Mario and Paulo to see their five acres of chardonnay, his downcast expression told the whole story. He took a shovel and dug up the roots of a healthy vine.

"I don't like to bear bad news, but I have to be honest with you," he said, putting his hands on both of their shoulders. "What you have here is phylloxera. You've done a very nice job with this vineyard. You should be proud. But I fear your work is all for naught. You can try pulling out all the affected vines, and I would do that – definitely. But if it follows the usual course, there's no stopping it. You'll end up starting over with all new vines."

When Marco learned what had happened, he was enraged. He confronted Mario and Paulo in the kitchen.

"You had Masson out to tell you about my vineyard?" Marco shouted. "What do you think he knows that I don't?"

"He knows about phylloxera," Mario said defiantly. "He's seen it before and you haven't. And it's *our* vineyard – you gave it to us."

Marco's face grew red. "Not yet I haven't. You have to produce grapes first, and you haven't done that."

"With the vines *you* gave us?" Mario shouted, irate. "We're never going to produce. You gave us vines that got phylloxera. What are we supposed to do about *that*? It's not our fault."

"What you're supposed to do is plant new vines. Do you think everything always goes well in a vineyard? You're too young to understand what persistence means. You have to take the bad luck with the good, so start over."

"Easy for you to say. We've worked two years. I'm not starting over. And fuck your vineyard."

Marco, his neck now deep red, was speechless.

"It's not fair," Paulo said, not wanting to seem timid. "Those were your vines, not ours. You bought the wrong ones, and we're paying the price."

Paulo turned his back on Marco and walked away. Mario followed. Marco wanted to thrash both of them, but he knew they were too big for that. "You don't deserve what you've been given," he said to their backs. "You're both spoiled."

MARIO TURNED TWENTY just two weeks after the argument with his father. Through the summer the two barely spoke as Mario watched the five acres of chardonnay vines slowly yellow, vine by vine, and cease to grow. In August he went again to see Paul Masson.

"I'd like a job, sir," he said. "I'd like to help you make champagne."

Masson nodded and thought for a moment. "As it happens, I need someone to represent me at the fair coming up next week in San Francisco," he said. "My champagne is catching on, and I think you could do a good job of showing it off. You have a nice personality. If you bring me some orders back from the fair, I'll hire you on. In the meantime, will you help me move some equipment?"

For the next few days, Mario helped Masson move his champagne production facility from the Lefranc building on Santa Clara Street to the basement of the luxurious Vendome Hotel a few blocks away on North First Street. Every step of the way, Mario asked Masson questions, learning everything he could about Paul Masson champagne. When he got his first paycheck, he rented himself a room near the Vendome and, with an advance from Masson, bought a suit so he could make a good impression at the fair.

On Mario's second day in San Francisco talking to fair visitors about champagne, the owner of a large steamship company happened by the Paul Masson display. The company's ships transported wealthy travelers across the Atlantic between New York and Europe, entertaining them in well-appointed dining rooms. Marco gave this man a glass of the bubbly and explained to him all the virtues of the Masson champagne-making method.

When he went home to San Jose at the end of the week, Mario took with him the largest single order in the history of the Paul Masson Champagne Co. He never again set foot in his father's vineyards.

Chapter 13

For Paulo, there was never a serious question of what he would do when the chardonnay vines succumbed to phylloxera. He would go talk to his friend.

Paulo and Robert Radcliff had met years ago at school, and at twelve they became best buddies. They did the things best friends do – joked, talked, horsed around, played cards and baseball. Then when they were thirteen, something new happened. One warm day after school, they were walking home and Robert took his shirt off. As they walked along, joking casually about this and that, Paulo found he couldn't keep his eyes off Robert's body. Then, before he knew it, a feeling came over him that he had never had – a desire. He was taken so by surprise that he pushed the feeling aside. But later, at home, it came back, strong as ever, not to be suppressed again.

The next time he saw Robert outside school, they were at the Castellani vineyards, where Paulo had invited Robert to spend the day. When they were up in the redwoods behind the house, where he was sure they couldn't be seen, Paulo put his hand around Robert's arm and said, "You're my best friend. I feel like we're ... really close." He pulled Robert to him and hugged him for several seconds. "Is that okay?" he asked, releasing his hold.

"Sure, I guess," Robert said, smiling. Nothing was said for the next few minutes as they walked through the trees. Then they stopped and Robert looked at Paulo, both of them smiling shyly. Robert hugged Paulo, longer this time, and then kissed him on the lips. "I love you too," Robert said. From that day, they could not be separated.

As Paulo thought for the next few weeks about what had happened, he began to take on guilt. Under Louisa's watchful eye, all of the Castellani children had been raised as Catholics, faithfully attending mass and catechism. As his guilt mounted, Paulo wondered what had happened to him, why he had these feelings for Robert, what God must think about his feelings. There was something wrong with him, he was sure of that – horribly wrong. Otherwise, God would not punish him in the strange way he did.

He was afraid to go to confession and tell this terrible secret. They would take him, put him in confinement, maybe torture him to get rid of these demons that possessed him. That's what they did to people like that. It never entered his mind to tell Marco or Louisa, and Mario was too normal to understand. Or was he?

One night, as the two brother lay in their beds in their dark bedroom, Paulo said, "You know what you said about girls?"

"What?"

"You know, about it getting hard when you think about girls?"

"Yeah."

"Well … what if it was different?"

"If what was different?"

"What if … you know … if you thought about a boy and it got hard?"

"About a boy? No, that's not the way it works. It only happens with girls."

"Well, what if it didn't?"

"I don't know what you're talking about."

"What if … you know. What if you thought about some boy you liked and it got hard. Would that be bad?"

Suddenly, Mario sat straight up in bed. He jumped to the floor and stalked over to Paulo, who was still lying down.

"Hey, listen. You aren't funny, are you? You aren't that way, are you?" he said. They could see each other's faces in the dark.

"I'm just asking," Paulo said innocently. "Don't get so excited."

"You got to talk to somebody about that," Mario said, trying to sound mature. "You have thoughts like that, you got to go to the priest. You go to confession, Paulo. Go this week. I don't want any brother of mine thinking thoughts like that. You promise you'll go to confession?"

"I don't have to go to confession."

"You promise!" Mario said urgently.

"Okay, I'll go. Don't get so worked up."

"Okay." Mario went back to bed. After that, neither of them approached the subject with the other for years.

But Paulo did eventually go to confession – about a month later.

"I think God is punishing me," he opened, when he was seated in the confessional.

"Why do you think that?" the priest countered.

"He's doing something to me. Every time I think about my friend, he makes … you know … he makes … I harden up."

"Your friend? You mean there's a girl you've been thinking about."

"No, not a girl. He's my best friend."

"I see."

"Well, what is it, father? I think God is saying I shouldn't think these thoughts about my friend. So he's making me get hard as a punishment, you know, to say don't think those thoughts, it's bad. But I can't help it. I keep thinking about him."

"I see. Well, you're very young. All sorts of things might come into your mind. It's something that happens to boys your age. Just remember, God meant man and woman to be together. If a man lies with a man, that's a sin. But what you need to do is meet more young ladies. One of them will make you feel the same way, someday."

"Really? So is it bad, what I'm thinking?"

"The sin would be if you did anything you're thinking you might do with another boy. As long as you don't yield to temptation, you can feel right with God. The devil presents temptations in different forms. This is yours."

That was Paulo's last confession. As the months and years went on, he realized that there simply was no way to reconcile how he felt and what he did with the strictures God seemed to impose. Slowly, surely, he knew he was falling out of favor with the church, out of favor with his family, and out of favor with God. It took years before he finally shed the guilt and decided that it was just his fate.

THE SUMMER PAULO and Robert had their first embrace in the forest, Paulo joined the Radcliff family for the August prune harvest, a ritual he repeated throughout his teen years – even when he and Mario were getting their vineyard started. He could never turn down the chance to spend a month with his friend. Robert's father was one of the first valley farmers to convert from grain production to fruit orchards. He owned a farm at Stevens Creek Road and Bascom Avenue, where in the mid-1870s he planted a prune orchard on ten acres. By 1885 his orchard was yielding almost $4,000 a season, and it didn't need irrigation.

The word about orchards spread, and almost overnight, the nurseries in the area couldn't keep up with the demand for fruit trees. Over a span of twelve years or so, from the early 1880s to 1892, the predominant land use on the valley floor turned from growing mixed grain and cattle grazing to fruit orchards. A grower could go to the California Nursery Co., run by John Rock and R.D. Fox, just past the county line to the northeast, and find apples, peaches, apricots, plums – a total of 1,600 varieties of fruit trees. And it was the French prune, *la Pruneaux d'Agen* introduced by Louis Pellier, that eventually became the dominant tree.

By 1892 Santa Clara County was said to be the preeminent horticultural county in the state, and the county's 22 million pounds of prunes constituted the principal crop. When phylloxera killed the vineyard Paulo and Mario had nurtured for two years, it came as second nature to Paulo, now nineteen, to go see his friend.

"Come work for us," Robert told him. "You can earn more than your father can pay you picking prunes and helping us dry the fruit."

Marco accused him of turning his back on the family, even as Mario had done, but Paulo took Robert's offer. It seemed time for him to break loose. That fall, for the first time, he did not harvest grapes in September but instead helped the Radcliffs dip prunes in a solution of lye and boiling water to make the skins crack and help the drying go faster. It was hard work, but working alongside Robert made it go fast.

It was the heyday of the small orchardist, for the recent discovery of lye-dipping and open-air drying had made small-scale fruit production profitable. Evaporating ovens, which required hand-turning, worked for large-scale operations but were prohibitively expensive for the small grower. In 1887 the prune crop was so big that it couldn't be sold without shipping it out. So the growers had no choice – they had to resort to drying the fruit in the sun. Using the lye-dipping process, the open-air method proved more efficient than the evaporators anyway.

When Paulo and Robert began working as a team in the drying sheds, they pushed each other, taking quiet pride in their quickness and efficiency. They would wait next to a three-by-eight-foot drying tray as another worker used a wooden paddle to stir the hot lye solution in its huge iron pot. As the white foam disappeared, another man swung a metal basket of freshly picked fruit over the pot, then lowered it slowly into the boiling liquid. The contact of acid on fruit created a low hiss, and then the basket would be raised again on its counterweighted arm, swung over a drying tray and dumped.

That's when Robert and Paulo would go to work. Wearing gloves, they spread the prunes out on the tray, taking care to give each piece of fruit the space it needed to dry in the hot sun.

When they finished spreading, they would pull another big flat out and place it on top of the last one, to get ready for the next basketload. It was tiring work, and by the end of the first summer, Paulo and Robert could do it better than any other team in the shed.

One day, Paulo and Robert were leaving the dipping shed when they overheard a comment from one of the other hands, who was slouched against the outside of the shed, talking to his spreading partner: "I don't much like working next to queers, do you, Dave?" It was loud enough that Paulo and Robert both knew they were supposed to hear.

They walked a few more paces before Robert stopped and went back. "If you don't like it here, you can leave," Robert said. "I can arrange that."

The man looked at Robert, picking his teeth with a straw and a smile playing on his lips. "Your daddy must be real happy with you," he said.

"You want to shut up or you want to work here tomorrow?" Robert retorted.

"I don't really care," was the response. The man didn't show up at the dipping shed again.

B.J. Radcliff, Robert's father, noticed his and Paulo's hard work and rewarded them. At the end of the season, he sat them down in his kitchen and laid out a proposal.

"I know a patch of land out three miles west of here, 40 acres, that I can get for $100 an acre," he said. "These places are going fast – there's not too many like this still in grain. If I buy it, will you two turn it into an orchard?"

The two friends looked at each other, each waiting for the other to speak.

"We could do that," Robert said finally, "but what do we get?"

"You get the land. As soon as it's planted, I'll turn over the deed. Then you pay me back from your profits until I get the $4,000 back. It's all yours after that."

Paulo nodded. "This sounds something like the offer my father made my brother and me three years ago," he said. "But I feel better about this. Prune trees don't get phylloxera, do they?"

Radcliff chuckled. "You can deal with the pests. Nothing eats the roots of these trees. This is something that could get you boys started," he said. "I know you'll do well with it."

B.J., a widower, had never made a comment about the nature of his son's relationship with Paulo, but Paulo always had the feeling that as long as they didn't talk about sex, he was not going to disown his only son over it.

Paulo's own parents were another matter. For the last seven years Paulo had spent August with the Radcliff family, sleeping in Robert's room. He had never pretended to be attracted to girls. It would be odd, Paulo thought, if his parents didn't know his secret by now. But he was not about to bring it up.

He didn't have to. Shortly after Paulo returned to Montebello Ridge after the prune-drying season, he informed Marco and Louisa at dinner of B.J. Radcliff's offer and his plans to form a business partnership with Robert. He was prepared for an outburst, something like the bitter one precipitated by the failure of the chardonnay vineyard. But he found Marco resigned, Louisa stoic in the face of his announcement. He had been out of the house now for three months. Maybe they had already adjusted to his absence and "written him off," he thought. But later, after Louisa had retired for the night, Marco came to his bedroom.

"You and Robert," he said, "you'll be good partners. I've seen you two together and I know … well, I just know it will be okay. And it's okay with me. I've had a sign. I've known …" He nodded, smiled a little.

"You mean … it's all right with you … about Robert and me?" He couldn't believe his father would take an accepting attitude over something like this.

"It's all right. I had to tell your mother. She was …"

"When was that?"

"A year ago, maybe two. She took it hard. She didn't want to face it, but I knew. Carlo told me about it."

"Uncle Carlo?"

"You should talk to Carlo. Catch him before he turns in. He'll have some advice." He nodded again, and then said, "I'll always be here if you need me."

Left alone, Paulo tried to reason out what had just happened, and he wondered what Carlo could have to say. Hesitantly, he went to Carlo's room and knocked.

"Yeah?" came his uncle's gravelly voice.

"It's Paulo."

"Oh, Paulo. Come in, come in. I was just ready to go to bed, so you caught me in time. What is it, Paulo?"

"Uh, Pop said … I don't know, he said you might have something to tell me – about Robert and me going into business."

"Tell you? Oh, Paulo, I don't know. You seem to be doing okay. I know you'll do well. We'll miss you in the vineyards, though. You're a good worker, Paulo, better with the vines than Mario. You like the fruit trees, yeah? Well, that's good. Nothing wrong with that." He chuckled and smiled.

"I think Pop thought ... He said you told him ... about Robert and me."

"Oh, that. Well, somebody had to. That's for sure. Marco's not so fast to catch on sometimes. I didn't want him, you know, holding that against you. A family needs to stay close." Carlo looked at the floor, and fell into a long silence. Then he looked at Paulo. "It's my story too, Paulo. I have those feelings. I always did. But back in Italy, you know, back then it wasn't talked about. I never dared say anything to my mother. It would have killed her, after Marco left and all. But it was one of the reasons I came here. My friends were giving me a lot of ribbing about not having a girl. I just didn't want to go on pretending. I thought I could start over here, maybe find someone. But the work here, it always kept me too busy. Not much chance to get out." He chuckled again in his quiet way.

"Carlo ... you should have said something. I could have used your advice."

"Paulo, it's not something I ever talk about. I don't know how. It's been so long now ..." His eyes began to get red, and he put his hands to his face, unable to speak.

Paulo sat on the bed next to him and put his arm around his uncle's shoulder. Carlo began to cry, great long sobs. Paulo sat there with him and they held each other and let their tears flow, talking long into the night.

Chapter 14

The Foard Ranch, West Side
May 1899

AFTER MARCO DID WHAT HE COULD to keep Mario and Paulo in the vineyards, and both of them still left, his daughter Camilla said, "Don't worry papa – you still have three children at home." She wasn't thinking that she would be the next to go. The way that happened caused Marco the greatest pain of all, and in the end, it taught him the hardest lesson of his life.

It all happened so fast that later, it seemed like a blur to Marco.

Camilla always had an affinity for horses. She used to make any excuse to ride down to the Foards – to get her horse shod or go riding with Jeffrey's wife, Lorna, or just to socialize. One day when Camilla was nineteen, she was visiting the Foard ranch when a young man arrived from Monterey. He was bringing a black mare of his up for breeding, and his name was Joaquin Robles Amandillo-Wheeler.

When Wheeler saw Camilla, with her raven hair and dark, long-lashed eyes, he thought right away that he had met the love of his life. They met on Eli and Rebecca's front porch. They talked. For several minutes – neither of them knew how long – they were completely unaware of everyone else around them, including a thin, fiftyish man, dressed a little shabbily, his hair long and jet-black, standing in the barn doorway, watching them. When Camilla at last mounted her horse and bid Joaquin and the Foards goodbye, she also failed to notice that as she rode away, the man in the doorway was talking to Joaquin and beginning to raise his voice.

In the Santa Clara Valley this man was known as Juan Villegas. The son of the late Antonio del Costa and Esperanza Amandillo, of Monterey, was 52 years old. Since his birth and disappearance, and after all attempts to locate him had failed, the Amandillo-Wheeler family had gone on with their lives only seventy miles from San Jose, but in a world apart from Juan's. In time, George Wheeler learned from Guadalupe's father what he needed to know about the running of the ranch. At the same time, he developed the vineyard in Carmel Valley and built his winery there. George and Guadalupe had two sons and two daughters. The sons, Randy and Raul, had both married, building their own homes on the estate, sharing the family wealth and giving their parents five grandchildren. The youngest son of Randolph and Juanita Amandillo-Wheeler was Joaquin, the man Camilla had just met.

Although George and Guadalupe remembered well the kidnapping of their nephew, they did not repeat the story to their children, and they seldom spoke of it themselves. Few in Monterey even knew that Esperanza had given birth. In time, after Guadalupe's parents died in the 1870s, the story faded away. Joaquin and his siblings had never heard it.

On the day Joaquin arrived at the Foard ranch with his mare, Juan Villegas had come with a friend to see about purchasing a horse. He knew horses and was well familiar with the ranch, having been there often during the days of the horsecars to take delivery of Percherons for the line.

When the well-outfitted Joaquin rode up and asked him the whereabouts of Jeffrey Foard, Juan directed him to the residence and then asked his name.

"Joaquin Amandillo-Wheeler, from Monterey," Joaquin said with a smile. "And you?"

"Juan Villegas," Juan said vacantly. He stared, open-mouthed, hardly believing the words he had just heard. Through all the years he had harbored Antonio's story, the lie his father had told him, Juan had fantasized often about presenting himself at the Amandillo ranch, demanding what he knew should be his. But he had never worked up the nerve to take a single step in that direction. This was the first member of the family he had ever met.

While Joaquin did his business with Jeffrey and talked with Camilla, Juan watched from a distance, trying not to attract attention, deciding what he should do. Finally, as Camilla rode off, he shook off his fear and approached Joaquin.

"Do you know who I am?" he asked.

"I'm sorry," Joaquin answered, taken aback. "You told me your name – Juan, was it?"

"You're from the Amandillo-Wheeler family in Monterey. You'd be the grandson of George and Guadalupe."

"Yes," Joaquin said. "My grandfather passed away three years ago but my grandmother's still with us. Do you know her?"

"I never met her. She's my aunt."

Joaquin stared at him. "Your aunt," he said flatly. "Uh, you're mistaken. My grandmother doesn't have any nieces or nephews."

"No, *you're* mistaken. She had a sister, Esperanza. I'm her son."

Joaquin looked even more confused. "My great-aunt, Esperanza? She's been dead 50 years. She didn't, uh, she never had ..."

"Fifty-two years. What are you trying to tell me, that you didn't know your great-aunt had a son? You're not telling me you don't know about Juan Costa. Has the lying gone that far, that you people ...." He stammered, trying to find words. "That you would wipe out the memory of one of your family members entirely?" Juan was getting loud.

"Now hold on," Joaquin said, his voice louder but still calm. "I don't want an argument with you, but you can't come up to me and just start making wild claims. I never laid eyes on you before today. For all I know you're just some ... some charlatan."

"Oh, a charlatan. Well, fancy-pants, you can go back to your big palace in Monterey and tell everybody you met Juan Costa, the son of Esperanza Amandillo. Tell them that and see what they say. Tell 'em you met the man who should have title to the whole place. Tell 'em you met the rightful owner. Then see what they tell you." Juan spat on the ground and walked away. Joaquin, not knowing what to think, watched him go but didn't follow him.

CAMILLA CASTELLANI DIDN'T TELL her parents about Joaquin for a few days, but she kept her memory of him in his stylish riding breeches on his big roan stallion. She visualized his face and his smile as she woke every morning and as she went to bed at night.

The result of their first meeting was a date to go riding the following week with Joaquin and the Foards up the trail to Black Mountain. Camilla thought her father might not mind too much if he knew that Jeffrey, Lorna and Eli were included. She knew she was playing with fire, but she didn't care.

Camilla knew what her father never talked about, that he harbored a quiet dislike of anyone he saw who looked or seemed Mexican. He was uncomfortable being around Mexicans, didn't even want to share the same breathing space with them, and it had been like that ever since Marco's father was cheated out of his nest egg by a Spaniard in Abruzzo when Marco was seven. Camilla knew bigotry when she saw it. Down deep, Marco also knew it, and he didn't care. His father had been cheated and he had been cheated, and that was that. Louisa and the rest of the family knew his feelings and knew the subject could make him explode, so they were careful to avoid any possible flare-up. But Camilla's feelings for Joaquin were too powerful – maybe even love at first sight – for her to forget about him. She was going to take the risk.

Marco knew what he was doing when he bought his land on Montebello Ridge. Besides being good for grapes, it was as far from the centers of San Jose, San Francisco and Monterey as he could get. There were a lot of dark-skinned descendants of Californios in those dirty towns, and Marco visited them only when necessary. He didn't care what color a man's skin was – his own was dark enough – but he usually limited his associations to English-speaking Americans, Italians and Frenchmen. He hired Chinese laborers at harvest time, and he considered them good, hard workers.

Within a few days of learning about the riding date Joaquin had with Camilla, Marco knew Joaquin's family history – he made it his business to know – and he fumed. His daughter was associating with a Mexican, and that set off alarms for Marco of the very loudest kind. Marco confronted her, but she had prepared a strong defense.

"What do you know about this man – have you met his family?" he began.

"I know he breeds horses, he dresses well and he has money. I don't know if I'm interested in his family," she said defiantly.

"You don't know anything about a man until you've met his family."

"That's your opinion. You're a bigot. You haven't even met him, and you don't like him because he's Mexican."

Camilla had never spoken to her father in that way. He turned red in the face. "What do you know about bigotry – you're a child," he said. "These people are not like us – they're liars and cheats and are not fit to live with us. They have no values."

"What values do you have – the values of hate and ignorance? Are those the values you want to teach me?" She was shouting now, and she was red in the face, too. She stalked away and disappeared for the rest of the day.

Marco knew he couldn't prevent her from keeping this date, especially since his friends, the Foards, were also to be part of it. He was always wary of betraying his prejudice with friends, knowing how he would be regarded if they knew. He wanted to avoid any direct unpleasantness. But he knew there was no way he could duck this one.

Marco decided to confront Joaquin directly. When the young man came to get Camilla for the ride to Black Mountain, Marco would be there on his horse, ready to ride with them. He would make it clear to this Spaniard that he was not welcome as a suitor.

Louisa tried hard to keep her husband from interfering.

"Why don't you just let it alone for now?" she said. "You haven't even met him yet. How can you be so sure of yourself? And besides, this romance may fizzle out on its own."

"It's going to be snuffed out, and I'm going to do it," Marco said. "He won't like tangling with me. If you think I'm going to let this Spaniard into our family, you don't know me very well."

"Mexican American," Louisa said. "The Californios have a proud tradition."

"Spaniard," Marco said.

Marco's plan fell apart the next day. As he worked with Carlo among the vines, trying to assess which had been fatally affected by phylloxera, Louisa came calmly walking down the row of vines accompanied by a well-dressed young man wearing tapered riding pants, with jet-black hair combed straight beck from his forehead. He was one of the best-looking men Marco had ever seen, but he obviously had Spanish blood. He had tanned skin and a look to him that would have attracted women. Marco felt his back stiffen.

"Marco, this is Joaquin Amandillo-Wheeler," Louisa said. "He's come to see us."

"What can I do for you, Mr., uh, Wheeler?" Marco said, not moving from where he stood. Joaquin came toward Marco, smiling and offering his hand. Marco looked him in the eyes and stood his ground, keeping his hands on the shovel he was leaning on. "Well?"

Wheeler's smile disappeared and he lowered his hand but kept his gaze on Marco.

"I wanted to introduce myself," he said. "I've met your daughter, Camilla, and ..."

"You're a month late," Marco said. "You should have come before you tried to seduce my daughter and I would have saved you the trouble. Camilla isn't interested in knowing you any better, or in seeing any more of you."

"I don't know about that," he said. "She's told me she ..."

"You're not welcome here, Mr. Wheeler, and I want you to tell Camilla you can't meet her any more."

"No, I won't be doing that," he said calmly. "If Camilla doesn't want to see me, she'll have to tell me."

"And she will. Is there anything else you want?"

"I don't understand why you're so angry," he said.

"I have a lot of work to do today, Mr. Wheeler. If you don't mind, I'll get back to it."

Joaquin looked at Marco for a few seconds, nodding slightly, then gazed around the vineyard for several seconds.

"Phylloxera," he said. "It's a nasty infestation. It took our Carmel Valley vineyards five years ago. We're just coming out of it." Marco was taken off guard.

"What do you know about phylloxera?" Marco asked.

"Root lice – kills the vine from underneath. You just have to pull the vines out – there's no saving them."

"Tell me something I don't know."

"From what Camilla tells me, you're the master when it comes to wine grapes. We've had some good years in Carmel Valley and we will again."

Marco stared at him, beginning to see past his smooth manner. There was a certain grit in his inflection.

"Your vines … have phylloxera now?" Marco inquired.

"We've been clean for a year. We started working with Arthur Hayne from the University of California. When he went over to France he found a very specific variety of rootstock was resistant – the Rupestris St. George. It works best in California, and it's all we plant now."

"I read about it," Marco said. "Paul Masson uses it, says he thinks it works."

"It works all right. We have a new shipment coming in next week. Should just about replace all the ones we lost."

They stood in silence for a minute or so, looking around at the vines, neither of them knowing what else to say. Finally, Joaquin spoke.

"I'd like it if you would come ride with us on Sunday," he said, "up to Black Mountain. It's a nice ride."

"I know the ride," Marco said, trying to think of all the reasons why he should resist Joaquin's smooth approach and make him leave the family alone. Finally he sighed.

"All right," he said, "we'll ride to Black Mountain. Be here at 6:30. It's best in the early morning."

Marco wasn't happy with Camilla for not explaining that the Wheeler family grew wine grapes. He felt put in an awkward position, but he wasn't sure why.

Chapter 15

SUNDAY WAS A PERFECT JUNE DAY, the fog lingering in the trees just a bit when Marco went out to the barn around 6 a.m., the sun just about to hit the tops of the three huge redwoods that shaded the Castellani home. Joaquin rode in on his roan at 6:30 beside Jeffrey and Lorna Ford. Eli Foard, the old horse trader, who was now 91 with a face full of wrinkles and snow white hair, brought up the rear. Camilla came out in her riding clothes to greet them. Her horse was already hitched in front of the house, and Joaquin dismounted to help her mount.

"Nice day for it," Marco said to Eli, ignoring Joaquin. "I haven't been all the way to the top of the ridge in a few years. How're things on the ranch, Eli?"

"You work too hard, Marco," Eli said. "You should do what I do – let your kids do the work."

"My sons work hard, too," Marco said. "Just not for me."

"They'd be here if you needed them," Eli said. "Besides, you've got a big family."

Marco saddled his horse and the six of them started up the trail. There were three vineyard families above the Castellanis now – Raponi, Nicoletti and Daffin – and above that, mainly scattered oaks, some madrone and wide open slopes, a broad meadow at the top. As they rode, Joaquin stayed beside Marco, telling the story of how his grandfather had courted his grandmother, gradually winning over his great-grandfather, Don Joaquin Amandillo. He told Marco about his grandfather's adventures in China and near-death experience at sea. But he said nothing about the death of Esperanza Amandillo. When they crested the highest knoll on Black Mountain they all dismounted and had their lunch. They had a good view of the San Francisco Bay and could see the fog just obscuring the higher ridges, the ones that blocked a distant view of the Golden Gate.

Joaquin pointed the opposite direction, toward Loma Prieta. "My great-grandfather, Don Joaquin, owned 22,000 acres beyond the peak in that direction," he said to Marco. "He traded some of it to get the Carmel Valley vineyard land," he said. "It extended from the ridge line to the ocean as far as you could see, all the way to Monterey. You know, it's the most beautiful, wild country going south – not that vineyards aren't beautiful, too. Every year in July we ride toward El Rio Grande del Sur, from the Carmel Mission to the San Luis Obispo Mission along the coast, camping along the way. You should join us. How about it?"

"I have work to do," Marco said. "I can't just leave my vines for days at a time. That's for rich people."

"You're as rich as we are," he said. "You have good land and a wonderful family. And an especially attractive daughter." He eyed Camilla, who smiled shyly.

Two weeks after that day on Black Mountain, Louisa and Marco made a trip to Monterey to meet Randolph and Juanita Amandillo-Wheeler, Joaquin's parents. The Castellanis were introduced to Joaquin's grandmother, Guadalupe. The Wheelers accommodated them in the best guest room of their rambling hacienda, the same house where the first Don Joaquin had entertained Captain George Wheeler, and Randolph and Joaquin took them out to the Carmel Valley to see their vines on Rupestris St. George rootstock, which seemed to be thriving. They treated the Castellanis to meals of abalone and crab.

Marco returned to Montebello troubled. He had a dream of being lost at sea, in a huge ship alone, with no rudder and no sail, and threatening monsters looming on all sides. He awoke sweating and thrashing about.

Three days later Marco was in his barn and heard voices. He went to the door to look out and saw two wagons rolling in, Joaquin driving one and Julian, one of Joaquin's father's men, driving the other. Marco walked slowly out to meet them. As the wagons pulled to a stop, he saw that each was loaded with rootstocks.

"I brought 3,000 of the Rupestris St. George," Joaquin said. "They should give you a start of about three acres. We ordered too many. We'll help you pull out your old vines and put these in. Or we could take them back to Carmel Valley – it's your choice."

Marco was stunned. He told Joaquin it was out of the question – he couldn't possibly accept such a gift.

"It's not a gift – it's an exchange," Joaquin said, clearly ready to counter the argument. He held up a couple of the rootstocks. "When you get your first yield, send us some of your Zinfandel grapes and we'll make some wine. How about it?"

Marco was about to continue his objection, but just then he saw something that brought him to a full stop. There on one of the rootstocks, squarely between Joaquin and Marco, was something he recognized but couldn't quite name, like a suppressed memory come back to the surface. The sun was glinting off it, washing over his face. He reached and picked off the vine a little bronze crucifix on a chain. He looked it over carefully, not believing. But it was as real as it could be. It was the same one Father Dorian had given him, the one he had thrown into the Fontana del Moro in Rome so many years ago.

He stood speechless, looking at the crucifix, then looking at Joaquin's puzzled expression, looking at Camilla and Louisa, who had come out to see what was happening.

"What is it?" Camilla finally said. Marco felt tears coming to his eyes.

"It's a sign," he said. He allowed the tears to come, standing there almost helpless, and then put his arms out to Camilla, and she came running. They shared the warmest embrace he could remember in years.

That afternoon they started pulling out the dead and dying vines. Marco called out Michael and Adamo to help him, along with Joaquin, Julian and Carlo. The six of them pulled up eight rows of vines that day. Over the next few weeks they finished the removal, tilled the soil and planted the new rootstocks where the old ones had been. The Castellani vineyards had a new start.

Mission Santa Clara
September 1899

CAMILLA AND JOAQUIN's wedding day was warm and sunny. It was Indian summer on the Central Coast. The Mission Church was decorated with chrysanthemums of all colors. Carriages were parked in front. The two families were there – Randolph and Juanita Amandillo-Wheeler, Joaquin's two sisters and his two cousins, his aunt and uncle and his grandmother Guadalupe. All the Castellanis came, including Mario, Paulo, Michael and Adamo, as well as Carlo, Sara and Linc, the Foards, the rest of the Grayson family including Jack and Lucy Lee, the Pelliers, the Lefrancs, the Massons, and a few dozen other friends. Brother Linus and Brother Michael also attended. Even Leland Stanford's widow Jane ventured down from Palo Alto.

With the guests in place, Marco led Camilla down the isle as Joaquin waited at the altar, a guitar quartet strumming the wedding march. The ceremony was ready to begin. But before the priest had spoken half a dozen words, a commotion erupted in the back of the church. Amid the shouting, Juan Villegas came stalking down the isle pursued by three ushers, his long hair blown into a tangle and a rifle in his left hand.

"You want to have a wedding?" Juan shouted as he reached the middle of the church. "You want to have a show for all these rich gringos? Okay, have your show." As an usher put a hand of his shoulder he wheeled violently around, wielding his rifle as a club and knocking another usher off his feet. There was a gasp from the audience in the pews. The other ushers shrank back for a moment, giving him room.

"Isn't it funny that they didn't invite the black sheep. They didn't invite the mystery nephew, the one they never talk about, the one that should have owned the land. No, they didn't invite him, did they? Well, there's a damn good reason for that. See this?" He waved a few sheets of yellowed paper in the air. "If they all knew about this, they wouldn't be so proud. Maybe there wouldn't be a wedding. Maybe they'd have to think about that other wedding, the one they covered up, the one between my mother and my father."

By this time several of the men were beginning to close in on Juan from all sides. But just then a shrill voice stopped them.

"Stop. Stop. Stop it all," came a voice from the front pew on the groom's side. It was the voice of seventy-one-year-old Guadalupe Amandillo-Wheeler, standing and waving her arm, then almost teetering over. Her son Raul, at her elbow, caught her and propped her up. It took several seconds for the church to quiet down. "Take me to him," Guadalupe demanded in her resolute but quavering voice. Raul and Randolph looked at her, then slowly escorted her back up the aisle toward Juan, who was now motionless with the rifle dangling his right hand, his arm slack.

When Guadalupe was directly in front of Juan, he looked at her and she looked at him calmly for a few seconds, and then she smiled – a broad, open smile – and put her right hand on his arm. "Yes, I think it is you," she said. "Hello, Juan. I'm your aunt Lupe. I used to take care of you. You know, when you were still with us, after your mother … well, after the accident." The church was silent now. "You have the same sweet face. I'm glad you've come back."

"You're glad? You try to murder me and then cover up any trace of my existence. Then you say you're glad?"

"No Juan, it wasn't that way. I don't know what you've been told, but it wasn't that way at all. We loved you. We all loved you. When you were taken we looked for you but we couldn't find you. Someone took you away and we looked for the longest time. That was so long ago."

Juan stared at her for several seconds. "You're lying," he said in a low voice.

"No. I'm so glad you've come back. You're part of our family. Come, let me take that for you." She gently took his rifle in both hands and he released it to her. She handed it to one of the men at her side. "Come sit with me. We'll watch the ceremony together and then we'll sit and have a long talk, you and I. We have a lot to catch up on. Come on." She motioned for him to follow her and took him by the hand. Hesitantly, he began to walk with her and let her lead him to the front pew where a place was made for the thin, weathered man dressed in work clothes. Guadalupe took her seat and Juan, after looking at her for another long moment, sat beside her, eyeing the others suspiciously. After everyone had settled back in their seats, the ceremony resumed.

THE WEDDING PARTY and the guests went from the church to the Vendome Hotel, where Paul Masson himself supplied the champagne with a dinner of pasta, seafood and Mexican dishes. While Camilla and Joaquin received their guests, Guadalupe went with Juan to a quiet place where they talked for two hours.

After the toasts and the cake, and after the dancing was well under way, Marco went out to the deck for some fresh air. He closed the glass door, but he could still hear the music and celebrating inside. He went to the railing, thinking of his mother and father, and of his uncles and aunts in Controguerra and of the songs they would sing. In the distance he saw the fading light on the western foothills, where the new plantings were giving his vineyards a fresh start.

Louisa found him in his reverie and took his hand. He looked at her and felt a rush of warmth as he took hold of both her hands and kissed them.

"We have a good thing," he said. "God has been good to us."

Louisa smiled, nodded and put her head against his shoulder.

"Pop, could I have a drink of champagne?" It was the voice of fourteen-year-old Michael, who was walking toward them from the dining room with his godfather and namesake, Brother Michael of Villa Maria.

"He wanted to try mine, but I thought he'd better ask you," Brother Michael said.

"Here, have a sip of this," Marco said, handing his son his half-full glass. "I don't think you'll like it."

Michael took the glass and drained it. "It's good," he said, licking his lips.

"All right, but no more," Louisa said.

"Marco, when is that winery of yours going up?" Brother Michael asked. "I'm starting to think it's just a bunch of talk."

"One day soon," Marco said. "It's going to happen. But we have to have a new crop of grapes come in first."

"Pop, I'll help you build it," Michael said.

Marco smiled at him, his eyes starting to glisten. "Yes," he said, "I think you will."

Epilogue to Part Four

JAMES LICK LEFT $700,000 in his will for building an astronomical observatory. The Lick Observatory on Mount Hamilton, east of San Jose, was completed in 1888 and given to the University of California. In 1887 Lick's body was reburied under the site of the telescope. The glass-sided horticultural building that Lick originally planned to give to San Jose was eventually bought by a group in San Francisco and stands today in Golden Gate Park as the Conservatory of Flowers.

The younger Henriette Pellier, Marco's romantic interest, married Pierre Mirassou, a handsome winemaker from France, in 1881. The descendents of Pierre and Henriette Pellier operated the Mirassou winery in San Jose until 2003, when the Mirassou brand was bought by E & J Gallo and the San Jose winery closed. One descendent, Steven Mirassou, continued to make wine commercially in the Livermore Valley northeast of San Jose.

In 1902, three years after Camilla's wedding, the new Castellani vineyard had its third leaf and began to bear a significant grape crop. That was also the year Marco at last saw his winery built. The building materials – mostly bricks – and the winemaking equipment, including presses, bottling equipment, tanks and barrels, were a gift from Mario, Paulo, Camilla and Joaquin, who pooled their resources to give Marco a fiftieth birthday present he would never forget. The entire family helped pick the site for the building, 150 yards uphill from the family home, and they all pitched in over the next few months to help build it. Marco and Carlo did most of the heavy labor with Michael and Adamo providing a lot of help. On Christmas Day that year, after attending Mass, the whole extended family including the Amandillo-Wheelers helped dedicate the place. Brother Michael said a prayer and Paul Masson again sent a few crates of champagne. Two or three years thereafter, the Castellani label made its debut.

Paulo and Robert expanded their orchard holdings, eventually acquiring 640 acres north of Saratoga Avenue and Stevens Creek Road and south of Homestead Road. They planted their acreage in prunes, apricots and peaches, most of which they dried and shipped east.

Mario, while still Paul Masson's protégé, acquired his own vineyard land in Saratoga near Masson's new mountain winery, La Cresta, and he began making still wines under the Masson label in a partnership with his mentor. When Masson retired, Mario split off and established his own label, applying the marketing skills he had learned from Masson. Mario married Lucinda Della Maggiore, daughter of another Italian family from San Jose.

Camilla and Joaquin eventually took over part of the Amandillo-Wheeler estate in Monterey, although they kept close ties with the Castellani family, and included all of them in family celebrations and holidays. They had five children, four of whom grew to adulthood.

Juan Villegas, after proving to the family's satisfaction that he was Esperanza's son, was invited to the ranch and offered a position handling the horses and a piece of land with a small one-room adobe. He took the land but not the position, and he lived there quietly for the rest of his life.

Michael and Adamo eventually took over operation of the Castellani vineyards and winery on Montebello Ridge and doubled the acreage, acquiring majority ownership after their parents died. They cultivated a wide range of varietals and built the Castellani wine label into one of the brands most favored by hotels and resorts nationwide. Michael never married, and Adamo's children eventually inherited the estate.

Finally, there's the matter of Marco's crucifix. It became family legend that its appearance amid Joaquin's rootstocks was God's miracle for Marco, and it's tempting to let it go at that. But for accuracy's sake, it has to be revealed that it was Louisa's doing. Once, early in Louisa's acquaintanceship with Marco, he talked about having been abandoned by God and having thrown his crucifix into the Fontana del Moro. Louisa, devout as she was, immediately went on her own to the fountain, looked for an hour and finally located the crucifix. All those years she kept it, knowing that one day God would put it to use. The chance came when Camilla confided to her that Joaquin was bringing the rootstocks. She gave the crucifix to Camilla and had her plant it on a prominent vine when Joaquin arrived with the wagons. That Marco discovered it himself, Louisa always thought, was divine intervention. She and Camilla took the secret of that plot to their graves.

Miracle or not, the crucifix never brought Marco all the way back to God. After grudgingly entering the mission church for Camilla's wedding, he finally consented – for Louisa – to attend Mass on special occasions. But that tested his comfort level. He could still never bring himself to speak with a worshipful voice to the God who had rejected his most fervent prayer, the one he offered on the day of the hailstorm in Abruzzo.

Fact and Fiction

This is a book of fiction. I have created the major characters with the intent of portraying a place and a time – California in the late nineteenth century – as realistically as possible. Although many characters are fictional, some are historical. Although most of the places are real, a few are fictional. Although a few of the events are historical, most are fictional. In no case have I deliberately taken a historical character out of context or given him or her attributes that seem inconsistent with the real person. Here are the specifics, part by part:

Prologue: The characters, place and story are historical. The details of the scene are imaginary.

Part One: Joaquin, Carmelita, Esperanza and Guadalupe Amandillo are fictional. George Wheeler, Joseph Meadows, Antonio del Costa, Eusebio Garcia, Ricardo Gutierrez, Garson Jenkins and Charon are also fictional. John D. Sloat, Thomas Larkin and John C. Fremont are historical. The war between the United States and Mexico is accurately described.

Rebecca, Eli and Catherine Foard are fictional, as are all other members of the Foard-Benedict wagon party. The Donner-Reed party and its members are historical. James Clyman, Jim Bridger and Lansford Hastings are historical. The dates, events, motivations and route of the

Donner-Reed party are described as accurately as possible. Although the Donner-Reed party met other wagon trains on the trail, no interaction ever occurred between Lansford Hastings, Jim Bridger or members of the Donner-Reed party and the imaginary Foard-Benedict party, either in Franklin, Missouri, or on the trail.

Part Two: Charles Grayson and his family, the Marbough family, Pastor Whitaker, Humberto Rico, Edward Malley, Hamilton and John Cable, the Foard family, Joe Parsons, the Contreras family, Sheriff Phillip McTavish, David Soto, and Marshals Harvey Davenport and Gordon Hecht are all fictional. Henry David Thoreau, Secundino Robles and his family, Antonio Sunol, Father Real, Andres Castillero, Henry Halleck, Thomas Berkey, Thomas Fallon, Peter Burnett, William Wallace, Anastacio Garcia and Tiburcio Vasquez are all historical. Louis and Pierre Pellier and Pierre's wife Henriette are historical, as are Antoine Delmas and his sons Delphin and Joseph, Etienne Thee, Jose Narvaez, Charles Lefranc and Louis Prevost. The Borregas Tavern, the Diablo Saloon, Clayton's Restaurant and Rancho de las Vacas are fictional. The description of the New Almaden quicksilver mine and its history is accurate, as is the role of the Pellier brothers in the history of Santa Clara Valley orcharding and winemaking. Francis Murdoch was a San Jose newspaperman of the period, but he had no interaction with anyone resembling Charles Grayson. Otherwise, his history is accurately described.

Part Three: Changtsu village is a fictional location in the real Kwangtung province, where most of California's Chinese immigrants originated. Lee Ming Tao (Jack Lee) and his family, Zhou Lin, Charlie Wong, Ah Bing, Ah Chong, the Foard and Grayson families, Clayton Phaneuf, Antonio del Costa (Jorge Villegas), Juan Costa (Juan Villegas), and Dr. Enderle are fictional. Marcelo, Charles Crocker, Samuel Addison Bishop, Thomas Dunn, Ng Fook,

J.J. Owen, Mayor Breyfogle, Charles and Thomas Reed, and John Heinlen and his family are historical. The history of San Jose's four Chinatowns is described as accurately as possible. The histories of the Transcontinental Railroad and of the anti-Chinese climate in San Jose are accurately described. John Heinlen's role in building Heinlenville is historically accurate with the following exceptions: He had no interaction with anyone resembling Jack Lee, and there is no evidence that he knew the Reed brothers or that either Heinlen or the Reeds participated in redeveloping the former downtown Chinatown.

Part Four: Controguerra is a real town in Abruzzo, Italy. Marco Castellani and his family, Father Dorian; Antonio, Louisa and Sara Fanelli; the monks of Villa Maria, the Foard and Grayson families, Jack Lee, Huang Bai, Robert Radcliff and his family, Joaquin Amandillo-Wheeler and his family, and Juan Costa (Juan Villegas) are fictional. James Lick, Father Aloysius Varsi, Charles Lefranc and his family, Pierre Pellier and his family, Henry Naglee, Delphin Delmas, Paul Masson, Arthur Hayne, Samuel Bishop, Frank Fisher, Francis Spencer and Leland and Jane Stanford are historical. The Lake House was a historical social gathering spot. The history of San Jose's first electric trolley, the history of the phylloxera plague and the early days of the Paul Masson Champagne Company are accurately described. The Stanford stock farm and vineyards and the founding of Stanford University are accurately described with the following exceptions: No one resembling the fictional characters was involved, the Stanfords had no role in building Montebello School, and there is no record of the university's receiving a contribution from local residents during its financial crisis.

– D.D.

Acknowledgments

Among the hundreds of books, articles, documents and online sources that I consulted, three were especially helpful. Bayard Taylor's *Eldorado* presents a vivid first-hand portrait of the San Francisco Bay Area at the time of the gold rush. Connie Young Yu's *Chinatown San Jose, USA* describes the histories of the four San Jose Chinatowns in compelling detail. *Like Modern Edens* by Charles L. Sullivan tells the engaging story of the early winegrowers of the Santa Clara Valley and Santa Cruz Mountains. In addition, the finely drawn and lettered booklets of F. Ralph Rambo gave me much useful information and flavor.

For research assistance, I'm grateful to the staffs of the San Jose Public Library California Room, the Monterey Public Library California History Room and the San Francisco Public Library San Francisco History Center. Several friends and family members read and commented on early drafts of this book, and their comments helped make it better. They include my wife, Stephanie Dugdale, Eric Brazil, Bill Stacy, Sandra Small, Debra Korbel, Helen and Jim Brady, and Patricia Reed. I also received significant encouragement and support from Matthew and Rebecca Tryon, Benjamin Tryon and Sigal Gavish. Elin Kelsey and the members of her Thursday morning writers circle provided innumerable helpful suggestions and welcome support. Judy Anderson ably designed the cover, maps and families chart. Finally, the book would not have been possible without the astute judgment and knowledgeable advice of my editor, Steve Hoar.

– D.D.

CPSIA information can be obtained at www.ICGtesting.com
Printed in the USA
BVOW030119110413

317872BV00001B/1/P